THE ROOM OF LOST THINGS

STELLA DUFFY

virago

VIRAGO

First published in Great Britain in 2008 by Virago Press
This paperback edition published in 2009 by Virago Press

Copyright © Stella Duffy 2008

The moral right of the author has been asserted

A CIP catalogue record for this book
is available from the British Library.

ISBN 978-1-84408-213-1

Printed and bound in Great Britain by
Clays Ltd, St Ives plc

Papers used by Virago are natural, renewable and recyclable
products made from wood grown in sustainable forests and certified
in accordance with the rules of the Forest Stewardship Council.

Mixed Sources

Virago Press
An imprint of
Little, Brown Book Group
100 Victoria Embankment
London EC4Y 0DY

An Hachette Livre UK Company
www.hachettelivre.co.uk

www.virago.co.uk

Stella Duffy is the author of eleven novels, and many short stories, she also writes for radio and theatre. Her story *Martha Grace* won the 2002 CWA Short Story Dagger Award. *State of Happiness* was longlisted for the 2004 Orange Prize and she is adapting it for a film to be produced by Fiesta Productions. *The Room of Lost Things* was longlisted for the 2008 Orange Prize and shortlisted for Stonewall Writer of the Year.

Her website is www.tartcity.com

Praise for Stella Duffy

'Stella Duffy strides into a whole new league with her lyrical, gritty, deeply affecting journey into the heart and soul of south London' Manda Scott

'A book for anyone who's ever lived and loved in London. Always surprising, always moving, and as fresh as tomorrow' Neil Bartlett

'Oscar Wilde's Happy Prince, when turned into a statue, witnesses the real lives of the dwellers across the city, his subjects. In this book, Stella Duffy too sees the many peoples of the Metropolis, hears their authentic voices – inner and outer – picks up nuances, hopes and desires, pain and spurts of joy, acceptance and stoicism and the need for connection. I don't know how she does it. Extraordinary' Yasmin Alibhai-Brown

'Without doubt, this is Duffy's best work so far' John Harvey

For Faisal,
with thanks.

One

Winter. Monday morning. A sofa is placed at right angles to the road, it blocks a third of the footpath and people make their way around it in both directions, one way hurrying for the bus, the other for the train. For the most part they do not complain – for the most part, a sofa in the middle of the street is the least of their worries. It is raining, it is cold, it is January and another year has begun, with gritty sleep still to be rubbed from the eyes of the last. The sofa is exactly 3.15 miles from the statue of Eros, as the crow flies. The crow that sits in the bare branches of the buddleia, picking at ants, screaming at small children. The sofa is slightly closer to the Houses of Parliament, the Savoy, the Royal Festival Hall, the river. This sofa also sits exactly halfway between Brixton and Camberwell, on a road that runs parallel to the bulging Thames, below the tube map's blue water line, signalling a destination black-cab drivers rarely appreciate.

Robert Sutton gets up at six thirty, every working day. Winter mornings harder than most, no sunlight to help him out of bed, arthritic knee and aching back and that burn on the back of his hand from the shirt press still not healed and a fortnight since he did it. He walks from the front room, where he sleeps, to the bathroom to the kitchen, same routine six mornings a week. Same on the seventh too, but an hour later. Robert has tried sleeping in on Sundays but it

1

doesn't work, fifty-odd years starting at six thirty have taken their toll.

Dan has been sitting on the sofa for almost an hour before Charlie comes to join him, shambling across the road, not waiting for the traffic lights, not waiting for the cars either. Charlie takes the other end of the sofa, carefully settling his bony behind on the thin cushion, wary of inner-sprung surprises and the damp from last night's rain. He runs a bloodied hand over the fabric, seeing the dried blood now for the first time, caught in the crevices of his skin, wondering what it was in the night that caused him these cuts, the potential of pain. The sofa covering reminds him of the thick curtains in his grandmother's front room, they hung there for years, vertical threads of yellow and green running through the dark red, fading to a dirty puce in their twenty-year effort to keep sun from the carpet, block out the draught, hold the room always in a late-afternoon gloom. Charlie's Nana Fisher said she'd been given the curtains when she was stationed at Windsor in the war, said she saw Princess Elizabeth in *Aladdin* one Christmas, that the soldiers on sentry duty had to put up with that Margaret Rose, no better than she should be, dropping gravel stones on their tin hats from two floors up, said the curtains had been hanging in the castle itself until the old Queen, the one who was the Queen Mum, thought better of it. Charlie couldn't see the Queen dancing round some wartime stage in tights, reckoned there was more than a pinch of Nana Fisher's salt to that one, but he quite liked the idea that the winter curtains blocking out the dangerous sun in the old woman's Bermondsey flat had held in a more treacherous light during the war.

Robert makes a cup of tea and very lightly burns two slices of toast, Anchor butter, Robertson's raspberry jam. At seven he turns on the radio. He is not interested in the news, that he gets from his paper, later in the day. The radio is on because half an hour is too long in this flat with no sounds other than his own.

Charlie nods to his mate, opens the can he has lifted from his pocket, takes a long pull on the body-warmed beer, before holding it out to raise aluminium good health to his friend. He follows Dan's eyeline to the halal meat and veg shop on the corner opposite their stop. An hour ago the new owner began the process of opening for the day, setting up the display stalls, half filling the pavement with a supermarket-challenging variety of vegetables and fruit, the whole a precarious mountain of old crates and a fake grass of exhausted green.

By seven forty-five, Robert is shaved, washed and dressed, making his way through the back alley to the front of his shop, key in the lock, heavy metal blind rolling up for the day. He smiles at the young woman clicking past in tight heels, nods to the men behind the counter of the kebab shop over the road, chip fat heating already for the pre-school rush. At seven fifty-five Robert turns his sign from Closed to Open, takes his place behind his own counter. Ready.

The halal shop owner has nearly completed his display.

'Doing all right,' Dan offers, his voice quiet, beaten down by the morning noise, the idling bus, the overhead train, the screaming baby in the traffic-jammed car. Charlie looks up, across the road, unsure. Dan tries again, shaking his head to clear a path for his own words, his mind a pea-souper of stolen beer and old voices, long since separated from the mouths of their original speakers. He blinks twice and his head drops a little further forward, hanging off his strained, stubbled neck. Eventually he turns back to Charlie, accepts another can of Special Brew, the thin and dirty thumb of his free hand marking a line to the corner shop. 'Doing all right. The new bloke. Nice display. Bright. What that corner needs.' And here he halts his staccato, takes in the view again, the late winter morning, the grey sky, old grey brick, dirty grey road and the vibrant red peppers, repeating with a confirming nod, 'Bright.' Dan opens the can, puts the pull tab in his pocket where it sits with the others from the past few days, they clink lightly when he moves, as if they were keys, as if he had a door to lock. He takes a long suck on the contents made frothy by Charlie's loping walk, waits for the liquid to travel down his throat and then, as if it gives him permission to speak, he launches in, holding the can and holding forth. 'Fumes. I told them, bloody fumes, get into the potatoes. Have to cover them up. Green potatoes, going to kill you, kill them too. Red peppers next to green potatoes. All wrong. But did they listen? Did they hell, bloody fools. Meat yes, meat fine, wouldn't tell them what to do with that, wouldn't dream of it, their meat, halal, kosher, whatever, not my meat, none of that, don't care. Do what they like with their own meat.'

Charlie nods, listening hard.

Dan continues, beer can arcing the force of his argument, his other hand batting away the words and ideas and images that sit beside him, getting in his way when he'd rather not see them, pictures that elude him altogether when it might be nice to have some company, when the night is longer than it should be and it's too hard to wait until Charlie arrives. 'Their meat, they know what to do, no argument. But I grew potatoes. My allotment, Streatham, by the line, the track, the railway line track . . .' Dan's words back on track, he takes a moment to smile at the bright blue bird to his left, the blue that is clear to him, invisible to anyone else,

4

pauses in gratitude and then continues. 'That was back – you know, back – before she, back . . . and . . .' Deep breath, another mouthful, makes it, finds the end of his phrase. 'I grew potatoes. Bloody good at it, bloody good. Grower. Growing. I know, the fumes . . . you can't put them out on the street. Look at that bus, look at it!'

And Charlie turns his head to the halted 345, disgorging half a dozen schoolchildren, kids crossing the road in front, diesel fumes pumping behind.

'Potatoes soak that up. Starch. Chemical thing it is, chemical. Soak it up. Kill us all they will, all of us.' Dan ends triumphantly, his point made, a sentence finished more or less where he wanted it to end. Sinking back into the damp pile of the worn and rotting sofa. 'Stone cold dead.' Offering it as an observation to the young Asian man who now walks past, pushing on to the dry cleaner's at the corner beyond the train station, ten past eight already, and this meeting too important for a hurried arrival, flustered and late.

The two men sit back, cans to mouths, beer to gullet, breakfast in hand, day begun.

Two

Robert placed his advertisement in the *South London Press* in December, not expecting a deluge of replies. In truth, he wasn't hoping for a deluge of replies. He placed the advertisement knowing it was a beginning. The beginning of a leave-taking, the beginning of his going, he didn't expect to be ready for a while yet, placing the ad was a start. Robert has always been thoughtful and painstaking, some have seen it as slow, others as committed, determined. He has never yet promised to turn over a suit in two hours flat. It can't be done, not well. Other cleaners might promise the world – or a morning suit before midday – Robert Sutton only ever promises what he can deliver. No more, but definitely never any less. A careful man who makes sure to think long and hard before his actions, he knows only too well that actions have consequences. So he doesn't expect many replies to the advertisement, and – because he wants to take his time taking his leave – doesn't much want them either. The advertisement has precisely one reply.

Akeel Khan walks flustered into the shop. He's fifteen minutes late. Someone pulled the emergency cord at Embankment, someone else tripped a security camera at Stockwell, then – because he was taking out his annoyance on the pixilated, and brutally decimated, images of goodies and rather more baddies on his mobile's latest download – he

6

missed the bus stop and had to walk half a mile back. He waits just five minutes after shaking hands before putting in his offer. Seems he has it all worked out.

'OK, listen, I'll come and work for you – work with you – for a few months? Learn your way, what it's like round here, and then I'll take it off your hands.'

Akeel makes the offer as if it's a generous one, and Robert can see why the young man believes he's doing him a favour, Loughborough Junction is hardly the finest example of South London's regenerative skills. There is a pause and to fill the silence, Akeel asks, 'Have you been here long?'

'All my life.'

Then. Alice Sutton gave birth to her only child in a blacked-out room in the house of the McDougall flour people. Great big house, gardens dug over, a courtyard with a fountain the girls could see but not visit, water that waited but did not flow, and a double dormitory arrangement for a dozen South London girls moved out to the country, the old house made into a place of safety for pregnant women nearing their time. Alice never found out if it had been commandeered or given willingly, but the lady of the manor was nice enough in a stick-up-her-backside kind of way, and anyway, God knew they'd enough of the bombs, of the dirt and the dust of town, most of the girls would have agreed to be moved out even if all London – what was left of it – had stood at the gate trying to stop them. Alice's parents' home, just off Kennington Park, was no place to have a baby. Twice in a row they'd been hit, one bitter week, lucky not to have been caught in the worst of it when the shelter in the park took a direct hit. Alice knew one RAF bloke who swore blind it wasn't an accident on the Luftwaffe's part, they'd been fed wrong information on purpose, the fat man on the other side of the river thought the rubble of Walworth and

St Olave and Kennington a fair trade-off for the Houses of Parliament and Whitehall. That lot had never had any respect for south of the river. Looking at the looted remains of her parents' home, searching plundered wardrobes in vain for her dancing dresses, she wondered if the politicians didn't have it right. Only that night though. Alice had never been one to bear a grudge. But she did mind losing her dresses. And then, her bloke back on his one weekend's leave, she lost her figure as well.

So there they were, all in together, this frosty weather – six women to a bedroom originally intended for one child, others in the nanny's room next door. A gaggle of factory girls, a few WAFs, another who'd been on the Ack-Ack guns, wouldn't shut up about it, so sure she'd done more than the rest of them. Which might be right in terms of night shifts, but everyone knew the Ack-Acks weren't much cop anyway, and if that mouthy army girl didn't give over, Alice was going to have to let her know. She had no qualms about speaking her mind, no qualms about much really, though this having a baby lark wasn't quite what she'd planned on. Peter Sutton had been away the better part of the past two years, which had, as it turned out, suited Alice fine. But then, on the single weekend's leave he'd managed, she travelled halfway up the country to see him, all the way to Darlington station when the southbound trains were stopped and the only thing to do was head north from the other end. They had not quite five hours together, and now Peter was a prisoner of war and Alice a prisoner of their kid.

Alice's baby was born in the middle of the night, just before four o'clock, and all through the dark the woman in the next bed had kept time with her, contraction for contraction, groan for groan. Come the morning Alice wrenched herself out of bed and walked the slow, uncomfortable stretch to the cold bathroom, sick of lying there in her own sweat and ache, the urge to wash, to comb her hair, only just overcoming her passion to sleep. Besides, it was nearly seven thirty, there was no way that hard-faced bitch of a nurse was going to let them sleep the morning away, she might give them a day in bed after a hard night, but the curtains would be open any minute, cold light and her baby's birthday let in. Her baby. Alice shook herself, that was going to take a while to get used to.

She made it to the end of her bed and took a breath, harder than it looked, this walking malarkey. The woman in the bed beside her did not have a baby in a cot. The woman in the bed beside her lay cold and quiet and alone without the silent blue-black baby that had been taken from her in the night. And Alice, who always wanted to say something rather than nothing, always thought it better to acknowledge than to hide, looked down as she hobbled past and said, 'Strange int't? There you are, wanting your baby – I mean, you really wanted him, didn't you? And you didn't get him. Here I am, never much fancied a kid, God knows when I'll get my old man back, and still the little bugger's screaming blue murder anyway, mouth like the Mersey Tunnel. Funny how things work out, eh, love?'

The woman in the next bed turned away, wondering if the tears would ever come. She never forgot Alice.

Robert Sutton never forgot the woman either, or her stillborn son. Alice had already picked out the names for her baby if it turned out to be a boy – Anthony John. One for each grandfather, keep 'em both happy. Later that day she asked the silent woman what she'd been planning to call her child. The woman whispered out the names, choking with the effort of naming her dead newborn. Elizabeth Rebecca or Jake Robert. There were a few raised eyebrows in the room at the Jake and the Rebecca, but Alice had asked and

9

anyway, there was a war on, all sorts rubbing along together, no point making a fuss. And so, because Alice wanted to do something nice for the woman she never met again, her own baby was given both that poor little mite's names as well. Down at Holy Trinity in Eltham they christened him Jake Robert Anthony John Sutton. The child was always called Robert. He wasn't a Jake.

Alice had no problem telling that story to Robert. She told him when she took him home and tucked him up in the bottom drawer in her parents' back bedroom. She told him when Peter Sutton finally came home, demobbed and so thin, tired and too angry to tell Alice about Germany and Poland and Czechoslovakia, holding tight to the pictures in his head and letting the lost years seep out in watered whisky and occasional swipes at the Yanks, the time it took them to wake up, to do the right bloody thing. Those swipes made contact with Alice's head on more than a few occasions too. She told Robert again when, a fortnight after Peter Sutton had thrown himself under a train at London Bridge, she packed up the pair of them, and left her parents' home, the one they'd been moved to after the last bomb had really done for their own place, and came back to South London. Of course Eltham was officially South London, sort of, but it was more like Kent really, not proper town. Alice wanted to be within reach of the river's dirty dip, a walk down East Lane market, or Bon Marché in Brixton, on a good day, when she had money to burn. There never was money to burn, but Alice toasted it anyway, a pair of shoes for the boy, a dress for herself, a glossy French lipstick, kiss-me red.

In June 1946, the not-so-young mother with a quiet little boy rented a room just off Coldharbour Lane, the slow curving stretch between Camberwell and Brixton. She claimed a space in a house of cracks and crevices, directly across from a half-gutted terrace, the front façade gone, the inside walls and their striped fleur-de-lis wallpapers exposed to the street. They had a room on the top floor, with a shared kitchen and bathroom one flight down. Alice didn't bother to cart the pram all the way up, left it in the hall for the neighbours to complain, they'd moan whatever she did, no point making it easier for them, she scooped up her baby like an old bag of shopping and made the climb. Lot of exercise, good for the figure. The old lady who owned the house told her it was a wee way from the house where Dan Leno used to live, Charlie Chaplin rehearsed up the road with the Eight Lancashire Lads, round the back was where Fred Karno had his Fun Factory. She was dead proud of the place. Alice didn't care so much about the music hall, or the aspirin factory, or John bloody Ruskin, but she did like that Annie kept the rents low and the front door unlocked, and the people and the noise below were much more like home than Eltham's open fields.

Alice started Robert off in the cleaning trade, she was at the steam laundry down the road for a few years, dirty sheets for clean, soiled towels for white, nice bunch of people to work with, long as she worked hard and kept at it. After all, people were always going to need clean clothes. Then when the shop came up at the junction, she begged and borrowed from all sorts to get together a deposit, made a dozen different promises, and took it on. Even with everything they could scrape together as well as her great-aunt's money, things were very tight for the first few years. Alice quickly learned to get Robert behind the counter, as soon as he was able. People liked the kid, liked that Robert could keep his mouth shut.

★

11

Now. Jake Robert Anthony John Sutton is a cleaner. Dry cleaner. He takes the stains and the tears and the messy secrets and makes them go away. But Robert remembers who brings them in, the soiled articles, the broken zips, ripped dresses, old suits, he checks the pockets for lost lists and letters, and he knows what his customers are trying to hide, cover up, make good, make do and mend. Alice could never have done his job for long, wouldn't have been able to keep her mouth shut. Wouldn't have wanted to either. He did, he does. Look and listen, listen and learn, keep it all in. All his life.

Three

Robert has lived on Coldharbour Lane all his life, and above the shop for most of it. Sometimes it feels longer than the sum of all the adult lives he knows, same place, same routine, keeping going. And sometimes, rarely, it feels like no time at all. No distance from boy to man, single to married, married to divorced, boy to husband to father and back again, just Robert, on his own. As if it all happened while he was out the back, removing stains, mending tears, pressing perfect creases into other men's shirts.

Akeel Khan is nicely dressed, nothing too flash, smart enough. Robert flicks through the young man's references and CV, though in truth, far as he's concerned, the simple fact is that some people can run a business and some not. You get in, you get your hands dirty, you make a few mistakes, if you've got an ounce of common you learn and get on with it. After all, it's your money – or the bank's, almost always the bank's – that you're pissing away. Still, he can't really see why this lad would want it.

'This isn't a young man's job, son. Not nowadays.'

'What's wrong with it?'

'Nothing at all. It's just . . . well, got a degree, haven't you?'

'Mr Sutton—'

'Robert.'

'Robert, I'm from East London, I have Pakistani parents,

of course I've got a degree. But you don't go to university to get a job, do you?'

'No idea, lad, not my idea of a picnic. What do you go for then?'

'To grow up? Work out what you want to do?'

Robert frowns. 'And you took three years to work out you want to own a shop? Open six days, fifty-two weeks a year?'

'I have to start somewhere. I don't want just one shop, I'm not going to be behind the counter all my life.'

'Oh, right. Got a mogul on my hands, have I?'

Akeel's smile is both shy – for appearance's sake – and proud, because that is exactly his dream. He quietly mouths Inshallah, taking his time, guarding himself.

Robert shows Akeel out the back, where freehold slips into leasehold as the shop blossoms into the cavern of a railway arch. He names each of the massive machines, taking care to point out the cost too, so this lad knows how much he's taking on and that Robert will not be robbed – if he says yes.

'That monster, twenty grand. Stainless steel drum, know why?'

'Runs on gas?'

'And?'

'Perc and gas – bad combination, it'll rust if it's not stainless.'

Robert nods, pleased the lad isn't totally ignorant, continues the tour. 'Shirt machine, five grand second-hand, if you're lucky. Those two, another ten each. Over here, spot station. Presses there, that one, the old press, been here longer than I have.'

Akeel doesn't mind old, not if it works. He looks to the peak of the arch, the old brick. 'Any problem with damp?'

Robert slowly folds his neck back, following Akeel's line

of sight. 'We used to get up there on scaffolds, every second year, me and a mate, few of us sometimes. Damp-proof, spray, the lot.'

'Used to?'

'Gave up about ten years back, hasn't made a blind bit of difference.'

Akeel smiles. 'So it was a waste of time, all those years?'

Robert brings a hand up to rub his neck, eyes level again. 'Couldn't say. Maybe it was a waste, maybe it's why I don't need to do it now. All I know is, come Saturday, you can't see this arch for the white of hanging shirts, but I've never had a single complaint about brick dust, not on one of 'em.'

A train storms overhead, and while Akeel can feel the noise, rattling around them, sending a rumble through his feet, Robert is right, the warm air is as still and airing-cupboard sweet as it was before the train.

'Is it expensive? The lease?'

'It's not cheap.' Robert watches Akeel calculate time and space and mortgage, totting up the machines, and now adding in the extra rent. 'Unless you've any friends at British Rail?'

Akeel shakes his head.

'Me neither, more's the pity. It's a space-hungry business, you can't borrow your mum's old washer and call yourself a cleaner.'

'No, I'm just . . .'

'I know. Working it out.'

Robert leads Akeel out to the thin courtyard, an L-shape running along the side of the shop to the first arm of the arch, backing on to a row of old lockups curving west to Brixton, north to Victoria. He explains about the flats upstairs, the top one he lives in, the middle is used for storage, both come with the freehold and, in truth, either might be worth more than the business itself, the stupid way of property prices right now.

15

Akeel nods in the right places, tries not to look as if he's already made up his mind, as if the sales pitch is what's making the difference. He's not surprised when Robert asks what he studied.

'Biochemistry.' Robert raises an eyebrow, Akeel ignores it. 'I liked science at school, only when I got to university, it was way harder than I'd expected. I lasted a term, had a massive argument with my parents, then transferred to philosophy and history. Better really, stopped them looking at me like I was a terrorist in training.'

'The teachers?

'My mum and dad. Though philosophy's not been all that much use for getting a job.'

Robert shakes his head. 'No, well, maybe not. But you know, all this – it's a bit ordinary, isn't it? I thought you young ones were all desperate to work in computers – IT and the like – you're a bright lad, clearly, shouldn't you be producing videos or recording some bangla band—'

'Bhangra.' Akeel grins, surprised. 'And you know about it, how?'

'Radio. I listen.'

'To bhangra?'

'Documentary. You'd be surprised. Wouldn't something like that be more interesting, at your age?'

'Can't stand that music. Rubbish, innit?'

Robert knows he needs to leave the shop, is getting too old for the sheer grind of daily physical work, but he still finds himself stalling, unsure how to let go. 'I don't know, aren't there any places round your way you'd be happier taking on?'

Akeel looks at the older man, wonders what he means. Maybe exactly what he said, round your way, a shop in Stratford or Bow, out as far as Leyton or Plaistow. Or perhaps he means round your way where there are more of your sort. More Asians, less black, less white, less mixed. Or perhaps he simply thinks it's a long way to come, over the river. Akeel takes the face-value option and explains himself. The big plan, the chain of shops, the need to make a start, find a way in. South London prices. He doesn't mention the hunger he feels for something else, something as yet unclear, a hunger he hopes will be sated if he settles, does well, makes good.

'You could go and do a course.'

'I did one when I worked with my uncle.'

'And?'

'It was all right. There're always courses. Correspondence, night classes.'

Robert smiles, was offered a postal diploma in 'Modern Stain Management' just last month himself.

Akeel is still explaining. 'But I want to get on with it, really, and on-the-job training's best, right?'

'Can't find it in Stratford?'

'Yeah. But my mum'll come into a shop in Stratford, my aunties will check out any place I have in Bow, all my cousins will come in if I try Leyton. And my father would keep checking wherever I was over there.'

'He won't come here?'

'My father doesn't do south.'

'Still, nice they care, your lot.' Robert nods.

'That's one way of looking at it.'

'Not yours?'

'Not always. I don't know anyone round here.'

'Safer to make mistakes without them all watching?'

Akeel blinks. 'Something like that.'

'I'll be watching.'

'Yes.'

The two men stare at each other, both waiting. Eventually, slowly, Robert nods. 'Don't sell a lot of the *South*

17

London Press in Stratford? Just happened to come across a copy, did you?'

'I'd already worked out this was a good area to try.'

'I might not be ready to move for a bit.'

'Good, I'll need time to sort myself out too.'

'Right then.'

'Right then.'

Four

Monday night. The Poet of the 345 journeys on this bus every day. It is what he does. Other people have jobs or children or families, some have all three. He has had them too, once, maybe will again, he cannot tell. But for now, what he does, is journey on the 345 bus. He sits upstairs when he can and talks to the world, he sings sometimes as well, Marley mostly, Mr Bob, Sir Bob, messenger of Jah. He too is a messenger. He tells the world. Sometimes they listen, sometimes not. He is not frightening, does not want to scare people, not with intent. But the Poet does have a huge voice, deep. Profondo. He studied music once, remembers learning the terms. Capriccio. Grandioso. Obbligato.

It is evening, early evening, but winter, so it is dark. The Poet likes the dark. He enjoys summer and sunshine too, he was made for sunshine, but when it is dark his bus takes him past other buildings, warm homes, he can look in, to the lit windows and the illuminated lives. A woman walks past him to one of the few empty seats, this time of night, so many people on the way out, on the way home, on the way. The woman heads towards the back of the bus. The Poet likes to sit in the middle on the left, from here there is a better view into other people's rooms, top floors, balconies. The woman is pretty, the Poet turns to smile at her, she does not smile back, she is tired from her work, a day of talking to people, a day of sorting out their problems, now she wants to get

19

back to her own life. She is reading her telephone. Time was, people read books on buses, papers on buses, now it is all telephones, all they read, all they say, all all all of it.

'And now it is the telephone, is it not? My Queen, my dear sweet young Queen.'

Marylin Wright is startled by his voice, she'd seen him watching as she walked by, but had not expected the man to talk to her, talk at her. Nor did she, in her forties, expect to be called a young woman. She is caught between irritation and pleasure at the attention.

'Time was, my Queen, that all the people read were books and newspapers, now it is the telephone, always, every way. Will you read a telephone book? Hah – a telephone book? Is that what you're writing, reading?'

Marylin does not reply. A health visitor, she works with people like this man all day, wants time to herself now.

The Poet of the 345, though, is not ready to let go. 'So my Queen, daughter of the Nile, daughter of Nubis, for you are she, fine and young and black, and God knows, oh Jah, only God knows, he has plans my young Queen, he has his plans . . .'

Marylin frowns, continues her failing attempt to ignore him.

The Poet only smiles and opens his mouth to sing. 'No woman no cry, oh oh oh oh no, no woman no cry . . . ai ai ai. No woman no . . . no . . .'

His song drops in volume as the bus driver brakes, stops altogether at the stop just after Loughborough Junction. A young man gets on, far younger than the orator, climbs the stairs with his friend behind him, they have Irish accents and the Poet of the 345 greets them warmly, he has always been fond of the Irish.

'So, my young friends, yes indeed, yes indeed. The only

country, the only country where civilisation will be, the only country is that called Ireland. Ireland yes. Yes.'

The Poet pronounces it ire-land. Perhaps it is not just his accent.

Unlike Marylin, the young men are not disturbed by the Poet, there are two of them and one of him, and it's true that the man speaking, song-speaking, story-singing, has a lovely voice, he sounds like that poet bloke off the TV, deep and slow and very smooth. The Poet has a voice that sells expensive coffee, overpriced brandy, rich mellow caramel chocolate. His accent shifts from what the kids in Marylin's flats call Ja-fake-an, to roundest-vowels old-fashioned BBC, and back again as the bus travels on. This bus that began its journey in Peckham and will end in South Kensington. This bus that travels from black to white to black to brown to white to white to white and back again, brown again, black again, crossing the lost River Peck and the enclosed Effra, touching estates and trees and looking over fences into lawns and car yards and parks and the fast dirty Thames and the new apartments and the old old flats and poor men wanting and credit-card havens waiting.

The Poet of the 345 makes the whole journey there and back again. Sometimes twice, three times in one day. It is as much his home, this bus, as the place he sleeps at night. Whichever of the many places that may be, when there is no home, there are so many beds. The Poet wonders about Jesus' Father with his many-roomed mansion, perhaps He too understood the joys of life on the street. Certainly the Son had his desert days, though the Poet thinks that forty nights in a cool dry cave is not quite the same as a week on the Embankment last November. He catches himself, shakes the hint of blasphemy from his shoulders, sends up an apology and a smile, and looks down to the street as the bus stops again, swaying with the weight of moving people, a twist in the road, the bus, his bus, his 345, switch-beaten by the bare winter branches that lean into the street.

Marylin gets off at Brixton police station, walking round the corner to the Portuguese deli, something nice to eat for her short walk home, something as a treat for her long day, and the Poet lifts his voice to the closed window and calls out after her, past the condensation and the fogged breath as he sails away west, 'God bless you, my Queen, bless mama, bless – peace – love. My word. My word. Ai, Jah bless.' And then quietly, to himself, 'My word.'

Five

When Akeel comes back for a second look he brings his wife. Small, dark, very businesslike. It doesn't surprise Robert at all when Rubeina tells him she's a maths teacher, looks like she doesn't stand any nonsense. Later they have tea and biscuits, and Rubeina softens, laughs with Robert about his good work, and the look he'd given her when he was handing over the books. Have schoolteachers always terrified him? He wants to answer only when they're as pretty as she is, but he's not sure how she'd take it, with that dark red headscarf marking her out. He notices the matching dark red nail polish. Not too austere then.

The couple stay for more than an hour, Akeel running his hands over the machines, trying out the new press and the old, Rubeina watching Robert with the customers, studying the flow in and out, people and money, dirty and clean. It's just past the end of school-time when they're ready to leave, Akeel gathers his papers together and stops to look at a yelling, squealing mass of youth outside.

Rubeina asks, 'Do you get any trouble?'

Robert shrugs, the slight lift releasing a slow shower of fine dandruff flakes to his knitted cardigan shoulder. 'Depends what you mean by trouble.' He nods toward the group, fifteen-year-old girls with intricate hair weaves and half-inch nails, high chunky heels on their black school shoes, fifteen-year-old boys looking years younger than the girls, pants hanging low, double layer of black and blue hoods shading their bum-fluff faces.

'There's always kids, shouting, showing off. Don't think I was any different.' He looks closer at Rubeina. 'Were you?'

To her credit the young woman allows Robert to make her blush, 'We never got up to all that much. Not as much as we wanted to, anyway.'

'Few of us do.'

At the door, Robert answers their next list of questions. He stopped doing shoes years ago, hardly anyone bothers to get them fixed these days, not when a new pair are so cheap. The keys though, he can teach Akeel the cutting, nothing to it really, just take your time, no rush. So much of it to do with not rushing. There's been a bit more family business since the police clamped down on the druggies, past few years. Then again, dealers go to weddings, attend funerals, they wear suits too, usually nicer ones at that, bit more disposable cash, tend to get their things cleaned more often as well, who's to know the follow-on value of a black market economy? Certainly things out in the street, the junction itself, are looking better, tidier than they have in the past ten years. Plastic flowers in chained hanging baskets at the station. Though Robert's not sure a tidy street is always the best way to judge an area. Anything can be swept away, doesn't mean it hasn't happened, isn't lingering, a stain in the fabric. He has to admit it's a damn sight better than it was on that hot Saturday in '81, when what began as a distant murmur became a louder hum and then a clatter of boots on tarmac, batons on shields, stones on shields, a black and white riot flowing over the banks of the Effra.

It was a few years after Alice had stopped working in the shop with him, and Robert had – against his own better judgement – taken on an assistant to help with the Saturday rush. He was used to the weekend panic, when half the area seemed to get up on Saturday morning and only then realise there was a suit, dress, shirt or three-layer ballgown they absolutely needed by six that evening, please, help me out, Rob, Robert, please? Be a gent, play the white man, come on, mate, give us a hand, brother. It wasn't a new phenomenon, though it felt more pressured since Alice gave up work and he had to deal with it all himself. His wife Jean had an office job up in town, and no intention of working a sixth day as well, and without Alice a part-timer had been the only solution. Seema Banjee was five foot nothing, thin as a rake, and so softly spoken that even Robert had to ask her to repeat herself, when it was just the two of them behind the counter and he had the radio turned off. She could, though, hand-press a fine cotton shirt in seventy-five seconds flat and that was something Alice was happy never to have to do again. Alice was upstairs sleeping as she did most afternoons now, Jean had taken Katie up town to get the girl a new swimming costume to help encourage her into the cold waters of Kennington Lido, and Robert and Seema listened to the radio with growing concern.

'Lock up.'

'You what, love?' Robert turned from radio, he'd been staring at it as if vision might make sense of the words he was hearing.

'Lock up. No one is coming in today. Not now.'

Seema was right. It felt like just before a thunderstorm when the birds turn quiet and clouds hang low enough to bring on headaches. There was no one crossing the junction, no kids hanging around outside the Green Man, the newsagent's over the road had pulled down their shutters half an hour ago.

Then, slowly, the hum became a murmur. Seema went outside, began struggling with the faded old awning, folding it back in on itself, ready to close the front door. This was before Robert had installed the roll-down lock-up, they still had the metal grilles to fold back and padlock to their settings, which always took a good five minutes. The murmur became a rumble, the rumble a stifled roar. And from round the corner, wielding a table leg in one hand and a brick in the other, outrunning the sound of police sirens by three minutes at most, came a young man. The shop had two plate-glass windows, one on either side of the central door, wide and welcoming. Robert didn't think the lad even saw Seema or himself, just the tempting glass, newly cleaned and whole.

Then Seema turned from the padlock she was clicking shut, shoulders back, neck thrust forward making her look even shorter than she was, and yelled up at the boy, 'Don't you dare!'

Robert froze, frightened for Seema, for himself, his shop, his mother upstairs sleeping, his wife and daughter out there somewhere picking up bits of bright nylon for the little girl.

The lad – because he was just a lad – looked down at Seema. 'Wha'?' A West Indian elongated *a*, falling into the missing *t* of his South London childhood.

'This is my shop. Don't you even think about it!'

The young black man looked at the name above the door – Robert Sutton. He looked from the small brown woman to the frowning white man, felt again the weight of the table leg in his sweating hand, heard the boots coming closer, and nodded. 'OK. Yeah. OK.'

The bloke smiled at Seema, didn't look at Robert a second time and ran off, down towards Camberwell, losing the table leg at the second-hand furniture shop and then the brick by the chemist's. Robert's shop window remained whole, unlike many of those five minutes further west. Over the next couple of weeks Robert noticed quite a few of the local youths had better trainers than usual, and several of them had noisier, smarter versions of those hand-held computer games they played as they waited at the bus stop, school bags dropped to the ground, heads bowed in concentration, thumbs flashing, voices raised in whooping derision as another player crashed and, presumably, burned.

Robert looks out through the glass now, the school kids have moved on, over the road to the kebab shop, two of them will buy halal chicken, the others will eat chips, grainy with salt, slick in brown sauce. 'There've been changes, but they're not always things you can see.'

'How d'you mean?' Akeel asks.

'Not all changes are physical. Things happen in the world, right? And those things get on the news, the front pages. Queen Mum dies, some bloke walks on the moon, miners go on strike. We watch it on telly, see it in the papers, and it doesn't matter if you think it's got nothing to do with you, it still gets into your life. It changes people, how they walk, where they walk. Changes what they wear. Because of that, it changes my business.'

Akeel looks at Robert. 'Our business?'

Rubeina takes her husband's hand when Robert answers, 'Maybe. Possibly.'

'You really think the political climate makes a difference to your work?'

'Course it does. Bank of England measures in sterling, I measure by how busy I am of a Saturday afternoon. People take better care of their clothes in good times, stands to reason. They'll always need cleaners, yes, but sometimes it's a luxury, and others a necessity. It all depends on the cash they've got in their pockets.'

Rubeina can't help herself. 'And how busy are you?'

Robert's lower lips rolls into a half-pout as he makes up his mind. 'You'll see. If it works out.'

This is what the young couple have been waiting to hear. Akeel feels the colour rise in his face, his heart beat a little faster. 'You will sell to us?'

'If I think I can trust you to do a good job. I'm going to need you to show me that. I'm too old for this lark, but I'm proud of my shop, I don't want you thinking I'm aching to get out.'

'No, I—'

Robert doesn't let him finish. 'Bollocks. 'Scuse me, love,' he adds, nodding to Rubeina. 'I know what you think, lad. You think I should be glad to sell up, move off somewhere quieter, less traffic, less building work . . .'

'Well, it's not as if there's a Starbucks on every corner round here, is there? I mean,' Akeel hastens to add, 'not that I think that's a good thing. Starbucks. Necessarily.'

Robert shrugs. 'Maybe not. And maybe one of those swish coffee places would come in handy, spill a few drinks, clean a few suits. Maybe I'd've done better further up the road, closer to the tube. But there's something about a cross-roads, people coming through, traffic all the time. How old are you, son? Twenty-five?'

'Twenty-six.'

'Right, well, you need a step up your ladder. And maybe this place'll be that step for you. But there's a lot more here than just a shop on a corner. Not all of it good, I grant you. Not all of it bad either.'

They meet twice more and Robert agrees to take on Akeel as apprentice-partner, and potential owner. Robert says it will take a year and that knowing the job takes a lot more than a few bits of paper certifying you can tell the difference between two batches of chemicals and the meaning of half a dozen symbols.

'You're asking them to bring you their dirty laundry, son, they're going to need to trust you. Take longer than six months, that will, longer than a year, but at least give them the respect of the seasons. Besides, January now, if I only teach you winter and spring, you'll be lost when all those summer frocks come in.'

Robert can't offer great money. Since Seema left he's always worked by himself, and he likes it that way. He's trying to get rid of the business, not expand, it's not in his budget to pay out extra each week, but then he figures his asking price can be a little higher when they make their final deal. When the details have been hammered out, on the late afternoon of their fourth meeting, Robert makes a cup of tea, a celebratory one this time, the men shake hands across the counter, and Robert invites Akeel to step behind to the other side. They hardly know each other. It's a beginning.

Six

Tuesday morning. Akeel runs up the stairs from Blackfriars tube to the overground, taking them two at a time, a pole vaulter leaping the horizontal. It is 8.29, if the 8.34 to Wimbledon arrives on time he has almost five minutes to pick up his double espresso, single caramel shot, and then grab a forward-facing seat on the left-hand side of the train. Akeel likes his routines, infuriates Rubeina with a desire for order and arrangement, bills paid on time, holidays booked, meals with their parents or friends planned weeks in advance.

'Akeel, we don't even have children, we don't need to book our holiday six months in advance.'

'Why not? This is a good deal.'

'Yes and what if we want to do something spontaneously?'

'Like what?'

Rubeina glares, and bares her teeth, growling at him, 'It wouldn't be spontaneous if I knew!'

He kisses her forehead as he leaves the house. 'You work out what it is, let me know and – please God – we'll have plenty of time to fit it in because everything else is already so nicely organised.'

'I hate you.'

'I know. You'll be late tonight?'

'Second Tuesday. Staff meeting.'

'I'll make dinner.'

'We're both going to be late.'

'I'll make easy, fast, keep-you-happy dinner.'

'Boiled potatoes. Lots of butter.'

'OK. Bread and butter too?'

'White bread.'

Akeel groans, agreeing. 'If you want.'

'I do.'

Rubeina hoists her overloaded teacher's bag on to her shoulder, wraps a pale blue scarf over her hair, tucking it securely in at the back, where Akeel would like to kiss her neck, where neither of them have time for him to kiss her neck, and walks down the stairs to the front door, her car keys jangling at each step. 'I love you.'

'Yes.'

Akeel likes to be on time, he sees it as showing commitment, both to Robert and to this new plan he has created for himself, the action plan that will take him from his parents' son to his own man, a business-owner in his own right. Being on time is as important as not walking under ladders, avoiding cracks on the pavement, never speaking of his hopes without adding Inshallah. Being on time will give him grace, bring him luck, make it all work out. The shop is a first rung on a long ladder, he needs to make a good start.

Akeel is an East Londoner, born and bred. He discounts that half year in Pakistan when he was fourteen, it was not one of his best, his mother sick, his father preoccupied, Akeel sent off to an aunt and uncle and a raft of cousins who didn't want to share and didn't want an English boy living with him any more than he wanted to be there, not for the first few months at least. Then, just as he had become used to it, the land, the light, just when the cousins had accepted him and let him into the secrets of their world, he was sent home to Stratford in time for the clocks to go back and school finishing in the dark with a long bus journey home.

And then there was more hassle at school, from the other Pakistani kids as well as the white ones, calling him country boy, village boy, the just-made yokel to their city-wise lads. Akeel remade himself very quickly that winter, upped the London in his school accent while keeping the elegance of his newly fluent Urdu for home, made himself the classic city rudeboy, two personas at least, both of them underpinned by the East London in his heart, that heart in his mouth, heart in his vowels. As an East Londoner, it is Akeel's duty to deplore the river crossing. He quickly learns that crossing London entails the same problems as travelling cross-country. Akeel has family in Liverpool and Manchester, he knows it is in latitude not longitude that British transport stumbles and sticks, catches and stops. In the first fortnight Akeel tries many different routes.

On Monday he takes three different lines, red, black and blue, and then walks down to Loughborough Junction from Brixton, but the falsehood that is the Bank interchange takes too long and the most obvious route is immediately discarded. The next day he tries the DLR to Lewisham and then a bus to Loughborough Junction. It's quiet, with the added childish thrill of any train with no driver, but the bus trip is an unmitigated horror. The single-decker is crammed first with Lewisham kids shouting at each other in the flesh and on their mobiles – mainly black, mainly loud, all talking in some street slang Akeel probably wouldn't understand even if they weren't shouting. The second half hour he is hemmed in by Dulwich brats – almost all white, and all shouting on their latest-issue phones in the slummy-BBC mockney Akeel had always assumed was invented purely for the use of TV actors. He arrives at work thirty-four minutes late and in a foul mood and Robert, already opened up, already on his second cup of tea, remarks that even a view of the lovely girl on the front of the Cutty Sark can't be worth fifty-odd minutes in the company of teenage hormones. On Friday Akeel gives up and yields to the train. Like most Londoners, he submits to the overground only when he has exhausted all other options.

That first Friday morning, the train at first slows and then stalls on Blackfriars Bridge, Akeel is pulled from the view of his watch and a late minute ticking past by two seagulls staring into his carriage, staring at him. He passes the next minute watching the choppy Thames below. And the third, and the fourth. He admires the sweeping curves of St Paul's for a fifth and sixth minute, marvelling at the height and engineering of the dome. He counts people on the Millennium Bridge, watches Tower Bridge slowly raise its arms to a waiting boat. The train eventually moves on and Akeel, heart rate steady, breath calmed by the water, plenty of room to sift through the games on his mobile, no one beside him to jog or disturb as his brutal thumb decimates another enemy line, realises he has found his route. A plan confirmed when he passes the coffee cart on his way back that night, evening latte and dark chocolate brownie to fortify the extra ten minutes' walk home.

This morning Akeel sits in his seat, coffee in hand and stares out at the river. Until now he'd never paid it much attention, it was just there, bends to be travelled round, bridges crossed under duress only, but since working with Robert he has started to think he might learn to like it. Robert knows things about the river, facts he offers up while showing Akeel the finer points of spot cleaning, stain removal. 'All those flash new buildings by Albert Embankment? Reclaimed land. Ought to be careful, that lot, river might just rise up again and take over their swish glass office blocks. Happened before now. When I was a kid, used to be a tower there, before they made it part of the Festival of Britain.' Adding for Akeel's

33

look of incomprehension, 'Back when we still thought there was something to be festive about. Great bloody thing it was, made bullets they did, shot drop or some such. My mate, Tom Hunt, always threatening to climb it. Never did. Died years back, lung cancer, fifty-two. No age at all, never climbed the flamin' tower.'

The stories Akeel's parents tell are of another country, India before Pakistan, Pakistan apart from India, the making of a new country, and then leaving the new one to come to this old one. That new life versus this new life. All his childhood Akeel listened to his parents planning to go back for good, make this holiday the last, this return to England the final return. He hears them making those same plans now, but he knows they probably mean it this time. Akeel has been back home with them plenty of times, for weddings and parties, funerals and festivals, travelled to stay with relatives, journeying alone and with his cousins. He does feel an attachment to the land, the tastes, the smells, the sounds, but his parents came from India and then from Pakistan, Akeel comes from London. This city divided by its twisted river is his home. He loves East London, likes the noise and the people, the old and new with even newer still, and now, because of Robert, because of this shop, Akeel likes the river as well. He won't say he likes South London, not yet, it's too big to judge so soon, in not quite two weeks. But with the new job he crosses the river every day, and Akeel knows Robert is right, a regular river crossing is the gift of South London.

Akeel sips his coffee, sweet caramel in bland milk tempering the espresso bitterness. He looks to his left, follows the Thames bending at St Paul's and then round again to the other side behind Tower Bridge. He watches seagulls fly above his stop-start train and swoop down to the river, back up to the cold sky. He sees a rubbish barge emerge from beneath the bridge, its massive cargo of city waste in sealed and private containers dunking it low in the water, and it makes him think of dead people, in their sealed and private containers. A third of the way through his coffee, the train shudders into motion again, moving slowly off the bridge, waiting for the train ahead to speed up, switch points and direction, another four carriages to come in from the opposite side, a heavy load of daily commuters to tip out. Akeel looks down as the Thames slips away behind the Tate and then the train pulls him on, faster, past swathes of new building work, hiding, changing, remodelling – the same process Robert has described happening fifty years ago and fifty years before that, and certainly for fifty years to come. He sits back and waits for the next round of his game to begin, five minutes before he gets to Loughborough Junction, a row of opponents to kill off with sword and stake, he could easily get to the next level between now and then.

Seven

Wednesday lunchtime. Up the hill and due south, just over a mile from the shop, Helen Goff is thinking there is no sadder sight than bacon rinds left on a plate with half-eaten egg. She really should have done the breakfast dishes earlier. At least the children are quiet, for now. Used to only the little one at home in the daytime, the two older children had restless nights and woke complaining of aches, runny noses, their temperatures high enough to keep them at home, and Helen's morning feels like a full day already. Fifty minutes ago, Emily's insistence on the Hungry Caterpillar for the eighth time was edging her close to tears, as was Simone's repetitive whine – the thumb-and-little-finger-in-mouth singing to herself that once seemed so cute, now just grating. Just for now though, the girls are fed and soothed, the television once more pressed into nannying duties. An hour ago Helen eventually dragged Freddie from harassing his sisters and off to his own distraction of choice – a computer game that involves ambushing marauding villains, then arranging their heads in serried rows on glittering pikes.

The big old house is quiet but for the electronic voices in far rooms, the ticking of the central-heating timer, and the distant shush of the water tank. Helen thinks she could do with a bath, a long slow one, filled with calming bubbles, soft music and candles to complete the chocolate-advertisement effect. Instead she kicks aside the head of a butchered

Barbie and starts on the dishes. Breakfast dishes and a few pans from last night's supper sprawl across the shiny new granite surfaces in varying states of soaking, draining, and dishwasher gleaming. She turns on the radio and the repetitive music relaxes her tight fists as she moves rapidly through the room, on one level methodical and clear, this pile then that, this action, then the next. On another level she is maniacal, any activity, any displacement to stop her head, shut up her head. She flicks the music louder and then realises she won't hear the girls if they call, turns it down again. Just the tiniest gap for her thoughts to enter and they pour in, crowding through.

What is she doing here? This shiny new kitchen, this perfect house. Over two years ago she promised herself she would leave, make her case, plain and clear, and just get the hell out, but Andrew persuaded her to try one more time with him, with them. She can't recall exactly what he said or how he convinced her – not enough to make her feel better about being here now – but she very clearly remembers the joy on his face when she backed down, said yes. The mask of joy with which he only just managed to hide his look of triumph. Then Simone was born and it was too late, she was trapped again. Perfect tiny baby and all the attention and exhaustion that entailed. Last summer she had just about walked out, had actually been pulling a bag down from the wardrobe, when Emily hobbled all the way upstairs on her sprained and bandaged ankle, simply to give her the still wet painting she'd been working on for the past hour. 'Our Family', with a green-shaded Helen standing lopsidedly right in the middle. Now here she is again, plunged to her wrists in dirty, greasy water, feeling the tears well up behind her eyes, staring blindly out into the cold, manicured garden. No idea why she stays and no idea how to get away.

Four years in this house. In the beginning it seemed full of

37

possibility, empty walls that have slowly been buried beneath the children's pictures, deep cupboards now filled to over-flowing with their combined mess. This house once felt so close to town and the parks, all the places she could go, the new things to see with the two little ones, before they multiplied to three, before it became all she could do to get them up and dressed and fed and off to whatever meeting or lesson or playgroup demanded their presence for another hour. By the time Simone was five months old the park had long become just another fenced space Helen walked round while Emily dragged on her arm and Simone tried to attack other children. One day, before the route changed to St Pancras, she and Freddie spent two hours watching the Eurostar speed past at fifteen-minute intervals, from the soft green of Brockwell Park and on to Paris.

Helen has always wanted to live in Paris. It was on her long list of things to do when she finally grew up and left home. She did go there once, for the day, took the seven o'clock train and went for lunch. It was an adventure. She walked around the strange, beautiful city and thought of staying, imagined herself someone else. She built a precious fantasy where she took an apartment in Montmartre and just walked around every day, free of the demands on her time and her conscience. She thought she would understand Paris simply by being there. It was what she'd imagined about London too, when she first moved to the city, that living here would mean she'd come to know it, simply remembering which tube to take without looking at a map, which bridge to cross to avoid the queues, where to eat that wasn't full of tourists, would make her part of it. She knows now that isn't true, knows that the most she understands is her own collection of streets and no more, her bus and tube and train routes and little else. Knows she has made herself a London villager just like anyone else who makes their home in a single small area because the city is too big to allow more than a corner per person. But Helen still has the shiny bright fantasy that another city, a brand new place, might offer her the escape that London promised and never returned.

At three in the afternoon, on that day in Paris, she made her way back to the Gare du Nord. She couldn't stay because she'd promised to go and pick Freddie up from his school play rehearsal at eight that night, and staying out so late was a big deal for him and she knew he'd be excited by the potential of the play, waiting to tell her his lines. She had promised and Helen never broke her promises to the kids. Not so far. Andrew breaks his promises, coming home too late to say goodnight, or leaving before they even get up in the morning, but he's their dad and in many ways it seems they expect it, expect him to fail to be there for them. Claire breaks loads of promises too, but Claire is their mum and the children are used to her not only breaking promises, but forgetting she ever made them in the first place. Claire has the whole world to think about, all those poor people to save, and her own children are clean and fed and happy and that ought to be enough for them, more than enough when there is so much suffering out in the real world. Because Claire's work is Very Important and what she does Really Matters.

But Helen is the nanny. She is the person and the place the children take for their truth. So she never breaks her promises and she never forgets and she is always there, and sometimes she is grumpy and sometimes she is tired, and after four years she hates the constant demands of her job and she despises this big old house and she knows that she is starting to dislike the kids too, some of the time, some days much of the time. Andrew and Claire and Freddie and Emily and Simone love her and they need her and rely on her. That's what Claire says, when she's telling the press how they couldn't cope without Helen. She is their Helen, that's what Freddie says. My Helen, that's what Emily says, and Simone sibilantly echoes her big sister, thumb in mouth, new words wiggling their way over her tongue. She holds them all together, that's what Claire's mother-in-law says, not quite able – or willing – to keep the disapproval from her voice. They wouldn't cope without her, that's what Andrew says. So Helen doesn't know how to leave, how to get away, but she knows she wants to.

Then there is a wail from upstairs and a yelp from Simone and a blood-curdling scream from Emily. Helen pulls off the rubber gloves, leaves them floating in the water and hurries upstairs. Hurries slowly. Slower by half than she would have hurried two years ago, slower by far than the leaping run she would have made in the first year. They have never yet killed each other, these siblings who fight so hard, she doesn't expect it will happen now. Cereal scrapings and Simone's crusts swirl around the pink thumb of the right-hand glove and then they bob together, floating in the warm greasy water.

Eight

It is the end of Akeel's third full week of work, six twenty on Saturday evening, the sun gone and a damp chill settling on the road outside, kids hurrying home just to rush out again, couples back from the supermarket with their shopping, a ready-bought pizza and DVD for the night, lottery tickets held in hopeful hands, stacked three-deep on waiting mantelpieces. A dozen of the lottery hopefuls round this way have no chance of the dream coming true this week, Akeel has already found their random-number prayers in forgotten pockets, the wasted tickets handed over to Robert, who has a system for disposing of pocket-remains. Akeel imagines the system involves nothing more complicated than the bin bags waiting wet in the alley. Robert is cashing up, Akeel washes a busy day's accumulation of teacups out back. The two men have only just managed to shut the front door, turn the open sign to closed, have not yet brought down the heavy metal rollers that will lock in the clothes and hangers and racks and chemicals for the quiet of Sunday.

It was six fifteen before Robert finally said goodnight to that one last customer, whose presence allowed in the next one last, and the next one last. Robert Sutton has been kicking people out of the shop late on Saturday evenings for coming up to fifty years; today is no exception. Except that it is also Akeel's birthday. Robert shouts through the thin wall separating the ordered front from the private chaos of the cavernous back. 'Oi! Lad!'

Akeel lets a cup slip back into the water, wondering how long it will take for Robert to make the leap from calling him lad or son to using his name. Or maybe it'll never happen, he's noticed the older man has a love, darling, dear, poppet, mate, guv, lad, son or sir for just about every customer who comes through the door.

'You get off, I'll finish up here.'

'You're all right, I don't mind. I like to leave it tidy. Makes Monday morning easier to cope with.'

'No argument from me, but we've been going solid since first thing this morning, you had no lunch break to speak of.'

'Neither did you.'

'But I'm used to it, and I don't have a wife waiting for me with a cake and candles. Bugger off.'

Akeel just shakes his head and turns back to the cups on the draining board.

'I'll finish this, then I'm gone.'

And Robert is pleased to have his offer turned down.

Akeel pulls on his coat and Robert locks away the last of the coin bags in the safe.

'She'll have a cake for you, Rubeina, will she?'

'We don't really do birthdays.'

'How d'you mean "we"? You and her, or your lot?'

Akeel twists his scarf inside his coat, the close confines of the shop front made narrower with his layered winter bulk. 'No, not "my lot", we do birthdays same as anyone else. Everyone else.'

'Not everyone.' Robert contradicts. 'Wife's mate was Jehovah's Witness, they didn't do birthdays. Some of those weirdy sects don't hardly do anything.'

'We do, my family anyway. My mum loves birthdays,

always made a big fuss when we were little. But they're back home in Pakistan just now.'

'Oh right. I see.'

Akeel doubts he does, explains that he and Rubeina save their celebrations for anniversaries, their engagement, their wedding.

'You'll get more as you get older.' Robert stands up from the safe, rubbing his arthritic knee, the thigh bone only just connected to the knee bone. 'They crowd you out after a while, all the dates you have to remember, or can't help but remember. When you're a kid, the only thing you care about is your own birthday, and Christmas of course – or whatever it is you do?' Robert adds, a barely visible nod to their cultural differences.

'Eid.'

'Right. That one. And you're a kid, so you look forward to it and you count the days and it's special, because there's really only one or two days a year that matter, when you're little. But get a few years on you . . .'

'And there's more?'

'The year's full of them. As you say, your wedding anniversary, and then women always remember when the two of you met, and woe betide you if you don't. First date, first kiss, they go on and on. Course, after that, there's your wedding anniversary. Then you get the kids' birthdays, their wedding days. People start to die, late if you're lucky, early if not, so you get the death days too . . .' He shakes his head at Akeel's grimace. 'Those are anniversaries an' all, son, no denying it. See? Starts off just you and Christmas, ends up a year full of the bloody things.'

Akeel adds a black knitted beanie hat to his winter armour, fastens the top button on his coat, he might not be rushing home to cake, but he does want to get there eventually, has learned enough about Robert's habits in the past weeks to know he needs to make an obvious move, and soon. 'So I've got that to look forward to. Meanwhile I'm not all that keen on making a fuss about being another year older.'

'Twenty-seven? You go and enjoy yourself, pick up a nice bottle of wine and get home.'

Akeel shakes his head, it's not even a month yet, he doesn't know if he can be bothered, then it's out of his mouth anyway. 'Ah, no – "my lot"? We don't drink?'

'That's just for the extremists though, right? Those are the rules everyone breaks indoors, Catholics on the pill, Jews eating bacon, got to be some of you drink.'

'Yeah, but I'm not one of them. And I can't see Rubeina letting me get away with it in the house, even if I did want to.'

Robert takes a moment to consider the possibility of never having enjoyed a single pint, and finds he just can't see it. 'Not a drop?'

Akeel is hot now inside the heavy winter coat, wants to get out into the cold, start the journey back, clock ticking towards six forty, torn between home – with or without cake – and wanting to explain. Always that uncertainty whether to elucidate or to allow the ignorance. He pulls the hat off again. 'OK, there was this one time . . .'

Robert grins, clicks his fingers. 'Go on, my son!'

'It was an accident. First year at college, I was staying in halls of residence and there was this girl, Sarah, we got on well, used to share food, tea, coffee. We ate a lot of toast. Anyway, one night, Sarah had a glass of something, I thought it was lemonade. I'd just got in, run up the stairs, I was thirsty, grabbed the glass, downed it.'

'And? Bolt of lightning? Pillar of salt?'

'It tasted off, so I spat it out. And she was laughing too hard at the look on my face to mind I'd wasted the last of her vodka and tonic.'

'Nice girl.'

'She was a good friend.'

'You didn't want to give it another go?'

Akeel pulls a face, his lips turning down at the memory. 'It wasn't good.'

Robert smiles. 'Hated the taste of bitter at first, believe me. But I learnt to like it. Well, you had to, didn't you?'

'That's what I don't understand, people go on about how alcohol is an acquired taste, why bother sticking with something you don't enjoy?'

Robert considers Akeel's question for a while, the lad has a point, and then a smile comes to his face. 'Ah, but not all that many people have it so good first time in bed, do they? Doesn't stop them trying to get used to it though, does it?'

Akeel bursts out laughing, a barrier broken between the two men, his voice loud and warm in the fluorescent-lit room. 'That's the first time anyone's ever been able to answer that question so it made sense.' He pulls on his hat.

'You're right, lad, on your way. See you Monday.'

Akeel crosses the road and walks up the stairs to the platform at Loughborough Junction, grateful for the cold outside, the damp air cooling his cheeks. He waits for the train, glad he bothered to explain to Robert, pleased the older man was interested, able to listen. But he thinks, too, about where the divisions are, they've gone three weeks with no argument, no disagreement. Akeel wonders how long that can go on, how polite they really want to be, where Robert's cracks are going to show. And his own.

Robert pulls at the soft cord of his old brown trousers to check the keys are jingling loose in his pocket, then follows Akeel outside, locks the front door behind him, opening the box that houses the mechanism for the wide metal roller, just a turn of the key to bring it down, grateful that the days of closing up by hand are behind him now, his old shoulder muscle tear pulling a little anyway, even with this gentle action. Robert will not be sad to leave behind this part of his business, the routine physicality of it all. He padlocks the roller at the bottom, both sides, checking – as he always does – that the locks are tight and safe. He lets himself back into the shop by the side door, and spends another half hour in the now-enclosed front, pottering about, putting away the last of the week's work, gathering together the bits and pieces that Akeel has cleared from other people's pockets, taking them upstairs to sort them, put them away – as he explained to Akeel, just in case the owners remember what they have lost.

Robert has always enjoyed the shop at this time of day. When he was very small, before Alice bought the cleaner's, he'd loved to look into the back of other people's shops. The newsagent's, the grocer's, the bakery, all had a dolls' house fascination for him, what else there might be behind the counter, what else a stockroom might hide. Then, when Alice took over this shop, he found security behind the counter, even more so once he'd closed up for the night. In the old days there'd been a metal grille in front, he could still see out into the street, which meant any late customer could see him inside too, see him and stand at the window and then beg and plead until he either upset them by walking away, or gave in, reopened the doors, unlocked the till and put his evening off by another half hour as he repeated the entire closing-up process all over again. The metal roller, though, shuts off the shop front so it's like any other room in a house – any other windowless room. Robert likes it, held in his own space, held into his own place.

All the last jobs done, he turns off the lights in the shop, checks the machines in the arch and treads upstairs to his home, stopping in at the storeroom on the first floor as he

46

goes, the forgotten leavings of customers' pockets set aside for safekeeping. There is a slow-filtering sense of disappointment as he walks back into his flat. Robert can't imagine living with anyone again after all these years. Once Alice was gone, and then since his Jean and Katie moved out, he became accustomed to his own company, happy to leave a room in the morning and find nothing changed when he comes back in the evening. While knowing no one is going to finish his crossword has its appeal on work days, when all he wants to do is sit in front of the telly and eat his dinner and have a beer or two before going to bed, on Saturday nights there is always – even at his age, even after all this time – a quiet sense that he should be doing something else, anything else.

The Saturday night out. Robert loved it as a teenager, and then when he and Jean were first married, finishing up work late on a Saturday afternoon, hurrying upstairs to wash and shave. Afterwards, all clean and polished and sharp-crease pressed, he'd take Jean out somewhere nice, make a proper night of it. They went dancing at the Locano in Streatham, Jean liked skating too, and Robert, hopeless on the ice himself, had been more than happy to watch her twisting and twirling, right little Sonja Henie. Other times it was out to the pictures at the Elephant or Brixton, up town to see the lights at Christmas and have a frothy coffee, feeling so flash, the pair of them. Even after Katie was born he and Jean had still tried to get out of a Saturday, Alice would babysit, and later, when Katie was old enough, all four of them used to go out together, often only over the road to the Green Man, maybe just the one drink each if things were a bit tight that week – but Saturday night had always been a time to get dressed up and go out. Alice in her red dress, Jean with her smart crocodile handbag and Katie with a bag of crisps, sucking up her weakest of weak shandy through half a dozen straws, every one of them blue, always blue.

Robert wouldn't want to go out now, even if he could be bothered to make a phone call, ask one of his old mates to meet him, and none of them living this way any more, not for years. He doesn't think the effort would be worth it, small talk on the phone, small talk in the pub, nothing much in common now, except age, old stories and complaint. So Robert doesn't make those phone calls. It's his own choice, he'd be the first to admit, but there is always that feeling – that teenage-boy anxiety – about stopping indoors on a Saturday night. It's the opposite of how he feels in the closed-up shop. Down there, the enclosure has a sense of security, upstairs though, Robert can see through the windows, hears the other lives going on outside, moving eagerly into the dark, and he feels far more cut off. It is seven forty. He pulls the curtains and turns on the telly.

In the green and yellow kitchen – the colours were Jean's choice – Robert warms up last night's casserole, listens to the trains crossing the railway bridge, over the road and on down south, hears the voices from the telly in the other room, and opens a second bottle of beer while he waits for the gas ring, one of just two that still work, to heat his meal. He wonders what Akeel's wife will be getting up for his birthday tea, if it's true they really don't make a fuss, or if Akeel just thought he meant a different kind of fuss. Surely the girl will have a present of some sort for the lad? Robert loved birthdays when he was little. The whole lot of it, cards in the morning, and something extra nice for breakfast, special jam maybe, apricot his favourite, a milky coffee, then his birthday tea after school, a carefully wrapped present waiting at his place at the table. Alice often got his presents slightly wrong – a set of toy infantrymen instead of the sailors he'd had his heart set on, a blue Corgi car not the red one he'd told her he wanted –

but even so, Robert loved it. Nana and Granddad coming over just for him, one or two mates home after school to share the cake, being special.

Robert spoons out the steaming casserole on to his plate, braised beef and carrots, two for one at Iceland, raises his bottle to Akeel, probably only just home, maybe not quite, walking up the road to wherever he lives with his little no-nonsense wife, walking home to someone else. Raises the bottle too, to Jean, who left him twenty-five years ago this year. Another anniversary. Then he makes the ten steps through to the front room and takes his place on the left of the two-seat settee, eats his tea in front of the telly, noting, as he usually does, that he wouldn't have picked any of those lottery numbers. If he'd bought a ticket. Which he never has.

Nine

Monday. Feels like spring. Just after ten in the morning, according to the long bank queue waiting in an aggrieved mutter in the street below. Stefan Corey stretches in his wide white bed, long legs and strong arms reach and turn, muscle definition pleasing him as he wakes, slowly returning to the room. Stefan loves to feel the strength of his body, this morning as every morning. Dull day edges its way round the tightly drawn blinds, no matter how carefully he closes them, a little light always manages to find its way into the room. Stefan doesn't object to light, on his skin, hitting the planes of his finely angled body – when he chooses to be lit – but on a morning like this, after a long night like that, he craves the dark. Holding a finger-cracked hand against his eyes and turning on to his side, he becomes aware of the body beside him, the young man beside him. Stefan stops, from thought to muscle to action to inaction, the briefest of pauses, he's not ready for conversation, for another person. The light is harsh enough, another human being would be far too much at this hour. He holds his breath and hopes for the best, that last night's excesses will still have the young man in their inebriate thrall. Too late. The boy sighs a stuttering breath of waking. He reaches a hand along Stefan's torso, Stefan's thigh, then the young man is twisting in the bed, up and down again, down Stefan's fine body, back to his groin, back to his cock.

Stefan lies still for a moment, contemplating the sensation, the young man's long blond curls scratch softly at his lower belly, the concave belly Stefan is so proud of, the belly he has worked to maintain every day, every single day, birthdays and Christmas included, for at least twenty-five years. For at least every day of this young man's life. On the wrong side of his mid-forties, Stefan is all too clear that the young man in his bed, legal though he may be, is definitely a boy. Twenty-odd is so very far away. The young man is there again, still so young, happily there again, his lips and tongue and hungry mouth, eager hands, back there again, but Stefan withholds his conversation and himself. Intentionally and naturally. This young man is perhaps twenty-one, Stefan is forty-six. He knows he looks forty-two maybe, thirty-eight on a good day, very good night, soft light, keeping those blinds drawn tight, but his body is definitely forty-six and his cock is even more certainly forty-six, he's had just over three hours' sleep and he simply can't face it, not even this readily offered, this very eager. He needs sleep and a healthy lunch and several papers to read and, above all, he needs his flat to be empty of everyone but himself and the cat, empty of the boy.

Stefan reaches an arm down to the blond curls and the smiling, hungry face looks up, eager, willing, happy to be in that bed at that time with that man.

'Good morning.'

'Good morning to you. I'm sorry . . . ah . . .'

'Mike.' The young man smiles, name loss no concern of his.

'Right, yeah, thanks . . . Mike. Look, I'm really tired, sorry . . . I need . . .'

'Me to go?' Mike sits up, one hand still resting on Stefan's thigh, smile running on his lips where half a minute before Stefan's flesh had held still. 'Sure?'

Stefan is sure, wishes he wasn't, but knows himself too well. 'Yeah. I have two classes this afternoon, two more tonight. I need to prepare.'

Stefan does have the classes, all four. His Monday afternoon and evening, get going, start-the-week classes, but he doesn't actually need to prepare them. Stefan can teach any of his classes at five minutes' notice, regularly does so when other teachers at the studio fail to turn up. Stefan never fails to turn up. His real preparation is time, and quiet, and no curly-haired boy in his flat. Lovely though the boy is, to look at and to lie with.

Mike needs no further prompting, has rolled from the bed, is pulling on his jeans, his T-shirt. Stefan knows it would be polite to offer coffee, a shower, breakfast. Either of his parents, each of his three sisters would have offered a glass of water at the very least, his big brother would probably have been up and made porridge for his conquest at seven in the morning. A lady conquest of course. But Stefan really doesn't want to offer, so unless the young man asks, he isn't going to offer, not even water. He does remember being twenty-one though and reaches for his wallet in the bedside table. 'Do you need some money?'

Mike looks down from the tight T-shirt he is stretching round his neck.

'Like for a cab?'

'OK,' Stefan agrees. 'Like for a cab.'

'That'd be great, thanks.'

Stefan removes one twenty-pound note, then adds another. The young man takes the first, hands back the second.

'Cab fare's fine. You want a coffee before I go?'

Stefan shakes his head. 'But help yourself.'

'Don't drink coffee. Bad for you.'

Stefan Corey, body-guru to a hundred or more wealthy

London wives and workers, grins. 'You're right. But sometimes, Mike, a little of what's bad for you, is good for you too. Moderation is the key to continued care.'

'You teach that?'

'No. I teach total abstinence and denial and transcendental pain. They like it that way.'

The boy smiles. 'Yeah, hard teachers are often the best, I mean . . . if you like that kind of thing?'

Stefan shakes his head, he knows where this is leading, has been there so often before. 'Sorry, I save that shit for class, the ladies like it . . .'

'Not the men?'

'Not many men come to my classes. And no, the men who do, don't like it, me coming on all Daddy, they find it threatening. It's the women who get off on being pushed. Pushed, pulled, pummelled. Part of their man–woman thing I think.'

'Don't they know you're gay?'

Stefan shrugs, thinking of one or two of his over-achieving regulars. 'I honestly don't think they care, I'm male, they're female, the dynamic works for them. But I leave the master-disciple bollocks in the studio, I don't mind acting it when they're paying, but I don't need to live what I teach.'

'In that case, can I take a beer?'

'Help yourself, there's a few in the fridge from last night.'

When Mike comes back from the kitchen he is already wearing his jacket, trainers on, laces double-knotted. He has a beer in one hand and a chunk of bread and cheese in the other.

'OK, I'm off. Thanks.'

'You're welcome.'

As the young man finally heads for the door, doing up his jacket, breadcrumbs spilling from chewing mouth to polished floor, Stefan feels his shoulders slowly fall, his stomach begin to relax, the tease of welcome solitude on its way. Then he sees Mike's pace slow, the hesitant turn begin.

'Would you like to . . . you know . . . I could leave my number?'

Stefan smiles, and then shakes his head. 'I don't do that. Sorry.'

'Nah, that's cool. Thanks for the beer.' Mike raises the bottle in salute and walks away.

Stefan listens as the young man closes the door to the flat, hears his fast feet running down the first flight of stairs, then the slam of the outside door. He pictures Mike moving out into the crowd on the street, past the bank queue, the too-young mothers taking their whining children into McDonald's, the old women who stand at the bus stop to chat as much as to wait for the bus. He imagines him crossing the road, four lanes of impatient traffic pouring out fumes and frustration, then pocketing the twenty and fishing coins from his pocket for a number 12 bus to take him across the river, back into Soho, back where Stefan found him last night. Good on him, with a week just beginning and a bottle of beer in his young hand, Stefan would have done exactly the same. If he didn't have the mortgage to pay, a gas bill due, a studio meeting to go to, classes to teach. If he, too, were twenty-odd instead of forty-six.

Stefan gets up, begins a half-hearted sun salute, gives up at the third down dog and goes to the kitchen where he drinks a long glass of unfiltered water. He reaches a slightly shaking hand to lift up the blind, looks down at the flow of people crawling away from Camberwell Green, the old trees and the littered ground that any day now will host an inordinate number of daffodils, Southwark council trumpeting its care for the community in the green and yellow of a spring rectangle. In the opposite direction the wheeling and limping and frightened propel themselves in varying degrees of ill health up Denmark Hill towards the hospital. All that shopping and talking and shouting and living already, too early, too many of them.

Stefan pushes the blind back into the window frame, blocking as much light as possible, and eases his body between the just-warm sheets. He pulls the duvet close to his chilled skin and stretches out across the mattress, his fine long limbs making it, marking it their own. Five minutes later, when the cat is sure the stranger with the big feet has definitely gone, she crawls out from her hiding place under the bed, leaps to the centre of the duvet, turns three times clockwise and then nestles herself into the edge of his thigh. Her man moves his leg to make more space for her and then Stefan Corey is fast asleep, alone. Just the way he likes it, the way the cat likes it.

Monday afternoon, Stefan Corey walks down Coldharbour Lane into Brixton, long arms pumping by his sides, smooth striding paces, head held high, face up to a grey sky so heavy with waiting rain it may well catch him before he slows for the tube. He could get any number of buses into town from the Camberwell end, but Stefan is looking good today, and a London bus, windows fogged with hair-product smears, offers little opportunity to display his charm. A quick smile to himself in the glass of a darkened pub door, then he looks down at his watch, quickens his pace still further.

The walk to the tube from his flat on the corner by Camberwell Green is a taste-bud awakening for Stefan, every time. First the deli, then its cousin bakery next door, never having confirmed if the owners are Greek or Turkish Cypriot, Stefan is careful not to question the particular Mediterranean provenance of the sesame-studded bread he buys there, enjoys for its white-flour wickedness. Then the

Chinese supermarket where bright-scaled fish glisten on the iced table, eyes wide at the shock of ending their lives next to the Woolworths in Camberwell. Round the corner to the bakery, fuggy with the combination of cooking and the two dozen people packed in, picking up a late lunch, later still because of the queue. Lunch that will now be eaten in the office from a plastic container, radiating the warmth of rice and peas, curry goat, extra gravy, always plenty gravy, as his grandmother would offer herself. Were she alive, and working in a shop on Coldharbour Lane. Stefan thinks not. His Grandma Corey could cook all the dishes of her childhood, but she didn't enjoy the process, saved it for holidays and Christmas, tradition and family dictating her hours by the stove. She didn't like to cook, but she could certainly sing, and when she did have to cook, for festivals, funerals, it was her voice Stefan recalled best, her joy in music just masking her boredom in the kitchen. Now, all four grandparents dead, and his father gone since ten days after his thirteenth birthday, Stefan still cannot walk past the bakery, which he does several days a week, without the spices slamming him back to childhood, the family of his past.

At Loughborough Junction he passes half a dozen gated businesses, each one carved out of an old railway arch, most of them holding car works or metalworks or woodworks. By the dry cleaner's he sees that the long-closed public lavatory is also up for rent, wonders how brave an entrepreneur would have to be to re-envision the red brick and metal grilles. Brave or stupidly rich. He drops off his shirts, smiling at the new guy working alongside Robert, young and well shaped, though too straight for Stefan to fancy beyond a glance, and turns back out of the shop, pushes paid bills through the open mouth of the postbox, rounds the railway bridge, the Control Tower takeaway, Guinness punch for a pound, fresh sorrel juice just under, and on alongside

Coldharbour Lane Mansions, dusty old flats slowly exchanging their squatters' ghosts for PVC windows and laminate flooring, curling Che posters replaced by tulips in IKEA frames. Stefan walks on towards the phone shops – old for new, sim cards replaced, no questions asked – the money wiring places, competing tunes blasting from the parked minicab drivers, and the nail bars, the barbers', the record shops, each one an example of the slow, not at all sure, urban gentrification that creeps in just before the Barrier Block, where Brixton proper begins and a dozen cameras steal his soul from every angle.

Above the hidden Effra, Stefan stops by the street entrance to the market, the babble of accents and languages reminding him how fast this place has changed, what was black and some white in his teens is now a landing site for all the Africas, any number of Portuguese and what sounds to Stefan's untrained ear like a good half of Eastern Europe. He remembers a Pentecost service with his mother's mother, the faithful grandmother, how she disapproved of speaking in tongues, insisting if the speakers couldn't translate for themselves, then it most certainly was not the same gift that was accorded the apostles when the dove-flames descended in that upper room and they went out into the market place of Jerusalem, speaking to each in his own language. Stefan knows a few market traders who seem to have that skill themselves, meanwhile he has an upper room of his own to get to and twenty extraordinarily lithe middle-aged women offering themselves in willing submission. He checks his watch again, there is time for a cup of coffee. And a cake. Maybe. He pats his stomach, feels the muscles taut. Cake, yes, but not cream, not much.

Ten

As Stefan is descending into the tube, Marylin Wright is running down the escalators at King's Cross, twenty-five minutes from Brixton if the Victoria line is running a good service. Marylin is in a hurry, pushes past tourists standing on the left, studying their *A to Z* as if their lives depended on it, arguing about where to change. On another day Marylin might choose to help them, she likes to be a helpful Londoner, dispel the myth, and she loves the tube, savours its brave, first-in-the-world depths. Today, though, she has spent all morning listening to people who don't do her job tell her how to do her job, writing down new protocols and old practice as if a masters degree in economics entitled a young woman half her age to explain exactly how to deal with yet another death-defying patient, hanging on to life months and years after their prognosis has run its course. As if there could be a protocol for changing the dressings on ulcerated legs and kneeling at the amputated feet of an old woman crying for the children who never visit. But Marylin likes her job, so she attends the courses and ignores the coursework, and now she is hurrying to make sure that Mrs Patricia Ryan of Denmark Hill has remembered to lock her front door and turn off the gas. If Mrs Patricia Ryan has remembered she has gas, last month the old lady forgot to pay the bill and spent a week without hot water.

At Oxford Circus a group of teenage girls boards the

carriage, atoms of arrogance and fear, they are moving too fast to get a fix on any one for more than a moment at a time. Marylin looks across to the tightest knot of young women, each girl fiercely, briefly, illuminated by what she is yet to become. The fat girl who will shed her excess flesh with a growth spurt at eighteen and emerge shocked and scared into a world of eager men. The bright girl who cannot show her depths, hides how much she knows with a veneer of nasty sophistication and cleverly controlled wit, just funny enough to make the other girls laugh, never funnier than the boys. Marylin watches this girl and her heart sinks, so many years after the first horse's hooves, the smashed windows, the cracked glass of the heavy ceiling, it is heartbreaking to see this girl tone down her full brilliance in order to seem cute enough to the two lads sitting at the other end of the carriage. Marylin listens as their south London accents rise above the tube rumble, taking in each voice with its matching imported *innit* and the twisted *is it* – both phrases statement not question, exclamation not question mark – along with the *aks* she says herself, as has been pointed out by helpful management consultants, and still Marylin chooses not to reposition her consonants. In the spin of raised voices she recognises the religious girls who attend church every Sunday and cry for Jesus to love them, hungry for his blessing both in body and in spirit. Just as during the week they also ache for the boy up the road to love them and truly believe he could save them too. These girls already know they'll need both the boy from up the road and the one who comes down from the cross on Sunday morning.

Marylin shakes her head, annoyed with herself, wishing she didn't mind their noise, wishing she didn't think the girls needed to shut up, but as the train moves towards her home, away from the parts of the city that are almost only white and certainly mostly tourist, she hears the wish echo through her head. Shut up, be good, behave well. You are a young woman. You are a young black woman, mixed-race woman, not-white woman. They are looking at you, and they judge you harshly, judge us harshly. She and her girlfriends were once just like them, playing loud music on the bus, taking up too much space even though each one wished individually to be smaller, thinner, cackling secret jokes, a group of constantly shifting focus so that one day she was in the inner sanctum and another day, with no warning, she was far on the outside. Marylin wishes she could sit these girls down and ask everyone else in the carriage, everyone over the age of forty or even thirty, to tell their own stories of being loud and wild and delicious, how they too were sure they were the first ones to be this special, but she stops herself, because it would not be nice, and anyway, the girls would never believe her. As she walks up into Brixton Road where a posse of the hungry, the homeless and the strung out wait to politely request her spare change, Marylin hears the girls behind her, still giggling about the boys they left behind when they changed tubes at Stockwell, boys that don't come to their church. A boy from a different church always was a very enticing prospect.

Marylin turns left out of the tube and on to the market. She picks and pays for a couple of just-ripe mangoes, thinking it's been so damn long since she had a particular boy or man to think about, where he worshipped, if at all, would be the least of her concerns. On the corner of Coldharbour Lane, right where the Saturday Christians usually position their loudspeaker, she sees a young couple arguing, alcohol and local illicit substances having taken their fight to a higher level. The usual passer-by interest in any street theatre has become a loose semicircle of head-tilted pedestrians, each walker paused in mid-movement, bodies still facing the market or the tube or the Ritzy, faces twisted to the fight. The passers-by, not quite passing, wait long enough to see the woman land a punch, the man parry a blow, the ever-present siren wail, and then they move on. Marylin turns down Coldharbour Lane and thinks of her full working day tomorrow and the days after, and remembers she has never been very good at sharing, plans to eat both these mangoes herself when she gets home, and will be pleased to do it alone. Maybe a man wouldn't be that useful after all. At Loughborough Junction she waves through the glass to Robert in the dry cleaner's shop, old friend of her Aunty Irene, makes a mental note of the fit young man standing beside him, and decides on a bus the rest of the way to Camberwell, there's a 345 at the lights, she'll be with Mrs Ryan ten minutes sooner. If she's really lucky Mrs Ryan will have remembered she was coming.

By five thirty Marylin is done for the day and on her way home. Twenty minutes of fast walking and she has turned her hunger for the heavy mangoes banging against her thigh into a salivating yearning. She turns off, away from the fried chicken shop, the halal butcher and what was once a useful post office and is now another empty room, down the short stretch of her own quiet road, pushing back the heavy gate to the squat block sitting in fat Victorian splendour, the culverted Effra flowing on beneath, its moisture slowly seeping up through drains and diversions, cracked Victorian piping and thick London clay. Marylin has been walking up the four flights of steps of St Anne's Residences since she learned to walk. From the street it is impossible to imagine the Babylonian ranks of garden that climb the balconies along each floor, but having attained the fourth floor, looking towards her own door where the steps open to the balcony, green growth is all she can see. One neighbour has masses of geraniums, buds that will soon be fat red flowers, another offers fifty or more snowdrops hanging their heads round a dozen early tulips. Curving over Marylin's own door is the old climbing rose that Romeo-leaps three floors from the converted basement, so the fat petals of the amber rose can criss-cross her front window with its thorny branches, while the deep roots assiduously drain every nutrient from the ground, reaching into the foundation stones of the building, its beginning.

St Anne's Residences were built in the 1890s, the work of a handful of London philanthropists, old men nervous of camel's humps and needle's eyes. Most of the original inhabitants of St Anne's, the mothers especially, had worked in service, before their marriages, before their babies. The first woman ever to live in Marylin's flat had been pastrycook to the editor of *The Manchester Guardian*, and she'd seen plenty of views from fourth-floor windows before, Berkeley Square and Grosvenor Square, but what she'd looked out on in the past had never been her own world. From the new flat in St Anne's, this first tenant looked through the back bedroom window to her children's school, then the street, the shops, the fields beyond, and back in again to the spreading, branching railway line. The families arranged along the streets off Coldharbour Lane had always rented their homes, but in blocks like St Anne's they were also renting, for the first time, a view of their own people as well.

Twenty minutes after turning her key in the door, Marylin has put away the morning's notes in a special folder she keeps for the purpose, not likely to be opened until she next attends a similar course. She has been through her list for her rounds tomorrow, added a new note to Mrs Ryan's file reminding herself to call the old woman's GP, she is halfway through a large glass of red wine. She stands at her kitchen window and, leaning over the sink, peels the first mango by hand. She eats in big mouthfuls, juice running down her chin and fingers, dribbling to her elbows, she sucks her fingers and the fat seed, mouth full of warm fruit flesh, looking out to the city and the early evening lights, catching the sparkle from the western rim of the Cyclops' Eye as it slowly turns tourists in the dark.

Eleven

'What's up, laughing boy?'

'Nothing.'

'Rubbish. You've been staring out that window like a lost soul all afternoon. It won't get any better for looking at. Like a pretty girl.'

'What?' Akeel turns back to Robert, interested now.

The older man smiles, big hands hugging his mug, the swollen arthritic joints on his index and second fingers looking more like his mother's every day. 'Pretty girls. Start off the best they're ever going to be, all downhill from there.'

'That's a bit rough.'

'I'm kidding, lad. Sort of. But you know, those model types, they don't exactly age well, do they?'

Akeel shakes his head, still not used to Robert's sweeping dismissals and generous endorsements. 'I don't know, maybe not.'

'How about Rubeina? First time you saw her? Did you know straight off, or did she grow on you?'

'Well, given what I saw was head and shoulders, four in a row, I'd say she grew on me.'

Now it's Robert's turn to look confused.

Akeel explains. 'It was arranged.'

'What? Proper – all set up?'

'Not entirely.' Akeel shakes his head. 'Not the way it

always is on those TV programmes, screaming kids and furious parents.'

'Son, nothing's like it is on the telly, we'd all be inside or insane if our lives were that interesting.' Robert looks out at the rain blurring the street, glad to be inside, driers humming behind them, nearing the end of their cycle, the warm air they've been pumping out to the back alley turning cool, pleased to have someone to talk to. And surprised to be pleased. 'Go on then, tell us.'

'Not much to tell. My mum and dad knew her mum and dad, my parents were back home, they met Rubeina who was there on holiday too, sent her picture back to me to see if I'd like it.'

'And did you?'

Akeel nods, a slow smile. 'She was gorgeous.'

'And now?'

'I love her.'

'Course, but you're used to how she looks?' Robert downs the last of his tea, quickly, wanting to get on and make his point, a bead of tepid liquid hanging on the side of his lip. 'Bet you don't see it first thing in the morning and last thing at night like you used to.'

'Well, no. We've been married for nearly five years.'

'There you are then, point made. Doesn't get any better for looking at. What if you hadn't liked the look of her, though?'

'She wasn't the first girl I'd met. There were a couple of others.'

'And?'

'Neither of them liked the look of me.'

'I see.'

'I doubt it, I don't imagine you've got any idea what it feels like to know that you're being actively considered as a potential husband from the very first meeting. We get introduced, no one in my family has to be with someone they don't want, but all the same, you're still being judged. And you're judging them too. I went to dinner at people's houses, lovely meals, everyone making a real effort, and then, several times, I just didn't . . .'

'Fancy the girl?'

'Or I did and she didn't fancy me. I know it might sound odd to you, but it really did feel like a market sometimes.'

'Don't be soft, it's not odd, it's the same for everyone.'

'No it's not, white girls don't do that, weigh you up, they don't need to, not any more.'

'Bollocks, lad, you want to take your blinkers off. We all do it, the lot of us, you meet someone, and you try it on, your future, start to imagine what it might be, it's only natural.'

'Didn't feel natural. It felt like hard work.'

'Nobody ever said nature was easy,' Robert says. 'That's why they call her Mother.'

Akeel had really liked Malika, had been falling in love with Malika, but then, when it didn't work out with her, he'd imagined himself content with Alisha, happy enough. Except that neither Malika nor Alisha wanted him. Alisha went for a doctor, she was training to be one herself, it probably made sense, and Malika informed Akeel that he was neither religious nor political enough for her. She wanted a proper Pakistani boy, not a British boy stuck, as she saw it, somewhere in between. Akeel couldn't quite call it heartbreak, knew they'd not really been close enough for that, but it had felt close enough. A rip, a tear perhaps, if not an actual break. He thinks of the first time he met Rubeina, her knowing grin. No other phrase for it, absolutely knowing, and in control too. Even five years ago, two years from finishing her own degree, eighteen months younger than him, Rubeina did not do holding back, not around her own family, not even around his. She was very pretty, clever, his mum and dad would be delighted if it worked out, two families happy to come together, and he wasn't going to be turned down again. It wasn't the rush of desire he'd felt for Malika, or the bond with Alisha, but it worked. In the process of making the effort to win her, Rubeina won him – Akeel knows he fell in love before she did, expects he'll probably stay there longer too.

Robert is asking why he's been looking out the window, what's worrying him, Akeel doesn't know where to start. The fight he had with Rubeina this morning about the crazy hours he's working, the three hours it takes him travelling to and from the shop every day, the not-so-mild panic he felt coming on when Robert left him alone for half an hour at lunchtime. How much he wants it, all of it, this life he doesn't quite feel adult enough to move into, husband, father one day, Inshallah, businessman. His own father had two children at his age, his grandfather even more. Akeel wants to be adult and responsible, and wants to run away from it all at the same time. He doesn't say this though, explains the immediate problem instead, his cousin's wedding coming up. The best man's speech he hasn't even started yet, too tricky, the bringing together of English and Pakistani families, white girl and brown boy. Rubeina's been nagging for weeks and yet he still sits in the train, on the tube, every morning, playing games on his phone, fearful not finished, not writing his speech.

'Even the ones who don't agree with the marriage, they're coming anyway, they all want to get a look at the English girl.'

'Fireworks, were there?'

'My mother says his mother's still unhappy, and I don't suppose Angela's family are any keener than ours, and everyone has some old uncle who blurts out the truth at some point.'

67

Robert laughs. 'That's my job, that is.'

'And I have to make this speech, and I don't even want to go to the wedding. I don't like weddings, there's always so much pressure to have a good time.'

Robert looks at the young man in front of him. Really takes him in, chewing on his lower lip the way he always does when he's thinking hard, and then nods his head, agreeing with himself. Decision made.

'Follow me, son. I've something to show you upstairs.'

Robert unlocks the door to the room above the shop and ushers Akeel in ahead of him. The first thing that strikes Akeel is the smell. It's the smell of charity shops, jumble sales, second-hand stalls. The smell of thousands of people letting go, forgetting. Dead skin-cells dry in emptied pockets, licked-finger DNA lingering on dog-eared corners. The room they are standing in has the same dimensions as Robert's front room above and the shop below, but it isn't a room any more, it's a tiny warehouse. Divided into three narrow alleyways by floor-to-ceiling shelves, more shelving against each wall, almost blocking all the light from the window, two bare dusty bulbs hanging from the ceiling. And on every metal shelf is a box or file, each one named, dated, all the boxes different sizes and shapes, from shoeboxes to those proudly displaying their capacity as equal to 24 tins of Heinz Baked Beans, every box flush with the wedge of its shelf, each one in its own order.

'What's this?' Akeel asks.

'What we've to clear out if you want to turn this into the luxury flat your missus is so keen on getting all that rent from.'

'You said it was a storeroom.'

'It is.'

Robert smiles, disappears behind a shelf, comes back a moment later with a wide, flat cardboard box. He shows

Akeel the label on the side, plastered over the exact number of Jammie Dodgers the box is meant to hold, it reads in Robert's careful writing: WEDDING SPEECHES, JUNE '76–MAY '02.

'This, son,' Robert speaks quietly, looking round the room with an obvious pride, 'this little lot, is what people leave in their pockets.'

Twelve

Outside the shop, the four buses that have been queuing at the lights greet the green and screech past, in the opposite direction a 345 stops, allowing a middle-aged man singing about the Queen of Judah to get off, and fifteen-year-old Shannon Dobson to climb on, throwing her half-smoked cigarette behind her. The Poet stops to pick it up, it is burning still, and smells of a young girl's mouth.

On the front of the dry cleaner's shop on the corner, the faces of unknown men picked out in plaster look down from the building's façade, calmly observing the singing man as he crosses the street, no concern for lights or cars, no interest in their rules. Above these faces, in the upstairs storeroom, Akeel Khan takes the cardboard box Robert Sutton offers him, pulls back the lid and flicks through the pages inside. Typed pages, handwritten pages, photocopied pages. White A4 sheets and thin airmail blue, the backs of envelopes and the insides of cigarette packets. White sheets that have crossings out, and yellowed paper with faded alternatives pencilled in the margins. Pages that were printed soberly with care and the best-intentioned thought, and those written in anger or sorrow or simple insobriety. Pages covered in outpourings of love, and those that really don't know what to say, or how to say it. Robert, and Alice before him, kept them all.

'Summer, you see.'

Akeel looks up from the speech he's reading, Lee praising his mate Dean's choice of bride, while also suggesting her own choice of bridesmaid isn't bad either, not that Dean's known for making that many good choices.

'What's summer? What?'

Robert points to the box. 'Wedding speeches. We get them in the summer, every year.'

'I don't understand.'

Akeel shakes his head, leaves Lee's speech on a shelf and takes another from the box, this one about Lola and Joseph, meeting in the market, making their union more legal than their stock. Here the writer has added a scribbled note to himself – Pause for laugh!

'What is all this?'

Robert points to the box. 'That's when the weddings are, aren't they, usually? Summer. Not this cousin of yours, obviously, not if it's soon enough for you to be worrying about your speech, but mostly, right?'

'I suppose so, but . . .'

'Keep up, son, now, say the wedding's in summer, best man or groom, father of the bride, whoever, brings in his suit, he's not going to be wearing it until the next wedding at least, glad to get rid of the bloody thing most of them, fathers of the bride 'specially, now it's done and dusted and all they've got's the bills to face – he leaves the speech in his pocket. Bob's your uncle, or best man, as the case may be.'

Akeel lifts the box again. 'All of these? All speeches?'

'Well, girls do speeches these days too, but I reckon they must keep 'em in their handbags. Pockets on lasses' clothes are never as good as ours, no depth, and they're always more worried about line, aren't they? Used to be a different matter when things were made properly – a nice costume, like Alice used to say, well cut to fit the body, not remaking

71

your body to fit the clothes, one size fits all – and it never does . . .'

'Robert,' Akeel interrupts, 'you were explaining about the speeches?'

'Right. Yes.' He runs his hand along a shelf, checks for dust, rubs the soft grey from his fingertips to his trousers. 'Most of that lot are your best-man speeches. A few grooms in there an' all, some fathers of brides, not too many, maybe they remember to keep theirs, or the wives do – new wives, brides' mothers – for a keepsake? But yeah, mostly they're best men.'

Akeel still can't quite take in what he is holding, let alone the room full of boxes around them. 'You keep them?'

'Alice started it. Collecting, when she was working down at the laundry, I kept it up once we took over here. Family tradition.'

Robert looks at the shelves surrounding them, the heavy metal racks, the second-hand bookshop smell of old paper and fingerprints thick in the room. 'Hung on to all sorts, Alice did, not half what they found at the laundry mind, more than one dead baby turned up in those sheets.' He turns slowly, admiringly. 'You couldn't fill a room with just speeches, not even a little room like this.' Robert points out another box, the label BUS TICKETS/TRAIN TICKETS in a careful rounded hand. The progression of Alice's ageing scrawl leads them over the shelves as the dates on the boxes rise through the fifties, sixties, turning to neatly lettered labels when it reaches Robert and the seventies. He indicates a shelf in the corner, two boxes labelled JEWELLERY. 'A few rings. Though mostly they're asked after.' He nods, recalling. 'Used to be a lot of hankies, not so many these days, tissues took over. Alice used to give them back all lovely, washed and ironed, nice sharp triangle for the ladies, rectangle for the men. After a while, she got tired of doing the work for them, gratis. What she said was, most people couldn't remember what they'd left in their pockets, and that was why they never thought to come and ask. Do you?' Robert breaks off, waiting for Akeel's answer.

'Maybe not, depends on what it is. We probably only remember what we've lost if it matters, don't we?'

Robert nods hard, glad Akeel seems to be getting it. 'Exactly. And things like these – speeches, well, when they're done, they're done, aren't they? Once you've got over being nervous, said the words, got a few pints down you, chatted up the bridesmaid . . . you're not likely to remember, are you? Alice thought it was more trouble than it was worth, coming upstairs, leaving the counter while she searched out whatever someone said they'd left. Or thought they'd left, half the time people come in and swear blind they've left their lottery ticket or bus pass in their pocket, then find it a week later under the sideboard.'

'But she started storing things?'

'Not like we had any room out back in the arch, you know how full it is, even more now with the big dryers. So she'd always have to come upstairs if they asked, after a while she got fed up with it, took to saying, "No, not found a thing." No matter what it was they were asking about.'

'And it was all this organised?'

'Dear God no, Alice was no housewife. Boxes all over the show, labelled, yes, but a hell of a mess, up and down the stairs an' all. When Jean moved in though, we took the flat upstairs and Alice moved down here. We had to take the presses out of this room, they'd been up here all that time, hell of an effort that was, why we didn't bother using it as a flat in the first place, too much like hard work. Anyway, once it was clear, she made this her place.'

'And used her front room for storage?'

Robert brings his hand to rest on the shelf beside him, it

73

is a proprietary hand, a proud hand. 'No, I did this, after she died. Alice kept all the boxes in here, but no room for a system with her armchair and sideboard, telly on top. I put in the shelves, sorted it out. Gave me something to do when she'd gone. I had all this time left over.'

Akeel wonders at Robert's evident pride in what is at best hoarding, and at worst maybe theft. 'But surely all this stuff belongs to other people? Didn't she feel bad about keeping it? These things are probably really important to someone.'

'Why leave 'em in your pocket then?' Robert shakes his head. 'Nah, lad, your average best man'd be more likely to think he left the speech screwed up on the bridesmaid's bedroom floor, wouldn't he? Than in his top pocket?'

'And what do you think?'

'Same really, more or less. If they don't care enough to check their pockets when they drop the stuff off, it's not my lookout.'

'But what if someone left something that really mattered?'

'It's all dated, son, open your eyes, if anything came in that really mattered – anything anyone wanted to tell me about, mind – I'd be able to put my hand on it in no time. Have done once or twice, though you'd be surprised how few ever ask. Maybe they think they left their bits and pieces somewhere else, or maybe they don't know they've lost it. Think that's more likely, don't you? People don't even know what they've lost?'

The two men look around the room, a screeching magpie swoops over the tiled roof opposite, a speeding cyclist narrowly misses Dan and Charlie crossing the road, helping each other back to their sofa from the off-licence, a child screams in the street and his mother slaps away the noise.

Robert holds out his hand, asking for the box Akeel is still holding. 'Give it here, you're going to be late home.'

'Can't I see more?'

Having felt the temptation of the room, Akeel isn't ready to go yet.

'You can take that pile with you, have a look through, see if there's anything useful. If you like. If you're careful.'

Akeel looks down at the box in his hand. 'Feels a bit weird. They're not mine, are they?'

'Not anyone's, not any more. Lost property.'

'Maybe I could just take a few? See if they've got any jokes?'

'They've all got jokes, believe me. Most of them are rubbish.'

'You've read the lot?'

Robert shrugs, 'Skimmed mostly, just in case.'

'In case of what?'

'Can't really say. Think I just thought, I ought to have some idea, you know, what they said. I figured if there was anything in this lot I ought to tell someone about, it would be obvious.'

'And was there?'

'Once or twice.'

'Like what?'

Robert grins, 'You don't get me that easy. That's part of the job too, you'll learn, keeping secrets. Go on.' He waves a hand at the box. 'Take a handful off the top. If you don't find anything that suits, you can always come back and have another go tomorrow.'

'Like a library?'

Robert ushers him out of the room. 'Only I'm not telling you to shut up.'

'Not much.' Akeel smiles over his shoulder as he walks down the stairs.

'That's right, not much.'

As he leaves that night Akeel asks Robert about his own wedding, if the speeches were good then.

75

'Not bad, son. The bad memories started long after the wedding, usually do.'

They stand beside the roller as it shudders round and down to the ground and Robert explains about the wedding in Kennington, the church so badly hit during the war and looking like nothing outside, but pretty enough inside to shut Jean's mum up, not that anything could keep her happy for long. The proper wedding she insisted on, but then a reception to make Alice proud, over the road at the Green Man. Robert looks at the old pub opposite, newly made flats now, hemmed in by a triangle of railway bridges. 'That place has seen some parties. Now look at it – luxury flats? With the trains starting at five in the morning? I don't flamin' well think so. Bloody good reception though, we had, a lot of beer and a big old fruit cake, and just a stumble across the road to get home. We were stopping with Jean's mum and dad then, but we had our wedding night here, in the flat. Alice thought it'd give us some peace.'

'I suppose you carried Jean over the threshold?'

'I carried her right over the bloody junction. Across the road, through the door, up two flights of steps to the flat. I was in love, lad. Makes you strong.'

Thirteen

August 1965, Robert Sutton was coming up twenty-two, Jean Swanson turned nineteen in the April, Helen Shapiro was on *Juke Box Jury* and Robert knew the Byrds outclassed the Beatles, no question. Robert didn't much fancy Jean when they first met, he was clear the girls he liked were the ones he and his mates called 'real women'. Breasts and hips, in and out. All the girls Robert and his mates knew wanted to be little like Jean Shrimpton, thin like Audrey Hepburn. He could see the attraction, but Robert turned fifteen in 1958 and for his birthday Alice took him to see *Houseboat*. She'd always liked the look of Cary Grant, and in the dark of the Empire, Robert discovered Sophia Loren. Everything about her appealed – hair, eyes, breasts, hips, legs – the whole shebang. So for seven years Robert pursued women who look like Loren, or Bardot, or Lollobrigida, and he did so with a considerable degree of success. Robert Sutton's fancies ensured a good number of South London's loveliest young women avoided their younger sisters' Twiggy-induced anorexia. Until Jean Swanson came along.

Jean was small, and fair, more mouse than blonde, closer to skinny than thin, in winter her skin faded to a waxy pallor and people were always asking if she felt entirely well, in summer she veered from white to pink, pale freckles speckling her bird's egg skin. She had no breasts to speak of, no hips at all. She dressed well enough, but not showy, around her neck she wore only the plain gold cross she'd been given as her cousin Carol's bridesmaid. She was not at all Robert's type, and still she shone. Even Robert, scanning the room for cleavage that evening – as every evening – could see that the girl was shining. What he didn't know at the time was that Jean was shining for him. She'd been watching Robert Sutton for some time.

Jean first saw the man who was to become her husband when she walked past the shop, early in the morning on her way home to Kennington, after a night out with her mate Susie Erskinshaw. It was warm for spring, and she decided to walk instead. St John the Divine wasn't far down Loughborough Road, she could see the church steeple between the roofs, and she'd walked home from St John's often enough. This way she'd also get a chance to walk past the flat that Susie's oldest brother had just been offered on the estate. Nice flats, all new and bright, some of them with views clean over to the river. If Susie was lucky, and her brother took the flat instead of going off to Australia the way his wife Hazel kept threatening, she'd be able to get herself on the list too. A home for life and no chance of getting kicked out, pretty much all Susie wanted really. And a bloke and some kids of course.

When Jean crossed the road with the Green Man behind her, Robert was outside unlocking the shop, starting his day, and he smiled as she went past. It was an ordinary smile, the smile Alice had been drumming into her son ever since she took on the business, a smile that draws in customers, not every day, every smile, but simply because you've been nice to them once, they're bound to come back eventually. Some of them will come back often enough to make it worth doing, smiling. It wasn't a flirting smile, there was nothing of Jean to flirt for, not in Robert's eyes. So he smiled and continued his unlocking. One padlock, two, the big old keys to the main door. Maybe he said something about the nice day, the early warmth in the air, maybe not, years later neither of them could remember, but Jean walked home making plans.

She asked Susie if she knew the lad in the cleaner's at the junction, got more than she bargained for in answer when Susie's dad told her a few stories about that Alice Sutton. Jean added a pinch of salt to what she heard and then made an effort to have a word with one of the lads Robert went round with, a mate of her cousin Vic's, someone she could talk to without seeming too keen. She found out where they went for a drink, what pictures they liked, and then Jean started going to those places too. Just to look at first, to make sure that what she thought was lovely on a bright sunny morning was as good on a muggy evening, a damp night. After a month of watching and looking, she decided it was, he was. Robert Sutton seemed quiet and self-sufficient and he looked as if he knew what he wanted, but didn't shout about it like so many of the lads. Jean knew what she wanted too, and she thought they might do well together. So she made her play. From the girls she'd seen him chatting to, chatting up, Jean understood she wouldn't win him with her figure, she'd have to win him with herself.

They started to talk in the pub every now and then, meet on the street – always an accident he thought, always by intent she knew – and then there was something else she liked even more, a slight reticence, a sense that Robert was holding himself back. At first Robert's restraint made him more attractive, there was more to uncover, more to find out. It became less appealing as the years wore on, once he was hers, Jean wanting to know all his thoughts and Robert with no idea how to tell them, to be the sharing husband she started to ask for in the seventies, demand in the eighties.

79

Later, it wasn't at all desirable that her husband and the father of her child should hold it all in. Until the day she wished he'd never said anything, and she had never asked.

The following May, when Robert watched Jean walk down the aisle, he knew she'd made the right choice in picking him. He knew, too, that he would never again sleep with a woman with high breasts and wide hips, feel a fullness of body and desire straddling him. In truth, standing there in the church, watching Jean's dad walk her proudly towards him, he had to admit he minded, a little, not a lot. In the nine months they'd been together – three months to fall in love, five to make it serious, and then just three weeks to sort out the wedding – Robert had given up his fantasies of the dream woman, and fallen in love with a real one. As Jean walked to him in white, her silver-wire glasses shining beneath the veil, he promised himself he'd do his best.

Alice and Edna sat up front on opposite pews, visions in shop-bought apricot and home-made sky blue, each woman watching her only child, each despairing at the state of the union. Edna Swanson sighed, and raised her perfectly ironed and initialled hankie to her eye, thankful for three small but united mercies. First, her Jean had always been tiny; second, empire-line dresses were all the rage this year; and third, she knew the priest well enough to get two hours spare for an unbooked wedding on a spring Saturday. Father Dickson, gentleman that he was, hadn't even raised an eyebrow. Now all she had to hope for was an overdue birth and they might just get away with it. Edna shuddered, and promised herself another half hour in the Lady Chapel as she moved over for her husband to join her. Still, pub reception or not, at least the lad had a job. Maybe he even had a future, he could certainly support Jean, it wasn't as if clothes were ever going to start cleaning themselves.

From her side Alice looked to Robert and smiled encouragement, family like that, he was bloody well going to need it. Not that she blamed Jean, not at all, poor little bitch had come to her in tears, terrified to tell her own mother about the baby. Like Alice herself though, never a thought of getting rid of it, though Alice had given enough encouragement, as obvious hints as she could manage without coming right out and shocking the girl. She liked that about her prospective daughter-in-law, that she was willing to take it on, her responsibility. Bit of spunk about her, nothing wrong with that, though you'd have thought the whole bloody lot of them were going to hell in a handcart the way Jean's mother had carried on.

First everyone was summoned to Sunday dinner in best bib and tucker, wading their way through a mound of dried-out beef and undercooked potatoes. Then, while a bitter apple pie slowly burned to a crisp in a spotlessly clean oven, the choice was made, the day picked, the vicar's wife consulted in hushed tones, and a wedding dress turned out within the month. But Alice wasn't having it all taken out of her hands, said as they were family now, couldn't she help out, maybe do the reception? She noticed Edna wasn't so keen to argue once Alice said she meant to pay for it too, and the old man looked positively bloody grateful. But not at that church hall. Alice put her foot down, and then, with Peggy and Jessie, her old mates from Walton's laundry, she spent the best part of two days churning out gala pies and cheese straws and Scotch eggs and God knows how many sausage rolls. Even this morning, Jessie had been cutting the crusts off egg cress sandwiches to keep her ladyship happy. Now if the bloody vicar didn't get on with it and give them a chance to get a drink down themselves soon she didn't know what she'd do. Alice's cross-your-heart corset, reining her in and letting her loose in just the right places, was itching all to hell.

When Robert and Jean pledged their troth to each other and, silently, each to the little one between them, they did so in love and desire and hope. Hope of making it all the way, hope for the baby they hadn't planned but didn't really mind either, hope that they'd be happy. And they were, for a long time. What they didn't know then was that though Jean could make Robert love her, once things had changed, she couldn't make herself keep loving Robert. Years later, Jean told Robert everything would have been so different if she'd only got a bus that morning, not walked past the shop, not made the effort to see what she could see. He knew she was right, and he knew that in the end, while she was packing and crying into her suitcase, she probably wished she had got a bus, or gone home later in the day, had a lie-in at Susie's, run the risk of Edna's wrath and an accusatory dig as she asked if they'd had a 'nice' night out at the dogs.

But Robert is still glad Jean walked past that morning, he has never stopped being grateful for that first smile. Jean is one of the best things that ever happened to him, no matter that it didn't last.

Fourteen

Half a mile east and eighteen years since his mate Lee made a complete cock-up of his best man's speech at his wedding, Dean Dobson is trying to sleep, he had a late night last night, and the one before that, late bloody week really. Two hours ago he heard the boys come in from school, heard Gina tell them to shut up, not to wake their dad, he's been working late. Dean feels bad about it, but he didn't tell her to leave them be either, didn't get out of bed and say hello to the kids. He was knackered, is knackered. And there's a night's work ahead of him too. Dean flops back against the mattress, the pillow that smells of Gina's perfume and, more recently, his own sweat. He always sweats like a pig when he's knackered. Dean's been dog tired for years, feels like. He was fine as a lad, could keep up with anyone, then he did that job in Brazil, caught some bug or virus or something, and he doesn't think he's ever felt the same since. It was a hell of a bloody trip.

Then. Sat on an upturned bucket in the hotel shower. Dean has no fucking idea why they have buckets in every bloody bathroom in this place, but they do. Every bathroom he's been into anyway, and he's been in a few in the past month in São Paulo, hardly anything staying in his stomach, he's had the shits most days. They've done what they were told, him and his mate, sticking to the food they know, but out here he reckons even the bloody KFC is extra-spiced to cover the taste of the rancid chicken, if it is chicken. He's never had any meat on him anyway, but Dean reckons he must have lost a stone since they've been here, two weeks too long and counting. Yeah, he's been in loads of bathrooms all right, but none like this. Someone else's hotel room that he's been given a key for and told where to be and where to wait and when to go and what – exactly – to do. Minute for minute, hour for hour. Dean sits on the bucket in the sweltering hotel bathroom, smelling someone else's sweet-acid piss, staring at the dirt on the floor and the mould on the walls and the crossbow in his hands. The place is a mess, it must be even cheaper than Dean and his mate are paying for their hotel two streets away. Dean and his mate. Only it's Dean sitting here on the bucket and Lee waiting in their hotel room. Then there is a click outside, the slow grate of a key in the lock. Dean stands up, quiet as he can. The bloke on his way into the room has been drinking all afternoon, rum and Cokes in the bar downstairs. He's having trouble turning the key in the lock, got it in all right, but the action of turning is what's knocking him out, left or right, clockwise or anti. Dean can hear him cursing on the other side of the door, is tempted to go through and unlock it himself, welcome him in. He doesn't, stands carefully and quietly, looking past the edge of the bathroom door. The old guy comes in, slams the door behind him, and does exactly what any other bloke of fifty-five with a drink problem would do when he finally gets back to his own hotel room, sighs and farts and unzips his jeans heading straight for the bathroom and a piss. He practically has his cock in his hand when he sees Dean waiting, ready, holding the blade, slices.

Now. Dean sits up carefully in bed, not wanting the kids to hear that he's awake, pulls the duvet tighter to his bare chest and lights up. He pushes the bell-patterned nets aside and looks out at the back garden, has smoked half the fag before his hands stop shaking. It pisses him off that getting sick over there was dragged back into his real life, because in truth he'd sat there on that bucket and waited to do the job and he'd bloody well done it and done it well. Dean had never done anybody before. He never did anyone after either. He knew he might, if he was ever in the same position again, but he intended to make sure he never was. Stupid and eager and a chancer at eighteen. Yeah, sure him and Lee would go over to Brazil and bring back a kilo each. Why not, the kind of money they were offered, and it would keep that firm sweet, they would owe him. At eighteen Dean already knew far too well how useful it was to be owed rather than owing.

Dean and Lee left together, flew to New York for a night, running up and down the subway platforms at 42nd Street like lunatics, not their first time out of the country, they'd both been down to Spain, Dean to France for cigarettes, tobacco, beer runs. But this was New York City, just like it looked in the films. Then on to Brazil, where they'd picked up the couple of K, got it back to their hotel room easy enough, tossed a coin to see who would wear it home – Lee. Dean was so fucking relieved when he saw Her Majesty's profile grinning up at him, but then next day, when they went to buy their return tickets some cunt came up, grabbed Dean's passport and money, straight out of his hand. The gun he held made it easy. Dean would fight any bugger, no worries, not scared of glass or blades either, but only a complete twat thinks he can fight a gun. Anyway, he knew the bastard, bloke was mates with the same firm that sent them out there. Dean knew even as he handed over the passport and cash that it would only be a matter of hours before someone else turned up, offering a deal, a job, in return for the passport and a ticket home. Knew right then that they'd been set up from the first.

Later that night, in the bar, Lee on rum, Dean on beer, and not much of it, waiting, watching, the message came through about who and how and where. Dean didn't know the old bloke, but he knew of him, knew he'd fucked over the people he'd been working with up in Scotland and had come out here to hide. But the Glaswegian lot had a connection with the firm Dean was working for, and shit, why did these arseholes ever think there'd be anywhere to hide? Dean was never going to get like that. Not so attached to any one firm that they could hold him, and never pissing anyone off either so they wanted him done. That night in São Paulo he promised himself he'd only ever depend on the one bloke he could truly trust. Himself. Anything else was for idiots. The kind of idiot who let themselves be tempted the fuck out here by a few grand and the thought of a favour owing and didn't consider what else would be owed. Last time. First and last time. So he picked up the blade and he picked up the pass key and he waited on the bucket and he did the bastard. Clean and fast. No one was going to miss him, the bloke was a cunt, everyone agreed on that, but no one wanted to be the one doing the job either. Dean had been well used and he knew it. But now they owed him, and they knew it.

It's almost twenty years ago and Dean hardly ever thinks about it any more, not when he's awake, hardly thought about it from the first to be honest. The bloke had shat on so many people, he must have known it was coming round sometime. But Dean hadn't liked being set up and he made sure the home firm understood that when he got back. They held up their hands and agreed and handed him an extra grand for his pains. Then they slapped him on the back for a job well done, smoked some weed together. Dean left knowing they were calling him a white bastard behind his back, just as he hated the spades himself. Mutual loathing, mutual respect, and whatever else they could do for each other. Dean had made himself a few friends for life.

Lighting up another fag and looking into the back garden, watching for that bloody fox with the nerve to come right into their garden in the middle of the afternoon, he remembers the ravenous hunger that hit him the minute he left that hotel. He'd gone to pick Lee up and on the way he had to stop for a burger and a milkshake. Trusting McDonald's where he couldn't trust the Colonel, shoving the food down his throat, none of it even reaching his stomach it felt like. Lee had wanted to go for a beer, but Dean needed more food, and then more. Ate a fortnight's worth of tight stomach and gritted tension, ate until he calmed down enough for a beer and another and another.

Not many people know about that trip. Dean still feels a bit of a wanker for getting taken, and maybe he feels a bit funny about the bloke, what he did, what it means. He told Gina a few years after they got married, the baby over at her mum's, late in the night and both of them pissed, she wasn't too worried. She knew a bit, enough to understand that getting himself fucked over out there was way worse than anything that might happen to him at home, lose your passport in London and there were any number of blokes you might have a quiet word with to get another one, something Dean deals in himself these days. Lose it over there and the trades you'd have to do to find it again, you might as well take the blade to yourself. She'd been more worried about the idea of him coming back to England with the gear, thought he was a bloody fool. But even now Dean remembers the elation of taking off from São Paulo, coming home well away from the States, long round trip and Lee all taped up, the pair of them walking through customs at Heathrow, easy as can be. The joy of coming home. Yeah, they might have got done, it happens. Even when you think things are sweet with security, all tied up, it does happen sometimes, but the worst was over. The boys were home and they were

87

happy, walking through customs with a spring in their step and an easy confidence in British justice.

Dean sits back on the bed, pushes the pillows up behind his head, flicks through yesterday's *South London Press*. Home paper, home boy. Another five minutes and he's up. Passing his little girl's bedroom as he walks down the hall, their fifteen-year-old angel still not home and his bloody lighter sitting on her dressing table when she'd promised him she wasn't smoking any more. Down the end of the hall and into the lounge, his two boys mucking around on the floor in front of the telly, Gina's smile lighting the room when she sees he's awake, stepping over the rolling tangle of Sammy and little Lee to give Dean a kiss.

'Shannon's just called from the bus, God knows why she can't walk anywhere. Kettle's just boiled and there's chocolate digestives, two for one at Somerfield, your tea'll be a while yet.'

It's nothing, what she has to say to him. And it's plenty for Dean. He puts an arm round his wife's bloody good body, three kids or not, lets her lead him through to the kitchen. The boys yelling behind them, smell of Gina's chicken casserole in the oven, potatoes half-peeled and a head of that purple broccoli stuff on the side. Gina's trying to get them all to eat better, they've both been watching those telly programmes about kids' diets, want to do the right thing. Dean puts his hand on his wife's neck, pulls her close, they kiss. He hasn't cleaned his teeth, her lips are dry, it doesn't matter, São Paulo is long gone, his concerns those of an ordinary family man. The fox that's been digging up the back garden, his suit to pick up from the cleaner's, Shannon's admiration for dodgy bands, the racket his boys are making, and what a damn shame there's no holiday pay in his line of work, but fuck it, Gina's lovely. Still. More so maybe. He's bloody lucky really. But he could do with a night indoors.

Fifteen

Tuesday evening, closing time. Akeel has spent the day going on about the storeroom upstairs and Robert is glad to see the back of him. Finally got the lad to shut up about it by simply refusing to answer any more questions. No more about Jean, no more about Alice and her storeroom, no more about Dean bloody Dobson and God knows what he'd found in that little bugger's pockets over the years. No more and work to do, can we just get on with it, all right? All right. He knew he'd probably upset him, the lad, but there were only so many questions Robert could take, so many he was prepared to answer. Every one of those boxes with another memory, another story to tell, and Robert not ready to have a go at many of them, not yet, not by a long shot. Pops into the storeroom on his way upstairs, half a dozen coins to throw into the wide jar he keeps by the door, coppers only these days. Funny that, most of his customers so much richer now in many ways, cars and tellies and holidays abroad, but the forgotten change in their pockets worth so much less.

Robert Sutton is nine years old and he stands behind the door to the middle front room, watching Aunty Elsie through the crack between the two big old hinges. The door has been painted many times and around the hinges the enamel paint has flicked off in chunks to reveal rusting metal beneath the layers. Aunty Elsie, who isn't a real aunt, just a being-polite aunt, wears a flowered housecoat over her dress whenever she's here, and in her own home too, when she nips over the road to the shops, and under her outdoor coat when she goes down the market. The only time Robert has seen Aunty Elsie without her housecoat is on a Sunday when she pops in on her way back from church, having swapped the faded violet of protective cotton for the soft mauve of her good church hat and matching gloves. Aunty Elsie wears a thin gold cross around her neck and she wishes Alice would too.

Aunty Elsie comes in once a week on a Tuesday afternoon to do the alterations, she's already there when Robert comes home from school, wading her way through a pile of ripped pockets and fallen hems, putting in careful darts, letting out tight seams. Elsie Finch left school at fourteen and took a place with Madam Isabelle in Maddox Street. Court dressmaker, everything by hand, not a machine stitch in a single frock, as Elsie never tires of saying, trousseaus and going-away costumes and the finest silk camiknickers too. Elsie is a few years older than her friend Alice, never married, never found any fellow worth it she says, and so she's not had any children of her own, which might be why she won't have little boys under her feet, getting in the way. If children are to be around the place, she likes to see them busy. So Robert watches from his hiding place and somehow, even though he's there for half an hour or more, Elsie doesn't seem to notice him as she stitches or unpicks, tight-stretching a hem around her hand. She always has the wireless on in the background, her own tuneless humming a constant accompaniment to her actions, hands dusty with tailor's chalk and mouth full of pins.

Robert is not watching Aunty Elsie because he's interested in the art of taking in and letting out – though even at

90

nine he can see there is a magic to her work, an alchemistry in fixing and fitting, make do and mend – Robert is watching the pockets. Elsie checks the pockets of every new garment she comes to, feeling for fluff and crumbs, and for coins too. Between them, cleaning, pressing and tailoring, Elsie and Alice reckon they find enough change in pure coin for a week off in Sheerness once a year, or would do if the coin didn't need to be kept back for the electric and the gasman, for Robert's school shoes and Alice's stockings. Alice checks the pockets before she cleans, Elsie checks them before she mends – mending before cleaning, so the old hemlines are washed out, new seams ironed into place. Robert wonders how old he'll need to be before he is allowed to check pockets, and then maybe he'll keep a few coins back for himself. The women have an agreement. It's Alice's shop, her business, her risk, so she pays Elsie by the piece for the tailoring work, and they split the coins seventy/thirty. That's what they tell each other, but Robert, who peers from behind flaking hinges and has learned the art of standing silently on stairs by half-open doors, knows better.

He's also seen that while the women take care of the coin, there's a lot else they take from the pockets. The shopping lists and the notes to the milkman, the letters and the unpaid, never-paid bills. Alice hangs on to everything, you never know, she always says, never ever know. It's all piled in together, a jumble sale of forgotten possibilities, and Robert so wants to get in there and sort it out. He's nine years old and he has a fierce desire to keep things in their place. He cannot keep Alice in her place, keep her to himself, keep away the visiting uncles and their bottles of dry sherry and the shrieking laughter from inside the Green Man as he waits on the step with a bottle of lemonade and a straw that he's too big for now, not a little boy any more, except that sucking the fizz through the straw feels good, feels better than to wait indoors by himself. Robert imagines he could find order in those pieces of paper, checking what comes in and what goes out, watching Aunty Elsie throw two coins into the pot and one for herself – Robert has sharp eyes and sees the shape of the coins as well, two pennies in the pot but a threepenny bit in the hand. When Alice is out, or upstairs making their tea, he likes to look through the messy boxes, reads other people's shopping lists, makes up stories for why bread has been crossed off, lard left on. Robert reads the lists of other people's cupboards and imagines the lives they come from. There's a mother in the kitchen, she wears a housecoat like Aunty Elsie's, only hers was new this spring, and the cotton is still crisp. There's a father down the back of the garden, he's putting in stakes to ward off the foxes and digging up new potatoes to go with a grilled chop for his tea, he's hung up a chunk of fat for the finches, inside a little sister is playing in front of the brand new electric fire, the one with a fan inside that makes the plastic coals glow red like real flames, and then there's Robert himself, the big brother, coming home from the shops with everything on the list, Mummy and Dad proudly smiling, that's our boy, we can trust him, our lad. All the way up the shops and back and not a penny dropped on his way.

Robert Sutton is nine years old. He knows for a fact that most of his friends don't live in the world their teachers and school books like to pretend they do, but he likes to pretend they do. Because that world, where there is a mum and a dad and a little sister and the pictures on Saturday afternoons and cake on Sundays after church, that world is ordered and tidy. Robert has fun with Alice, she's a laugh, much more exciting than any of the other mothers, but it isn't the same as it is in the books. It doesn't feel like the lives he imagines when he sneaks a look at the letters and the lists Elsie lifts from the pockets she is preparing to mend, and every now and then Robert thinks he would quite like that life instead. The neat and tidy one, with potatoes growing down the back of the garden, and a dad just home from work, a lamb chop waiting for his tea.

Sixteen

As Robert locks the storeroom door, Patricia Ryan walks round Ruskin Park on her slow progress to church. It is ten to seven, and she'll be late if she's not careful. That health visitor, the coloured girl, kept her longer today than she liked, too many questions, not enough answers, and now she is running late. Walking slowly late. Patricia walks slowly, it is safer that way. She knows what happens to old ladies when they fall. A bone break here, a fracture there, and it's the hospital chaplain and someone from Social Services clearing out your flat. In summer she walks to evening mass through the park, heading west into a warm low sun. Tonight though, it has been dark for half an hour, and while she can see through the iron railings that the early crocuses are up, it will be a month or two yet before the park is open late enough for her evening walks. She hopes she will remember the way by then. Novena, confession, novena, mass. She likes the rhythm of it, loves a good novena. The same novena she has been making since she was fifteen, a Daughter of Mary. Patricia thinks she has been making this novena, but she cannot be sure. Five years ago Patricia Therese Ryan began living almost entirely in the moment. The way the young people talk about it, the way that pre-retirement course had talked about it, living in the moment should be a joy. To Patricia it is more a sorrowful than a joyful mystery.

She is seventy-five, seventy-six in three months' time, and for half a decade Patricia has been aware she is losing things, pieces of herself dropping away, left behind and not missed until it is too late to find them again. She has become an old woman, and Patricia knows that while old women are supposed to forget where they left their hairbrush just ten minutes ago, they invariably remember every last detail of their first dance dress. Patricia was a nurse for coming up fifty years, specialised in geriatrics for the last twenty, and if there's anything she doesn't know about old women, Patricia can't remember what it is. Which is the point she thinks, perhaps, because while Patricia can't remember the hairbrush, or the hairpins, or even where the mirror is half the time, she can't remember the dance dress either. She knows she did use to remember, used to know all her own stories, now she isn't sure if the stories she has left belong to her or someone else.

Patricia Ryan knows that every story needs a beginning, a middle and an end. Miss Hawkins taught them that and she always believed it. Patricia used to send letters home based on the beginning–middle–end principle. A full four-page letter every week until her father died in 1982, each one carefully structured to tell her whole story, Monday to Sunday and back round again. Now, though, Patricia has the middle and end but no beginning, or perhaps an end and a beginning, but she cannot quite recall the middle that connects them, if there is a connection, if there is a middle. She is not sure. But she knows it is getting worse, and she knows what will become of her, she knows the nothing that will become of her.

And so, every evening that she can, Patricia goes to a weekday mass. On Fridays she adds in a novena to the BVM and makes the first mass on Sunday mornings, holy days of Obligation, maybe the occasional Saturday evening thrown

95

in for good measure. Patricia isn't asking for much, just an easy death, in the not-too-distant future. Or quite soon actually, that would be nice, though she doesn't want to ask for too much. Patricia Ryan's life has been one of learning, and the greatest lesson has been not to expect too much. Meanwhile, though, she has cleaned up her flat, everything is neatly arranged, willed her few goods and savings account to the two nieces and four nephews who can rarely be persuaded to visit, and she's ready. She hopes God is too. Patricia is on her way to ask Mary the ever Virgin to intercede, walking alongside Ruskin Park as she does every day and hopes to stop doing in the not-too-distant future.

Not that the Holy Mary has achieved a great deal in Patricia Ryan's life to date. The longed-for young man did not grow into a loving husband. Patricia Ryan's short-lived marriage was both brutal and empty, Frank left her for an English girl after four years. Four years too long with a barren fool he said as he picked up his bag and took a loaf of bread from the pantry, the only loaf of bread. Patricia didn't mind him leaving, she thought she would have been happy without him if the baby they had both hoped for had ever arrived, she'd have been quite content in the little flat, she and a child. But ten days after Frank's departure, her period came again, regular as tears. They never divorced, Frank didn't even bother to ask, knew Patricia better than that, but eventually he found himself a willing priest, who had need of some contribution to a church roof, and the priest found his way to an annulment, and that was that.

Still, the Virgin did help with a job. Frank left on a Friday evening, Patricia went to church on both Saturday and Sunday mornings, added an extra decade of the rosary for every month of her time with Frank, and when she went into work on Monday, not only was Matron delighted to hear that Patricia Ryan was willing to take on a few more shifts, she also offered her a permanent night shift, six days on, two days off. The younger girls didn't want it, night shifts played havoc with their social lives. A month later she moved into the nurses' home. When the hospital decided to make a few flats available to senior nurses, Patricia Ryan's name was at the top of the list, and when she eventually retired, Patricia simply moved from the nurses' block to the housing association flats one street further up the hill. They needed a resident nurse to maintain their sheltered-housing status and, just turned sixty-one, Patricia was fit enough to take it on. Thanks to the BVM's intercession, Patricia Ryan held on to the job, with a free flat and a small allowance on top of her pension, for eight years, only retiring fully on the day after her sixty-ninth. As everyone said, she was certainly entitled to a rest.

She was, but she didn't want it, didn't know how to rest, didn't know what to do with herself. Took to walking the park once a day, then twice, three times. Patricia read Ceefax and Teletext every morning and it was only when she realised she'd been rereading the green-print pages not once but three or four times a day that she knew something was wrong. She bought a school exercise book, three new pens in different colours, took some notes, made a few comparisons, and now Patricia Ryan understands it is all going very wrong, far faster than she had expected. She leaves yellow stick-it notes all over the flat to remind herself what she has done, pointing out that yesterday was Monday, so today must be Tuesday, that she is wearing one pair of tights, she does not need another, that it's only spring and she probably needs a coat. Patricia has nursed people like herself for years, she knows the day will come when she looks at the note she has written and cannot tell if she can't read, or she can't write, when it will be impossible to work out the meaning of the squiggles, and her own words will have become another language. She is living in the present tense and it is harder work than anything she has ever done.

Back at his flat above the shop, above the storeroom, while Patricia heads west into her future of yellow notes, Robert puts a lamb chop under the grill for his tea.

Seventeen

Wednesday. A week later. Robert has been quiet all day, sitting at the side of the counter, sorting through the post and bills that arrive before Akeel, staring out into the road, mostly silent. This is a new side to Robert, in the past months there've been plenty of times Akeel's heard Robert exclaim aloud, furious with something in the paper, angered by the lying politicians or the pandering journalists. Other times he's been a joy to watch, having a go at that Australian nanny, a third of his age and Robert delighted when he can coax a broader smile on her face, lecturing her on London sights and the state of Britain. Akeel is also used to lengthy explanations regarding the correct placing of a tailor's tag, a perfectly smooth nap, a realigned crease. What he's not used to is quiet Robert, silent, closed, drained. Akeel wants to ask what the problem is, if he can help, if it's to do with the room upstairs, if Robert feels he gave away too much too soon. Akeel would like to be generous, but asks about mortgages instead, interest rates and no reasons.

A woman is crossing the road, heading for the door. Robert sees her and suddenly he's off his stool, pushing Akeel into the back room, behind the partition.

'Wait there. Wash up or something.'

Akeel turns away, Robert's words a sharp order, in contrast to his door-opening smile, and the woman shuffles her plastic bag into the shop. 'Don't think you've anything to pick up today, love?'

'Just my letters. I have my letters.'

'Let's have a look.'

The woman speaks an English that is as Eastern European as her clothes. The headscarves and swathes of winding cloth Akeel sees and tries not to see when he has no change for the women begging in the tube. Or when he has change and can't be bothered giving. Or when he's already given his change to the woman in the morning, the one with the dark-eyed child on her hip, and has none for the next woman and her skirt-clinging children in the evening. The begging women Akeel sees every day on the tube, the women who make him uncomfortable whether he is feeling generous or not, sympathetic or not. The women with their puff-cheeked babies tied to the breast, their covered heads and open hands, always with children, never with a man. The women who might be Rubeina if he looks closer, or his own mother if he doesn't. The women who make him want to try harder, be a better husband to Rubeina, better son to his parents, better father to any children they may have one day, please God. The women who remind him how lucky he is to have a warm bed he doesn't want to leave when the alarm goes for prayer, clean clothes to travel in, a full day to tire himself and be paid for the privilege.

Rubeina says he's an easy touch. A young woman came to their front door one night, told Akeel her kids were at home up the road, all she needed was five quid for the electricity card, she'd bring it back first thing in the morning, soon as she could get to the post office, not taking the piss, honest, she only lived up the road, number 56, she'd be back in the morning. Akeel gave her two five pound notes and then listened while Rubeina told him off for giving away their hard-earned money, these women go from door to door with the same story, anyone more likely to give money to a woman, a mother. Anyone gullible like him. Akeel answered he knew it probably was a scam, and maybe those women in the tube were scamming him as well, with their hip-held babies, and probably that bloke outside Bow tube with his can of Special Brew and dog on a long frayed string, but that's not the point. Akeel doesn't have to beg and he doesn't have to lie to get money and sometimes, not every day, but sometimes, that makes him grateful and glad and very fortunate. So if all he does is give a few quid every now and then to a stranger who feels obliged to lie, who truly thinks that sitting on a cold pavement in winter is an easier option than having a home and a job and a wife – then yes, he'd rather be gullible, rather take the chance to offer charity than not, make a blessing than not, give than not give. Rubeina listens, marks a few pages of Year Eleven's algebra test, tells him he's an idiot, that she loves him. And will he give her ten quid too? He does, with a kiss.

From where Akeel stands out the back by the tea things, the rinsed but not washed cups, the saucer full of used, dry tea bags, he can just see past Robert's shoulder to the woman by the counter. Akeel waits, the cups remained unwashed. He watches the woman put her hand into a Pacific-blue plastic bag, this one creased from weeks of use as her hand-bag, and pull out a dozen or more papers. Robert takes them from her and starts to place them in order.

'Right, what've we got . . . gas and electric, council tax, phone. They always come at once, don't they? Like buses, only not as welcome.'

The woman nods and Robert continues. 'Bank state-ment? Enough to pay them all, right off?' He shuffles through the papers until he finds the statement, completes several mental arithmetic sums, all of them subtraction, and comes eventually to a narrow-numbered total. He checks the calendar on the wall by the till, fourth page of the year and already tired with the annotated details of chemical deliveries and tailor's collections. 'When d'you get paid next? Tuesday is it, or Thursday?'

'Thursday.' The woman's unassimilated *th* migrating to a *d* as it leaves her mouth.

'Best put that BMW on hold, eh? Give us your cheque book then.'

For the next ten minutes Robert maintains a steady flow of chat about the weather, the pair of trainers he's seen hanging from a high chestnut branch in the park – some kid'll be in for it, police trying to do something about drug dealers along Coldharbour Lane. The woman seems to say yes and no wherever she feels Robert needs it, on the occasions he leaves a long enough pause. Two customers come in and out, one stays to chat briefly, gets short shrift from Robert and leaves banging the door behind her. When the payment forms and cheques are written, Robert slips them into the correct envelopes, takes her stamps one at a time, and places them carefully in each corner.

'There you go, darlin', in the postbox and you're done.'

'Thank you.'

The woman leaves, and Akeel comes into the front of the shop again, eyebrows raised, waiting for Robert to explain.

'Don't get any funny ideas, son. I'm not a bloody charity.'

'So . . .?'

'Look, she was here one time, they wanted to cut her gas off, got herself in a right state, three kids, no bloke. So I called them for her, their mistake anyway, not hers. Now she brings in the bills, I fill out the forms, write her cheques for her, no skin off my nose. Always want to keep your customers sweet.'

'Right, and does she bring in a lot of clothes to be cleaned?'

'Winter coat every autumn. Not as if I'm paying the bills. You'll see, Alice always said there's a lot more to cleaning than just hiding the dirt. Whether you want to keep up that side of it or not – that'll be up to you.'

Akeel isn't convinced. 'It's just . . .'

'Listen, lad, if we're going to get on all bloody year or however long it is, you can't be asking me about every flippin' move I make, yes?'

'OK. Sorry.'

'No, don't be sorry, just don't . . .' Robert shrugs, shakes himself, looks at the clock, then at his own watch, still only five fifty, time's passing too slowly this afternoon. He jerks a thumb back towards the arch. 'There's a load of pressing to be getting on with, don't have to leave it all till morning.'

'And what are you going to do?'

'Pay your bloody wages. Cheek of it.'

Akeel pauses, thinks about what he really wants to say, starts to speak and then shuts himself up.

Robert sighs. 'Go on then, out with it.'

'I just wondered if maybe you feel like you've told me too much? Showing me what's upstairs?'

'Haven't told you the half of it, lad.'

'Well, you know . . . just if . . . if that's what's upsetting you . . .'

Akeel knows there is more, but doesn't know how to ask for it, and Robert has so much to say, and can give voice to none of it. And so, because he wants to deflect, remove himself from this particular conversation, because the younger man is still waiting, Robert begins cashing up for the day, explaining how that Australian girl got his goat first thing this morning. Akeel thought he had been doing his usual chat and smile, but she'd infuriated Robert no end, just as she was leaving, looking at the front page of Robert's paper, saying how scary she found all this terrorist stuff. Robert told her London had lived with terrorism for years, floods, riots, bombs, the lot. It wasn't news. But he was telling the girl's retreating back.

'It probably does seem like a big deal to her,' Akeel says.

'Well, why?' Robert asks. 'Of course it was terrible for the people actually hurt, the bombs here, what happened in New York. But how many did that really affect? In their day-to-day life? The families, friends of the dead or injured, I grant you, but not everyone, not really. Look, after those bombs up in town, half my bloody customers were in here, carrying on about how it was all different now, but at the same time they were picking up nice clean clothes for a do somewhere, or a job interview, and getting on with it all just the same. If it was true that everything had changed, they wouldn't be haring off for a fancy weekend away, would they? They would have been as changed as they said they were.'

Akeel takes a shirt from the pile ready to be pressed, carefully checks the state of the collar, slowly folds and unfolds cuffs, picking his words, treading carefully.

'There was a lot of fallout, not always what you'd expect. Rubeina was attacked – the week after the bombs here, had her headscarf ripped off, right in the street, one bloke hit her, a few others were trying to have a go as well. Only stopped when the police came along. Since all this stuff has happened, the guys – the white guys – who've always had a go, think they have a better excuse.'

Robert rings up the last of the receipts, nods and shrugs in the same movement, agreeing and not. 'Exactly. That's my point. Your wife getting attacked upsets you, course it bloody does. But it really happened.' Robert walks past the younger man to the sink, running their cups under hot water, scrubbing at them like the dishcloth might help him explain better. 'But a lot of all this fuss is down to the politicians and their like stirring it up. They can call this a war on terror if they want, but it's nothing like a real war. You ask Alice's uncle, two years in Burma, poor bugger, he'd have told you what a real war is, what we've got here is nothing like. And that's what gets me, because it's fear-mongering. And then you get a kid like Helen going on about someone else's grief as if it's her own, but it isn't. She's stealing other people's grief. Like there's not enough to go around.'

Akeel looks down at the floor, a pile of old tickets and plastic tags in a dusty pile by his left foot. He has felt fear, in the street, real afraid-for-his-physical-safety fear. But there's something else going on here, this isn't what he's come to recognise as Robert's usual late-afternoon moan, spat out over a cup of tea and his cheese and onion crisps and the soft shuffle of the little hand to six. He picks up the old tags and tickets, drops them in the bin, reaches for his coat.

Robert stops him before he gets to the door. 'Hang on, lad, I've something to ask you.'

'Yes?'

'D'you fancy having the shop to yourself on Saturday? You could get the wife in to help you, keep you company. Do the pair of you good. I need to go off for the day. All right?'

Robert asks as if the only answer is yes.

Hours later, in his flat over the shop, above the boxes and the files, above the counter and the till and the piles of ready tags and tickets, Robert rereads the letter he received this morning, trying to understand what it says, trying not to believe what he reads. Eventually he folds the letter and puts it on the sideboard. He will take it to the storeroom eventually, there is a box in which it belongs. He attempts the prayer he learned as a child and still can't bring himself to recite fully – now I lay me down to sleep, now I lay me down to sleep.

Robert lays himself down, he does not sleep, he pulls a blanket round his chilled body, watches pale car lights shift across the ceiling, thinking about fear and anger and grief, the places where the three meet, what happens when they do.

In a Stratford bedroom Akeel and Rubeina are talking about the shop, Saturday, the first day they'll be there together. She's wondering when she'll get the kids' homework checked, will probably have to work Sunday morning instead, but there's no point mentioning that to Akeel, he's too excited – and nervous – about them taking over for the day, being there together. And he needs a break from Robert too, Rubeina knows he's still upset by the old man's anger. They talk in the dark about the times she has been scared and the times he has. They talk about how they want their children – when they come, if they come, please God – to never be scared, never be afraid. And then, out of a sleepy silence, Rubeina adds she never wants her kids to be the cause of someone else's fear either. Akeel says it hadn't occurred to him that their children might be the bad guys. Rubeina knows he won't have thought about it, how children can always go wrong, make mistakes, choose mistakes, no matter how hard their parents try. She smiles that Akeel hasn't ever worried that some bad might come from their good, says it's one of the things she likes best about him, his innocence, his hope. And she kisses him, not at all innocent, though certainly hopeful, and they make love.

Eighteen

They are making love, rutting, shagging, screwing, fucking. Silent and hot in the room at the top of the house, heat born of contained friction, minute movements all held in. Her hands grasping, arms encompassing his body, his flesh, holding him to her, into her. A slick of saliva running between them when he moves his head away, turns to breathe, to gasp aloud and she wrenches him back, covering the sound with her tongue, teeth, swallowing his exclamation, biting through a vocal passion that would have them found out.

When Helen comes she is not soft or pliant in Andrew's arms, she is sharp and aggressive and when, through the strength of their smothered pushing and rocking, she comes with him, often with him, it is a hard, held, moment. She has heard other women speak of orgasm as a melting, a rush, a join, and often in their tone, Helen has heard a sense of something within that experience that is tender, precious. This is not Helen's experience. Her experience is that fucking Andrew is sharp. There is a fear she might cut herself, has cut herself, on the edge where she falls into pure body, only body. This is what she likes, liked since she met Andrew, had an idea she might like before she met Andrew. An idea confirmed in their first-ever stolen sex, confirmed with each subsequent fuck. Like this one.

Two o'clock in the morning and Andrew leaves Claire

asleep, climbs to the converted loft, Helen's loft. Her middle-of-the-night body is his domain, his and hers. Helen knows it is purely luck that her own and Andrew's bodies are a fortuitous fit. Like most women of her generation she has had many more lovers than her mother did at the same age, certainly more than Andrew at her age, she has tried and tested and she understands that much of the fierceness of her coming with Andrew is merely to do with an accidental geometry, their lucky fit. Like a perfect pair of jeans found in an unexpected shop, not easily given up no matter how worn or old. It is not skill, this glorious sex, it is simple chance. She is fortunate in this, in the same way she is unfortunate that Andrew is not her partner as well as her lover. He is the only man she has found this ease with, sometimes she thinks he must be the only one, and that fear is as effective a deterrent to her return home, her dreamed-of move to Paris, her ending this stupid and future-free affair, as any.

Helen doesn't think Andrew knows how good their bodies are together. He understands from his side of the skin that barely divides them, has told her how this feels for him, but she has not given her own story in return. She lives in his house, is paid by his wife, cares for his children, comes when he calls, often – as now – in the middle of the night. But she wants to keep something back for herself, and so Helen has not told Andrew that the sex she has with him is her best. She has not told Andrew about the diamond edge, that it feels like they are slicing open and cutting through. She has not told him of gutting, spilling, forcing, breaking. For a start, Helen knows these words sound too harsh, and Andrew is a nice man, he would not want to be doing anything to hurt her – he is not doing anything to hurt her – and Helen knows how these words sound, but she has no others. It is that good, that much.

She comes, he does too, he rolls from her body, checks his

watch and they kiss. They have held their mouths against each other, have clashed teeth and smacked lips, this is the first time they have kissed since he came to her room twenty-five minutes ago.

'I have to go.'

'I know.'

'I don't want to.'

'I know.'

'Good night.'

'Sleep well.'

'I won't.'

'You will.'

He does.

When Helen and Andrew first began this affair, she thought it might mean the end of the job, and she wouldn't have minded. She'd only planned to be in London six months, time to save some pennies and get out to the rest of the world, the beginning of Europe at least. Helen had packed her bags and left Sydney to the sound of her mother's tears, heading out for foreign accents, foreign men and the ubiquitous sidewalk café that four years of badly taught French had assured her was her due, fresh croissants at one end of the continent, Greek beaches at the other, and any number of new experiences between. There's a café ten minutes up the road with chrome tables outside, where she sometimes stops having dropped the older kids off at school, but there's no way the slide down Denmark Hill to Herne Hill can be compared to Paris or Rome. Helen knows it's all her own fault, she got herself stuck in love, right at the beginning of her adventure. Back then, she thought all she had to do was fall out of love and find someone else to pay her wage, in many ways the beginning of the affair with Andrew looked like the end of the job. After four months in the Tomlinsons' house, just heading out of a not-too-bad

London winter, she had almost a grand saved in her travelling account, it was clearly time to move on. Shagging
Andrew wasn't the most obvious method of handing in her
notice, but it would do for a start. There was no way she'd be
able to stay long in a house where she was putting the boss
to bed as well as the kids. Then the clocks went back and the
nights grew longer and, just as she was starting to think
London evenings couldn't get any stickier, Andrew asked her
to go away with the family. Not the travelling she'd intended,
off with a girlfriend or five or none, stopping where they
could, moving when they wanted, picking up some local
blokes and getting to see the real Naples, authentic Athens,
true Dublin, pill and condoms as double-sided protection for
the young women who never understand that sleeping with
a total stranger might be the unsafe part of sex. Andrew was
offering a proper holiday, children in the fully staffed Kid-
Klub five hours a day, evenings to herself, a whole fortnight
at the kind of white-sand beach resort than Helen had never
even considered visiting. Claire had a case to work up, she'd
be glad Andrew had some company while she was working.
So they went on holiday, nuclear family plus one, and Helen
agreed to stay two months more and then another two and
then it was nearly Christmas and then she was in love, and
then Claire was pregnant with Simone, then another year
passed and a few more holidays and another winter and then
it was too late.

Helen is very good at starting things, terrible at finishing
them, has never dumped a lover in her life, always relied on
their boredom or fear or partner coming along and timing
the end for her. And now, her fourth summer in London,
she still has no idea how to end this one. She doesn't want to
break up with Andrew, she just doesn't want to be living
with Andrew and his wife and their three children any more.
Claire works twelve-hour days saving the world, Helen stays

at home and shags Claire's bloke. She's no cuckoo, doesn't want to kick Claire out of the nest, has no desire to supplant the sainted hard-working mother in the children's hearts, feels awful about what she's doing – whenever she isn't with Andrew. Helen is absolutely not interested in the life of a Herne Hill housewife, she does want a life and a man and a place of her own, and she wants to be moving on, all that world still to see, and her mother's Christmas phone calls sounding more and more lonely, her brother's accent stronger as he mocks her for sounding posh, poncey, Pommy.

Unfortunately, in addition to all the other things she desires, she also desires Andrew. Balding Andrew. Andrew with the slowly increasing paunch and terrible line in silly-accent jokes, jokes that aren't funny in his own Mancunian voice, and even less funny when he offers them in Claire's London vowels, or the crap Aussie he always attempts when pissed. Andrew with his red wine breath long before the end of the evening, beautiful crinkled-eyes smile. Andrew who has the small tummy of a middle-aged man, the tummy that no amount of working out – and Andrew does no amount – will get rid of. Helen loves Andrew's tummy, finds it both comforting and sexy. She doesn't want to stay and she doesn't want to go. Stuck and trapped, wanted and loved, and lying. Amazed she hasn't been found out.

In the beginning the affair had all that potential – for good and bad, for hiding and being found out – like smoking dope at school, or stealing from her brother's wallet. There was also the recognition and remembrance. She remembers now that when she first started sleeping with Andrew it was similar to how she'd felt when she was shagging her dad's apprentice, Matthew. Matthew, who'd been coming on to her since she was thirteen, whom she slept with at fifteen, when he was twenty-seven. Matthew who still doesn't seem old, even thinking back, just illicit, and exciting. What she recognises is guilt, and how much she likes it. Dirty, scab-picking self-loathing is one of Helen's greatest skills.

She has thought a lot about what she gets from these rela-tionships. It's certainly not merely the sex, though that was good with Matthew, is wonderful with Andrew, even when placed alongside the honest discomfort of being his servant, putting his dirty washing in the machine, doing his dishes, feeding, bathing his children. Beyond the practicalities of the relationship itself, there are the other, private totems of an affair. These are the feelings she recognises and, even as she mocks herself for being so crap, so *rubbish* in the English parlance that has colonised her mouth, feels at home with. The late-afternoon loneliness of a wet Sunday. Guilt without remorse. Carrying on regardless. Family men in both cases, good husbands, fathers, and each man wracked with desire and pain in his dealings with Helen. Which is of course another component of the interest she feels – Helen as temptress, Hellenic Helen, available Helen.

On Friday night she stands in the wide, bright kitchen helping Andrew's children eat their dinner, wine chilling in the freezer because that's how Andrew and Claire like it when they get in from work, and when he comes home and takes the just-poured glass from her hand there is a look and a smile, and when his already-wrinkled eyes crinkle even more, Helen knows he does this for her, smiles just for her. In a way – in almost enough of a way – it will do. For now.

Nineteen

Friday night. The Poet is on the upper deck of his bus. At Battersea Park he asked the Buddha's blessing on the city, and now he is happy, his people are climbing on board, these are his people, this is his land.

It is late, not quite chucking-out time at the pubs, but close. His fellow journeyers are also merry, laughing, chatting to each other or on their phones. Always the sound of people on their phones. Half-heard conversations filling the top deck and the Poet begins to sing, 'Because they're cold, they are as ice, they are willing to sacrifice . . . just to keep Babylon in gold. Golden Babylon, gold in Babylon, Babylon the gold. Babylon the whore, Babylon of Mesopotamia, land that will rise, will rise again.' The Poet turns to the young couple behind him, nodding and smiling at their embarrassment. 'Oh yes, oh yes, you two are shy, you too are shy, too shy hush hush eye to eye too shy, two shy, shy you two. And why are you shy? Why I ask you? I shall say unto the Lord who comes and takes what he will, where he will, why the shy? They were known unto each other, the dark beauty and the other. Oh yes, they were known. Whatever, whatever . . .' His speech slows as the 345 stops outside Stockwell tube station. The bus driver climbs down, his shift over for the night and the Poet watches him go. The driver has also been on this bus for five hours, they have shared the shift, but the driver does not turn and he does not wave. He never waves.

113

'Whatever, whatever . . .'

The Poet does not pronounce the *whatever* like a young person, not for him their new century *whaddeva*. His vowels may roll from the lilting Jamaica of a cinema Bacardi advertisement to the smooth rounded RP of the old-fashioned BBC, but the consonants are constant. The new driver climbs in, locks himself and his cash tin into his corner seat and the bus rolls on. Up Stockwell Road and past another of those old pubs turned into bars for the young people and the passing-young who have colonised the Poet's streets.

Stefan Corey is inside one of these bars, leaning against the counter, getting in another bottle of wine for Mike and himself. Stefan meant to go straight home after work, but he bumped into Mike in Soho and one thing led to another and now here they are, stuck between Brixton and Stockwell, having rather a lot to drink. They meant to eat Portuguese, made it as far as this bar. Stefan returns with the fresh bottle, beyond the smoked glass windows he can see the red of a traffic-stalled bus, Mike gets up from the table to help, the glasses are filled before either man is back in his chair. This is a good night getting better.

A hundred yards down the road the bus stops again, three people get off, none get on. The Poet looks into the eye-level upper windows of the Portuguese club and sees older men, his own age, drinking and talking together, small beers and smaller coffees, eating little oval cakes of fried cod. Once, last winter, he left the bus, needing to pee, got off at the stop after this and walked back to the ground-floor café beneath the first-floor club, asked behind the counter if they would let him use the conveniences, he has seen the gentlemen upstairs, they must have a bathroom for the men, perhaps he could use it now? If the sweet Queen behind the counter did not mind? Izabel was alone in the bar and her English less sure than the Poet's. She did mind, but she didn't say so. She called to the kitchen for her mother to come mind the bar while she led the Poet upstairs. Where he peed, washed his hands and, before he followed her back down the stairs again – Izabel waiting outside the door to stop him interrupting her father and his friends – the man asked her what they were eating. She told him, *pasteis de bacalhau*, he said it sounded good, she said it was. Fishcake, codfish. When he left the restaurant she passed him a fishcake from a plate on the counter, wished him goodnight, watched him go feeling both guilty and glad as the doorbell took back its welcome. The Poet enjoyed his gift at the bus stop, waiting for the next 345, blessing the young Queen who had passed it to him despite the snarling glance of her silent mother. Blessed her mother too, for who knows? Who knows indeed? What and when and who? Only the Lord. And he isn't telling.

Now the Poet sits in his seat on the left-hand side of the top deck. It is a Friday night, there is Brixton to get through yet, Loughborough Junction, Camberwell, on to Peckham. Any one of those places might offer succour and a snack. If there has been something good on at the Academy the young people will be leaving in high spirits, they will want to share their good fortune. The Poet may get off the bus then, give those young people someone with whom to share their joy. For now he hums, his teeth ringing with the possibility of song.

Twenty

Dan comes to the corner with a bunch of narcissus, their scent thick and a little too sweet, the stalks dripping sap where he has ripped them from other people's front gardens. One of them still carries its bulb, perennial no more. Charlie passes over a can and the two men sit back on their sofa. The early morning sun, edges towards warm, softly picking out the grey in Dan's beard and the scrappy buddleia pushing up from the cracks in the platform above their arch, the light climbs a minute degree above Shooter's Hill and slams into Robert's front room window, turning his thin nets white, opaque.

Akeel has his own keys, last night Robert talked him through it one more time, then wished him good luck and said he was looking forward to hearing all about it first thing Monday. Clear out, lad, time to go home. He will be gone before the young man arrives to open up this morning. Robert walks away from the sun at his front-room window and into the bathroom, runs the hot tap to its most extreme temperature and pictures Akeel waking up in East London, a young man, eager to get his hand in the till, his feet behind the counter, his name over the door. The water running almost too hot, Robert holds his shaving brush under the narrow twist of steaming heat, soaks it thoroughly, then swirls the brush anti-clockwise on the concave cake of soap sitting his shaving cup. The day he started shaving was the first time he knew himself truly separate from Alice. A fifteen-year-old boy with a face full of bum-fluff and half a dozen true whiskers, Alice had caught him scraping at his face with her leg razor, took one look at the shallow grazes he'd already made and told him to get his coat. 'Up the road, now.' She took him to the barber's, led him to the chair in much the same way she had when he was three years old and she'd finally handed over his curly head to the shears of her mother's approval, nodded to the barber and told him she'd be back in half an hour – 'I can't do this. It's down to you.' She walked out the shop knowing that wouldn't be the last time she had to ask a man to teach her son what she couldn't.

Thirty minutes later Alice was back with two good pork pies, moist and sweet with slow-cooked jelly, a sticky bun to follow, and her little boy had his first man's secret to keep from her. Torn between heartbreak and pride, she chose a celebration tea, thanking God Robert was a boy and she didn't have to explain towels and belts and pains to a daughter. Her own mother had silently handed over a pamphlet entitled *Private and Special*. Private she understood, special never made any sense.

In that half hour Robert learned the value of hot water to open the pores, the exact lather and bristle action ideal for bringing up each whisker from under the skin, and the smoothest stroke a barber with forty years' experience could teach. Not for Robert a lifetime of rasping at his skin, scraping off dead cells and the top half of a recalcitrant whisker. From that day on he was a bristle-and-blade man and proud of it. As proud today as he had been the first time he'd managed to get through the whole process without cutting himself, a good four weeks after the hands-on lesson. Just as proud, though possibly less interested in looking at the face, lined now, bloodshot eyes, narrowed lips, the introspection of his daily mirror commune.

Robert is on his way. He has never much liked train journeys. A certain type of traveller believes this is the best part of a trip, sitting on the train, nothing to do, all the time in the world. But for Robert that's the problem, all the time in the world and nothing to do but observe other people. Watching others turns his gaze inward, and Robert no longer likes to look inside. As the train ploughs on north, Peterborough gives way to fields so bright with yellow rapeseed that they hurt his eyes. He tries not to listen to the laptop tapping, mobile-phone ringing, teenage giggling around him, he tries to sit back and just take in what he is seeing, Robert wants to see what is outside the window, really see it. He knows he is supposed to mind the rape fields, the shock of fluorescent yellow, is expected to damn it as an intrusion into the English countryside of his youth. All the newspapers say so, the radio phone-ins insist that his England, the one he loves, the England forged through the fire of war and the dark winters of depression, shines true only in small country pubs with real ale and home-made pork scratchings. But Robert doesn't care whether his ale is real or not, never has. He can't bear country pubs with their glaring locals, low ceilings and dog hair on every seat. And anyway, he likes the splatter of yellow across the land. It reminds him of the young girls at the bus stop in the morning, watching them take off their too-heavy coats on warm spring mornings, revealing soft skin and pale flesh, pretty like Katie always was for birthday parties, Christmas mornings. Robert feels no more connected to the countryside than he expects a County Durham farmer to be at ease down the Brixton end of Coldharbour Lane. He didn't like all that green when Alice forced him off to cub camp in the Ashdown Forest, and his senior rail pass doesn't make it any more appealing now. But this new yellow actually glows, from miles across the land, and Robert does like a light in the green.

Just before Darlington, Robert takes the letter from his pocket, the one he received on Wednesday morning, with the words he couldn't believe, and checks again the directions he has indelibly memorised, all the while trying so hard to forget. From outside the station he takes a taxi to the hall. Not a church hall, but a public building, a Memorial Hall according to the plaque on the wall outside. A hall in memory of those who gave their lives in the Great War, now used for amateur theatricals and Weight Watchers and for this, a humanist funeral. Robert's first humanist funeral, not that he's been to all that many religious ones either, Alice's parents died within a year of each other, he first of pancreatic cancer, she seven months later, exhausted from the years nursing her husband, both were buried from the old church in Eltham and carted out to Falconwood, to lie within roaring distance of what became the wider A2. Alice visited for a few years, flowers on birthdays and Christmas Eve, but after a while she just didn't feel like it any more, didn't know if it was right anyway, to keep bothering them. They were dead and that was probably just as well, after all they'd had to put up with – not least each other – she ought to leave them to get on with it. Robert never went to the cemetery again, though he sometimes waved to the grandparents if he happened to be on the way down to the coast. Not often. Jean liked the seaside, Robert loved the river, he was never too fussed about pebbles and horizon and sticks of rock.

They'd taken Alice up to Norwood cemetery, his Jean and Katie were still living with him then, and the three of them had followed the hearse from the Co-op funeral people up the hill to Norwood. They were met by the last two of Alice's old mates, a second cousin Robert didn't have a name for, and long-term customers who, though Alice hadn't been downstairs in nearly three years, remembered her from the old days and turned out to show their respects. Robert thought it was a shame, if she'd died ten years earlier there'd have been a great turnout, as it was there were barely enough bodies to fill the first three pews. He told Jean it wasn't fair, all the people who'd have come to the funeral years earlier should still have been there, Alice couldn't help what she'd become, but it was as if she'd already died, cut off from them all in her room over the shop. Jean said it was just his grief talking and he should be grateful for the people who were there, but Robert knew it wasn't just grief, it was much closer to anger, and he held his lips together so it didn't spill out again.

As for other funerals, there'd been an old school mate, killed in a road accident, and the chap who used to deliver his chemicals, almost a mate himself really, Christmas cards and a drink on a summer Friday night, and that young son of Jean's friend. That one was the worst. Robert figured he'd been lucky really, to get to this age and only have half a dozen important funerals to count, there'd have been another one no doubt, had he ever known his father. And now this funeral. The one he's come all the way to Darlington for, a standard return in his pocket, not enough notice for the advance super saver. Not enough notice at all.

After the too-quiet humanist woman has spoken, while Robert is wondering if she is a minister, if that isn't a contradiction in terms, a girl, twelve or thirteen maybe, climbs to the lectern and sings a song. Three short verses about the happiness of home and the warmth of return. She looks familiar, she looks like someone else. Then he listens as several people, all adults, speak about the dead woman. Each one holding themselves very carefully so they don't cry, not yet, not until they've said the words, until their hard, honed sentences have been clearly heard. Robert understands the need to be clearly heard, he tried to do the same at Alice's

120

funeral, but broke down halfway through and Jean had to finish the speech for him, taking the crumpled piece of paper and making sense of his scribbles, while Katie guided him back to his seat, trying to help him hold it in as the tears and grief and pain came flooding out so he thought it would never stop. Now these people are talking about the dead woman's humour and her generosity. Someone remembers the amazing birthday cakes she made. Someone who was a student of hers says she was his greatest mentor and, even though Robert thinks the lad seems very young, this clearly matters, because from where he sits at the back of the hall he can see lots of heads nodding and many people turn to their neighbour for a quick hug or hold of a hand. Only one person talks about what killed her, praising her ability to keep going with disease, not in spite of it. And the dead woman's mother says how privileged she's been to have had this daughter in her life, how glad she is that the daughter chose her to be her mother. Robert thinks it sounds kind of the wrong way round, and then thinks about it again and decides it probably makes sense.

Afterwards Robert waits with the others signing a book of condolence, leaving his signature and his sympathy. When he stands back from the book, the dead woman's mother looks up from the other side of the room where she is being comforted by her husband, she sees Robert, and there is a look between them, very quick, then someone else leans in to her, to express their sorrow, and Robert leaves. By the time she looks again, thinking to come over and say hello, he has already gone. Outside the hall, briefly, Robert stands close to the hearse where the coffin now lies, a spray of deep blue cornflowers on top. He'd like to reach out and touch the coffin, he thinks the wood should be warm, soft the way good wood sometimes is.

★

On the way back to London, Robert finds himself looking out the window at the yellow fields, aching for the still quite young woman who has died leaving those children, and for the people collecting for the cancer charities in the foyer, and for the woman who spoke last, the dead woman's mother, so calm, not a single tear until she sat down when her whole body convulsed and she retched out a single sob. He'd wanted to hold her then, make it better. Now he stares out the window, aching too for himself, the dead woman's father, sitting alone at the back of the hall. Robert says good-bye to his daughter Katie and nobody hears the farewell.

The soft green of the country is a balm for his tired eyes. With no newspaper to waste the time, he reads the order of service and the poem the young man read out. Even after he puts it away one phrase keeps coming back to him, 'silvered like hazy London skies'. Robert doesn't know if they're really silvered or not, the skies of his city, couldn't say it was a shade he'd have picked if asked, but they are certainly hazy. The whole country is, outside the train window, late April pretending June. Across the aisle from him is an old bloke – properly old, he's got fifteen or twenty years on Robert. He watches as, with slow and steady intent, the old man gets a young woman beside him to put down her book, turn off her phone and talk to him. Only for half an hour, but still, it's a conversation. She tells him about her husband's job and her own, her gran who lives up in York, who she's been to see. The old man talks about his time in the war, how he proposed to his wife down a crackling line from Italy, all the while knowing he had the lovely Maude back in Leeds, a little older than him and far too much fun to be wife mater-ial. Well into his eighties, the man is flirting with the young woman, and Robert wonders what it might be like to share such easy confidences with a stranger, offering truths with-out a shop-counter confessional between. In his business he's heard people's stories, the ones they tell him, the ones they leave in their pockets, but it's been rare for the people on the other side to ask for his story. Not that he'd ever do what this bloke is doing, flirt with a girl fifty years his junior who'll be getting off half a dozen stops before him anyway. He isn't sure he'd want to either, but he has to give the old bugger his due, he's the brass neck of a bloke half his age.

At King's Cross, Robert makes his way to the local overground and waits for the train home. When his train finally crosses the water at Blackfriars, Robert feels a shift, something comes unbuttoned near his heart, and he cries through the Elephant and the full five minutes more to Loughborough Junction. That night he has a corned beef sandwich for his tea, thick with butter, on doorsteps of white bread, and he raises a can of lager to Katie's memory, glad he made the trip to see her off, and sorry, as he always is.

Twenty-one

At two in the morning Robert is pulled fully awake by screaming from the street below. At first, in his half-sleep state, he assumes it's the throat-ripping call of the local foxes, prowling bins and each other. Then he hears words in the screams, violence in the words, listening as the mobile soap opera passes beneath him, an endless argument that rolls back and forth across the junction, under the railway bridge where the two tracks make their perfect St Andrew's cross beside the Nation of Islam mosque over the garage. They are outside the shop again, gearing up for another lap, the junction separating south-east and south-west, a lodestone for tears and night-fights and car crashes.

'He's fucking what?'

'Doesn't matter.'

'I said, he's fucking what?'

'He's got a problem.'

'I'll say.'

'It's a problem, right? It needs sorting.'

'He needs sorting. You fucking need sorting. I'll sort you, I'll bloody sort you.'

'He needs help, I want to help.'

A junkie, fucking addict, user, bloody user, well not in my house, not under my bloody nose, no way, no fucking way, you get that through your stupid thick head, no way, I mean it, no way. And so it had gone on. He isn't, he is. It's not my fault, yes it is. It's your responsibility, it's nothing to do with me. You don't love me, I love you too much. You don't trust me, how can I trust you? You care more about him than me. You do, you do. And back again to the perennial he isn't, he is, he bloody well is. Round and round.

Robert wants to get up and look out the window. He'd like to put faces to these alarm-clock voices, but he stays in bed, knows better than to make himself the target of joint ire, knows to wait until the women are across the road. The big shutter downstairs is good and strong, well worth the excessive amount he paid for it, but it doesn't need any more dents all the same. When he does steal a look at them, crossing at the corner, away from the shop, Robert casts them as a mother-daughter combo. They could be age-disparate sisters, or even just old friends in a shared flat, but the vehemence of their words, the passion with which the 'it's always my fault' is slapped back sounds far closer to the matrilineal line as he understands it. As his mother and her mother, his wife and their daughter played out in their own fashion. And the two women go on, from after one until just before three.

When Robert first moved above the shop with Alice, a six-year-old boy sleeping in the bedroom of the top flat while Alice slept on the settee in the front room, the middle flat still chock-a-block with boxes and packing, cleaning chemicals and the heavy old presses, the only thing that disturbed his night's sleep was the persistent peep of the early blackbirds in the old trees behind the shop. Later, he and Jean made the break from her parents' back bedroom, and Alice was happy to get her boy home again. It took a solid two weeks to remake the two flats, the clearing of the middle one to make it habitable as Alice's home took the bulk of the time. With the combined force of three blokes brought back from the Green Man and Robert's youthful vigour, the huge old presses were finally carried down to the arch, one made it, the other didn't, was sold off for scrap. Robert pictures that old press as he stretches in bed, doesn't doubt some stupid City type would probably buy it as art these days. They shifted the rooms around upstairs as well, the back room became Robert and Jean's bedroom, or 'love nest' as Alice insisted on calling it, worse when she said it in front of Jean's mum, which she did as often as she could. When Katie was born they moved Alice's massive old sideboard downstairs, made a box room from a corner of the front room, and bought a brand new three-piece suite in time for their first Christmas as a three-generation family, ordered from Morleys in the summer and paid off weekly until they brought it home with the tree and the tinsel.

It was long after Alice died, nearly three years since Jean and Katie had gone, when Robert finally accepted his family weren't coming back, that he eventually moved the rooms around to satisfy himself, and only himself. He removed the thin partition wall that had created Katie's room, came forwards himself from the back bedroom to sleep in the front room, easier to get to the kitchen, easier to watch telly late into the night, easier not to sleep alone in the now-sagging double bed he and Jean had bought together in the Walworth Road in 1976. It was only once he'd made his choice to sleep in the front, made the choice, as with so many of his decisions, as if it could never be revoked, that Robert realised the noise from the street would become his new night companion. The late buses and early trains and bin men, the pub parties and fights, and now, more lately – or perhaps just more obvious lately – the corner-stopping, kerb-crawling, ordinary-bloke-and-hooker combination that never ceases to surprise him. Such ordinary blokes. Such ordinary tarts too. Despite the noise and the regular intrusions into his sleep, Robert is glad not to be alone. The mother and daughter fighting through the night offer him a kind of comfort – a place in other people's lives, a different argument, a space where he is neither instigator nor engaged, safe on the sidelines, witnessing. And for that, if not the lack of sleep, Robert is grateful, finds bearing witness so much less painful than giving it.

At three thirty, when Robert is dozing again and Coldharbour Lane is as quiet as it ever gets, the two women make their way home. They walk down Luxor Street to their shared flat on Flaxman, the dark and damp basement flat in an artisan-crafted, perfect arc of a would-be regenerative terrace – if only the developers could get rid of the likes of these two. They sway back, loving each other now, the alcohol intake turned to sugary sentimentality, the mother remembers a night of fireworks in Burgess Park, acid at the back of the daughter's throat recalls too much candy floss on a sweltering summer day at the Lambeth Country Fair, the mother's swift retch and vomit, over in a minute, and less remarked upon, takes them both back to a coach and ferry trip to Calais, the shocked faces of the stuck-up wankers sitting across the aisle when they pulled out their cans at eight in the morning. The women are too engrossed in their memories to see two men in the dark of a railway arch, Charlie and Dan curled top to toe for warmth and soundly sleeping off another day on their sofa. Down the steps to the flat and a fumble for keys in the daughter's pocket, a sugar butty each before they go to sleep, thick with salted butter, gritty between the teeth. The daughter helps her mother into bed with the user boyfriend and tells her she loves her. The mother says she was always a good girl, my very good girl.

Twelve hours later the mother wakes brutally hungover and furious already, that arsehole she's sleeping with was out of bed before her and has nicked her purse from the bedside table. Her daughter's right, he's got to go.

Twenty-two

London is full of parks. Flower-free Green Park, Regent's Park with mosque and roses, Hyde Park for horses and football games and lost cars trying to find the best way west, Kensington Gardens caught between Peter Pan's magic and Diana's Folly. These are the parks too big to miss and so open that nervous strangers feel easy, their Central Park Reservoir mugger fears assuaged, though the less trusting still hang tightly to bag straps, leave their passport in the hotel safe, carry just the right amount of cash. Tourists walk these very public parks and, having moaned about the tube and decried the unintelligible bus routes and been aghast at the prices and disappointed with the weather and horrified by the litter and appalled at the dirt and let down by the taxi drivers, they finally find a moment in green to take London in and let it charm them.

Londoners rarely visit these charming parks. They are central and therefore too far from home for most. They are too nice. Real Londoners – rarely born in the city, generally imported, still pining on occasion for the dales or the downs or the moors or the Tyne or the bush or the veldt or the Pacific – walk Hampstead Heath, run Brockwell Park, skate Ally Pally, brunch Clapham Common, climb Crystal Palace. They kiss, rut, frot and darkly, secretly, fuck in these places too. Too wide for fencing, too deep to be seen, the evening green provides solace and frisson for London transplants, be it summer dry, winter crisp or wet damp wet. Wandsworth and Streatham have their commons, Tooting and Gospel Oak their lidos, Battersea the children's zoo, Greenwich the Meridian, and Peckham Rye remains the astonishingly prosaic setting for Blake's visions. Each has its acolytes and 'my park' advocates, those who will happily pile the whole family into the car, drive half an hour or more, circle the car park like a waiting vulture pouncing on the two-hour slot with a glee only a fellow city-dweller could appreciate, before finally beginning their walk, their picnic, their play.

There is a third shade of London green, this one more usually claimed by the born Londoner. The Londoner for whom seventy acres is an enormous space, who is perfectly happy not in the country, who values the view of city and houses and parked cars and the never-ceasing call of sirens. This Londoner loves their local park. A field, a children's play area, a landscaped garden, planting that varies with the seasons, never the years, a one o'clock club with a stack of faded plastic toys, and, more often than not, a pond. Londoners like a good pond. Ducks, Canada geese, pigeons the size of squirrels, squirrels brave enough to jump on baby buggies. This park is fenced, walled, gated, railed. It sits behind houses and backs on to schools. It is known to locals, and usually only to locals. Council-managed, locally utilised, photocopied 'Friends of' posters at the gates, padlocked between sundown and sunrise.

Ruskin Park is one such place. High-fenced tennis courts with old nets slung so low the ball gets over every time, gravel football pitch for added knee-grazing, new–old bandstand, and the bowling green turned to meadow as the men that cared have died. There are cheery Special Brewers by the south-east gate from nine in the morning, sitting in the shade of their Narnia street lamp, dogs on their laps or at their feet, slavering the secrets of the thieving squirrels. On a north-east bench, dedicated to the memory of Michael O. Coleman, there is the sleeping man, who makes this bench his bed, all day, every sunny day, stretched out in his business suit, his glasses Eric Morecambe-askew, briefcase for a pillow. Perhaps he has no job to go to. Perhaps this is his job.

Named for the poet, though Ruskin left the area long before the park came into being – the rail lines brought people who spoiled his view, women among them no doubt, with their dark, disturbing femininity – Ruskin Park is the perfect example of a local green space. It is used by local workers as a shortcut to Denmark Hill or Loughborough Junction stations, it is used by non-locals as a shortcut to the hospital. It has a train line at the bottom of the hill and small children twist supple necks backwards from swaying swings to wave at drivers who are far too busy with leaf-heavy lines to wave back. The park borders the vast disunity that is King's College Hospital, in wartime these fields were an overspill open-air ward, tents of the injured and damaged slept beside the chestnuts, bandaged ghosts fluttering in the branches. Lucky the jogger who has his heart attack here, with the fertility specialist and the chemo nurse and the lunchtime porter all running close behind. This particular park is opposite the Maudsley, home to some of Britain's finest psychiatric enquiry, which means the dancing qui-gong man receives slightly more focused attention when he begins his slow routine in the centre field at seven thirty in the morning.

This is Robert's park. He has been coming here since he was a boy, just as Alice made Kennington Park her personal garden as a girl, and Akeel ran the track at West Ham Park every night for two years of his teens, back when athletics had seemed a possible option, and running around felt like running away. Robert and his mates played here as kids, he and Jean played at being grown-up here. Robert has never joined the Friends of Ruskin Park, or read its history at the Carnegie Library opposite, the Minet further north, he does not receive the Herne Hill Society newsletter, itemising the hopeful fates of the bandstand and the bowling green and the public toilet block. But he did make love to Jean here once, in the bandstand, on a chill February night when the old timber was damp and the steps were something to trip up in a heated passion. Later they rolled together on the wet grass of the bowling green, and this park was Eden. That is all the fate Robert needs to know.

Robert grew up when the shops were what you walked to every day, and the bank twice a week with takings heavy and hopefully not too obvious in your hand, when you walked to get the tube to go up town, and walked back from the bus garage when you came home late at night. When Robert was young, a daily walk was a purely middle-class occupation, for the likes of those who had a car to do the rest. Even now, simply walking round the park seems a bit daft, though this year he has found himself tempted more often by the green, and the hope of colour. Since sitting unnoticed at the back of Katie's funeral he has found the green helps. Not a lot, he doesn't believe anything could help a lot, or should help a lot, but the blatant new growth gives enough tiny solace to make the trip worthwhile. And anyway, how much he uses the park now, or has failed to use it in the past, is not the point, what matters is that Robert knows it is there, within reach, his piece of green. With a view of Big Ben's face, not clear enough to see the hands, but the face yes, and the Houses of Parliament, Post Office Tower in behind, and Centrepoint of course, St Paul's and that flamin' stupid Gherkin thing, up to Highgate, and now, astonishingly, the new Wembley arch. All the way from south-east to north-west with the arch clear as day. On a clear day.

This is a clear day. Four clear days in a row, warm and

bright, a promise of summer and very welcome. On the Sunday after Katie's funeral and then the following Monday and Tuesday evenings Robert walks the park just after seven, having locked the shop and brought along a can of lager for sustenance, and he makes some decisions. He has been planning this plan, thinking these thoughts for some time, Katie's funeral – utterly unexpected, and so brutal – has encouraged him to get on with it, get on with the move. His little Katie and her half-life, and he with all of his, the past he doesn't want to think of and a future that could be as lonely as the years since Jean and Katie left. Robert cannot do that any more. He cannot be alone any more. Akeel has been a good start, he likes the lad, but there is a lot to sort out.

Robert has always found it easier to think while moving, to make choices on the hoof, and if he doesn't have anywhere specific to go, no banking to do, no bread to buy, then the park is at least a reason to be moving. Akeel is doing all right, living up to his own promise. Robert has to admit, all the lad's hopes and plans for the shop don't sound quite so Mickey Mouse now he knows Akeel better, has seen a bit more of him, at least he's not frightened of hard work. The setting sun is warm on Robert's shoulders, as if making an effort to remind him it is there, has always been there.

London, the central city, the old city, down the hill and flat in its basin, is perfectly lit by this hour of saved daylight, it looks warm and soft. Robert passes a gent, older than himself. These days it hurts Robert to see men older than himself, what he reads in their wrinkled faces, balding heads, stooped shoulders, too close to his own story to look for long. The man is perched on the edge of a wooden bench, in full three-piece, waistcoat and tie, looking over the lower line of trees, south and east towards Battersea Power Station. He is suited and booted in black, shoes shined with more than just spit and polish, looks as if he has spent the afternoon at a funeral, as if his evening will continue the same. Robert shudders as he walks quickly past, shrugging off the man behind. On Sunday evening there was a kissing couple on the bench by the rose garden, a pasty middle-aged man and a page-3 girl sitting on his lap, the two of them linked at thigh and breast and mouth. On Monday the same bench was empty but the tree beside it offered its trunk as a resting place for a young pair, one white, one black, kissing and holding on to each other for dear life. Tonight when he reaches the bench again, an older couple are jogging past, they're followed by a tiny dog, five feet behind, smaller than an average cat, its cartoon legs scrabbling to keep up.

When eventually he has walked enough – Robert doesn't know if there can be an enough for this grief, but he also knows his sorrow's journey has nothing to do with what he wants – he turns downhill to head back to the shop, jingling the change in his pocket for his dinner from the kebab shop over the road. As he turns, Robert sees a young couple notice the Wembley arch for the first time, they smile at each other as if this discovery is theirs alone. The wheel sparkles as it turns, the pods catch and splinter an evening light that has journeyed all the way from Ealing. The bowling green is overgrown, the meadow field is ready to burst with wild flowers, the petals of narcissi and daffodils already turned to burnt paper. The evening feels soft, and ready. And, heading for home, knowing it is home, Robert thinks he is ready too. It would appear he has made up his mind.

Twenty-three

Four weeks on and what should have been late spring has vaulted into globally-warmed midsummer, billboards promise quick getaways to lifelong memories, customers complain about the heat along with their usual preoccupations of tube, buses, Lambeth governance, while Robert responds with his latest irritation that it's just not right to have to watch the football with his windows wide open and a new-bought fan churning stale air around his front room. Akeel and Robert have been listening to customers' holiday dreams all week.

'Where do you go for holidays, Robert?'

'I don't. Not since Jean and Katie left.'

'But did you? Before?'

'Went to Spain with Jean, couple of times, she loved it there.'

'You didn't like the food?' Akeel asks, hint of a smile.

'Bugger off with your cheek, loved it. Paella? Tortilla? Pata negra?' Robert pronounces each word with exaggerated commitment to the accent. 'Brilliant. No, it's the getting there. You sit on the plane, crammed in with God knows who, all of you breathing the same air, desperate to get away, and between here and there it's all delays and false starts, worrying if where you're staying is anything like it says in the brochure, bloody kids running riot up and down the aisle. Then you've got six days to relax, before you turn round and go through the whole palaver all over again. Only worse, because now you're sunburnt and broke and you've got a week's work waiting at home. Give me a coach down to Margate any day, least you get to have a good look at the driver before he turns the key in the ignition.'

Akeel thinks back to all those flights to Pakistan, endurance tests, every one. A dozen or more trips as a child, fewer now he's married, Rubeina and work taking up his time. Less reason to visit, and the added disincentive of paying his own way, his parents no longer so eager to foot the bill, though just as keen he should keep going back home. Home. The house his parents still live in, the Stratford house they moved to when he was eight, Akeel believes that is home. The house he lives in with Rubeina, that's home. Now, halfway through the year, this shop is becoming home as well. The messy cavern of the railway arch where the real work happens, standing at the spot station tamping out stains under Robert's ever-critical eye – a gentle repetitive beating which reminds him of his grandmother beating out her washing on smooth rocks, a memory he thinks is probably half true, half Discovery Channel – all part of the unexpected comfort of being behind the counter, being on this side of the shop. As Robert says, the Englishman's home may be his castle, but the shopkeeper's counter is his moat. These places are home. Pakistan was a holiday destination for boys like him, cousins mocking his accent, aunties judging his clothes, uncles shaking their heads at his prayers, everyone over there so sure he was English, no matter how often he was called Paki here. At home in London there was family and school and mosque and friends, the order changing with the day of the week, or the moon, or the season, but an order that was known, planned for, welcomed or endured. In Pakistan, though, everything was mixed up, so many people wanting to know him, to tell him the old stories and new ones, pump him for return dates only days after he'd arrived. Akeel has heard white friends complain of familial excess on a visit to Uncle Arthur for Christmas, the relatives in Bradford or Basingstoke who demand blow-by-blow accounts of London life, and isn't it time to settle down, and aren't you putting on weight? Everyone's family with the same ability to get under the skin and drive the visitor crazy, but the journey back home takes a lot longer than a day trip to Basingstoke, and gives the traveller far more time to sit with his worries.

As a child, Akeel spent the trip to the airport nervously practising his vowel sounds and working out how not to get laughed at when he arrived, while Wasi, his cousin who usually travelled with them, was jumping up and down, craning his neck for the first view of the mini Concorde, Akeel's dad driving and cursing under his breath as the boys made him miss the exit to the car park yet again. Later, in their teens and travelling alone for the first time, Akeel's nervousness was edged with an extra tension – torn between feeling embarrassment when Wasi insisted they find somewhere to pray, almost never the quiet corner Akeel would have preferred, and yet also proud of his cousin who ignored the stares and simply got on with it. And once he was praying with Wasi, Akeel had to admit it did feel good, special for its very ordinariness. An exaggerated special because half the time Akeel didn't pray at home, not always, his father did, and Akeel was supposed to, but he missed one or two prayers most days, more as he grew older. Hardly any of the Muslim boys he knew at school made all five every day, just Wasi. Though Akeel also noticed how most of the boys who made a big deal of not praying at home often really liked to pray at the airport, carefully taking out a compass and rolling out the prayer rug some old uncle had forced on them, blessings offered up. Praying at the airport felt like a dare to the same guys who also drank beer on Saturday nights and kissed girls they had no intention of ever loving.

Wasi went on Hajj when they were eighteen, moved to Pakistan at twenty, terrified his mother and Akeel's parents with his long letters home about the evils of Western life and then, after a period of silence in which everyone expounded their own theories about what he was doing – except for those who smiled quiet and knowing, more worrying for their silence – Wasi confounded them all by coming home, married to and already pregnant with a French girl who had no intention of converting from her own Catholicism. His mother cried for two days. Then she shrugged, thanked God for the safe return of her only child and started making clothes for the baby, a martyr to her knitting needles. Soon afterwards Wasi declared his intention to go into politics, to show 'these people' that a young British Muslim could be religious and political and still not conform to any of their tabloid stereotypes. Akeel knew Wasi understood exactly what was meant by those stereotypes, he'd lived them long enough before coming home. Unlike Wasi, Akeel had been frightened rather than excited by the sound of the training camps some of the older kids went off to, leaving as boys at the beginning of the summer holidays and coming back men, the aura of whisper and danger surrounding them, and attracting any number of willing white girls, and a few brown. Working with Robert, hearing the older man's endless opinions, Akeel has been thinking more about his own views and he finds it disorienting, like the childhood flights back home and the different accents and his cousin's utter certainty. Making the effort to find this shop, planning to take it on, that feels brave, important, and yet he knows that to many of the young men he grew up with, to young men like Wasi, it is straight and normal, and worse, probably just boring. Akeel is relieved Wasi hasn't ended up more political still, that they've both avoided the path taken by several of their old friends, choices no one really talks about now, not in public, rarely at home. Yet he also wonders if maybe he'd be a better person if he did take a stand, decide what he cared about truly, launch himself into it. Like the Jehovah's Witnesses in their house-turned-church by the bus stop, making an effort to get their point across, actively taking their beliefs out into the world. Vocal witness rather than standing silent.

Akeel moves on to untangling and stacking a nest of coat hangers, listening now to that Australian girl telling Robert how she misses the beaches back home, and Robert countering with stories of the Serpentine and Hampstead ponds and Richmond.

Helen is not convinced. 'It's not the same though, is it?'

'Didn't say it was, but it's not as if I'd go to Sydney and start asking where's your version of St Paul's, would I?'

She shakes her head. ''Spose not. Haven't been to St Paul's yet, keep thinking I'll take the kids, but . . .'

Robert doesn't give her a chance to list the excuses. 'Monument? Somerset House? Rotherhithe Tunnel?'

'Tunnel?' Her rising inflection sounding even more incredulous than usual.

'Don't laugh, Brunel that is, well worth a look.'

She's smiling now. 'I will, honest, go to St Paul's I mean, one day. Don't know about the tunnel . . .'

Helen likes Robert, she repeats chunks of his lectures in the mass emails she sends home, she doesn't mind him telling her off, reminds her of her granddad, though she suspects Robert thinks of himself as more fatherly than grandfatherly.

He continues. 'Pie and mash, girl, that's what you want, tell them about that when you go back home. Pie and mash and liquor, that'll put a smile on your face.'

'Oh no, I did do that, the green stuff? It's rank.'

Robert looks to Akeel, who winks at Helen. 'Nah, boss, she's right, it is rank.'

As Helen heads across the road Robert shakes his head. 'Daft bint.'

'What?' Akeel asks.

'Having an affair with those kids' dad, saw them in the park couple of years back, couldn't keep their hands off each other.'

'How do you know it's still going on?'

'Well, if you'd got your whole life ahead of you, and your job was picking up someone else's cleaning and wiping the noses of someone else's kids, and you were pining for Woolloomoo-bloody-loo or wherever it is you're from, you'd have to think there's a good reason to stay, wouldn't you? Besides, the silly bugger left a love letter she'd written him in his pocket. Found it a year or so ago.'

Robert leads Akeel out the back, unloading the biggest dryer while Akeel gets to work on the shirt machine. They raise their voices over the hum of engines.

'Why didn't you give it back?' Akeel asks.

'Who to? He never comes in, probably had a heart attack when he realised he'd lost the damn thing. And how embarrassed would that girl be if she thought I knew, bleating on about how she fancied him and all the rest of it?'

'You didn't have to read it.'

'Wouldn't you?'

Akeel stops. 'Yeah, probably.'

They smile, complicit, unloading, folding, pressing.

'Go on then,' Robert says. 'How'd it go with that best man's speech? Liked the jokes, did they?'

'It was OK. A bit quiet, I think register offices always are.'

'Meant to be, aren't they? Those God-botherers want to punish us for leaving their bloke out of it. Bit different from your wedding do, I bet? All noise and fuss and carry on?'

Akeel knows what Robert imagines – heat, dust, music, colour: the still-frame kaleidoscope of every film ever made about the subcontinent – they were his own confused expectations too, before he went to his first back-home wedding. It helped him understand a little of what Rubeina must have been going through, all her family weddings had been in Britain, it was his parents who'd insisted they have it back home, her own wedding was the first she'd been to in Pakistan. Akeel thought she was in shock for weeks afterwards, Rubeina said it was more like months. The shock of the old in the new, the unusual in the commonplace, and all of it seen through the eyelash filter of her politely downcast eyes.

'Sort of,' Akeel answers. 'I mean, everyone has family to deal with at weddings, don't they?'

'Certainly do. Mine was the mother-in-law. Who's yours?'

'Aunty Nur,' Akeel answers without hesitation. 'Sits at the back of every gathering so she can complain we're not doing everything right.'

'That one sounds like my mother-in-law too.'

'And my mother's brother-in-law who won't eat anything unless he knows exactly who it's been prepared by and how.'

'Religious?'

'No, just always on a diet.'

'Fat?'

'Oh yes.'

Both men laugh.

'Go on, who else?' Robert asks.

'Mariam. Used to be Mary. Converted when she married my dad's cousin, and forever telling my girl cousins they're asking for trouble because they don't cover themselves enough.'

'Don't they?'

'Some do, some don't. I think she just wants them to do everything like she does.'

'Converts always do go a bit overboard.'

Akeel lists the others. His businesswoman big sister never off her phone and always complaining that the rest of the family don't understand how hard she works, the gay cousin pretending he hasn't found the right woman yet and everyone colluding in his lie, the squealing children, spinning and fighting in three languages and at least as many dialects, all of it underscored with the utterly specific smell of mountain air and open fires.

The end of the work day comes, and while Robert locks himself inside for another night, Akeel heads home to his wife, thinking about their wedding. He remembers his shock when he saw Rubeina for the first time after the mendhi. Brought in and seated on the stage opposite him, dressed in her deep orange and gold, fingers made claws with a combination of henna and dark red polish on false nails, shoulder-length hair long and full under her veil from the addition of fat hairpieces, her beautiful dark skin waxen under a thick dusting of white makeup. Akeel knows now that Rubeina so wanted to laugh at the look on his face, a repeat of the horror she'd seen in her own mirror when she caught a glimpse of the mannequin the makeup women had made of her. But she couldn't look at him herself, not with her head bowed for almost three days, partly because of the protocol her chaperone cousin insisted on, partly from the sheer weight of the gold necklaces and earrings Akeel's parents had added to her wedding jewellery. Afterwards Rubeina told him she'd spent three days starving while he'd been indulging his existential thoughts, impossible for her to eat on that stage, with the white makeup and the fake hair and the hennaed hands and the heavy gold bowing her down. At the time he'd simply thought she was doing a good job of looking like a dutiful wife, had been impressed with her acting skills. Later, in the middle of the nikah, exhausted already by the surging people, unable even to catch Rubeina's eye, Akeel was struck by an acute sense of separation. Later still, in the car again, closer to Rubeina but unable to look at her face, to see her clearly, Akeel kept returning to this feeling of something quiet and very separate within the chaos. That evening, in his father's village, facing the barrage of a thousand rose petals, thrown with such ferocity he felt Rubeina wince as they hit her painted face and hands, he stood beside his wife, looked at her lowered head, her covered hair, heard the breath of everyone around him and, for the first time in his life, felt he understood community. The shock of it, the bliss of it, was that even though he felt intensely alone and separate, he was not lonely. He looked to his father and saw the man was older than he remembered, studied his cousin's face and saw new lines there, watched his sister's little boy kicking his friend beside him – the individuals that were the group. Akeel wondered how old he must have been when his parents' languages gave way to his own East London English. Was it school or home that fed him the everyday words, so that now the village voices sounded accented to Akeel's ear, when it was his own father's accent in these strangers' mouths? And then there was more to do and more to say, people to thank, words to speak, still more to eat, exhaustion and irritation and hungry to be alone with Rubeina. Akeel knew this feeling of separation would pass, was passing, even as he noticed it. But having stood there, a witness to the group, the group witness to him, he was certain that, somewhere in all this, he had been blessed.

Akeel sits on the tube heading east to home, his real

home, and wishing there were more chances in life to experience that private blessing, wishing it were possible to know a precious stillness in his everyday life as well. Wishing too – as his mobile screen flashes LOSER at him again and again – that he were better at *Death Trap 8*. Apparently level 12 is amazing.

Twenty-four

In the morning Marylin stops at Robert's shop to leave a bag of clothes, she smiles at the young Asian man behind the counter, he is polite and friendly enough, but he's not Robert. Marylin has known Robert all her life, knows he's been talking about selling the shop for the past year or so, she understands he probably needs to move on. All the same, she works every day with bright personable adults who gave up their work, or were made to give it up, and somehow gave up living as well. She wants to tell this to Robert, explain that, tired as he is, he might want to keep going a few years yet. Instead she takes her green ticket and puts it in her purse, exchanging weather-remarks with the young man, noting how little she likes change, unwrapping an ice-cream bar as she goes, mouth already watering for the caramel at its centre. Akeel watches her cross the road. Every time he sees her she's eating or drinking. He thinks she's stunning, sexy, full – the way she wears those tight tops and wide skirts and always those high, high shoes, like a woman from the fifties. And then he thinks of Rubeina, slight and bright, and he feels guilty. Though he still watches Marylin until she's out of sight.

Ten minutes north of the junction, Marylin walks along the wide concrete wall that is the base-pillar for the block of flats she's come to visit. The building she is trying to enter has a closed-in entrance, an intercom to each of the flats and a reinforced-glass security door firmly shut in her face. When Hazel Erskinshaw first moved into her flat on the fourth floor, this estate was considered hot property. She'd wanted to emigrate to Australia but her husband had been tempted by these new flats with their view clean over to the river. Mrs Erskinshaw, whose husband has been dead almost twenty years, is still not sure the view was worth it. Those post-war architects promised a community of homes offering warmth and safety, windows on either side of the bordering blocks, to catch both morning and evening sun, but the designers hadn't accounted for a yearning for earth, or that even an indoor bathroom could never make up for the opportunity to scrub your own front step, sluicing away the detritus of the week into a gutter just two feet distant. With no step to scrub, the ladies of the brand new Loughborough Estate had no reason to meet outside for a natter, and when skateboards and scooters took over the raised space out front, the ladies retired to their individual back balconies, each woman marooned on her own little concrete peninsula, looking down to the patch of rough grass below. Mrs Miniver and Mrs Mills might well have owned the streets they walked down, ruled their neighbours' kids with a smack round the ear and a dusty barley sugar from an apron pocket, but they did so from their own doorstep, with the safety of their own home behind. Once there were no matriarchs to rule the path, the kids ran riot, and in an illegitimately brief generation those kids grew to men and women, and now the flats Marylin comes to as health visitor have been repainted and made still more private, each wrought-iron gate and grille a set of perfectly pretty prison bars. Then the security gates were installed downstairs and the buzzers on the doors and pass keys in the lifts and now the building is hermetically safe, the pock marks of a hundred satellite dishes offering the only way out.

Marylin is visiting Mrs Erskinshaw, who at seventy-one is far too young to be locked away on the fourth floor, embalmed in total privacy. The flat at the end of a row never has passers-by, only intentional callers, and Mrs Erskinshaw had long since grown out of people who make the trek to see her for anything other than their work. Today, Mrs Erskinshaw is Marylin Wright's work. So Marylin stands by the security door and shouts her name into the speaker. Shouts it once more, and then spells it out for the woman three flights up.

Marylin Wright has had to spell her name almost every day of her life. Both names. Though it's true she sometimes doesn't bother, and people usually get the second one right. Wright. Marylin was born on the sixth of August 1962, the day after Marilyn Monroe died. Audrey Wright wanted to name her baby Marilyn Monroe Wright – that's what she said, what she actually wrote was something slightly different – and then the midwife persuaded her otherwise anyway. Said it might not be such a nice thing all your life to know you were named after a dead woman, and no better than she ought to be. The midwife said that at least if Audrey just gave her the first name then no one need know, not unless the babe grew up to be the kind of girl who wanted to say. She told Audrey she'd learned, over the years, to see the child in the baby, the adult in the child. Audrey was a well-brought-up young woman – despite clearly having mislaid her wedding ring somewhere along the line, that Woolworths gold wasn't fooling anyone – so she didn't laugh at the older woman's wise words, though she didn't take them very seriously either. The baby was named Marylin and Audrey took her home to St Anne's Residences and the flat she didn't share with Mr Wright.

Right from the start, Audrey and Marylin were a good

146

combination. There were plenty of people down Railton Road very fond of Audrey Wright, and as long as she was happy, no one saw the need to comment, certainly not in that first winter after she'd brought the baby home, when Audrey, with no income as such, had still, come Christmas, left a small stocking outside each of the front doors on her landing, with love from Audrey and Little Marylin. Audrey had a good heart, and that's why there was no talk about Mr Wright, or not enough to notice anyway, not enough to mind.

As her daughter grew, Audrey explained that while there was no Mr Wright, there had been a Mr Aubrey, and as she quite rightly said, Audrey Aubrey would have been a terrible burden. As it was, Mr Aubrey was a kind man who sent money a few times a year and a proper present at Christmas and remembered without fail the Monroe–Hiroshima anniversary birthday, Audrey had no complaints there. Besides, Mr Aubrey already had a wife and children of his own somewhere off on the other side of the river, a brown-skinned wife like the brown-skinned Mr Aubrey himself, possibly even black-skinned, if the photographs he'd once sent of Marylin's three half-brothers was anything to go by. Audrey met Mr Aubrey at a dance, she'd never fancied a dark man before, but Mr Aubrey had been special enough to give her a baby, and special enough to help out with a bit of cash for the child every now and then. Mrs Aubrey didn't know about them of course, which was as it should be, according to Audrey, not the wife's fault things had turned out the way they had. Their little secret, hers and Marylin's and Mr Aubrey's.

It was on Marylin's first day at school that she first understood that she and Audrey had different-coloured skin. The skin on Marylin's arms was a pale, middle brown, peppered with the same tiny freckles that smothered Audrey's own

147

pink-white. To Marylin the freckles were a meeting point between herself and her mother, joining the dots, but Audrey left Marylin at the school gate and within the first hour a dozen or more children had asked about her dad, where he was from, why didn't she look like her mum – until then Marylin thought she did. The children didn't ask from rudeness, they just wanted to know, many of them had mums and dads whose skin was different too, but Marylin didn't know enough about Mr Aubrey to answer the questions honestly, and no one in the flats had ever asked before, and when Audrey picked her up after school she somehow knew it wasn't a question she should repeat. Marylin was four and one quarter, she didn't want to hurt her mother's feelings.

Marylin knows to wait, sometimes Mrs Erskinshaw has taken fifteen minutes to get to the door. Last time she came to visit Marylin suggested Mrs Erskinshaw might consider giving her a key, to save time and pain, but the offer was ignored. Marylin watches a mother and child crossing the road, late for school, shouting at each other. She still finds herself yearning sometimes for that time before the rest of the world stepped between her and Audrey, remembers sitting on Audrey's lap, fingering the precious Marilyn Monroe clippings and truly believing she might grow up to look like her namesake and Audrey pointing out that the real Marilyn had changed her own hair from brown to blonde, so it certainly wasn't impossible. Marylin is a health visitor for an Inner London borough, she knows she is expected to take a stand, to care about the people first and about the politics espoused by her council a very close second. And she does care, she is a freckled, mixed-race woman living alone in South London, she rarely sees herself on television, never at the movies, has only two or three times found matching characters in the books she borrows from the Tate Library on Windrush Square. Marylin knows she is under-represented, actively hidden more often than not, but she wonders too if perhaps her white colleagues think about it a bit much, ask her opinion too often 'as a black woman'. Can't she just have an opinion as Marylin? Or can't they imagine? If they get it wrong, how bad would it be? They'd make a mistake. So what?

Now Marylin stands at the bottom of a block of flats in the Loughborough Estate, waiting for Mrs Erskinshaw to get up off the sofa, for the older woman's ulcerated legs to stand the pain of her enormous weight, for her to stagger to the door, down the hall and to the buzzer where she will let in that coloured girl who has come to change the dressing on her leg. Mrs Erskinshaw wishes they'd send her a white health worker, but this morning, in that first half hour out of bed before the pain really set in, she took out the nice china for this Marylin girl anyway. They'll have a natter and a cup of tea and a biscuit. The coloured girl brings biscuits, which, Mrs Erskinshaw has to admit, is nice of her, she doesn't have to, plenty wouldn't bother, or stay so long to talk. Unlike Marylin, Mrs Erskinshaw does have children of her own, three of them, all grown up now, but they don't visit much, very busy her children, and, rather like the first health visitor who came to Mrs Erskinshaw just the once and then found a way to get the woman off her route, none of them are very good with the stink of gangrene. Mrs Erskinshaw doesn't notice any more, and Marylin prides herself on not giving in to it, Audrey didn't smell too good at the end either.

'How's the leg, Mrs Erskinshaw?'

'Not good, but then, what is? Been watching the news all morning, God knows what we're coming to.'

Marylin carefully unwraps the now-sticky bandages from Mrs Erskinshaw's leg as she talks. 'What news, Mrs Erskinshaw?'

'Bloody Arabs, love, all terrorists that lot.'

'Oh.' Marylin leans back slightly as the last of the bandage peels away from the wound in Mrs Erskinshaw's leg and the stench of old pus and flesh rotting on the bone rises up to her face. 'Not all of them.'

'Enough, girl, enough. Your lot didn't come over here and start laying down the law, did they?' Marylin is saved from replying when the smell reaches Mrs Erskinshaw, and the old woman stops, disgusted and embarrassed by the way her body has let her down. 'Stinks to high heaven that does. And me, who used to love a dance.'

Mrs Erskinshaw shakes her head and reaches for another of the custard creams Marylin has left close by. While the old woman dunks and sucks at the biscuit, Marylin cleans the wound, listening out for the tiny, biscuit-gagged groans which are Mrs Erskinshaw's only concession to pain.

Before she leaves, Marylin washes the dishes, and then leaves the biscuits and a fresh pot of tea beside the doily-covered milk jug, all within easy reach, close to Mrs Erskinshaw's remote control. Her son thoughtfully paid for satellite earlier in the year, so now his mother has ten news channels to choose from, each one more sensational than the last, none of them the same as an actual visit from the son, but Mrs Erskinshaw knows her boy is very busy. Marylin sees herself out, breathing shallowly until she is safely back down on the ground, taking in the welcome fumes of the street. At the corner she looks through the shop window to see Robert ringing up someone's jacket on the till, and she waves through the glass. He's a good-looking man for his age, she thinks, as she walks on home. Audrey's sister, Marylin's Aunty Irene, always said so, and she was right.

Twenty-five

Just before midday Akeel checks his watch, raises his eye-brows to Robert who nods back, taking over from him at the till and counting out the change for their impatient customer. So many impatient customers, as if another missed train really will mark the end of the world, of the day. On the other side of the partition Akeel washes, then rolls out his prayer mat and begins to pray. These days Akeel kneels in a curved corner of the arch, remade for his prayer. For the first few months he cleared a space every time he wanted to pray, sweeping to make sure it was clean, then washing, then prayer.

By early spring, when Robert had had enough of waiting for Akeel to put things back and then rejoin him in the front of the shop, he shouted his question the minute he heard the crack of the younger man's knees as he rose from the floor. 'Why the hell do you have to move everything around every time?'

Akeel took a deep breath, he'd been waiting for this, felt his feet heavy as he pulled himself through to the front of the shop, rehearsing every discussion he'd ever been through on the subject of time and space for prayer, arguments he'd made himself, testing his parents' limits, arguing with Rubeina who is stricter than he is on almost every point. Akeel walked slowly past the boxes and bags, stacks of hangers, the rinsed teacups from the morning, tap dripping methodically into the stained sink, rounding the partition wall that separated the messy secrets of the shop from the marginally tidier façade the customers saw, forcing his arms to stay at his sides, holding back his pointing finger that itched to make the argument before his mouth could begin.

Robert didn't give him a chance. 'Why don't you just clear a space and leave it cleared?' he asked. 'It's not as if you're only at this praying lark once a week, is it? It's daft taking ages to move everything around every bloody time.' Robert paused, a moment for his first words to sink in, another to dig where he knew it would hurt. 'Unless you just can't be bothered? Don't really want to learn your trade?'

Akeel shook his head. 'You know I do.'

Robert nodded, his point made. 'Well, come on, lad, think! You're not dopey, don't act it, it doesn't become you.'

Since then Akeel has taken a space at the back of the main shop building, just where it opens into the railway arch, where the layers of wallpaper roll aside one by one to reveal the shop in a dozen previous incarnations. He vacuumed the frayed carpet, washed the skirting board that edged the small space, and in doing so began to take the building for his own. These are the skirting boards he will replace when he takes over, this old patch of carpet will be removed and the bare boards beneath exposed, new ones put in if necessary, no doubt it will be necessary. A new window out here would make such a difference, even with the low level of light that filters in through the narrow, overgrown yard outside. He could clear that yard. In time, with a little more capital, that partition wall can go too, he'll replace it with another, further back, dividing just the arch from the shop, opening up the whole ground-floor space, then the clean and pressed clothes will be set on racks in plastic overcoats, so the customers can see it all, everything open and bright like cleaners' shops in American films. Akeel's material dreams rise up in hand with the prayers and good intentions from a floor that will be his. Inshallah.

Now that they are fully into summer, and while Akeel still hears Robert's questions as if they are barked orders, he is starting to decode the intonation, to differentiate aggression from interest. Not that it's always clear. Akeel comes back to join Robert in the front of the shop and Robert begins.

'So, listen, all this prayer – can't you do it later?'

This is easy. Akeel knows this one by heart, and he's starting to think he understands the answer as well. 'There is no later. If I don't make this prayer – today's salat al–zuhr – then it's gone. That one chance to pray now, today, is gone.'

'You must miss it sometimes? What if you're on the train? Or your watch stops?'

'There's a dispensation for travellers. But as far as your watch stopping, well, you're in charge of your watch, aren't you? If the alarm doesn't go off, and you don't open the shop in time, you're responsible, right?'

'I don't need an alarm,' Robert answers. 'I've got the trains, no way I'd bloody sleep through that noise.'

'But if you didn't get up, and you had customers waiting – you'd be responsible, not your alarm, not your watch.'

'Fair point. So what happens if you do miss a prayer then?'

'I feel bad about it.'

'So it's guilt then, like the flamin' Catholics. All your religions are just based on guilt.'

'It's not the religion that makes me feel bad. I do,' Akeel explains, omitting to add that Rubeina is perfectly capable of making him feel awful too. 'Just the one chance to make the midday prayer, when it's gone, it's gone.'

'I don't know, I can't see God caring all that much whether one bloke in the back of a shop in Lambeth prays on time or not. If you think God exists, surely he's got better things to worry about than you praying?'

153

'It's not up to me to say what He cares about or not, we are required to make these prayers.'

Robert stares at Akeel now, shaking his head, trying hard not to let out the sigh that will mark him as an older man confused by the certainty of youth. Tries. Fails. Sighs. There is an uncomfortable silence between them that Akeel dares to break, marking another shift in time. A month ago he would have just got on, started a displacement activity, the cup of tea, the folding of garment bags, the counting of wire hangers into ten and twenty-five-unit lots.

Now he reaches for the teacups, but he asks as well, 'What, Robert?'

'Just worries me, as it happens. When people think they know what they're meant to do, what God wants or Jehovah or Buddha or Allah or whatever you want to call him.'

'Just the one name.' Akeel's voice is quiet now, steady.

'Listen, son, I'm not having a go, not at you specifically, I don't get any of them. I only ever knew one prayer as a boy – the one that starts "Now I lay me down to sleep" – and I still couldn't get more than a line of that out, even if I wanted to. It's all just been made up after all, hasn't it? By blokes like me, or you, ordinary blokes, who just one day up and got inspired, yes?'

'You could look at it like that.' Akeel is careful here. There are lines he will not cross, be tricked into crossing, people he will not admit his own confusion to.

'So who's to say who's right? Which one got it right? Might be the science-fiction rubbish that Hollywood chap follows for all you know. Thousand years' time might be we'll all be doing whatever that actor fellow does for Christmas.'

Akeel shrugs, his hands up. He understands that faith and no faith have nothing to say to each other. One faith talking to another, there he can find discussion and argument, as well as bigotry and ignorance. But in his experience, the discussion between faith and no faith is a very short one − I believe, you do not. End of story.

'We might. But for now, this is what I know. Anyway, I don't see the whole world getting Scientology. It's all a bit . . .'

'Hollywood?'

'Yeah, that.'

Then there is a run of customers. Given half a chance, Robert could expound on the ebb and peak of customer flow, the pre-work peak, the after-school rush and the five-minutes-to-closing jam, these are all obvious, but Robert has long been aware that there are other causal influences at work, and he is teaching Akeel these signs as well. A just-poured cup of tea will invariably bring a customer with a missing ticket and a variety of unclaimed items. A half-eaten dinner, the healthy greens quickly consumed, that particularly meaty bit of patty or chop waiting, will occasion a visit from a member of one of the too-many local societies, asking about street crime or traffic levels or those two blokes who seem to have taken up permanent residence under the railway bridge. An apparent lull, when tea and a bite of cake would go down very nicely indeed while checking the calendar and sorting out delivery dates, all too often translates into querying phone calls, one after the other, then up to three customers waiting to both drop off and pick up, and a van outside, unloading chemical boxes under the eager eye of a traffic warden. It is over two hours before they get back to religion.

Robert has his question ready. 'So what's going to happen when you're in the shop by yourself? How're you going to pray then?'

'Ah . . . I'll do what every other Muslim shopkeeper does in Britain.'

155

'Which is?'

In truth Akeel hasn't really thought about this, he knows there are plenty of others who must have worked it out before him, assumes when the time comes, he'll do the same. 'I don't know. Take a long time to walk through from the back?' Robert doesn't look convinced, but Akeel warms to his own reasoning. 'What? You've never been in a shop waiting for someone to come to the counter? Taken ages to come through after the doorbell rang?'

'They might have been having a break, cup of tea, piece of toast.'

'Toast?'

Robert nods. 'Crumpets, Alice loved crumpets. We used to have a toaster out there, proper old one, before the pop-ups came in. She was always forgetting she'd put it on. She'd be talking to one of the delivery lads and then there'd be smoke and the stink of burnt toast half the day.'

'And on the clothes?'

'Not very clever. Threw it out in the end.'

'Didn't she mind?'

Robert smiles. 'Oh yes. So you reckon every time I go into a shop and someone's taking ages to come round from out the back, they've been down on their knees bothering God?'

'They might have been doing anything. You don't know.'

'And you do?'

'If I'd just finished praying myself? And they looked like . . .'

Akeel doesn't know how to describe the recognition without falling into Robert's phrase. Robert falls for him. 'Like one of your lot?'

'Yes, OK, one of my lot.' Akeel gives in. 'At least I could make an educated guess about why it took them so long to come to the counter.'

Robert raises an eyebrow. 'Fair enough, son. Course, they might just have been working?'

Akeel leaves the shop that evening wishing Robert didn't always have to have the last word.

In bed, in the dark, Rubeina has an even later word.

'Are you asleep?' she asks.

'No.'

'Why not?'

'Because you're not. And when you can't sleep you fidget, and you keep kicking me, and you keep asking if I'm asleep. Which is why I'm not. What's wrong?'

'Nothing.'

'Liar.'

'Akeel! Nothing, doesn't matter. Go to sleep.'

There is silence, Akeel waiting, his tiredness and now the concern her voice has engendered edging him closer to anger, but if she can hold out, he can too. 'Liar.'

Rubeina slides herself closer to him. 'OK, well.' She takes his hand, moves it to her belly. 'I think we . . .'

She waits for Akeel to understand what she's not saying.

'You're late?'

'Five days.'

'You're never late.'

'I am now.'

A siren screams in the distance, the last of the night planes coming into Stansted begins its descent.

'How soon can you . . .'

'Test? Now. If I want to – if we do.'

'Do you?'

'I could. I bought a tester.'

'OK.'

Akeel's agreement is too quick, he wishes he could bite it back, doesn't want to pressure her, to make it matter. It does

157

matter. Rubeina is out of bed and opening her drawer, she goes to their damp little bathroom, down the hall, tells him to wait there, to wait for her, in the dark. Now Akeel really does have something to pray for.

In his bed, in the amber light from the street, Robert listens as the last train clatters past his flat, hears a helicopter buzzing over Ruskin Park and thinks about prayer. About praying for his dead daughter, his dead mother, about praying for himself. He tries, opens his mouth for 'Now I lay me down to sleep', and then closes it again. The words will not come, he will not let them. And he doesn't suppose he'd believe in them even if they did.

Twenty-six

Dan loves summer. He spends the early mornings walking over Myatt's Fields, where the grass, unwatered, is following the daffodils' descent to biodegraded dust. Dan has not always lived in South London, but for a long time this has been his home. These streets, this land. He stops on the centre of the ground and looks around, a small flock of seagulls has taken over the flat patch, bordered on either side by rubble turned into handmade hillocks. He watches the birds and thinks how far they have come. It is years since Dan has been to the seaside, an age ago when he took his wife and three sons all the way to Cornwall for a family break, up to the west coast of Scotland, on one of the first ever package holidays to Marbella, sun sea sand and a row of hotels identical in size and shape to these squat Loughborough Estate flats, their view of warm water, not Coldharbour Lane.

He listens to the squawking, screaming seagulls, eyes closed, waiting, waiting until he hears the undertone of tide and then, arms flapping, mouth wide and cawing, he runs into the centre of the flock, an enormous bird, fifty times their size, rising on the wings of his dirty grey coat and an early-bird can of strong cider. By the corner a mother distracts her little girl from the sight of the crazy man, wishes again she could afford to leave London, and hurries the child along to nursery, the little arm tethered at the edge of its socket, pulled up and away by the adult hand that has to drop off her daughter, get to the tube, go all the way across town, and hopefully beat the Archway post office queue before she joins the rest of the workers in her office at the Whittington. It is a perfect morning, but only for Dan and the seagulls on the wing.

An hour later Dan is back on the sofa at the edge of the railway arch. His cushion has sunlight, Charlie's half is in the shadow of the old brick arch. They will move their placing in time with the sun. Dan likes the light, Charlie prefers a cool shadow. This is a different seat than the one they had in winter, that was taken eventually by the council, frost and rain having rendered it beyond rehousing, useful only for the dump, or for Charlie and Dan. The dump won. Fortunately the two men are homeless, home-free, in an area of active recycling. The streets spinning out from the junction are full of houses that have either been divided into flats, ready for students and nurses and other transient occupiers, or are in the process of recreation from old houses into new homes for first- and second-time buyers. These homes-to-be are on the lower end of the ladder, but they have good-sized gardens, lovely wooden floors once the carpets are stripped out, as they invariably are, and they make fine, stable rungs from which to reach up. So much so that every second Saturday Charlie and Dan could refurnish their corner from the pieces left on the street by their fellow citizens. Desks with the drawers off their runners, a television with good sound but no picture, new batteries still in the remote that has been Sellotaped to the side, half a dozen mother-made jumpers taking up too much room in the summer wardrobe, a good pair of men's shoes, bought for a funeral and now too sad to wear again. This is city recycling, no need for a landfill site, things left on the street in the generous knowledge that some-one else will always find a use for any item that becomes redundant.

Dan could not find another use for himself when he was made redundant at fifty-one, neither husband nor father were enough, and a property and life ladder that had seemed easy to climb in his twenties quickly became a spiral snake's nest with no hand-holds. Now the seagulls benefit from his inspired team-building techniques, and only Charlie knows of Dan's remarkable fluency in several European languages, and even then only when the beer has the better of Dan's tongue.

At ten thirty Charlie is asleep in the shade, and Dan is settled on his end of the sofa, mid-morning sun, sol, soleil, sonne soft on his grey coat, rubbing his aching knees and smiling down at his feet, blistered but lovely, inside the beautiful, almost-new funeral shoes.

Twenty-seven

'Friday afternoon then. See you then. Bye then.'

The woman leaves the shop and Akeel watches as Claire – Helen's boss, Andrew's wife, Freddie, Emily and Simone's mother – climbs quickly into the high carriage of her 4×4, locking the doors even quicker, and drives off to work, splashing leftover dirty summer rain on to several furious passers-by. One of the now-damp pedestrians is on her way to clean and polish the Celestial Church of Christ. Her loud anger is not entirely celestial, but it does make Akeel smile as he turns to Robert. 'Three thens?'

'You what?'

'Three thens. Right then, bye then, see you then?'

Robert nods, replacing the receipt roll in the till. 'What about it?'

'You were talking as if you couldn't wait to see the back of her.'

'Can't be doing with that one.'

'I thought we had to welcome all sorts? Isn't that what you told me?'

'Glad to hear you remember, lad.'

He does. Akeel has committed to heart everything Robert's told him about the area. He's completed three correspondence courses and already has one framed certificate ready to hang on the wall, expects to have two more by the beginning of next year, when Robert hands over and Rubeina can finally get her itchy hands on the building, clear the place, start the redecorating. Akeel still hasn't told her about the contents of Robert's storeroom upstairs, doesn't want her to judge Robert on this one thing, though he too is keen to clear out that ordered nest of crammed files and musty boxes. Putting things away upstairs, emptying pockets into files and boxes, continuing for now Robert's pattern of study and store, Akeel is careful not to stay long in the room, the weight of all those other lives pushing in too close, like a rush-hour tube journey where enforced contact brings strangers together, connecting them at elbow and thigh and shoulder for five long minutes, and then the rude breaking away again. All those city lives, meeting in a single touch, then nothing more.

'Didn't you say we always need to show a smiling face?' Akeel asks.

'And?'

'You didn't exactly ask how her holidays went.'

'Damn right I didn't. Look, she comes in twice a year, if that, only when the Aussie girl's too busy with the kids – her kids, mind you – behaves as if she's doing me some great bloody favour using my shop – your shop to come . . .'

'Please God.'

'If you like, but I guarantee you, come time to pick up, she'll find something to complain about, crease not right or some stain only she can see. 'Cept she doesn't have the bottle to do the complaining herself, gets Helen to do it for her, next thing you know, you see her on the telly defending some flamin' asylum seeker's right to stay in the country, when she can't even bring herself to pass the time of day with the man who runs her local shop.'

Akeel checks the green paper slip Robert has attached to the woman's now-folded skirt and blouse, suspicion confirmed, smile on his face. 'So you charged her for a suit instead of two casual items?'

163

'No skin off her nose, she'll be giving the receipt to her accountant anyway. Look and listen, lad, listen and learn.'

Akeel takes another step closer to danger. 'This over-charging, nothing to do with the fact that she's black? Black and wealthy?'

'You what?' Robert's reply is sharp now, though his eye remains on the calendar and catalogue he's checking for stock.

'Seems to me, most white people assume most black people, and Asian for that matter, are poor. And they don't like it when we're not, it makes them uncomfortable.'

'I think you'll find,' Robert pushes the words, his place, his people, not yet Akeel's to talk about with any authority, not by a long shot, 'Most white people round here are the poor ones. And whatever colour someone is, it's the show-ing off I find hard to take, shoved down your throat the way that one that does it, with the stupid bloody jeep she's driv-ing and that clonking great watch. Round here we don't think a Rolex is the be-all and end-all, we think it's a bit common, tell the truth.'

'So it's about money, not race?'

'It's about the lot, lad, you're kidding yourself if you think they're not all mixed up.'

Robert points at the group of schoolgirls outside, their screeching laughter and texting fingers an effective deterrent to the builders eyeing them up from the other side of the road. 'See? White and black girls, all in together, they speak the same, want the same, because they're from round here.'

'So it's about class, then?'

Akeel is picking, sticking at Robert. There's something here he's heard intimations of all year and doesn't quite get, doesn't know if he wants to get, but he does want Robert to say it.

'Class?' Robert shrugs. 'Maybe, I'm not sure I'd call it class, location maybe, where you're from, who you grew up with, mixed with. Truth is, I think those girls, black and white, have got a damn sight more in common with each other than the white girls out there would with some posh Home Counties tart. These ones, they're daft as a brush every one, and I don't understand a word they say half the time, but you can see – they all get on. And that's what we like.'

'We?'

'English.'

'Right. You English.'

'Don't take the mick. You know what I mean.'

'Not British?' Akeel asks.

'That's another thing altogether. The flamin' Scots and Welsh are far more fussy than we'd ever be about all that pure-bred lark. Here's Scotland, there's England, never the bloody twain.'

Akeel has heard exactly the same when his father and uncle argue over the exact location of the Kashmiri border. 'And the English never fought over what it means to be English?'

'Yeah. Obviously. But depends what you mean by English, doesn't it? Anyone's a Londoner, they're English, course they are. You get out to bloody Hampshire or wherever, Sussex, Surrey, they reckon it's only them, rolling hills and whatnot. The cities, the English in the cities, it's us who've had to make an effort, learn to get along.'

'Why?'

'Here's where everyone lands up, isn't it? The French did, Jews, Jamaicans, your lot, after the war, whoever. London. Manchester. Birmingham. Your mum and dad didn't make a beeline for the Cotswolds, did they?'

Akeel shakes his head, picturing his mother and father in

a thatched cottage, yellow roses round the door. His mother would probably love it now, wouldn't have known what to do with it thirty years ago. 'And there's a problem with them not going to the country?'

'Not a problem, no, but it can cause, you know . . . friction.' Akeel does know friction, he waits for Robert to go on. 'Look, immigrants,' Robert explains, 'because they go to the cities, for work, they're heading where the poor are. But the people already there, they don't see why anyone would want to move into what's rotten and falling down in the first place.'

Akeel has heard all the arguments plenty of times before. 'And because the ones who were already there don't understand why anyone would want to live in their grotty bit of town, it's OK for them to treat the newcomers like shit?'

But Robert won't have this. 'Your mum and dad, their mates, they joined in when they got here, right?'

Akeel shrugs. 'They wanted to be accepted, they kept their opinions to themselves. But they're also clear that this isn't really home, London still isn't home to them.'

'I grant you, and Sydney's still not home to a few thousand ten-bob travellers who moved out there in the sixties. Gazza didn't stop calling himself a Geordie just because he started playing for Spurs, did he? Course your mum and dad call over there home, but they live here.' Robert stubs his finger into the counter for emphasis. 'Look, everyone's scared of what's different, that's normal, but when people used to come here, thirty, forty years ago, it was to make a new life. Only the ones coming in now, they don't want a new life, they want to take us back to doing it all by the book, and they want to shut you up as much as they do me, I'll tell you that for nothing.'

Akeel does know. He has been berated by his religious cousin for not living a pure enough life, on the same day he

was abused in the street for his brown skin. 'There are fun-
damentalists in all religions.'

Robert nods his head so hard his shoulders move in timed
assent, a dandruff drizzle moving with him. 'Course there
are, they're just as pig ignorant, the dopey flamin' Christians
who think the world was made in seven days.'

'And they've got America on their side.'

'Granted.' Robert points to the pile of unopened boxes
behind Akeel. 'Let's get started on that lot.' Akeel lifts over
the first box and Robert cuts open the top as he continues.
'Believe me, there's nothing you can tell me about the Yanks
I don't already know, I grew up on rationing while we were
still paying off lease bloody lend. How d'you think they had
money for rock and roll, when all we got was Lonnie
Donegan and skiffle?'

Akeel passes Robert another of the heavy boxes, 'Don't
they say the roots of rock are in gospel music?'

Robert takes his old penknife to the top of the box. 'My
point exactly, son – religion, it's a dangerous thing.'

Then a scream of laughter comes from the group of girls
outside, one of them looks into the shop, checks back with
her giggling friends and pushes through the door, leaving it
half open, catching on the bell that sounds in the arch, she's
smiling at Akeel. ''Scuse me, but . . . you got the time, yeah?'
She is still smiling, and Akeel points to the clock on the wall
behind him, the clock she could not possibly have missed,
the clock that says they're already late for school.

Another girl pushes in past her, the door releases the
buzzer. 'So? Ellie? Did you aks him already?'

'No! My God! Shaniqua!' The first girl squeals and runs
out of the shop, hair extensions flying behind her, leaving
Shaniqua to turn to Akeel, she takes her time, looks him up
and down. 'My friend likes you.' She pauses, smiles again.
'You get me?' Grinning as she walks backwards out the door,

enveloped in another belch of laughter from her friends, Ellie's face maroon with embarrassment, their rudegirl voices reaching over the road to the builders, drawing plenty of looks, but only one brave whistle as they hurry away to their bus.

Robert grins. 'Mind you, young girls, they're fairly dangerous too.'

Twenty-eight

First thing in the morning, up long before the rest of the house, Claire, the Third-World-saving, Rolex-wearing lawyer, had left Helen a list of things to do for the day, taken her clothes into Robert, driven off to work with no idea of the water spray or irritation she left behind her. By the time Helen had the kids fed, washed and dressed, had stolen a kiss with Andrew, taken the two elder ones to school and dropped Simone off at playgroup, Claire had already spoken to two news reporters and three clients. By mid-afternoon Claire had dealt with two civil claims, one settled, the other discontinued, and was explaining the finer points of a third to two trainees. Helen meanwhile was leaving the now-tidy house, taking Simone with her to do some of Claire's shopping in Brixton.

Helen and Simone sit on the bus travelling down Brixton Hill, past the prison and Tesco, then that big church on the roundabout with the bar downstairs, the one Helen tried – and failed – to persuade Andrew to take her to. On the street outside Morleys the push of people has Helen longing to climb back into the relative calm of the 45, but like all others before and behind her, she straps Simone into her buggy and they surge forward anyway, past the dirty hot exhaust the bus pumps into the street, exactly at child-head level, and on to the footpath that seems to be generating its own heat. Almost four years in London and Helen still isn't used to the city furnace. Brought up to believe in cold grey London, she arrived in October and the long slow drag from autumn to April did nothing to dispel the Antipodean myth of a cold, grey North. It was only when her first July and August finally hit that Helen realised London too had its summer. Hot and sticky, the hills named for shooters and gipsies and a single high gate form a concave plate where the Thames, trickling in from the cooler west, slowly gains heat on its journey out to the wide flat east, until by August it has turned the whole shallow basin into a warm low-tide pool.

In time Helen learned to recognise the harbingers of heat, in particular the public massing in uncomfortable locations. Half a dozen young guys, each one in a double layer of hoodies, no matter the weather, standing together outside a block of flats off Coldharbour Lane. Four young women loitering on a scrubby piece of waste ground in the early afternoon, a group that by evening will have bred twenty or more adults, a dozen children, babies in arms, and three different sources of music. Half-gallon drums, sliced down their middles and turned into a street barbecue outside the minicab offices her other nanny friends, those with real London boyfriends and therefore real London stories, assure her is also a crack house. Barbecuing beef and frying onions, corn on the cob and plantain, mixed together with warm smoke, a Special Brew marinade, and the smell of hot tarmac steady beneath it all.

For the last three summers Helen has walked up Coldharbour Lane to get Claire's dry cleaning, or down Dulwich Road to take the kids for a walk in the park, followed by a swim at the lido. And she has never once stopped to ask about buying a hunk of grilled meat, a piece of corn from the minicab guys standing around their street-made barbecue. She has turned down the offer of 'happy belly' Guyanese food from the men at the car-wash place in the railway arch, where they've turned their back room into a temporary kitchen. She has never returned more than a grateful smile to the singing man on the bus who has twice told her she's 'too pretty to be walkin', no ring on that finger'. She has never stopped to talk to the young guys sitting smoking in the sun outside the Ritzy, and she's never got round to asking the old lady selling ackee and salt fish just what the hell it's meant to taste like, how to cook it, what – exactly – ackee is.

Helen's reticence embarrasses her, shames her, so she doesn't try harder to overcome it. She walks through these hot footpath worlds, and soaks in the smells and the noise, the people on the streets confirming summer. She thinks she could be walking through a village in Portugal or southern Spain, one of those places where everyone sits around on hot nights in the town square, the places on the travel programmes where foolish Brits buy derelict houses and then wonder why the locals laugh at them when they don't speak a word of the language. Except that if she were in Spain or Portugal, if she'd ever made it that far, hadn't stopped in London and traded her backpack for an illicit boyfriend, Helen might have had the courage to ask one of the black-dressed old ladies sitting in the shade what exactly she should do with this chunk of salt cod, which vegetables to cook it with, how it was made. Here though, because she lives just up the road, she thinks she should know already, understand ackee purely through the osmosis of geography. Helen feels like a tourist. She has a London bedroom, and a London job, and a London lover, but she keeps the price of a return ticket hidden at the back of her bank balance, just in case. A boyfriend with a wife, a promise to stay, and a ticket to go.

Helen could ask Claire about cooking, Claire makes food from all over, on the rare occasions she has time, she's a brilliant cook. But that Claire's good food so often tastes like dirt

171

in Helen's mouth, dirt and sand from grating guilt, and every time Helen finds herself getting close to Claire, close in the way two people might be when they swap a recipe or share a family story over a meal, Helen hates herself even more, both because she feels bad about cheating Claire, and that no matter how well she and Claire are getting on, she'd always rather be eating with Andrew anyway, sharing just with Andrew.

She pushes past another flirting man, and shakes her head, furious with herself. The clock tower on the town hall tells her to get a move on if she doesn't want to be late picking up the older kids from school and the shopping still on Claire's list and everything else that is needed to make someone else's home life more comfortable, in someone else's home, with someone else's child in the buggy in front of her.

In his own home, his own bed that night, Robert thinks about his conversation with Akeel this morning, maybe the lad is starting to understand after all, the place, the people. He wonders about telling Akeel what happened to Katie, if he might understand. If anyone might. The thing is, the thing that makes it so hard, is that there's so much to say, too much. So instead Robert complains about that lawyer woman and the heat and the noise and money and lack of it and what's wrong with this city and he says none of the things that really matter. None of them. Not really.

Twenty-nine

Another day, another potential lover denied, Stefan waking alone and delighted to be so, in the warmth of the afternoon, cat curled solid against his back. Coming to after a mammoth night of drink and dancing, excessive for a Friday, Stefan parading his body, not for the interest of others – though that was certainly there – but for his own joy. Tonight he has planned exactly the same again. Perfect itinerary for a long late summer evening, when the ten-thirty sky is still iridescent as he enters the basement bars and clubs of central London, the low-tide Thames rolling east just yards away.

The denied lover is Mike. This is a surprise to Stefan, not to Mike. Mike from the winter became Mike from the spring and now, apparently, is summer Mike as well. Not on a regular basis and only when Stefan agrees, but Mike who is more than a little in love with the older man, Mike who is a lot in lust with the older man, accepts Stefan's parcelling out of affection – for now. Mike believes Stefan just needs to get used to the idea of someone else in his life, in his home. Stefan has a lovely home, Mike quite likes the idea of sharing it. Mike is also a little in love with the idea of Stefan's life – creative, managing on his own terms, his own home, his own career, and never having to get up before midday. Twenty-one last month, Mike thinks Stefan's carefully ordered state of affairs is almost as attractive as Stefan's body.

It doesn't occur to him that Stefan himself had plenty of lean years, he is, after all, a dancer who now teaches. Or that the kind of involvement Mike would like to have in Stefan's life would alter the precarious balance Stefan has achieved and Mike envies. Stefan knows this, and finds it a little irritating, a lot flattering and, every now and then, when they happen to meet in the same club, find themselves in an equivalent state of inebriation or desire or chemical enhancement, he takes Mike home and they spend more pleasurable hours together. Last month those hours turned into most of a weekend. It was a first for Stefan, first in many years, and a coup for Mike.

And now, late summer Saturday afternoon, Stefan is walking hard to Brixton, shaking off the touch of want, striding forward, at ease in his own showered and scrubbed and carefully dressed body. An unbidden picture of Mike, blond and blissful on his back, on their backs, is pushed away as quickly as it comes. Stefan dashes into the cleaner's at Loughborough Junction, picks up his shirts from the fit-but-so-straight Asian guy, narrowly avoids being pulled into a long discussion about the mayor's many failings with Robert, who's been behind that counter as long as Stefan knows, and is so very skilled at turning two minutes of polite chat into half an hour of state-of-the-world, leaving Stefan no time to waste on his way to work. Between the corner of Atlantic Road and the gathering Christian storm opposite the Ritzy, Stefan charges past a dozen or more young women, they pour out of the hair and nail bars, on their way to another dress shop, the tube, an early cocktail. These are the Saturday girls he was so scared of as a boy. Now, a grown man, he can see the young women in all their shining peacock-preening glory. Long sat-for hair of tight weaves, wigs in impossible shades of red-brown and blue-black, three-quarter-inch fingernails of sea green shot through with gold flecks and painted into

174

blinking eyes, kissing lips, candy cane manicures. Stefan skirts another group at the corner, bodies poured and twisted into smooth Lycra and tightest jeans accentuating every dip and curve, full high arse cheeks and long deep cleavage. These are the dips and curves his white women clients are so eager to eradicate, will sweat and burn and whip themselves to remove, the same anti-hollows the black sisters and cousins are so proud of. Working in the no-man's-land between women's real flesh and their body-dreams, Stefan has an everyman appreciation of the proper shape for a woman – concave and convex. Every day in class he tells his ladies that the body, like the breath, must be allowed its own rhythm, out as well as in. They never listen and his bank balance grows.

On the corner of Atlantic Road, he passes the old guy standing alone in front of the fish market. The waiting man and his wide freezers of frozen fish, no apparent desire for, or interest in, customers of any sort. The man watches Atlantic Road walk by and Stefan turns into the market to check out an album he has on order, still not in yet, man, nex' day, nex' week, yeah? He hears his own accent rearrange itself for the contours of the conversation, changing words on his tongue, in his mouth, to suit the place his feet stand. Stefan leaves, hands light, wallet heavy, thinking what he'll teach that afternoon, who will make it to the class, if he'll be earning the full whack of his potential income or if the late holiday season has come already, and the wealthy women who make up the bulk of his classes will have taken their riches away to an island retreat offering self-actualisation along with substandard accommodation and mediocre food for twice the price they pay in London. Some afternoons Stefan wishes for a proper job, work he doesn't have to make for himself, someone else to pay his National Insurance, holiday pay, sick days. On hot days, hurrying to work, Stefan can find himself dreaming of someone else to send him home at the end of the week, pack him off after the long six days of gutting and cleaning and filleting tilapia, home to the wife and kids and a meal on the table. Some days Stefan feels the weight of what he has to create for himself as a dragging burden on his back, like the day he left school, the day he left home, the stultifying awareness that there is no one else to take care of him, that he has to do it all himself. But not today, thank the blue sky and the thick city sunshine. Today he knows that the smell of fish or old vinyl or stacked papaya or cheapest bubble bath or even well-loved books would be too much after a week, let alone a lifetime's work. Stefan sells himself. He can just about bear the smell of himself as product, and on good days, most days, he understands the fish would be too much. Round the corner, past Iceland, he shoulders his bag and walks down to the tube, a creature of habit in the skin of an artist.

Work, three classes back to back, training up the already-fit bodies that are about to go out on the town. His own body, already-fit, out on the town. Stefan meets first with Tony, an old friend he can always trust to have an extra tab, a little coke, some sulphur perhaps, a very little, just a little, Stefan is no longer twenty-five and while he might find youth attractive and – on occasion, often enough – they him, he does not have a young man's power of recovery. So it's only a few lines or half a tab, in exchange for which he'll buy the bottle of wine they share, they'll talk about old times, and then part. Tony home to his sixteen-year partner, who will not come clubbing, has never been at ease in a sea of male bodies, far prefers takeaway to take-home, while Stefan has his pick of London's nightlife. Alone, unencumbered by partner or rules, unfettered by anything other than his own desire and his watch and the classes he must teach tomorrow.

*

176

Tonight, this morning, just gone three, an hour from the slow fade into British Summer Time sunrise, Stefan is walking home from Brixton back to Camberwell. The N35 took him once through Camberwell already, but he was too sleepy to notice, too dance-blissed to spot McDonald's through the window and climb from the bus to home. So now he is walking back down Coldharbour Lane. The street is punctuated with minicab shops, he could wait for the bus to return in the opposite direction, but Stefan is annoyed with himself for missing his stop, and punishing his tired muscles for the failure of his mind. Stefan believes in discipline.

Halfway home, just past Coldharbour Mansions, an angry spit from the new flats that have phoenix-risen from the Green Man where Robert and Jean danced their wedding dance, a group of youths turns into the street from Milkwood Road. Five or six young men, one or two young women, Stefan can't be sure, they are standing too tightly, dressed too loosely to judge gender. They cross towards him, one of the girls arrives first, she is small, has a tight face.

'Got a light, mate?'

'Sorry. Don't smoke.'

Stefan doesn't stop, walks on, walks a little faster.

He crosses in front of Robert's shop, they surround him by a fenced-off patch of waste ground, ask for his wallet, his bag, his watch, his phone. Stefan hands over each item without complaint. He does not need to punish his body this much. They do.

When they have taken everything they have asked for, when he has handed it all over without fuss, without returning the threat – just as any well-trained Londoner would, many of them and one of him – the attack begins. A smack in the side of his head, from the left, from behind. Stefan whirls round and bashes back, his closed fist makes contact with a cheekbone, there is a yell, but there is also only one of him. Another smack to the head and Stefan stumbles, he is running now, sort of running, but it has been a hard night and he has twenty years, more, on each of these kids, because they are kids, it is kids who are kicking him now, kids who kick the kidneys, the back, the stomach, the groin as he falls to and stays on the ground, defensive position adopted as well as he can, hands over the head, arms covering the face. They are kicking him for being the batty boy he is. That is what they say, it is all they say. Batty boy. Boi. No one drives by, the street is silent but for the grunts and groans of exertion and pain. It lasts less than three minutes. Long enough. There is a call from beneath the railway bridge, one shout, another, and the kids, because they are kids, run off in the other direction, yelling and whooping. Stefan stays on the ground until he is sure they are gone, the smell of concrete and dirt close to his skin, dark iron in his mouth. And now there is a police car illuminating the corner in flashes of epileptic blue, and now it comes to a sharp halt with a burst of siren and Stefan is told to stay still, to wait for help and a young woman in uniform speaks on her radio and another young man in uniform asks the two men with cans in their hands what they saw, what happened, but Charlie does not speak and Dan makes little sense, walking through his Special Brew dream.

The rest of Stefan's journey home to Camberwell takes place in the back of an ambulance, followed by three hours in King's College A&E. There is plenty of time to tell the nice young policeman that he didn't recognise any of his assailants, doesn't know if he would again, to call his phone company from the payphone and cancel his mobile, wake up the neighbour, promise to have the locks changed in the morning. It is morning. His last call is to Mike. Stefan asks Mike to come and help.

★

On Monday morning, his bruises badges of dishonour, Stefan and Mike spend an hour in the dirty police station foyer, women crying and men storming and children on laps wailing, silenced with a kiss or a slap or both. Eventually, in a small office, Stefan's details are taken and his losses noted. Then, first page completed, the polite policewoman carefully fumbles her way through several uncomfortable sentences before asking outright the two questions that still embarrass her. What colour were his attackers? Stefan asks the point of her question. The uniformed white woman with a sheaf of papers in her hand smiles at the bruised black man and explains the boxes she must tick. White attackers against a black man, potentially a racist crime. Black attackers against a black man – and here she pauses, careful not to look at Mike beside Stefan – a homophobic crime? Mixed group of attackers and a black man – ordinary crime. Stefan tastes the iron count in his mouth again, says that he thinks the latter is most likely, though he's not sure how a couple of girls in the racial and cultural mix of attackers stops it being a gay hate crime. He's met plenty of homophobic women, homophobic white men. Or why one black attacker among half a dozen white ones would necessarily mean there was no race involved. The policewoman nods, she takes his point, and ticks her boxes anyway. Stefan adds that in his opinion it was random violence, just the usual degree of homophobia, coupled with a desire for easy cash and – more likely than not – the fact that he had a better phone than any of them.

Staring at his bruised face in his bathroom mirror on Tuesday morning, trying not to blame himself for getting hurt, wondering what his clients will think when he turns up tonight, bruises still the black side of blue, Stefan decides he'll ask Mike to stay another night.

Thirty

Two weeks on, a damp afternoon in a week of constant warm rain, Helen walks a fractious trio of children past a yellow metal sign pinpointing the exact time and place of an assault. Here. Then. Freddie asks the meaning and Helen says someone did a bad thing and the police need other people to say if they saw it or not. Freddie says he'd watch all of it if he saw a bad thing happen and Helen has no doubt he would. Up the hill, on the other side of the park, Marylin Wright is asking Mrs Patricia Ryan what she's seen this week, where she's been. The answers are as vague and insubstantial as Mrs Ryan herself, sharp wrist bones jutting from skin that has aged suddenly from old white to include an almost blue, mottled here and there with jaundice patches. Marylin asks the older woman if she's been eating, Mrs Ryan says she does like a nice biscuit with her tea. Dan is back on his end of the sofa under the arch. He has been missing for a few days, in body as well as mind. But now he is back, safe if not sound, and Charlie is pleased, though he does not say, handing over another can.

Robert finds he is pushing through his day yet again, hourly, counting down in ten-minute lots, stumbling against frustrations he would have shrugged off years ago, now finding their way under his skin. Skin that long ago lost any flush of youth, skin untouched except in handshake for too long, skin that blooms with scars and years and now, on the back of his right hand, something else, maybe a liver spot, the beginning of a liver spot. Surely Alice was far older when her hands became old? Robert is three months shy of his birthday. He is tired. Everything today sets him off, teeth grinding, molars pounding against each other in an attempt to ease the irritation.

He comes back from the newsagent's over the road, shaking his head even before he begins to speak. 'Still got that sign up, from when the funny fellow got beaten up last week.' Robert shakes his head. 'Reckon they ought to leave them all up, all over, fill the pavements with those yellow signs. Then we'd know what a state we're in.'

'You'd be walking round signs all the time.'

'Yes you bloody would, that's my point.'

Robert breathes noisily through his nose, in and out again, an old bull, grumbling at the fence, his every breath a snort of annoyance. Akeel takes a moment, hands still working at the seamed fabric he is folding and piling, mind tracing back through the past seven hours, looking for clues. Robert has been complaining all day, not enough sleep, too much work, even with both of them hard at it.

'Idiots, the lot of them. Done nothing about all this street crime, not round here anyway, politicians don't give a monkey's about the likes of us. Lovely building, pack of fools inside.'

Politics then, Akeel nods, this is safer ground at the moment. Akeel wants to tell Robert about the baby and is worried it's too early, the words waiting in his mouth to be revealed, looking for a place to be spoken, fatherhood made real in the telling. Nothing feels different yet, everything will be totally different soon. The last couple of times he's tried to bring up the subject of family, Robert has cut him off sharp, sent him out back into the heat and damp of the arch.

Akeel agrees about the street crime, doesn't mind disagreeing about architecture, ventures an opinion. 'I think it's a bit overdone myself.'

'Ever been inside?'

'No.'

'Well, shut up and listen, you might learn something. There's this painting, right on the wall, where you go in. A map of London. Don't 'spose people even notice it half the time, but it's got us on it. Lambeth, Southwark.'

'Oh right. Us.'

Robert darts a sharp glance as Akeel picks up the boiling kettle, he gestures out to the street, the same kids he'd yelled at this morning, now congregating by the door of the newsagent's. 'You want to start thinking of them as us, mate, if you don't think you're with them, they won't stick with you for very long.'

Akeel hands over Robert's cup of tea and Robert reaches past him adding more milk, the liquid emphasising his point, how he knows better than Akeel, is informed in the ways of painted walls and local communities and how much milk is required in a late-afternoon cup of tea. As milk slops into the cup, Akeel sees a slight tremor in Robert's hand and decides to leave it. From his parents to his teachers to his grandparents, now to Rubeina with this pregnancy, sometimes it feels like everyone thinks they have something to teach him, their job to explain, his always to be told. But it's too hot this afternoon. Too hot and too wet and it's getting into the clothes as well, damping out beautiful creases from carefully pressed warp and weft, leaving sharp lines limp. So not yet. He'll just listen for now.

Forty minutes later Akeel is cashing up while Robert sorts pieces for the tailor. Robert looks up from the bag he is packing with clothes too big or too small or too lovely to throw out merely for a torn pocket or fallen hem and asks, 'So you've really never seen Westminster up close?'

'Why would I?'

'School trip? Family outing?'

'We were city kids, teachers thought the best thing to do with us was get us out, Epping Forest or the seaside.' Akeel remembers children running wild on buses and trains, teachers yelling, Southend pier stretching on forever. 'And my father always said we were here now, we were Londoners.' Akeel takes on his father's accent, the emphatic hand. '"Sightseeing, Akeel, is for tourists, we live here. We can see it any time, any time we like." So we never did.'

Robert knows this is true, he hasn't seen as much of his city as he'd like, as often as he'd like to. 'Lovely building, worth a look. Belongs to us an' all, the people.'

Akeel's eyebrows raise, one after the other, slowly, as if he can't help it, doesn't want to, and yet knows the conversation had to come some time. Robert glares back. 'What's that for?'

'Doesn't that depend if you agree with what they're doing or not?'

Robert puts down the tailor's bag, walks round the counter to reverse the open sign and close the shop, leans his back against the door. 'I didn't agree with a bloody thing Thatcher did, not one thing, but it was still mine, that building, more mine than hers, she was only going to be there for a while, however long that lasted. I can go there any time, it's always mine. Ours. And that's special, that is, for all of us.'

Akeel counts out the last of the five- and ten-pence pieces into the small plastic bags. 'It's not that simple . . .'

'Yeah, it is. Where were you born? Bow?'

Akeel nods.

'And you're in Stratford now?'

'You know where I live, Robert.'

'You're having a laugh, lad, you're a Londoner. Cockney at that, course it's bloody well yours. You vote, don't you?'

'Have done.'

'What's that mean?'

'It means I have done. Sometimes.'

Robert's right hand slaps down on the counter. 'For God's sake, it's your right, your duty, you don't want more of that BNP lot getting in, do you?'

'Of course not. But why should they be more my problem than anyone else's?'

Robert sighs. 'Just because it is, lad. Mine an' all, because I'm a working man and it drives me crazy hearing that lot say they speak for us. But if no one else is, well, that's how they get in, isn't it? You've got to remember, lad, Mosley, Enoch, they weren't welcome in South London, we spoke out against them way back. Look, you got born with brown skin and that's the way it is. Like the funny fellow, Stefan, got born that way, didn't he?'

'Gay?'

'If you want, yeah. So you've got to deal with your lot. He's a poof, gay, whatever. He's got to deal with his.'

'What about you?'

Robert shakes his head. 'I've had my share, lad, don't you worry. What I mean, if you're not happy with it, do something, it's in your own hands. You're three miles from the Mother of Parliaments. Go and have a look, and when you get there, see this bit of London you spend fifty-odd hours in a week, how we're painted on to that wall – part of the fabric. That's something to be proud of.'

'But it still goes back to what I said in the first place – what if you don't like what they're doing there? What if you don't think there's much to be proud of?'

'Free country, lad, do something about it.'

Akeel closes the plastic bags, sealing in the coins and their smell of dirty-fingered metal. He speaks quietly. 'Those sui-cide bombers, they did something about it.'

'Yeah. They did.' Robert finishes his now-cold tea. 'Bastards.'

Then there are the shutters to be closed, the lights turned off, the side door locked and there is no time to say anything more until Robert and Akeel part in the hot grey evening outside.

Akeel turns, says, 'I didn't have you down as such a politico, Robert.'

'I'm a working man. If that means political to you, then I suppose I am. Far as I'm concerned, that building on the other side of the river belongs to me as much as it does to whoever the current idiot is in Downing Street.'

'I doubt that's how they see it.'

Robert nods. 'Well, I've only got my own eyes and I've only got my own choices. So those Houses of Parliament? They're mine. And that lot on the other side of the water? They work for me. Dear God, son, it's hard enough as it is, if getting this old has taught me anything at all, it's you might as well look at things as if you have some choice.'

'So it's all just about point of view?'

'Not all, no. But a hell of a lot is, how you choose to look at it.' Robert is used to Akeel now, notices things the younger man doesn't think are so obvious, the thumb and first finger rubbing together when he's agitated, the deep-ened track lines of the frown marks between his eyes. He tries again. 'Yesterday, when you were all upset because of those black lads yelling Paki. Sorry, but that's the word, right?' Akeel nods and Robert continues, 'Well, they weren't exactly inaccurate, were they?'

'As you said, Robert, I'm a cockney.'

Robert smiles, caught out. 'OK, granted, but you've got to admit, the words do keep changing. Used to be coloured

185

was the polite word, right? And calling someone black was rude, now it's the other way round. It's up to you how you look at it, how you take it.'

'No, that's not on, if you wanted to have a go at me, you wouldn't call me cockney, or Pakistani, you'd call me Paki. Wouldn't you?'

Robert looks at Akeel, this young lad, closest Robert has to a mate right now, and finds his shrug turns to a nod, an acceptance, a confession. Akeel is on a roll now, train times forgotten, telling. The times he's been called Paki in the street. The way the word has been said, is said. The way it is not descriptive at all.

'All my life, in this country, the word of abuse, for anyone with skin like mine, has been Paki. No matter if they're Indian or Kurdish or Iranian or I don't know –' he stalls, hands in the air, groping for a place on the globe – 'Fijian. The word's Paki. And eventually it begins to mean something else, you make the word mean something bad and say it long enough, it becomes something bad. You know, all the anger, and violence, the fear, everything that's in the news and the papers all the time now. It didn't just come out of nowhere. People are sick of it, of being picked on, harassed, sick of being made the bad guys. And I understand why some people want to take a stand.'

Robert nods. He knows. He is tired and angry and hurt, feels like he has been for half his life – maybe he has – and he wants to take a stand too. He looks at Akeel, close, clearly. 'So is this it? Your stand? Is it going to be enough for you, just to do well? The big business plan?'

Akeel breathes, his heart rate slowing a little, shakes his head, frowns. 'I don't know. Honest. I do want my own business, and I'm pleased it's going to be this one.' Robert interrupts. 'Glad to hear it.'

Akeel runs his hand over the shutter, street grime marking

186

out the ridges of his fingerprints. 'But I thought having this place, getting it together would help, would make me feel . . .' He stops, not sure exactly what he's saying, unable to articulate the fear he feels whenever he thinks about Robert leaving, a fear tempered with enthusiasm and excitement, but real fear nonetheless.

'Like you were making a difference?'

Akeel shrugs. 'Like I was doing something important.'

Robert knows this only too well. Knows its futility too. He wants to explain about fear and growing up and being a man and taking a stand, but there are no words he knows that can do this and so, instead, he sort of pats Akeel on the shoulder, a pat that is a forceful slap, meant to convey every-thing Robert knows about responsibility and fear and rage and getting on with it anyway. It is the first time he has touched Akeel since they shook hands at the beginning of the year. It means something.

Then Akeel goes to his train and Robert goes inside, locking the side door behind him, heads upstairs where he boils the kettle and doesn't draw the curtains and sits in the streetlight in his front room, watching television for hours and taking nothing in.

Thirty-one

Too early in the morning, when the air is sharp with new autumn, Akeel waits at Blackfriars for the train that will take him to the shop that will soon be his. He wonders if it will still feel like going to work when it becomes his own, the means and end of production, will it somehow also translate from work to career, workplace into mission. A brittle wind spikes up from the river and the Sutton train, rumbling downhill to a slow stop, comes to rest at platform 4. Akeel takes an empty double seat facing south, leaving behind the shore and the great bulk of St Paul's. In this bright sunlight, made harsher by the absence of warmth, the lines seem particularly sharp, the dome immaculately elevated, the single clock clean and clear.

Once, when he was a boy, just turned twelve, back before every second passenger was a paedophile or a terrorist, long before Akeel had downloaded the most excessive games his phone can hold to distract him from the journey, he travelled by himself all the way from Euston to Liverpool. Faizah, his mother, sat her eldest child on the train with sandwiches and a bottle of Coke and a quick word to the guard. Three and a half hours later, Akeel's young uncle met him at Liverpool Lime Street with Twix, plain crisps, and a late Eid present, a sharp new ten-pound note to spend all on himself, no siblings or cousins there to share it with. The beginning of a holiday weekend with his father's youngest brother and the new, sexy wife. Even at twelve, Akeel knew for certain Hasna was a sexy wife. This was before the young couple started having babies and with each baby found more faith, less time for the ways of the world, the people of the world. Back then Ahmed and Hasna were still so much in the world that Akeel's mother, settling her son on the train, had warned there was a chance that Ahmed – or even Hasna, God forbid – might drink alcohol over the weekend, and if they did, not a word was to be mentioned to Akeel's father, the elder brother who took his family responsibilities so seriously. Too seriously for Faizah sometimes, more than enough to do with her own children and her various siblings, wayward and not, faithful and not, let alone taking on her husband's collection as well. She whispered to Akeel that not telling wasn't the same as lying, not really. Hasna and Ahmed had moved away for a reason, they would come back for another, a better one. Everyone in every family didn't need to know every little bit of what went on. They weren't in a village any more.

Akeel didn't know it at the time, but his mother was speaking for herself as much as for the young couple. For her own hope that no matter what the direction of her children's lives, they would all find themselves together again eventually. In heaven, Inshallah, if not on earth. Though on earth would be nice too. Akeel pictures his mother at their last family gathering, the cousin's wedding when Lee's best man's speech for Dean Dobson had yielded such successful jokes, and considers how she comes alive in family groups. Where both he and Rubeina find the ever-present noise exhausting, she thrives on it. Where he can stand Thomas and Oliver and Clarabelle for an hour at most, and Rubeina will give a maximum twenty minutes to the songs of her childhood shrieked in the high-pitched excitement of the under-fives, Akeel's mother sinks back into family and lets it wash over her, luxuriating in genetic chaos. Faizah eats up family mess and joy and tantrums in the same way Akeel devours her food. She is a brilliant cook, proudly so, Akeel has been known to grab a couple of leftover samosas for the fifteen-minute journey home just in case he might be peckish after a four-hour meal, and, secretly, sweet chunks of lamb from the pilau rice in her fridge during Ramadan daylight. Not for years now, but not that long ago either.

The morning train stutters out of Blackfriars. The young couple he stayed with in Liverpool are now in their forties, Sister Hasna, whose full face Akeel hasn't seen for fifteen years, Brother Ahmed whose only conversation with Akeel these days is whether or not he makes his prayers correctly. The uncle and aunt who are now Brother and Sister, who used to speak Urdu and English, not necessarily in that order, who now speak Arabic, Urdu and English, definitely in that order. It seems to Akeel he could never perform salah well enough for Ahmed, wonders if he ever will. He tries, he means to, easy in midsummer to rise in the quiet and welcome the new day at an hour many people consider the middle of the night, plenty of time to go back to bed again afterwards, having done his duty and made his blessing. Akeel and Robert have agreed a transfer date of January fifteenth, and then what will he do with his prayer, in the late afternoon when the shop is busiest, when customers are most likely to want their evening clothes, queuing for his attention and the clock ticking to sunset. Akeel is aware these problems will come, he is not yet sure how he will deal with them. The train brakes at the southern edge of Blackfriars Bridge, Tate Modern imposing its solid width on the shore, filling his window, and Akeel lines up observant Muslim shopkeepers the length and breadth of Britain, sees each one lay out a prayer mat, checking direction and praying in perfect order, perfect time – the halal butchers', the newsagents', the photocopying shops, the fast-food places, the restaurants, the chemists', the dry cleaners', he looks further afield to the office blocks, the City towers, the hospitals, the kitchens, the Houses of Parliament, the night-clubs, the sweatshops, the morgues. Someone must have worked it out, someone must know better than he how to manage life and work and family and prayer, what order to put them in. There will be a website or chat room or blog that tells him what to do and how to do it. Akeel has every faith that there will be someone eager to tell him what to do. Akeel wishes he had every faith that faith alone was enough.

On that journey to Liverpool, he tried to count the church spires on the way and gave up at one hundred and seventeen. Now, as the train moves on through Southwark, Akeel looks at both steeples and cranes, asking which tells a truer story of this London – probably the cranes that will be lit for Christmas before they know it, lowered for the ghost of Churchill's barge passing on the water behind, stacking the city heavier and higher on top of itself. Just before the Elephant, the train passes a Salvation Army building, then the wide white façade of the massive church on the round-about, the one Robert still calls Spurgeon's, though the name out front is a different name, and it is, apparently, a tab-ernacle not a church. Akeel does not know the difference, he expects Robert does, but will not ask for fear of another lec-ture on the appalling standards of modern education. He will store his question, save it for a time when distraction is the better part of friendship, one of those occasions, far more frequent now, when Robert has been quiet for almost an hour, looking out the window at a grey evening, no words needed to explain the hurt his leave-taking has slowly ignited, a fire fanned by any opportunity for reflection. Just out of the Elephant, and the train passes the site, long gone

191

now, of the Borough Synagogue, then half a dozen more churches, all of them dark and cold in the morning, silent at night, and finally along Myatt's Fields into Loughborough Junction where the churches no longer have steeples or steps bowed from years of pilgrims' feet, cracked bells or bomb-damaged reredos. In the same way that the shop was not always what it is now, these new churches were not always places of worship.

Opposite the station entrance is an office-warehouse that now houses the gospel-fired singing of a hundred or more matrons every Sunday evening. Across the road and past another boarded-up pub is the old house with high steps that is home to a certain number of Jehovah's select Witnesses, waiting for their day and shoring up potential recruits for the count that will surely come. Halfway along the road, across from the cab drivers' café, is a long low thirties block, offices originally, now an evangelical ministry from which, on Sunday afternoons, a gaggle of modestly dressed girls spill on to the street and over to the newsagent for sweets and crisps and Cokes, the E-numbers and additives only marginally denting their perfect harmonies. During the week these girls taunt the hooded boys at bus stops with their raised hemlines and higher-raised eyebrows, but on Sundays their giggles are as pure as their starched white shirts, their only vices flavoured with pillars of salt and a vinegar sponge for Jesus' thirst. Back toward the station, down a side alley, carefully tended with hanging gardens of plastic flowers, waits the Celestial Church of Christ, offering the greater glory of barefoot humility and sacrifice. Then back in a loop, closer to the shop, the #1 Mohammed Mosque, red and white light-box high above the beat-and-spray garage, proclaiming a place of worship and sanctity, above and no doubt beyond the reach of paint fumes from below. The Nation of Islam mosque with its passionate American influence is no more comfortable to Akeel, no more like the faith of his father and grandfathers, than the stronger Arabic influence that is now making its way into the mosque his family has attended for years, but the sharply suited gentlemen and immaculately dressed women of the Nation of Islam are unfailingly polite, elegant in their practice. And, as Robert points out when the young man in black suit and polished shoes and dark sunglasses comes into the shop, salaam-alaikum for Akeel, barely a nod for Robert, 'Anyone who worships once a week in a good suit is a friend to the dry cleaner. No matter how they say hello.'

'Or not?'

'Or not.' Robert agrees. And rings up the man's cash on the till.

Akeel watches the brother walk away, down the street and asks Robert, 'Why is there so much God here, do you think?'

'You what, son?'

'Half a dozen churches, the mosque, all the religious buildings round here.'

Robert pulls on his jacket, time to cross the road for his paper and crisps. 'Alice used to say it was the crossroads.'

'So?'

'Suicides. Old days, they didn't bury them in the church-yard, with the good Christians.' Robert spits out both *good* and *Christian*, the words sounding far too much like judgement to stay in his mouth for long. 'Used to bury them at crossroads, on the way out of town.'

'Yes?'

'Alice reckoned it attracted the God-botherers,' Robert is heading for the door, his stomach rumbling. 'All those lost souls wandering round, looking for deliverance.'

'And did she think they found it?'

Robert is halfway out the door, wind whipping at his

thin grey hair. 'Nah, not Alice, no truck with God. That was just what she said brought them here, the religious types. Anyway, doesn't work like that, does it? 'Sposed to find salvation for yourself, aren't you? If you want it. Chocolate?'

Robert is halfway to the curb when Akeel nods his head. He does want chocolate. And he does think the salvation of lost souls probably takes more effort than the generous prayers of the found.

Robert comes back with Akeel's bar of fruit and nut, and then it's time get those big duvets out of the drier, fold and pack them for the morning, take a pile of things upstairs to the storeroom. A notebook that has been used for an address book, a bus pass, a small padlock with no key, a love letter from Carlie to Ignisious, her adoration spelled with an extra R. Robert keeps saying he'll start to clear the room soon, but until then it is important to hold on to things, continue emptying the pockets, carry on with the system.

Over chocolate and crisps, Robert tells Akeel about his mate Geoff who lived up the road when they were kids, how they went go-karting down Denmark Hill, the sting and stink of iodine on their knees, how it's all changed for kids now, so bloody different. And then it just comes out, the words Akeel's been wanting to say, not knowing how to say, worrying about saying. Rubeina is pregnant, he's going to be a father, they're having a baby.

Robert simply looks at him, and nods, saying, 'Better get on with learning the job then, lad. Keeping the till balanced's no easy thing on two hours' sleep a night.'

And that's it. No useful tips, no lectures on what, where and when. None of the suggestions Akeel was expecting, hoping for. He knows Robert is no longer in contact with his daughter, but at the beginning of the year there had been

194

plenty of stories of Katie as a child, as a baby, how it had been, working downstairs with a screaming toddler, a stroppy teen upstairs. And now nothing.

Akeel feels bad he let it slip, didn't give more preparation for the news. Here he is, a young man, starting his life, baby on the way, new career, and there's Robert getting rid of the shop, no friends that Akeel's seen, not really, and no family either. He didn't mean to rub it in, the difference in their lives. And in truth, half the time he doesn't want to acknowledge it's really happening, fretting about money and time and sleep. Don't all new parents go on and on about lack of sleep? He's been working out when the baby is due, how much time he might need to take off, how likely it is to be a problem for his customers, put off by a closed shop, the chance of losing those customers for always. He wonders if it would be stupid or rude or just obvious to ask Robert to come back and help him out for a week or two when the baby's born. Akeel thinks Robert would probably like it, thinks maybe he ought to ask, thinks maybe he ought to work out how to talk about the fact he's going to be a father as if it's the most ordinary thing in the world, surely it's going to become ordinary eventually. Of course Akeel wants this baby. Of course Akeel is terrified.

A week later, after six working days when neither of them have mentioned the pregnancy once, Robert watches a young man struggle out of the shop door, a bag of carefully folded clothes shoved into the bottom of the over-large buggy alongside a sweaty plastic bag of used nappies, two bottles, one half finished and exuding the scent of sweet warm milk, and a small sick-stained blanket, all crammed beneath the form of the sleeping child.

Robert shakes his head, watching the man progress across the street, 'What about you? Going to get yourselves one of

195

those swish pushchair things? Wheels up to your knees and too wide for your own front door?'

Akeel's smile is faint. 'Ah . . . I don't . . . no idea.'

'Come on, son, you must be planning? The pair of you? First baby and all? Getting yourselves organised.'

Robert loved this time with Jean, readying themselves for Katie's arrival, lying in bed, dreaming their future together.

'Well, yes, we are. Of course. Only . . . it's just . . .' The words stumble to a halt. It's hard enough to worry alone, let alone aloud. It's ungrateful too, he knows that, they watched Rubeina's cousin trying and failing to get pregnant for years before the strain and unhappiness finally eroded her whole marriage. Akeel shakes his head, reaches for a wrapping bag and hanger. 'Nothing. It's great. Really.'

'Wasn't meant to happen yet?'

'No.'

Robert smiles. 'There is a way to stop that, you know. Several ways.'

'Yeah. Thanks.'

'Still – horse, spilt milk, stable door, eh?'

Akeel continues with his folding and packing. For the past six months he's almost felt in control, and he's liked it. Akeel has been wanting this for as long as he can remember, always wanted to be with the men when he was a child, to follow his father and uncles to the mosque, to leave the women behind, go off with his older cousins. And now, some tiny thing hidden deep inside Rubeina has made him a child again. Fearful and irritable and seeing the future as a problem, not a joy.

The door opens and Mrs Ryan comes in, with her quiet accent and her wandering mind, and it takes both Akeel and Robert a good ten minutes to work out what she's come for and what she wants from them. The first two of those minutes she spends asking for a coffee bun. Eventually Robert remembers she brought in her winter coat back in March and he goes upstairs to find it for her, Akeel is left to make conversation about the relative merits of coffee buns and custard squares. Mrs Ryan is right, Robert says, as he comes back downstairs, plastic-wrapped heavy wool coat folded over his arms, it is getting chilly again, she'll be needing the coat. He charges her just the basic cost of cleaning, and she leaves trailing the scent of Everton mints and talcum powder behind her. Both men watch her go, they know there are two other crossings she'll have to negotiate yet, but at least they won't have to watch her terrifying progression once she's round the corner.

Akeel reaches past Robert to take their teacups out back. 'Thought we only held on to things for three months?'

'Mrs Ryan lives in a tiny flat I could fit into my front room, where the hell's she going to keep a winter coat?' Robert places a careful tick beside his last crossword clue and leans back against the wall. 'Sometimes we're cleaning, sometimes we're storage. By the time you've worked out which, they're a customer anyway. Might as well hold on to them, lad. Now about this baby . . .'

Akeel sighs. 'I don't want to talk about it. Honest.'

'Too bad. We're talking.'

Robert follows him out to where the kettle has just boiled for the third time in half an hour, this time, no matter who comes through the door, he is determined to turn water into tea. He's asking Akeel what exactly it is that the younger man is frightened of. Not coping? Not being good enough, man enough? He assures Akeel this is a good business, it will provide. Akeel sits down, the ripped yellow vinyl of Alice's old stool pressing through his jeans. He says how much he's been looking forward to taking over, making changes. And then stops himself when he realises what he sounds like, hurrying Robert away.

'I know what you mean, son. Course you have. So what's the problem?'

'I thought I knew what was coming next.'

Robert starts to laugh, Akeel interrupts him. 'No, I know things get in the way. It's just that I had a plan, for a bit.'

'You like your plans, don't you?'

'It's not just that, it's that it's all going to keep on changing. Because that's what babies do, don't they? They change things.'

Robert agrees there's nothing like a baby to put the kibosh on plans. He takes a mouthful of tea, reaches for the sugar and stirs in another teaspoon, he needs to be clever now. He says he thinks Rubeina's a lucky girl, most lads Akeel's age might be worried by a kid on the way, but it wouldn't be for the same reasons. Most young blokes want to muck around long as they can. Akeel, though, he wants everything sorted, he wants to look after her.

'Yes. I do.'

'When my Jean was expecting, once she got bigger and I could see the baby was really there, all I wanted was to take care and make good. See, when you're someone happy with your wife, it's not about feeling trapped or held back, that's not the problem, what it really is, you're worried you won't be good enough, all of a sudden you're back to feeling like a lad, not a man. And I hate to tell you this, son, but you're going to feel that plenty more before you get to my age.'

'Doesn't it ever stop?'

Robert thinks, takes his time, he knows the answer, but he's not sure he wants to say it yet, to say all of it. 'Changed for me when Alice died. I was forty-odd then, no kid, I grant you, but when she went, it was like a windbreak had been moved. Or a door left open. There was no one up ahead of me, no one between me and well . . . dead myself. I knew I was a man then.'

'And when your wife left?'

'When they both left, the girls, that really did it. No one ahead of me, and then, once my Katie . . .' Robert stops, looks out the window, into his cup. 'I told you she wouldn't see me?' Akeel nods, he's never yet had the courage to ask why Katie made that decision. Robert continues, 'Once she'd made her choice, it meant there was no one after me either, not really. Don't think I've ever felt more lonely. Or more old.'

Then the shop door rings and Robert gets up to answer it, walking through to welcome whoever has just come in, his pleased-to-see-you smile on his wrinkled face, his come-back-again demeanour in place, speaking quietly over his shoulder as he goes, 'You try and enjoy it, son, lad one minute, man the next, you'll miss it when it's gone.'

Thirty-two

Dean is on his rounds. He travels by foot, not for Dean a flashy car that will draw attention, he knows the limits of his work, has no need to make a fuss. He makes his meet, pockets the cash, keeps back his own share and gets on. Other blokes might want to make more of it – showing off with the car, the suit, the watch. Dean spends good money on these things, but it's always understated, careful. He's been inside a couple of times, when he was younger, but he's nearing forty now. He likes his wife, his kids, his home, his work. He likes his life, and as long as he doesn't overreach himself, things will stay that way.

Dean has been known to overreach himself of course. That Brazil job for a start, bloody lucky to get away with that one, and then a year later, feeling cocky, flush with youth and ambition, he took an extra step he shouldn't have and found himself going away for eighteen months. The place wasn't too bad, in Kent, easy for his sister to visit from her flat in Maidstone. That's when he got into running, not far, they were never allowed to go that far anyway, but every now and then some pronouncement would come down that the boys could go on a run, work off their energy, and Dean's name would be top of the list. He was good at it too, a long run out, quick stop at the phone box in that little village to make a call, even the most hard-hearted bastard screws generally let the lads make an illicit call every now and then, they were just lads after all, Dean only nineteen, and then a slightly slower step back in on the return. Harder to run with your shoe lining stuffed full of the wraps your generous sister has left in the change hole of the payphone, and Dean cultivating his image as something of a smelly-socked bastard, so no one's tempted to check his footwear when he comes back in. He'd liked the running, and they'd done good business inside, him and Karen.

There was one time though, the bastards'd had a good laugh at his expense. Dean and his mates called in for another bloody announcement, another bloody call over the intercom, and every call ending the same – IMMEDI-ATELY. Not please. Not if you can. Not if there's time, if you fancy, if you want. IMMEDIATELY. Like there's any other fucking place to go. Immediately it is. In that foot-dragging, slouching walk those halls recognise as speed and immediacy. The lads all standing there, for a good five then ten then fifteen minutes before they were addressed. How power works, keep them waiting, Dean knows that, has done the same himself, yes, mate, I'll be back in ten, course, babe, round yours in a half, no probs, on your door, eleven fifteen. Dean has always prided himself on delivering just in time and just a little late. Whatever it is they're wanting – a car, some business, a clean passport, a safety net – make them want it that bit more. Dean understands the power dynamic very well, and being on the receiving end pisses him off plenty. Which is probably their point.

That particular announcement was worth waiting for. Tomorrow morning, 7 a.m. sharp, cross-country run, ten miles, all for a good charity, some children's hospice, no one minds helping out the little kids. And Dean's mind racing off with all the other runners. Kent and cross country? He's fucking out of there, if not for good, then at least for the day.

Sorry, boss, got lost, sorry, mate, couldn't find my way, sorry that the A20 was beckoning and I made it all the way home before I remembered where I'm s'posed to be staying. That night Dean gave away his fags, a couple of T-shirts, and the quarter ounce Karen brought him in last time she came to visit. They'll stop your girlfriend kissing you, the kangas, but not your sister. Dozy bastards.

By the time morning comes, Dean has planned his route. Out the main gate of course, smile for the passers-by, give it a bit of work at the first set of hills and then fuck it, he's off. It's not a break for freedom, Dean's not stupid, but they must know he'll give it a go, and he's a fuck of a lot faster than most. Run two half-marathons in the past year and done bloody well in both. The locals love it, nice bit of rehabilitation. Parole board love it too, they still believe that National Service bollocks about tiring a lad out so he's got no juice to play come the night, fucking twats. Dean sells juice, he lives on juice, that lot have never run any distance in their fat lives, course they wouldn't know that doing it on a couple of lines is better still, heart pumping the fuck out of itself and body spinning with oxygen and adrenalin. Nothing nicer. Dean doesn't expect to get all the way home today, but he's made a couple of calls, Karen'll meet him at the phone box they've used before, half-dozen mini-bottles of JD for him, few grams to trade, he'll run back down, dropping them in safe spots as he goes, pick them up later in the coming weeks. He's well behaved, gets a lot of outdoor work, volunteers more often than not. He's only nineteen and the effort he's put into getting fit and working hard, especially the outdoor stuff, gardening and whatever, it looks good, looks like he cares. And he does, of course, Dean is nothing if not caring about his profession. He's a trader, needs a constant supply of goods and buyers. Dean has customers in abundance, captive audience, he needs to keep the goods flowing, this little day trip is another opportunity to build up his stock.

Six thirty up and dressed. Six forty-five, warming up, pissing off the other lads in with him, fuck you, you lazy fat sods, fuck you. Six fifty, come on, open the bloody door, where's the starting line. Six fifty-five pumped and pumping ready ready. Fuck the tortoise, here's your hare, mate, here I am, let me at it. Seven a.m. Doors open. Dean runs out on to the landing in shorts and T-shirt, him and half a dozen others, each with their plans, each with their day sorted, their week sorted, their life sorted. Smack bang opposite him is a fuck-off sign reading APRIL FOOLS!

And Dean takes it, and he smiles, he laughs with the rest of them, laughs at himself. Takes it, because not to would show them they've won again. And he's lost the fags he gave away and that quarter ounce, lost those two good T-shirts too. And Karen will've come all the way down in the rain and she'll be well fucked off, waste of bloody time for her. But Dean laughs and takes it on the chin, in the guts, up the arse. Takes it because if he didn't he'd look like more of a wanker. Takes it and goes back inside to get changed and every button, every zip, every scratch of the stiff fabric is a tear in his skin. It doesn't matter it doesn't matter it doesn't matter. Three years later when Dean is in a fight that comes out of nowhere, that is just a spilt pint and a too-slow apology, when he uses a smashed bottle to better effect than he ever has before, that's when this will matter. Not now, not in front of this lot, not where it can be seen and used. Dean Dobson has a good sense of humour, everyone knows that, it's one of his best attributes, he can laugh at himself. Now that's what we call rehabilitation.

Five years later Dean gets his own back. Works out which screw had the idea for the April Fools joke and follows the cunt home one night, bloke so twatted from a night on the piss he has no idea he's being followed, no idea what hits him when the blade slices through both Achilles tendons either. One. Two. And down.

Dean still likes to run, runs his rounds more often than not. First stop is a house just off the top of Herne Hill, one of those posh ones. Detached red brick with stained glass and a kind of porch at the front, as if an old couple might sit there and rock, looking down the hill to town, all those monuments clearly visible from the front of the house. As visible as the whole bloody inside of the place too, no nets up, same as most of the houses in this quiet street, anyone can just look right in if they want to. Dean never follows her into the front room, his meet, way too obvious. Just in the front door, into the passage – nicely painted in two tones of red, proper old hatstand and some big modern art thing on the wall – takes his cash, counts it, and he's off. She's all right this one, he met her through a mate of a mate, usual thing, got her to come along to his local first few times, and she did – brave enough, he'll give her that – after that he felt sorry for her, walking into the pub and looking so bloody lost, figured she stood out way more there, talking to him, than he ever did round her way. She doesn't call him often, once a month, if that. 'Just for parties, you understand.' Yeah, course he does, just for parties, and he wonders what mark-up she puts on his deal, a tenner he reckons. He sells to her for fifty, figures she'll make her mates pay at least sixty, fair enough, she's the one making the phone call. A quick kiss in the hall – both cheeks, that's the way she does it – then he's off, she'd have him standing there five minutes for small talk if she could, lonely probably. And that's as much as he thinks about her.

Then he's on to a couple of flats up the Camberwell end of Coldharbour Lane, walks downhill through the park, past that old Irish woman who's always talking to herself, stops in at the Portuguese deli for a custard tart, best when it's still warm, just baked, with one of their tiny espressos, hot and sweet. On to the flats. Dean was born in a place like this, covered walkway across the front to reach your front door, and a private little balcony round the back to fill with washing or geraniums or rubbish, as you want, but it's your own, that's the point. Rubbish chutes at the end of each row, dropping the bin bags down there and then screaming blue murder when Nick picked him up and threatened to put him in too, then shutting up to hear the sound of the bag falling and falling, scraping against years of God knows what, God knows who according to Nick, who never did stop threatening to tip him in, then the satisfying thump when the bag landed in the big bins at the bottom, even more satisfying if they'd tied it really tight, really full, knowing it would explode on landing. They dumped a cat down there once. Well, Nick did, Dean was too young to help, but the noise it made going down, and the scratches all over Nick's chest and arms, that was brilliant. Scratches that gave him away when Mrs Baird came over and told his dad they'd been having a go. Nick swearing blind they hadn't been near the bloody cat and his shirt buttoned right up to the neck, cuffs pulled down and done up for once in his life. His dad gave them both a hiding, Dean too, which wasn't really fair, especially seeing how the cat was all right anyway. Smelly, but all right.

Dean jogs up four flights of steps to the top floor of the block, windows on each landing, mostly cracked of course, and the steps wide and shallow to make it easy for someone like his dad even when he was properly getting on. No lift to worry about getting stuck, trapped in there with someone you didn't want to be there with, someone who didn't want to be there with you. Dean doesn't do lifts if he can help it, doesn't do any small spaces at all if possible, he's not getting shut in with anyone else ever again. They may not have the stinking lifts of the high-rises, these older blocks, but they still reek of piss. Dean hates it that other blokes piss in corners, in lifts and stairways, pissing like Mrs Baird's old cat. Never done it himself, never would. Nick used to have a go about how fussy he was, even when they were kids. Now Nick's the one with the proper job, commuting up to town every day from his place out towards St Mary Cray, Karen's still in Maidstone, three kids, all in their teens and a bit of a handful by herself, and Dean's here in Camberwell, up and down the steps, self-employed. They've all done well enough. Of course, Nick's got the house and garden, but you can get more space if you're prepared to live out of London – which Dean isn't. Still, his and Gina's flat is more of a maisonette really, and since the council said they could buy it, he's got a mortgage just like anyone else. Nick works for a bank, Karen's nursing, and Dean's running his own little business, just like any other good entrepreneur brought up in the eighties. His tax form says builder, who's going to question that? Not far off the truth either, there's not a lot Dean couldn't fix for you, given the time and money to do it. Their old man would've been proud if he'd made it this far. Proud, but not asking too many questions.

Dean knocks on a door, two from the end, walks into another passage, counts out some more cash, hands over another little pile of wraps, clingfilm-covered, and leaves. His customer up in Herne Hill might prefer a pretence of friendship, down in Camberwell it's strictly business. Dean checks his watch, walks on to his next meet, thinking about himself and his big brother, how it doesn't matter what they do to pay the mortgage, how different their paths, Nick still looks like shit in an old M&S suit that gets more creased as his day goes on. Dean likes an ironed shirt, a clean pair of trousers and fresh socks every day. Short sleeves in high summer, a warm jacket in winter, has a few nice suits, gets the lot cleaned and pressed regularly at Robert's shop. His dad started going there way back when Robert's mum Alice had just started up, hardly ever anything to clean, the old bugger just liked to get a look of Alice.

There's another drop off Loughborough Road, then just time for a quick pint before a meet in Brixton. On his way back he pops into a couple of the places the Brixton firm have a bit of a scam going with, picks up their monthly donation, nods to Robert as he passes the cleaner's, making a mental note to talk to the Brixton lot about the bloke Robert's got lined up to take over. They agreed years back with Alice not to take anything from her, some deal Dean never got the details on, but whatever it was, it held good when Robert took over too. His old man reckoned Alice was as good at deal-making as she was at wearing a tight blouse with loose buttons – or maybe that was the deal. Dean figures the Brixton firm'll want to have a chat with the new bloke when he takes over though, can't see them offering him any favours, black firm and new Paki owner, not likely to be any love lost on either side. And the Peckham lot too maybe, he'll be in for a bit of a shock, the new guy. Dean wonders if Robert will've told him to look out for them, put a little bit aside, either way, the Paki bloke's bound to be from a long line of shopkeepers, he'll know the score.

They don't talk much, the two firms Dean works for, one lot black, the other white – publicly, openly, they despise each other. Stupid white wide boys and lazy shit-head spades – that's how it suits them, the public perception, the family ideals, each to his own, this end of Peckham for the white boys, that side of Brixton for the black. Except of course they have to meet, they're businessmen, and for years now Dean has been the join. He never wanted to be just a dealer or just a thief, scrounging a living like all the others and wasting it in the Crown from Friday afternoon to Sunday night. Dean always had hopes and plans, but hopes and plans need financing. He knows his own abilities too, not born into the kind of family that would take him far – their dad was just a thief, no real connections – Dean needed to make his own. So he did, and because he started young and proved himself handy early on, and because both firms obviously needed someone to go between, Dean got the job. Something like, and nothing like, a runner. Smart enough to know when to stay out of trouble, but reliable and able to handle himself if he bloody well had to, with a sharp enough temper to just let it all go sometimes, a bit lairy, but smart, knows which side his bread's buttered on – in this case that's both. In one way, it's bloody good. On the other hand, of course, there's a hundred per cent chance for the bread to fall buttered-side down. Dean is very careful not to let it drop.

He meets the bloke he's been asked to have a chat with, passes on this bit of information and that answer, then heads home to Gina and the kids, keys and change making music in his pocket. Getting dark earlier now, and a bit of damp in the air too, feels it in his knees first, only bloody forty and he's an old man already. Gina's made a shepherd's pie for their tea and they sit with the kids, eating and trying to guess the answers on that quiz show the kids like. The boys moan they wanted chips, but Dean likes shepherd's pie, Gina makes it lovely, no lumps in the potato and loads of gravy to the meat. Dean covers the lot in salt, even though Gina always nags him about it, happy to be indoors with the family, happy with his lot.

Thirty-three

While Dean was jogging up and down his local streets, Helen was stuck ten yards from Robert's shop. Standing in front of the Somewhere Fried Chicken shop – like its sibling establishments across the city, the home location of the secret recipe employed within is anywhere but Kentucky – she checks her watch again, quarter past five. Helen has been here for five minutes and it feels like half an hour already. She's glad the kids aren't with her, annoyed she doesn't have her phone and starting to get cold. She pulls up the zip on her soft blue hooded top. This is not a hoodie, she is the wrong age, class, nationality and sex for it to be a hoodie. This is the pale blue hooded top she picked up as she rushed out of the house to catch the last post and get Claire's must-have-for-tomorrow dry cleaning. She ran out with two envelopes in her hand. One contained the household's gas bill and its accompanying cheque, written in what Claire believes is Andrew's unnecessary fountain pen flourish, invariably slightly smudged as he rips it from his cheque book too soon, the other envelope held two hundred and forty pounds in twenty-pound notes, and had Helen's name written on the front in the just-sharpened pencil Claire prefers for the shopping lists she leaves Helen every Thursday. This is the envelope now sitting in the postbox five feet from where Helen stands, while the gas bill remains in her cold hand.

She'd run down the hill, two envelopes and the dry-cleaning ticket crammed into a slightly-too-small pocket on top of her house keys. Andrew was home from the office all afternoon, working upstairs in his and Claire's shared study. The children had eaten and were, supposedly under Andrew's watchful eye, playing quietly together. That left perhaps three-quarters of an hour before the soporific effects of the organic additive-free dinner wore off and they began their usual fretful countdown to bath and bed. If Helen could get to the postbox for the five-thirty collection and pick up Claire's cleaning – a run achieved far faster without the children – then, when she made it back up the hill, she and Andrew might find a reason to be in another room together, away from the children, and before Claire returned home. She needed to talk to him, and she needed to do it in peace.

'Helen needs Daddy to help with the dishes.'

'Daddy has to talk to Helen about something important.'

Helen and Daddy haven't had a minute alone since the Thursday night last month when Mummy was away at a conference and Daddy and Helen took the chance to have sex – in Helen's room, the only one with a lock on the door – and then spent another two lovely hours watching TV and playing happy couples, a gorgeous evening, the ensuing night interrupted only by Simone having not one but two nightmares and finally needing to sleep in Helen's big bed with her.

And so Helen had been running and not thinking clearly and, pushing one envelope through the slot in the postbox, she turned swiftly to walk into Robert's shop. It took three and a half paces towards the shop's glass door before she stopped with an adrenalin thud. Helen looked down at her hands. Shit. Fuck. No. In her left hand was the envelope for British Gas, in the postbox was the envelope with her week's pay in cash. Some of the cash inside was to pay for the dry cleaning. Helen regularly uses her own money for household items, keeps the receipt, gives them all to Claire at the end of the month. The rest of the cash is hers, and it's in the post-box.

Helen glares at the postbox, checks her watch again, seventeen minutes past five. Claire is very good at making sure that Helen is never out of pocket, never paying for anything that is for the household. She's a very good employer actually, very generous. Helen hates thinking this, hates thinking how good Claire is, thinks instead about what the hell she's going to do now. She has been into the shop, Robert let her take Claire's cleaning on account until next time, he doesn't think the postmen will arrive before six.

'But the collection's at five thirty?' Helen's rising inflection making a question of her wail.

Behind his counter Robert shrugs. 'How many postboxes are there? You think they all get emptied at five thirty? That there's one bloke assigned to each one?' And even as he explains the unlikelihood of an on-time collection, he further warns that the chances of the Royal Mail bloke letting her take the envelope from the box are slim.

'Dodgy that. You might be anyone, mightn't you?'

'It's got my name on it.'

Robert carefully, too damn slowly for Helen's liking, folds up Claire's clothes, puts them in a plastic bag for ease of carrying, while she, half in and half out of the door, watches round the corner for the red van.

'So you say. But maybe you saw someone put the envelope in there, maybe you're nicking it?'

'Why would I do that?'

'What's in it? Money?'

'Yes.'

'There you are then.' He warms to his theme now. 'Be

211

surprised what people will do. Could be a drugs thing, couldn't it?'

Helen, who just wants him to shut up so she can sign for and take the cleaning and go back to standing as close as possible to the postbox, joins the young Asian guy in staring at him. The Asian guy, who Helen thinks is bloody good-looking, places the box he is carrying on the counter, screws up the wrapper from a chocolate bar and throws it at the bin, misses, stoops to pick it up and drop it in on target this time, asking, 'Drugs? In the postbox?'

'Why not? All the letters people never get, cheques and cash going missing . . . maybe this is how they do it.'

'Do what?' the Asian guy asks.

'Their deals or whatever. Cash in the postbox for the bloke collecting letters, he passes it on to the chap who actually delivers your mail, next day your crack cocaine comes through your letterbox, deal's done, Bob's your uncle.'

The Asian guy goes through to the back room, laughing. 'You should be writing those documentaries, Robert, not watching them.'

The older man passes the wide plastic bag to Helen, his hands are very dry she sees, with bitten nails. 'Good luck, girl.'

As she steps back outside to the constant noise of the street, the sirens and the trains and the buses and the screeching teenage girls, she hears him shout to the younger man, 'Documentary, I said, lad, real life, they don't write that stuff.'

Helen knows he is wrong, her cousin Phil who lives in Sydney is a writer. He wants to write films, but until it happens for him, he works for half a dozen companies and has written loads of documentaries. Apparently it requires real skill.

Helen has been standing here for twelve minutes. More

buses have gone past than ever roll up to the stop when she is waiting for one. The trains to and from the City have crossed the railway bridge three times. She hopes that if she speaks nicely to whoever arrives in the red van to take the post to the sorting office – she hopes it will be a man, Helen knows she is better at speaking nicely to men – that whatever the rules may be, they will give her back her envelope. Her week's wages. Helen has been so annoyed about not getting back to Andrew in time for the quiet chat and maybe kiss she had planned, so frustrated with herself for fucking up in the first place, that she hasn't really taken in the possibility she may lose her money. This thought occurs to her in the same falling-weight way that the realisation of posting the wrong envelope did – crushing, embarrassing, infuriating, self-hating. There is cash in that envelope, not a cheque. Twelve twenty-pound notes cannot be cancelled and given again. Helen knows for a fact that two hundred and forty quid is not all that much for Claire and Andrew, for her though it is loads. It is running-away money or Paris money or running-home money. It is one-day money. One day soon.

Five twenty-five. Helen has spent three minutes watching a small boy charge in and out of the grocer's over the road. Now the small boy climbs on to the bike he left leaning against the ATM sign and rides off towards Shakespeare Road. Like most other kids around here he has no intention of riding on the road, he is right it is unsafe for him to do so, it is also very clear that he is unsafe for pedestrians as he careers into a plump girl coming this way. She shouts at him, at this distance and with idling traffic at the lights in front of her Helen cannot hear what the girl says, but whatever it is, it has the boy off his bike and pummelling her with his fists. The girl pummels back just as forcefully, she is at least twice his size, though judging by her dress, a variation of the uniform from the primary up the road – the state school Claire and Andrew's children don't go to – Helen thinks not that much older. Then the girl breaks away from the boy and begins to run towards Helen, he jumps on his bike and is gone, following the cars and buses in the opposite direction to Brixton. The girl slows as she gets closer, her face is bright red, up close she does not look as white as Helen had thought, she is a pale Asian girl, stocky, lumpy. She is angry and close to tears, muttering under her breath in her little-girl voice. 'I fuckin' 'ate him, man. I 'ate him. Fuckin' 'ate him. Chah, fuck 'im, man, fuck 'im.' She glares at Helen as she walks past her into the shop and into the waiting arms of her father heating chip oil behind the counter where she bursts into tears. Helen wants to burst into tears in her father's arms too. Three minutes until they come to open the letterbox. It is five twenty-seven.

Three minutes that become five and then seven, then nine. Helen begins to wonder about the collection, maybe they will not come at all. She watches three different people post letters on top of hers. One young women opens a white plastic bag and shoves in hundreds of identical letters, each one franked with the same postmark, each one with the address carefully centred in the envelope's transparent window. Helen wants to ask her please not to put them in yet, not to run the risk of mixing her envelope in with all of these, but the girl scares her and so she says nothing, watching the deluge of envelopes slide in and drown her own. The girl has a swept-up weave of hair, pulled high on her head and very fake. She has long nails, impossibly long for the job of putting letters through a narrow slit opening, let alone for any other office duties. Each nail is brightly coloured on the nail bed, with a thin silver line separating the blue base from the green tip. It's definitely chilly now and the girl is wearing knee-length boots and a thick woollen skirt, but they are

214

her only concessions to the weather, her round and high breasts are barely held in a tight purple shirt unbuttoned to reveal half her cleavage and a promise of so much more. One by one, four young men come to the doorway of the halal chicken shop over the road, merely to appreciate the particular geometry of her form as she lifts another pile of letters from her bag. A middle-aged man waits to put his own letter in the box. He has just one letter in his hand, the young woman turns to see why he is standing so close, to glare at his proximity and, even though he apologetically holds up his single letter, she does not let him lean across, continues with her task. When she is done she turns and smiles access to the man behind her, then walks off, her high rounded arse the object of attention for every other man on the street. No, it would not have been possible for Helen to ask the girl not to put the letters in the box on top of hers.

Five forty and Helen realises she has never really looked at this corner before. How busy it is, how dirty, how old. Those weird faces above the shop window, cut or moulded into the tops of the frames. The constant flow of noisy traffic. She feels bad about judging the place, the area, judging it for class and race and money and aesthetics, then she judges anyway. She wonders how long the postbox has been sitting there, in that spot. Robert could direct her to a photo he has in the storeroom upstairs, found in someone's pocket many years ago, kept first by Alice and then by himself, a faded photo of the same corner from somewhere round the turn of the century. The century that turned before this one. There is a postbox in the photo, and what is now Robert's shop offers three shirts for 10/-. There is a lad in the picture, staring directly at the photographer. Robert could tell Helen all about the photo and the corner, but she'd never think to ask. Five forty-five and she watches people walking back and forwards across the railway bridge, city tigers pacing, waiting

215

for their train. Five fifty and a red van pulls up on the corner. She waves to the man getting out of the passenger door, who does not wave back. She explains her story to him and he shakes his head. He tells her they cannot just hand over post. She explains three times about the lack of address or stamp on the envelope, that it won't go anywhere anyway. The van is parked illegally alongside the postbox. The frowning man turns to his colleague who leans over from the driver's side, listens and nods, then tells his mate to start opening the box. The driver explains that they can look through the letters, but once they put them in their grey bag, then it's too late. In the box still, and she can have it back, it's hers. Once in the bag though, it's property of the Royal Mail and more than his job's worth. Helen knows. She agrees.

The little red door is opened, There are so many letters inside. So many letters Helen could have asked the girl not to post. Half a minute to scoop them into the bag, another handful, one more, and then, in the driver's wedding-ringed hand, there it is, her envelope, exactly as she described it, the sharp dark pencil, her own name. He hands it to her, she feels she should kiss them or something. If this were a movie she would, then one of the men would fall in love with her, it would be the beginning of a beautiful affair. The men drive away with their grey bag. Helen walks slowly up the hill.

Claire is home by the time she gets back, she and Andrew laugh at Helen's story as if it has all been a hilarious adventure. They feel sorry for her, Claire offers to give the kids their bath, Helen should go and have a rest, come down later and they'll have a glass of wine waiting for her, poor thing. Helen goes upstairs, hears them talking about her as she goes, laughing at her misadventure. Helen is crying when she reaches her bedroom door, she is cold and tired and she has had enough of waiting, of keeping herself waiting.

Thirty-four

It is late Wednesday afternoon, five months since Katie's funeral. Robert has not told Akeel about his daughter's death, he hasn't told anyone, he doesn't know if he has words to do so. Robert is scared that opening his mouth and saying it aloud will make her death more real than it already is. It is already too real. For once he is relieved not to have family, friends who will ask him questions and demand answers, he is glad of the silence that surrounds him. The words would break him apart.

Last week he received a second letter from Jean. The first had the bare details of Katie's death and the venue for the funeral, if he wanted to come. The second letter was longer, Jean apologised for not being in touch sooner, tried to find a way to put it nicely – and failed – that Katie had not wanted to see her father before she died. It was her choice, there was nothing Jean could do, the girl was dying, too soon, in pain, and Jean had to respect her wishes. Jean was sorry. For a lot of things. She hoped Robert was well. She'd seen him at the funeral, but when she next looked up he was gone and, anyway, she wasn't sure he'd have wanted to talk to her. Jean said there were a lot of things she didn't feel very sure about, she thought it was to do with the shock and the grief, she wished him well, she was sorry they had both lost Katie. There was no return address, no address for Katie's family. Robert read the letter wanting to hold his wife, the woman who had not been his wife for twenty-five years, wanting to hold her and kiss her and make love to her, to push away the disgusting pain of their joint loss with action and sound and fury and whatever he could find of passion. Instead he read the two pages alone, folded and replaced them in the envelope, putting it carefully in the correct file in the storeroom. His own file, on a corner shelf, behind several others, Alice's faded writing on the outside of the box, 'Robert Sutton, 1943 –' He turned off the light, hoped Jean's husband was being good to her.

The shop is shut. This is Akeel's big new idea, closing mid-afternoon on Wednesdays and dropping off deliveries for an extra two quid a time. Robert isn't convinced, he couldn't make home deliveries work when he tried years back, more fuss than the extra income was worth, but time and the spreadsheets will tell now. Yesterday afternoon Robert took the van keys off their hook above the sink and handed them over to Akeel, said he might need to borrow the van when he was moving his boxes and things out, but otherwise he had no need, gave the lad the papers too, and they sent the forms off to the DVLA. Robert is throwing in the van as a gesture of goodwill. It will be nice not to have to worry about parking and petrol prices.

The men have been making their plans. Robert will move out at the start of the new year. He's told Akeel about the place he's found, it's a quieter road than most round there. Southwark, not Lambeth, but you can't have everything and, astonishingly, he will finally have a river view. Robert has always wanted a river view, and he tells Akeel he's worked out how to claim it. He will get on with moving the stored years in the Christmas break, dealing with Alice's excesses, and his own, and by mid-January the place will be Akeel and Rubeina's, to do with what they will. Having made the southern trek to check out the property for herself, Rubeina is very keen for them to start renting out both flats, bring in a regular income to offset the terrifying mortgage. Akeel thinks they'll easily rent out Robert's flat, once all that old furniture is cleared it will only need a bit of paint and some new stuff from IKEA and it'll go fast. In any big city there are always people looking for homes, newcomers and returners and the broken-hearted and the just-together. Rubeina has made him watch enough of those DIY programmes to know that all anyone really wants when they move in to a new home is a blank canvas they can later make their own, plain walls edged in fresh white gloss, nothing too personal. Home-owners will proudly explain the provenance of the coal cellar and fire surround, but a rented flat is long-term temporary accommodation in which the current key-holders prefer to imagine themselves the only ever inhabitants, paint and disinfectant their tools of eradication. Every night Akeel listens to his wife's plans for the shop and the flats, for the name change outside, is delighted that her excitement turns it into their dream, but he also knows that moving will be hard for Robert. Clearing out the old, finishing his shop life. So Akeel is relaxed about the old man, older man, taking a little longer with the storeroom. Robert reckons it will take a couple of weeks to go through the boxes, he tells Akeel he intends to go through every single one and see what needs keeping, what might matter and what can go to the tip. Rubeina would dump the lot right now, but Robert wants to check, just in case there is a left-over memory that needs returning.

But not yet. For now, this evening, Robert sits in the dark shop. The front shutter is down, he has not bothered to put on the light. It is almost dark but for a sharp spike of light at the far left edge of the shutter, near the bottom, where two years ago a remarkably strong, crack-charged young woman

219

tried to lift the shutter from its moorings. She didn't get far, made a four-millimetre gap that now lets in the smallest amount of street light. Orange light that seeps from the entry point and into the gloom, a light that cannot stop, no matter that it has no reason to be there, is not welcome. Robert does not want light right now, he wants the dark and he wants to be here, he wants to sit in his shop and he wants to be alone. And he has exactly what he wants and it is not enough, it is never enough − not dark enough or alone enough or here, his shop, enough. There is always too much sharing, of time, thoughts, memories, light. Too much light. Robert is tired and he has had enough, he had not imagined divesting himself of so much could feel so weighty. He has signed away the van, will sign off the shop once both their lawyers have sorted out the paperwork, has started to plan what he will do with the accumulated years upstairs. And yet this giving away, releasing, does not bring with it the free-dom he had hoped for. Robert thinks now that perhaps there will be no liberation, no blinding flash of release when he finally leaves. He had hoped for more, nothing specific, nothing he has ever been able to name, just more. It seems now that he will simply have to keep going, differently, but keep on, as he always has done. He is nothing if not dogged − Robert tries hard and is consistent in his work; Robert has good application and the ability to work alone; Robert is a dependable boy. Robert is reliable.

Robert, the reliable and dependable, hard-working boy and man, reaches to his left, where the key-cutting machine stands. He stretches his arm right round the back of the heavy machine and, bracing his feet against the dusty floor, careful of the constant twinge in his lower back, the dull ache that any sharp movement will turn to shooting pains in his lower spine and down his left leg, bending close so the oily metallic smell is stronger, becomes taste as well as scent, he hefts the machine three inches away from the wall, then another two, deep breath, three more. Robert does not need light to do this. Now he stands and reaches into a recess at the back of the machine. He pulls out a shoebox, it is the right size for a pair of children's shoes. The box is heavy, with the clink and rattle of a thick metal chain. For a long time he sits with the box on his knees, then he carefully removes the lid. Inside are keys and, even in this strange light, the contents gleam like a box of Christmases past opened on the twelfth of December. These are new keys. Some never used, others just once. These keys have not sat in pockets or journeyed in handbags or waited on hall tables, in chipped mugs, hung from comedy key racks reminding the owner to hang it where it's plain to see, then they'll never lose this key. They have not yielded their gleam to years of tissues and dirty handkerchiefs and being dropped at the front door by clumsy drunken fingers. These keys have been cut, then carefully put away. Each one has a small label, the date it was cut and, where known, the owner's name and address.

Robert has been cutting keys since he and Alice bought their first machine almost forty years ago. Sometimes he cut them for people who came to the shop for that purpose alone, they were not regular customers, he did not know the stories of their clothes, the contents of their pockets, the origins of this stain on that expensive suit jacket. Other times he cut keys for customers he knew well. Enough to know they needed a dress cleaned urgently, for the sister's wedding up in Halifax, where their London clothes will be judged on colour, make and price, as well as size. The wedding that took them away for the whole weekend, the wedding that meant their house would be empty for two days and two nights, but could Robert possibly get the cleaning done before they have to leave, is there any chance at all of a home delivery? Robert often refused to deliver, not because he didn't want to help but because he simply didn't have time. He'd stay open another half hour, the half-hour extra was never as much hassle as the home delivery usually became, with parking and street names and hissing cats in allergy halls. On rare occasions he'd make an emergency home delivery, sometimes bending his principles for a customer he liked more than others, someone he felt he knew better than just their clothes size and job description and the shopping list they left in their pocket. Then Robert would stand at the door with a hanger and plastic cover in hand, or come into the hall, or wait to be buzzed through the safety doors of a big estate, and he'd look inside another life and wonder about it. And sometimes, just fifteen, twenty times in total, over this past lifetime of occasionally cutting keys, Robert would go back to see, to feel, to smell, what it was to live in another place, to live a different life.

The relationship between shopkeeper and regular customer is a varied one. Some simply come in with their goods, leave them, pay, pick up later. They may have been doing this for half a lifetime and Robert would know no more about the customer than he did the first time she came into the shop. Other people are happy to chat, pass the time of day, nothing important, nothing more than weather and headlines. A very few are actually keen to talk, discuss, engage, and occasionally these chats have become discussions which become friendship. A friendship that feels real and yet is totally arbitrary. Anyone could be the man behind the glass in the petrol station, anyone could come in and ask for a quartered and skinned halal chicken. Anyone could bring in three dresses, their mother's fifty-year-old dresses, asking do you think they could possibly be cleaned and mended and worn again. Anyone could then turn that transaction into a relationship, but most don't. Alice made friends with a dozen customers in as many years of business. Robert continued some of her friendships when he took over, and made perhaps another ten of his own. Always he stayed and they moved; a bigger house for the growing family, a smaller flat now the kids have left and there's no need for all these rooms, a council trade for a nice maisonette in Mottingham out of this bloody awful estate and away from these noisy roads, off to New Zealand or South Africa or India or Spain or Devon to try, try again. The ones that remain he will pass on to Akeel, like the van and the deeds and which drivers to be nice to, which to harangue. These customers are part of the shop's legacy, Robert has meant something to them and they to him.

People have said they'll miss him when they go, will pop in when passing. They do not pass, and they do not pop in, but Robert doesn't forget. Sometimes he wishes he could, there is so much he wants to forget, but it's all there. Kept in the files upstairs and in the keys of this small, heavy shoebox. It once held Katie's first pair of proper shoes, worn as bridesmaid for Jean's cousin's wedding. Silver shoes with a shiny buckle on the front, she loved them, wore them long after they were too small for her, kept them in the box for years. When she left home the shoes went too, but the box was left behind.

Robert is looking through the box. He is looking for a specific key, with a specific address tag. The tags have homes attached, stories attached. The owners have been at work, on holiday, a weekend away. They were not at home. No one was. No one is. Robert is.

Thirty-five

Saturday the fifteenth of October, 1983. It has been a long day and Robert is tired. He has been tired for months now, tired since Alice died at the beginning of the year, tired since Jean and Katie moved out in late summer, tired of being alone, and tired of grieving. Sitting in his flat above the shop, he feels the solid weight of people and places and things all around him, other lives, the ever-present scent of skin and discarded cells in the walls, the constant flow of other people's dirt through his hands that no amount of cash transaction or carcinogenic chemical can erase. All these other people he knows too much about, he understands, keeps their secrets, and no one left to listen to his. Robert has never been lonely before, no chance to be, he went from son to husband to father with no time between, he has always lived with other people, he has always lived with women – mother, wife, daughter. Now Robert lives alone and there is no clash of perfumes in the air, no warm red lipstick stain on the cup, no scent of powder on the pillow beside his, no long hair clogging the drain. Robert wants to unblock the sink, rewash the cups, sliding his thumb and forefinger over a greasy lip-print on the china's edge, complain that the place smells like a French whore's boudoir. Robert has been working all week and it is Saturday night and there is nothing to do, no vodka and lemonade to buy, no overflowing rubbish bag to throw out, no wife or daughter or mother to feed. He wants to smell other people's breath in the room, see that someone else's feet have left prints in the hallway, wipe away table-top crumbs from another's piece of toast.

He has been thinking about this for five days, since first thing Tuesday morning. The temptation has been there, shiny and new, offering itself, and Robert is so tired that resistance now feels impossible. He cannot stand up to himself. He pulls his shoes back on, not bothering with the laces he didn't bother with when he shrugged them off, picks up his jacket, checks for his keys in the left-hand pocket. And then he takes the other key. The second key he cut while chatting to Mrs Ryan about the weather and the queue-jumper in the post office, and the wisteria in Ruskin Park.

Patricia Ryan is at her aunt's funeral in Sligo. Robert knows this because on Tuesday morning she brought in her funeral dress to be pressed. Not cleaned, thank you, Mr Sutton, no need for that, it's been sitting in its bag in the cupboard since the last funeral, my own brother, just turned fifty, God love him, a pressing only, if you don't mind, that'll do just fine. At the same time she asked Robert about cutting her a spare key. She wanted to leave one for the cousin she'd be staying with, the dead woman's daughter. Oh I know she won't want to come all the way over here, poor girl, never married, never been anywhere, and now no one in the world but herself, well, and myself, of course, so I just thought, if I had one cut, I could leave it there for her, that way she'll know she's welcome. There's always a bed, a put-you-up really, but a place, so she's not alone. Course the poor girl thinks London's a hell-hole, and she may be right, but anyway, thought I'd offer, give her a chance to say no, everyone deserves a chance. Robert thought it was a lovely gesture. Knew he'd never accept a similar invitation himself, had turned down several since the girls left him, but the key was a nice touch, something solid to hang on to and make

225

the offer look real. So they'd talked about her journey and the coach and the ferry, what weather she might expect for the crossing, and without thinking about it at all, without actually acknowledging what he was doing, let alone why he was doing it, Robert had cut two copies of Patricia Ryan's front-door key, and kept the extra one on the sideboard all week.

Now the key is in his pocket and he is walking up the road to her flat. He knows where she lives, has written Patricia Ryan's name and address and taken her signature several times over in the old book Alice used to keep for payments, back when they trusted people to pick up their clothes one day and pay on another. So it's not as if he doesn't know where she lives, or that he hasn't talked to her about the flats before now, the state of the stairs she has to climb every day, the noise from that neighbour she used to have, the one the housing association only moved on after a good deal of complaint and not just from her, the view from her front window where she likes to sit with her tea of a morning. Now Robert is where she lives. He is inside the block and walking up the stairs and the key is in the door and his heart is racing, he has no answer for why he is here, what he is doing, there is no answer.

There is no answer when he calls out her name either. And so for two hours, Robert Sutton, who is all alone in the world, looks out the window at Patricia Ryan's view. He makes himself a cup of tea with Patricia's kettle and Patricia's dark blend tea and Patricia's mother's aluminium teapot, the one with a screw where the lid handle once was, the screw put on by Patricia's father, never a handyman, but useful all the same. Not a lot of couth, as he always said, but useful. Robert sits at Patricia's kitchen table and watches the city, trying to see it as she does. The view reaches down from the top of Denmark Hill, a good long view, nice quality of

226

afternoon and evening light to keep the dark at bay, acutely angled late sunlight picking out the tourist spots over the water. The block of flats is quiet tonight, it is early evening, perhaps her latest noisy neighbour is popping into the pub on his way home from the shops, readying himself to become the belligerent drunk that upsets Patricia Ryan so much, makes her so silently angry, that come Sunday morning she's doubts there is enough grace in the world for her to be worthy of the body and the blood.

When his two hours are up, Robert very carefully washes and dries the evidence, hanging the now-damp tea towel back on the rail of the cooker. It will be dry by Patricia's return on Monday. For two hours Robert Sutton breathes in someone else's life and sits in someone else's kitchen chair, the one with the back cushion carefully placed to make sitting easier. He opens the cupboards and sees that Patricia has two sets of china, one chipped and plain, the other delicately flowered and very pink, barely used. He sees she has bulk-buy ginger biscuits in packets at the bottom of the cupboard, though there are arrowroot biscuits opened in the tin. He reaches to take one and then realises that would be going too far, the tea was enough, maybe even too much, any more would not be right. Biscuits may well be placed temptingly on a plate, but you only take one when offered. Jean's mother had been very clear on the protocol of teatime.

That night in his flat above the shop, fish and chips and three cans of beer heavy in his stomach, Robert goes to bed with more ease than he has felt in weeks. He says his half prayer, 'Now I lay me down to sleep', breaks off there as he always does, and closes his eyes. When he dreams it is of someone else's kitchen and he is relieved to be in it.

Thirty-six

Now. Robert dips his hand into the box and pulls out a fist-ful of keys, sitting here all this time in the dark, his eyes pick up subtle shifts in colour, the metal is amber and gold, warmer than he expected. Most of the keys are single, not attached to any others, some of them are in sets and most have tags attached. He flicks through the addresses, Stefan Corey, the dance teacher, came in the other day, bruises all gone, but Robert suspects the scars are still there, he's lost weight, looks wary. Akeel has never understood how Robert can know so much about someone just from a few conversations a month, from their clothes, the way they behave in the shop, the things he has collected upstairs. Robert has considered showing him the keys, explaining the lives he has looked into, how exactly he knows the dimensions of Patricia Ryan's tiny flat, but he has chosen not to say. Unlike Akeel, Robert is very skilled at saying only what he wants to. He hasn't been to all the homes listed on the tags, but he likes to keep the keys. Sometimes it is enough to know there is the possibility of being some-where else.

Marylin Wright, Audrey Wright's daughter, Irene Hodges' niece, lives up the Brixton end of Coldharbour Lane. Her place is a turn-of-the-century block, last century, before the first war took the young builders and buried them in French graves. Robert hasn't been to Marylin's home for a few years, but there was a time, several years ago, when he would pop in at least once a month. A while after her mother's funeral, when Marylin was in the throes of sorting through Audrey's clothes – what to keep, what to give to charity shops, and, worse, what to consign to the bin for no further use – she brought three of her dead mother's dresses to be cleaned and mended, frocks with full skirts and extra petticoats, high-waisted, three-quarter-length sleeves. Alice kept dresses like that too, yards of material, starched underskirts, net petticoats – Alice said herself she was too old for them really, a load of old mutton, but she'd loved them anyway, her celebration dresses. Years later Katie dragged them in and out of her dressing-up box, later still they'd been thrown out when Robert finally understood that Jean and Katie weren't coming home. But when Marylin brought in her dead mother's dresses, and a new set of keys to be cut, Robert wanted to know her better. So he went to visit.

Robert has always been careful not to allow his desire to overtake sense. He would wait until a customer had told him they were off on holiday, away for a few days, until he was certain their home would be empty. He didn't mind cats, wouldn't risk dogs, and he could always tell the presence of pets from the state of the clothes. Marylin's home was pretty much as he might have expected, the only thing that really surprised him was the empty fridge, practically empty cupboards. Robert can't ever remember seeing Marylin when she wasn't eating, or had just finished eating, about to un-wrap a chocolate bar, open a bag of crisps, finishing off an apple, just on her way to pick up a patty, dumpling, fishcake. Marylin has always loved her food, loves to eat and, unlike so many of the young girls he sees today, or the ones he remembers from when Katie was young, she seems to have no qualms about it at all. She loves her food, and that love suits her rounded body, her full flesh. Just like her Aunt Irene, that girl, a real figure of a woman.

He stopped going to Marylin's flat the day he was sitting there in the calm of her darkened front room, just enjoying the peace and quiet, and he heard the front door slam open, feet rushing into the flat, doors banging and rocking on their hinges. Robert's heart was smashing in his chest, standing there behind the open door, terrified it was Marylin about to find him, and then more frightened still when he realised there was more than one person, young lads' voices, and not sober either, as they headed down the passage into the front room. They were just a few feet away when the voice came, his own voice, barrelling out of his terrified, thumping chest, a big, shouting, older man's voice asking what the hell these little buggers thought they were doing, how bloody dare they, he'd already called the cops, they were well in trouble now, just one more step, one more bloody step, I dare you, come on, one more bloody step. The voice was enough to scare them off. It scared Robert too, he'd never heard himself like that, like someone else, another man, a louder, fiercer, harsher man. A certain man. It was fear, he supposed, fear of being caught and fear of being hurt and fear of being found out. Robert waited a few minutes after the lads had legged it, his breathing fast and shallow, then went outside to the long balcony at the front of the flats. Ten minutes later he called the police from a phone box on the way home. Said he'd been walking past the flats and seen some lads haring out of a door, knew the girl who lived up there, didn't expect they belonged, maybe someone should go and check it out. Robert felt terrible that evening when Marylin popped into the shop to thank him, tell him how lucky she was that he'd been near by, had noticed the little bastards. How lucky she was her place was safe, though she was getting new locks put on the door, and she felt a little scared, to tell the truth, her home didn't feel safe just now. But anyway, she was very grateful to Robert. It could have been so much worse.

That night Robert went to bed feeling bad, of course, guilty, sorry, but there was another feeling as well. Something he couldn't help but smile at. Robert was proud of himself, of his big voice, of that territorial ferocity that had come from nowhere, pleased that some primal part of himself had reacted so strongly, choosing fight not flight. Though he was pleased, too, that the lads' flight meant it had not come to fight. And he never went back to Marylin's flat.

A few of the keys have no tag. Perhaps Robert didn't recognise the person he cut the keys for, or he didn't like the look of them, knew at first glance he wouldn't want to know their lives, or he was simply too busy, no time to write himself a note that would later turn into a tag, matching the new keys with the address provided by the customer the very first time they brought in their cleaning – and an address, please? Just for the records, in case anything goes missing, in case you lose the ticket. In case Robert wants to pop in. Not all the tagged keys have been used, but all of them once seemed worth keeping.

Flats are easier than houses. For all the dangers of friendly neighbours and communal stairwells, there is less chance a flat-dweller will be able to afford their own alarm, less likelihood Robert will open the door and set off a screaming noise, bringing the howling siren. He did once. Up in Herne Hill, not long after that lawyer woman and her banker husband first bought the place, before they had children, before they got the Australian girl in to live with them, Robert had been up that way, on a legitimate delivery, a few doors down. From his own van, waiting for the rain to ease before he jumped out with the bag of clean clothes, he'd

231

watched another driver pull up, the bloke got out and walked round to the back of his dirty white van, lifting out a box – wine by the look of it – and then walked up to the front door. He only tried ringing the bell a couple of times before he put down the box, fished a card from his pocket, put the box back in the van and drove off. It didn't take Robert more twenty minutes to get down to the shop and back, two new keys on one tag in his back pocket. The mortice lock was a little stiff, perhaps he hadn't filed it as well as he should, and then the Yale. Easy. And in. He closed the door behind him and as the Yale clicked shut the most almighty high-pitched siren started up. Robert didn't bother to double-lock the door behind him, was out of there quick as you like. Two days later the woman, the lawyer, came back to the shop with a whole new set of keys to be cut and a mouthful of complaint about the area, the people and the local police. Robert stayed clear of houses after that. He wanted to look and sit, be in a space where other people moved and breathed and lived, still lived. He was never in it for the thrill or possibility of being caught.

He steered clear of certain other places too, never been to that Dean Dobson's for one. Robert doesn't know much about the drugs the press are always on about, it's never really come near him, too young for the pills and such that Alice and her mates enjoyed during the war; the wrong age, and class, for the dope and more that followed in the sixties and seventies. He's certainly removed an eclectic range of goods from his customers' pockets – more than his fair share of small squares of lottery tickets folded into careful rectangles of white powder, little plastic bags of seeded leaves, the missing items no one ever asks to have returned – but he's not been tempted to see what those items do. He does, however, know something about gambling, and debt collecting, and a little about cars, he definitely knows that Dean Dobson always has a bit more cash than you'd expect from a bloke round here. Alice had known the old man Dobson, ten years younger than her, and in later years it's been obvious where young Dean got his talents. All right for a night in the pub, no problems putting his hand in his pocket for his round, not ever, that was one thing you could say for the Dobsons, the whole family, but you didn't want to get on the wrong side of the old man. As Alice said, 'A bloke who'd take off his little finger with a wood axe at the age of eighteen, just so he didn't have to do his National Service – he won't think twice about doing the same to you.' Robert kept out of the Dobsons' way as a boy, and had no intention of doing otherwise as a man, but it was nice to have Dean Dobson's keys. The keys to his home, and a duplicate set to that other flat as well, the one Dean rents privately, from a landlord as quiet as he is, the flat Dean doesn't talk about, just pops into every now and then, on his way, out on his rounds. If he mentions it at all, Dean calls the place his business centre. Less obvious than a lockup, and less common too, both reasons equally valuable to Dean. Robert would never use either of those keys, but he likes to know he has them, that there's one thing he knows that Dean Dobson doesn't.

Robert balances the heavy box on his lap and dips both his hands into the glittering brass. He scoops out a fistful, letting them trickle back into the box between his fingers, tags catching on his thumb and forefinger, strings reaching across his heart line and love line. There was a time when Alice fancied herself something of a fortune-teller, used to take up Robert's hand when she'd had a bit to drink and tell him stories of who he would be, her boy with his future waiting to happen. Robert rubs his eyes. In this dark room, with the tears that are falling, it's hard to see the names on the tags clearly. His hands smell of metal. With another scoop of keys Robert finds a tag he didn't even realise he was looking for.

Thirty-seven

Jean and Katie have moved out, and for just over six weeks Robert has spent his Monday to Thursday evenings in the Green Man. Weekends he finds it too busy, too many people wanting to say hello, or ask him how it's going. He doesn't want to say how it's going, it's going badly isn't the kind of answer most people want from a brief exchange in the pub, they want fine thanks, cheers, not so bad, bloody awful but damned if I care – let's have another. Robert does believe this will pass, that one day he will wake up and feel differently. One day he will come to in the morning and will not be surprised there is no Jean lying beside him, that the front room is as he left it when he closed the door, that Katie has not been playing her music half the night and littered the carpet with coffee cups and unfinished biscuits. He will not feel the urge to walk downstairs at seven thirty with Alice's morning cup of tea. Robert Sutton is a rational man, a successful small businessman, he understands that the passage of time will force him to accommodate these changes and eventually he will stop waking expecting to see what he knows is not there. But it is not that time yet. And while he has to work in the shop, spend anything up to ten or eleven hours a day beneath one flat too-empty, and the other overfull, where the floorboards do not creak unless he walks over them, where the sink stays empty for days on end, Robert does not have to spend all evening sitting in that flat as well. He does not have to do anything any more.

One evening, when he has soaked up almost as much whisky as he can bear, breathed in just about enough of other people's smoke, Robert stands up to leave and finds that standing is not possible. Robert Sutton's stumbling form attracts attention from the far corner, Ian and Irene Hodges cross the room to help him. This is not the first time they have crossed the sticky brown and red carpet to help Robert, the two men are not close mates, but Ian works at the taxi garage up the road, has known Robert for years, passed the time of day in the shop and put the world to rights in the pub many times over the past ten years. Ian and Irene have tried to talk to Robert since Jean and Katie left, asked him to come for a curry, suggested he might like a beer instead of another double, a half instead of a pint. Robert has stuck to his corner and pushed them away, along with anyone else who tried to sit down for a chat. Robert lives over the road, his work is over the road, he had his wedding reception here, if he can't be left alone in his own damn pub, where the hell can he be left alone. Robert is so lonely he could cry. His solution is to tell other people to piss off.

Tonight, as Robert stands swaying in the breeze of his own grief, his shoulders are held by his long-term acquaintance Ian. When they cross the road back to the shop, his hand is held by Ian's wife Irene. Irene's hands are bigger and softer than Jean's, all of Irene is bigger and softer than Jean. Robert has not held a woman's hand for almost a month. He held Jean's hand when she came back to see him, a few weeks after she and Katie had moved out, to check on him, see how he was doing. He wasn't doing very well, he told her so, not that she couldn't see for herself, but he didn't ask Jean to come back, and she didn't offer.

★

235

Robert and Jean always liked holding hands, right from the start, and when her mother and his long hours of work and the new baby and her father's death and Alice's illness tried to come between, Jean and Robert could always rely on holding hands. One reached for the other when they went for a walk, even just crossing the road to the shops or the pub, while watching telly at night, and in bed, always in bed. They'd held hands, too, the morning that Jean and Katie had left, neither Robert nor Jean knew how to let go, but she let go anyway. Katie crying on her mother's closed fist and eventually the tears worked like the all-purpose solvent Alice used to keep under the sink, the hands broke apart.

In the Green Man on the other side of the road, Ian reaches into Robert's jacket pocket and takes out his mate's keys, battles with three different locks on the side door. Irene climbs the stairs ahead of the two men, putting on lights and kettle, closing curtains, picking up newspapers and plates and cups. Robert is not a fool, he has a business to keep going, a daughter still to provide for, he has clearly been making an effort to look after himself, has made tea, corned beef sandwiches, beans on toast, scrambled eggs. It is also obvious that any more than a single mouthful has been beyond him.

Irene decides to do something about Robert. She is a generous woman, in heart as well as figure. Robert is invited over for Sunday dinner and, surprisingly, he arrives. He brings flowers for Irene, real ones, from the florist in Camberwell, not just the hospital shop, and a box of toffees for the kids. Kids in their late teens and not thankful, but Ian and Irene appreciate the gesture all the same. Irene takes to popping into the shop on her way into Brixton. She works in the sub-post office down the back of the chemist on Coldharbour Lane, and has her Wednesday afternoons off, gets all the family's shopping done then, her bits and pieces. Robert is pleasantly surprised at the offer of company, invites

Irene in, they have a cup of tea behind the counter, nice for him, someone to have a natter with.

The next time Irene comes by Robert tells her it's been quiet all day, he might shut up for an hour, would she like some company shopping? They could have a cup of tea in the market, a cake maybe. Robert's always liked a good custard slice. Irene is surprised, Ian hates shopping, never wants to come with her. When they first married she used to try to get him to come along, make decisions about what they'd eat in the week, what she should buy for the kids, but it wasn't long before she gave up, her husband's fingers drumming on one tense thigh, his other hand jingling the car keys in his pocket, his combination of disinterest and irritation meant that it was easier and, oddly, faster for her to go alone. Irene has been getting her shopping by herself for over twenty years, she is so delighted with Robert's offer she accepts immediately. Months later it occurs to her that if he hadn't offered to come with her she'd never have found her way to his bed. But he did, he does, she does.

Irene helps Robert get himself together, that's how she sees it, believes she is getting him back on his feet and out of the dark place he has been hiding. But when he is whole again, or as close to whole as is likely, when he is once more smiling at customers and passing the time of day and shouting at the thieving little buggers from up the road who try to run in and grab coat hangers off the counter, Robert tells Irene they have to stop now. He is lying in bed with her, the two of them naked, his head on her breast. When Jean left, Robert thought he would never again lie this close to a woman, couldn't picture himself doing it; what he now knows is that he couldn't picture it unless the woman was Jean. Irene is very definitely not Jean. She is big and broad and heavy, she is quite hairy. She shaves her legs and underarms, that much is obvious, Jean did as well, but Jean's body

237

hair was pale and soft, she shaved once a week if that, Irene's body hair is sharp and prickly, grows back at a ferocious rate. She has told him she shaves her legs on Tuesday nights now, so they will be smooth for him, late on a Wednesday afternoon. Robert doesn't care about smooth or not. It is a difference, he likes the difference, is glad to be with a different woman. He does not want to imagine he is making love to Jean here, wants to know for certain this is another woman, lets the touch reassure him, reaching down Irene's body and feeling the indentations where her bra cuts into the soft flesh of her back, where the elastic of her knickers bites into her waist, the faint ridges from the tight skirts she likes to wear that ride up, ruched at the widest stretch of her hips. Jean was always small and fine, she'd have been the first to say she never had breasts to speak of, just the one time when she was pregnant with Katie, and that extra vanished as soon as Katie was on the bottle. Irene certainly has breasts. Gina Lollobrigida breasts, Sophia Loren breasts, Robert doesn't want to think this, but can't help himself, the idea thought before he can stop it – Irene has breasts like his mother had when he was a little boy. Robert rests his head on Irene's breasts in the same room he made love to Jean and feels enormously lucky to have this time with this extraordinary woman. Irene whispers that Robert should have a garden, it would help him, it's not natural for a man to have nothing green in his life, to live so far above the ground, the earth. She suggests an allotment, a window box, a bloody pot plant even. Irene has never met a bloke with such clean hands. Though she does love his clean hands, kissing them, taking his fingers in her wide mouth. Irene is warm and generous and loving. Her belly has stretch marks and at her cleavage her skin is soft crepe, it is not young-girl skin, elastic and smooth, and Robert likes this best of all, that his lover's skin is not a girl's skin, but a woman's, that he is a man not a boy.

And being a man, and knowing that Irene is falling in love with him, Robert realises it has to stop.

He tries to explain himself, his certainty that he cannot do another wrong thing, not ever if he can help it. Irene doesn't know what he's on about, they're happy together, what the hell's wrong with that? Nothing and everything, of course they are having a good time, a lovely time, but Ian is his friend. Irene points out that Robert and Ian have a drink twice a year at most, usually when there's some big match on, what kind of friendship is that? Robert agrees it doesn't seem like much, but he doesn't think that's the point, the point is that while he is not yet divorced, he is no longer married, and Irene is. She hates him for doing this to her, for giving her hope of a different life, the kind of life where she mooches around the market with a nice bloke on the occasional late Wednesday afternoon and he holds her hand when they walk together. Robert has never yet held her hand in public, nor has he ever suggested she should leave Ian and come here to hold his hand more often, but they have held hands in this room, in this bed. Irene likes to hold hands. Robert doesn't tell her that Jean liked it too. He says he doesn't believe it would be a different life, that it would just be the same wrong life, tainted from the beginning, wrong for them both, wrong for Ian, and for Irene's children. She says she'll be the judge of what her children need and he agrees that's her right, but there are too many people to hurt if they let it go any further and Robert has decided it is better just to hurt Irene. Himself too, but he's used to that by now, used to hurting.

That last afternoon when Irene lies in Robert's bed he holds her hands in his, kisses the bitten tips of her fingernails, amazed still that her hands can be so different to his, so different to Jean's, kisses her eyes and nose and lips, and when they make love it is very good, feels right and important and

239

matters so much that Irene can't really believe he still means what he'd said at dinnertime, when she came in with her shopping bag and list and top button already undone, and Robert closed the door behind her and before he kissed her hello he said he thought she shouldn't come back to the flat again, she should go home to her husband because Ian is a good man and she has a good family and it's not right. When Robert finally makes Irene understand this is exactly what he means, even now, even after this time, here, in bed, she turns angry on him, bitter, nasty. Screaming and shouting and calling him all the names under the sun, most of which he agrees he deserves.

After a while the words end and Irene is just tired, all shouted out. Robert sits on the side of the bed, and Irene is crying, getting dressed, trying to put her clothes on, tights tangled, blouse buttons out of sync, up to the top before she realises, and again, and a third time before they're right, reaching into her bag for her comb, remaking her hair in the swept-up style she found at nineteen and has stuck with ever since, searching for lipstick and powder, redoing her face, replacing her face so she is ready to leave. At the door to the flat, Robert in his dressing gown, bare feet, still trying to explain, Irene throws the keys back at him, right in his face, landing a sharp bruise on his cheekbone, lucky it didn't get his eye. The keys he gave her to the shop door and to his flat.

They are the keys Robert holds now, in the near dark, in the front of the locked shop. The one set of keys in this heavy box that belong to him.

Thirty-eight

Sometimes it feels like the hardest part of the day is going to sleep, turning off the lights and lying down, stretching out. Robert has always been cold at night. Cold hands, cold feet, cold legs too, and arms, shoulders, back. Just cold, all through, even on the stickiest nights of August. Trouble is, he can't stand pyjamas, never could. When he was a little boy Alice used to come in at night and find his pyjama top up round his neck, half strangling the child, his bottoms screwed down at the end of the bed, lost somewhere between the candy-striped flannelette sheets and the pulled-up blanket, pale blue candlewick bedspread wrapped round his body, her mother's old eiderdown piled on top, its gold ribbon edging tucked under her son, as he twisted and burrowed through the night in the hope of finding some warmth. Alice called him her caterpillar boy, wondered aloud when he'd find his butterfly. Robert found Jean, who held him in bed and made him warm. Her skin to his, her narrow to his wide, her open and warm to his cold and closed.

The first night they slept together, properly the whole night, all through, lying together and even actually sleeping, eventually, was their wedding night. Robert had carried Jean over the road and up the stairs from their reception at the Green Man, Alice went to stay with her friend Jessie, give the kids their first night to themselves, she said to Mrs Swanson's pursed-mouth face. They spent their second married night together in the back bedroom of Jean's mum and dad's house. After all the recriminations and the preparations, they finally had a chance to talk to each other in the night, brutal fox calls outside, the animals leaving Kennington Park for their nightly excursions into backyards and bins.

Delighted to be in this place, beside her husband, Jean curled herself carefully, possibly shyly, into Robert's side, and recoiled far quicker, far from shy. 'You're like an ice block!'

'Sorry. I'm . . . shall I go warm up?'

Jean laughed. 'Where?'

'There must be a heater, or something, somewhere?'

'Don't be daft. If you think my mother would let you turn on the fire this time of year you've got another thing coming. "No fires in this house from St David's to All Saints. Not once, not ever."' Jean's impression of Mrs Swanson – Robert didn't think she was ever going to tell him to call her 'Mum', didn't think he could anyway – was all too accurate and Robert found himself even colder, a shiver down his back.

'Sorry.'

'Well, yes,' Jean whispered, 'if I'd have known it would be like this . . .'

The pressure of the pregnancy, the build-up to the wedding, the reception last night, the hangover he'd been pretending all day not to have, Robert's face fell from man to youth to little boy. Even in the dark, Jean knew what he looked like.

'You daft thing. I found out all I needed to know weeks ago, didn't I?'

'You did?'

'Yes, Robert Sutton, I think I did, and came back for more, or hadn't you noticed? Come here, let me spoon you.'

'What?'

242

Robert and Jean had slept together – with no sleep, no bed either – just four times. They took six months to even get round to making love, and it was on their third try, in the Ruskin Park bandstand, that Jean had been caught with Katie. They'd never yet slept together for holding, for closeness, for staying all night, for sleep. And while neither of them had been a virgin that first time, it didn't take Robert long to work out that what he knew about it all was a damn sight more than she did. Jean wouldn't tell him who the bloke had been, or when, just that it had been the one time and not a good time. He never asked again; they might have been new to each other, but not so new that he didn't understand there was no way he'd get an answer from her if she wasn't willing to give it.

They lay beside each other, shivering in the little bedroom, the sprays of flowers up and down the wallpaper such a bilious yellow that Robert swore he could see them in the dark, Jean pushed him over so his back was to her, and she took off the itchy pink nightie her mother had insisted she wear – 'You might have given it all already, madam, but there's no need to look like it in bed too' – and she wrapped her thin, naked frame around his, small breasts to his shoulder blades, little beginning-belly, beginning-baby, in the small of his back, her knees against the back of his thighs. Robert heard his 'Now I lay me down to sleep' in his head and prepared, as always, to repeat it, beating the cold with a mantra for the sleep so hard to achieve. Then, by whatever miracle of design or desire, for the first time in his life, on that night in May 1966, Robert Sutton fell asleep warm and he woke warm.

In the morning he turned to his girl, his wife, his bride, and he kissed her and was warm and happy and comfortable in that back bedroom with the yellow roses never seen in any garden. Robert was calm and easy, grateful for Jean and for the baby, grateful for his life. He hadn't felt this safe since he was a little kid, playing with boxes under the kitchen table in the top flat in Coldharbour Lane, watching Alice's feet as they sidestepped and foxtrotted round the kitchen, getting up a scratch tea of egg and chips for the two of them, no school or work or visitors to interrupt her undivided attention, basking in the glow of his own little shelter. That back-bedroom bed, with its sway mattress and sagging springs, was a shelter too. Until Mrs Swanson started up in the kitchen, and the wireless came on and it was Monday morning, one up, everyone up, and off to work, and he was more certain now, if that could be possible, they had to get out of that house.

That afternoon Robert talked to Alice about the shop and the flat, and by the time he got back to the Swansons' for his tea, he'd made up his mind. There was an almighty row with his mother-in-law, a bit of a sulk from Jean as well, but two months later the big presses were finally moved from the middle flat, Alice's boxes were stored in the front room where she was going to sleep, and Robert and Jean had taken over the top flat. Alice was good at knowing when to get out of the way, and it helped too that she slept in the front room of her flat, while Jean and Robert slept in the back room of theirs, no creaking floorboards to disturb the other. No creaking springs either, as Jean and Robert learned new ways, practised old ways, to keep Robert warm.

Since Jean left him, Robert has gone to bed cold. If he can be bothered going to bed at all, dozing on the settee easier than lying alone in the bedroom, even with all the noise outside. He sits in front of the telly, he drinks cups of tea from tannin-stained mugs, he watches programmes he hates and a very few he cares about. He rereads the paper and the things that upset him earlier in the day are still as infuriating, sometimes even more so. He listens to the noise that rises from the street and he hears the late and then the later buses and the last train and the constant keening sirens and the yearning foxes and, because he hates to be cold at night and because he hates to go to sleep alone, even now, after all these years, Robert puts off the moment of actually trying to sleep as long he can. Recently, there have been a few nights when he hasn't bothered at all, but then his back hurts even more in the morning and the boxes are heavier to lift and the tickets that fall to the floor are harder to reach, so the next night he lies down at least, because it is sensible and Robert is a responsible man and he wants to do the right thing. But when he lays himself down and turns out the light, the cold creeps in again and no amount of 'Now I lay me down to sleep' can warm him. He sleeps alone and is glad when the blasted planes begin their overhead route to Heathrow at five and the trains start at six and it's time to get up and get on and let in the daylight. Even in winter, when the sun won't rise until well gone seven, Robert opens the curtains anyway. The shop faces east and Robert wants the light to arrive as soon as it can.

Thirty-nine

The trains wake Robert before the light. He is used to this, for much of his life Robert has lived beside a railway arch, worked beneath it. He has walked down the back streets into Brixton market, seen arches transform from mere lockups to baby e-businesses and back again when bust inevitably followed boom. He has seen their bridges hit by buses, trucks and the eager spray of a hundred graffiti taggers. It was not until a spring morning in 1964 that Robert first saw the arches as beautiful. One early morning, walking down Coldharbour Lane, past the postbox, on an extended stretch to get Alice her paper from a slightly further shop than the one over the road, walk off a bit of the too-good Sunday lunch the day before, walking further merely because he'd woken with spring rising in his own body as well as the earth, Robert looked up from the street and saw the slow, wide turn of raised railway. He took in the heavy brick curve, forming Belinda Road on one side and a back alley for Coldharbour Mansions on the other, and he saw it was beautiful. He applauded the complex mathematics that took a squat rectangular chunk of red brick made grey by time and grime and carbon monoxide and the slow, stolid lives of generations of pigeons, and turned it into a smooth progressional arc. The long swoop of solid brick wall that had withstood years of pissing youths and fighting dogs and clawing cats, that offered shelter to the ever-present London garden of stringy buddleia, a sight that he must have passed a thousand times since he was a boy, and saw now as elegant, clean, beautiful.

Time changed Robert's understanding of what was beautiful and what was not. Jean became his womanly ideal. Then Katie came and irrevocably altered Robert's perspective, everything else compared against Katie for a reference of lovely. As fatherhood progressed, Robert found he no longer fully enjoyed the beautiful things for all the dangerous ones he noticed as well. The vast size of the buses compared to his tiny daughter in her pram, the speed with which car drivers took the corners, the steep gradient of the steps to their flat, the enormity of life stretching before her, the fact that he would only be able to hold her hand for such a short time of it. By the time Katie was three, they had a routine, just the two of them, out for a walk on a Sunday morning, give Jean a chance for a lie-in, catch up on her books and papers. They didn't go far, Ruskin Park to feed the ducks, Brockwell Lido in summer, getting there before it was too busy, a paddle and a play, an ice cream on the way home, Mr Whippy's Pied Piper tune announcing a cornet with flake and sprinkles a good three streets before they spotted the van, Katie on lookout from his shoulders. And every time they walked down those streets afterwards, when Katie was five, ten, twelve, sixteen, Robert had to stop himself picking her up, from swinging her high above his head, holding his daughter a long way off the ground, away from grazed knees and stubbed toes and stupid drivers and nasty boys and mean teachers and anything else that might hurt her, hurt his baby.

By the time Katie started school it was obvious there wouldn't be another child. They'd been trying since Katie was eighteen months but nothing happened, just Jean crying in the morning when she'd come on in the night. She was upset for a while, had been hoping for another baby, two

247

more maybe, a bigger family than either she or Robert were raised in, and Robert would have gone along with whatever she wanted, the baby need more hers than his, more her body than his. So they tried and nothing happened and the doctor said it was just one of those things and Jean asked Robert what he thought about adopting, and then Robert had to tell the truth, he didn't think about it at all, didn't want to either. Yes, they could be good parents for any number of other children, take them in, be loving and kind. They were good parents to Katie, everyone said so, they must be, even Jean's mother had grudgingly said it, but Robert didn't feel the same way Jean did, his Katie was plenty for him, she was high on a pedestal of Robert's creation, he didn't want her sharing prime position with anyone. Jean was disappointed, though in the end, especially once Alice was so ill, and things became very hard, it seemed it had been for the best, just the three of them after all, keeping it small, keeping it safe. But Robert couldn't keep it all together forever, he couldn't protect his family from the world always, even the best-built brick arch crumbles in time.

A mid-November afternoon and Robert catches Akeel smiling as he rings up the till, adding the day's takings, noting it on the screen for the week's calculations.

'You look like the cat that got the cream. Did we take more than I thought?'

'Yeah, there's an extra hundred quid I'm hiding from you. Going to sneak it out in my pack.'

'That job lot of duvets you thought I hadn't noticed?'

'That's the one.' Akeel pushes the last few buttons, turns off the machine. 'No, it's this,' He runs his hand over the till. 'When I was a kid, my sister had a shopkeeper's set. Most people gave us money for Eid, aunts and uncles and all that, it was brilliant, all the cousins used to come over and we'd pool what we were given, then spend it all down at the corner shop. Actually,' Akeel smiles again, 'they were Muslim too, the people who owned the shop, they should have been shut for the festival, guess they knew we'd be coming.'

Robert nods. 'Then they were good at their job. Know your customer, can't go wrong.'

'Anyway, at Eid, big Eid, after Ramadan, most children get cash, but our parents always gave us a present. One big present each. And one year, Leila got this shop set, with a till and little boxes of flour, tiny milk bottles . . .'

'Alice got Katie one of them. She wanted a dolls' house.'

'Leila did too, she hardly ever played with the shop, so I did. It wasn't so much the little boxes of foods, it was the till, pushing buttons. Rubeina says it's why I love video games and those ones I've got on my phone, I've always liked gadgets.'

'What? Just gadgets? You don't like the violence and the slaughter count too?'

Akeel grins. 'Yeah, a bit. The adrenalin rush mainly, but a lot of it is to do with the gadgets too. I like all that stuff.'

'Our first push-button telephone – after the old dial ones? I thought I was it, just making a phone call felt like I was one of the Thunderbirds.'

'Virgil?'

'Bugger that. Scott. Much better-looking.'

'Weren't you too old?'

'Nah, we just weren't as sophisticated in our viewing as you lot now, not enough channels to be sophisticated with. Or time, come to that. Not that the till's fully yours yet,' Robert adds, his own claim still there, the solicitor's forms upstairs waiting for the right day to be signed, the day Robert can bring himself to make his mark.

'I know, but, still, being here, knowing it's going to be mine, it does feel . . .'

'Safe?'

'That's the one.' Akeel nods and goes outside to lock the shutters.

Robert considers. He is not this boy's father. He has given enough warnings of overheads and insurance premiums, explained what tax and financial implications he can. It is not his job to also warn of heartbreak and boredom, sudden death and long-drawn-out losses that are not even noticed until they're gone, of the adrenalin rush from real life smacking you in the face. When Katie started talking about learning to drive, what he'd wanted to do was sit her down in front of a video of every car accident he could find, run it on a loop for a day or two until she was terrified of the power she would possess; what he did instead was promise her lessons for her eighteenth birthday. Father or not, Robert believes adult truths to be unteachable. Maybe even unlearnable, certainly his first loss did not prepare him for the second, the third.

Akeel comes back through the side door, keys swinging in his hand. 'I'm not stupid, Robert. I know standing behind the counter doesn't fix it all. But right now, it does feel safe, my future. Like I sorted this out – finding you, getting you to take me on – and we've made it work, between us, and now it's going where I wanted it to. Most of the time, I admit, I am scared, worried. But not today.'

Robert pictures his own hands on the padded leather driving wheel of his first car, the keys a constant assurance of his adulthood. Taking out a bucket and the chrome polish every Sunday while Jean got the dinner on, working on his second-hand cream and grey Zodiac until it shone. Robert had grown into the adult and done it himself, his own soap-sud hands playing the sensible dad he'd never had. He is too old to trust in that kind of security any more, there have been too many partings and funerals to believe in the comfort of years, but he remembers how he once believed age would bring certainty, and that his own disappointment need not be Akeel's.

'Fair enough, lad. You enjoy it.' Not that he can quite stop himself either. 'While it lasts. Bound to go wrong eventually.'

On Sunday Robert takes a walk up to Brockwell Park. He has not been here for years, the walled garden is smaller than he remembers, the foliage more dense. It's been raining for most of a week, but this morning is bright and crisp, clear out to Crystal Palace and well beyond, if he could climb that transmitter he'd be able to see right out to the Downs. The walled garden has curved walls too, mathematically miraculous straight lines edging into round. Robert sits, in sunshine that has no warmth, and watches the families and couples come and go. By midday his park bench has held a dozen other people, most of them older like himself, a few children who climb up and down in their short little wellington boots, muddy and unconcerned about the marks on the wooden bench or Robert's trousers, the children's parents apologetic or blithely ignorant, the mud there anyway. Around the time parents start calling their children to come and have lunch, two old blokes join him on the bench, cans in hand. Robert realises the men think he is one of them, he smiles at the thought, smiles and then grimaces, torn between anger and acceptance. Or he would be torn, if what he felt was that big. Acceptance then, he thinks, sinks further back against the seat, acceptance because he doesn't mind enough to move. Robert sits until a distant clock sounds two, and it is time to go back to the flat, make himself a bit of lunch. He gets up, the cold well and truly in his arthritic knee now, and leaves in winter sunshine. The park is full and other people's activity feels like a blessing.

As he walks downhill to the shop he feels happier than he

has in years. Giving up the shop, moving on, letting go – these decisions have lifted a weight from him. He will spend the afternoon sorting more boxes, clearing space, getting the place ready for Akeel. He trusts the young man, has come to like him. Robert wouldn't say he knows him well, but enough to know he'll do the job and take care of the shop. It's a good beginning for the lad, and it's not a bad new start for Robert either. He's been to his lawyer, spoken to the bloke in the dark suit about the money he's getting for the business, has his will all sorted, everything nicely taken care of. All he has to do now is get on with the packing, the clearing out. Even though he knows it will be hard to go, it is always hard to leave, it is definitely time. Robert is pleased with himself. He picks up a few cans of lager from the corner shop, he'll do some packing for a couple of hours and then have a little celebration. Raise a glass to himself, it's about time.

Forty

Patricia Ryan is frightened, she cannot find her way home. She has her key tied to a piece of string, which is pinned to the inside of her handbag, that health-visitor girl Marylin, she suggested putting it there, and it's worked fine so far, but now here she is, with her bag and her key, and still she can't go home. Unfortunately, while Patricia has the key nice and safe, she isn't sure which door it fits. So she is staying out until she knows, she doesn't want to try the wrong door, get into trouble, Patricia hates getting into trouble. She has been out all morning. She sat for a while with the two men on their sofa under the arch, one of them offered her a sip from his can, it was gallant of him, but Patricia knows better than to share viruses that way, Patricia was a nurse for a long time. There is a number she could attach to those years but Patricia cannot find the number. There are a number of things she cannot find.

Then she was in the park and then she walked past the hospital and now she is in the bank, she is sure of all those things. She is in the bank in Camberwell, it is warm here, and Patricia's flat, wherever that might be, is cold at the moment, she is not sure about turning on the heating, not sure where, how, if. She thinks it should be cold, the calendar on the wall says December and Patricia knows December is meant to be cold. Deep and crisp and even. Though why the shepherds and their poor flock would want to be all

253

seated on the ground in a foot or more of snow, she's never understood. Patricia looks out the window and sees that the people going past have coats and umbrellas and wonders if she should have those things too, if she did have those things. She looks down and checks again that she has her handbag. There is a bag on her arm, where it should be, and Patricia is pleased.

There are two women arguing in the bank. Patricia would have called them coloured ladies in the old days, it was more polite, black wasn't polite, women wasn't polite, coloured was, or dark, lady was certainly a nicer word than woman or female, and Patricia, who'd had more than enough of English rudeness about her own accent and birthplace, always wanted to be polite. Not long before she finished work, she went to a course and it was all explained to her, 'These are the words we use now', the words she is supposed to remember. Patricia is keen to hang on to words, especially as numbers seem to be missing today.

At first there was just a conversation and then there was an annoyance and then there was an argument. It started when the older black woman was explaining to the younger Asian woman behind the counter about her granddaughter, how she's been playing up at school and the parents have had enough, so they're sending her off back home, and the main reason this grandmother thinks it will be a good thing is that the girl doesn't know anything about village life, she's 'scared of sheep and goats and cows'. The black lady and the Asian lady both laugh at this idea, laugh that a London girl who is not scared of all the horrible things in this big dirty city should be scared of goats. But Patricia remembers – pleased to find the memory safe – that she was always scared of goats, they have strange slitty eyes. She doesn't think it is nice of the two women to laugh at the girl for being scared of goats, she wants to point out that the girl has every right to be scared of goats, goats are frightening, why is the devil called an old goat if not because they are frightening? But then the conversation moves on and the older black woman is telling the younger Asian woman how this same granddaughter, who is scared of goats and sheep and cows, walks around in next to nothing 'showin' too much o' her wares' and the women laugh again, as if what can you do about all these young girls, what can you do? After that another woman in the queue, a much younger woman, who is also a black woman, sighs and asks can't we get on with it. She is talking in a strong voice, quite posh, and very clear, and the whole room goes quiet and her voice is louder still when she repeats herself. 'Can we please just get on? This is a bank, you know? Not just a place to come for a chat?' Patricia can see she has a point, and some of the other people in the queue clearly agree, they nod, but they're not saying anything, people rarely do, no one ever said anything to stop Frank whenever he was hitting so hard, which was often enough. And the older woman turns round, and she looks the younger woman up and down, and the younger woman is very well dressed, it's not as if she's showing too much of her wares or anything else, she is wearing a nice suit and a good pair of shoes and a red umbrella, rolled and folded away, all neat and tidy. The older woman sucks her teeth and glares at the younger woman and nods at the Asian woman behind the counter and then clasps her hands tight round her own handbag, which she holds high beneath the shelf of her breasts, and asks, 'What your problem, girl? You think you English?' The way she says English Patricia can't tell if it is meant as an insult or not, but the younger woman clearly knows, and she answers very calmly that she is both English and Jamaican, and last she heard asking someone to hurry up in a queue when they'd finished their transaction five minutes ago was just sensible, wherever they were from. Some people in the

255

queue nod and some shake their heads like the young woman shouldn't be speaking that way to an older woman, and then someone from the bank comes over to where Patricia is sitting and asks her is she waiting for an appointment with the financial advisor, because if she is she needs to take a number, and if she isn't would she leave now please, surely she can see they're very busy? And Patricia, who has been perfectly happy for the past half hour watching the people in the queue, and who would quite like to hear what the young woman is going to say next, gets up to leave because there is really no point speaking to a financial advisor, not when the numbers are so far away.

When Patricia stands up her handbag falls off her lap and things inside spill out. On the end of a long piece of string is her door key, and on the key is a label, and the label has her address on it. Patricia can read the address and now she knows where to go. The label must have been there all along, she looks at the piece of thin card and follows the letters, one by one into a word and then an address. That was the health visitor's idea as well, a label for the key. Though she did say Patricia should maybe not keep the two things together, just in case. Patricia couldn't work out what the just in case might be, surely the two ought to go together, in case she got lost, gets lost? Patricia has been lost, the letters and the numbers on the label lost to her. And now, all of a sudden, they have come back. Patricia is going home quickly, while she is back with herself.

She makes it up the hill and to her own door before the really heavy rain starts and it is not until she is sitting inside and has boiled the kettle and turned on the heating – turned it on quickly while she knows what to do, fumbling in her own darkness – that she remembers what she went out for in the first place. Patricia sits at her kitchen table, looking north across the city. The view from her window is still as glorious

256

as it's ever been. All those buildings lit up, that big Ferris wheel, and the tall thin building at the back, that tower, the other one, with the dome, and the one with the clock. They are still there, they don't need names. They are still there. Patricia drinks her tea weak, without the milk she went out for. It's not too bad.

Forty-one

It is the Sunday before Christmas. Stefan is going home. He has, against the odds, against his own principles, spent the night with Mike, at Mike's flat. This is the fourth time he's done so in the past three months. Despite the younger man's wishes, Stefan has so far refused to discuss 'where they might be going', but he does acknowledge, even if he doesn't really approve, that he appears to have a boyfriend. Inconveniently and, Stefan thinks, entirely predictably, this boyfriend lives in north-west London. That is, the furthest, and least conveniently located, part of London from his own South-east. Now it is late Sunday morning, and Stefan has just entered a carriage on the Jubilee line at Finchley Road.

As he takes his seat, before the doors close and the outdoor-indoor train begins to move off and down, Stefan listens to the messages the driver is broadcasting. There are two London voices, both women. One woman is black, she asks you to mind the gap between the train and the platform. Her accent is low and she almost, but not quite, gives the word train two syllables. The other is white, hers is the accent that tourists believe all British people possess. Her message tells you the train terminates at Stratford and she sounds as if she means the Stratford Shakespeare comes from, not the Olympic destination. The black voice is low and soothing even in its warning, the white voice clipped in its delivery of destination. Stefan wonders what a brown voice might sound like, somewhere in between perhaps, an intimated warning with no certain destination. There is no certain destination either, in this thing Mike likes to call their relationship. Stefan can certainly feel a warning in his blood, the uncertainty that in the past has always made him run from anything more than sex-free friendship or plain fucking, but the warning is not stronger than the memory of Mike's skin on his, Mike's mouth on his, Mike's wanting and his own giving. It is almost ten years since Stefan was last in a relationship, he has successfully lived without one, been happy without one. The train plunges into the dark, the fluorescent lights make their presence known, it is Sunday midday and Stefan is looking forward to seeing Mike for lunch on Wednesday. Here we go again.

At Green Park Stefan changes to the Victoria line. He is followed into the carriage by a young black man wearing a deerstalker hat, a comedy Sherlock Holmes. Stefan thinks Shaft would have been a far better choice. The young man sits down in his cap and cape and, to the immediate tensing of facial muscles all round, produces a large CD player from his bag. He is nattily dressed beneath the outfit, Stefan can see this now, as everyone else looks away from the source of the loud noodling jazz and to the floor, the advertising placards, the shards of Sunday paper they are so glad to have picked up from the seat beside them.

At Victoria a young white man gets on, and sits beside the deerstalker, gleefully grabbing the last empty seat, placing his not insubstantial frame in position, staking his claim. Then he hears the racket at his side. He stares at the black guy, the black guy stares back. The young black man is impeccably, if oddly, dressed, and he is small. The white man is wearing jeans, tight white T-shirt, leather jacket, and is enormous. Stefan is hating this already, his mind races on to fists and boots and bruises and breaks, a trickle of bile forces its way up his throat, he swallows it back. Looks around, reminds himself it is day, and public, and he is safe now, his skin is whole and unmarked, he is fine. The man closes his eyes beneath his deerstalker cap, nods his head and continues to sway, ever so slightly, in time to the syncopated rhythm the entire carriage cannot now avoid. The newspaper readers, sensing danger, become even more interested in the print before them, second-hand BMWs and best ways to avoid the pitfalls of velvet still more enticing.

'Your music is very loud.'

The white man speaks quietly, not so much above the music as with it, in time.

The young black man slowly opens his eyes. He turns his head to the white man. 'Whagwan?'

Stefan's heart sinks. If the black half of this conversation is to be conducted in street talk, he really doesn't want to be called on to translate. And he agrees with the white man, the music is too bloody loud. But the black man is much smaller than the white man, a few years younger and, it now seems from the white man's surprisingly camp voice, a good deal more heterosexual. All Stefan's minorities laid out for him in one potential altercation.

White man repeats. 'Your music. It's very loud.'

Black man raises a single eyebrow.

Now the white man's voice is louder still, betraying the braying nasality of a public school education, along with a slight sibilance, which mark him out as both posh and poofy. Londoners throughout the carriage realign their prejudices, making the leap from one side of the fence to the other, but all too aware that, unless they can find something good to do at Pimlico, tea at the Tate, a Dolphin Square swim, they'll likely witness unpleasantness before the river.

The train stops and starts, there are more public announcements, people get on and off. The level of the jazz coming from the CD player continues unabated.

Furious now, the white man stands, leans down past the deerstalker cap and speaks right into the black man's face. 'Will you turn it down? You're disturbing other people.'

It is disturbing other people, and several passengers nod to confirm the fact. But then again, the white man is so much bigger than the black man, and if the white man's accent contains a lisp of camp, it also has the languid vowels of privilege. Stefan has had enough, he stands, comes forward on legs made shaky by the moving train and the fact that he very much doesn't want to get involved, as well as an image of himself he cannot push away, eye cut and swollen, lip ripped, tooth cracked. He wants to be back in bed with Mike. He really doesn't want this.

Stefan leans in. 'Man,' he says to the white man, 'back off, OK? And brother,' he adds to the black man, who doesn't take kindly to being called brother by a stranger, no matter how useful the intention, 'turn it down, yeah?'

The face beneath the cap turns up to the two older men, looks from one to the other, stares long and slow, up and down, adds the hint of a smile. 'Is it?'

Stefan shakes his head, the white man is getting angrier, the train pulls into Vauxhall. The black man turns off his CD player, stands, waits for Stefan and the white man to get out of his way, and walks slowly off the train, turning to smile behind him as the doors close, waving goodbye, mouthing 'batty bois' as he does so.

At Brixton, Stefan runs up the stairs out of the tube, rounding the yellow police signs warning of drug dealers and mobile-phone robberies in the area. Stefan knows both are possible, cannot walk down Coldharbour Lane without hearing whispers of 'Weed, hash, something nice, man, ari'?', he walks quickly past the minicab office where so many have stopped and been stopped, charges on past the copy shop, signs in the window offering *Professional Videos – Wedding! Christening!*

Funerals. He's pleased that at least they left the exclamation mark off the funeral offer, somehow it matters. He crosses the corner and remembers a boot to his kidneys, walks towards Loughborough Junction with that irritating jazz ringing in his ears, the taunting smile of the deerstalker boy in his mind. The little bastard would have been cute without the stupid clothes, Stefan thinks the white man thought so too. By the time he reaches the first railway bridge his fear is walked out. Tired from the tension of sitting on that tube and just waiting for it to kick off, tired from the relief that it didn't. Tired of saying no. He rings Mike, asks if he wants to come over for dinner later. Mike doesn't bother to leave a pause before saying yes.

Stefan walks past the dry cleaner's and remembers Robert is leaving soon, or maybe he already has, he can't remember when the new guy said he'd be taking over. Shame if he's missed him, he meant to say goodbye. He picks up more speed, the cold is too damn cold, turning down into Camberwell, he dashes into the Chinese supermarket for fresh fish and then the deli for herbs to go with the red mullet, sesame bread to soak up the sauce he will make, and fuck it, why not, two thick chunks of sticky baklava for dessert. He walks up the narrow stairs to his flat, a bus trundles past, shaking the old building, and Stefan thinks how he never wants to live anywhere where they sell only one nationality of food, where the shopkeepers all have the same accent. He unlocks the door to his flat, slams it shut behind him, puts on the kettle and some music – not jazz, not loud – chops herbs, heats oil for a sauce, runs the fish under cold water, begins to make dinner for his boyfriend. He looks down at the cat, twisting herself around his ankles, angry that he has been out all night and hasn't even bothered to apologise yet. Stefan crouches down, strokes the cat. There there, I'm home, I'm sorry. The cat walks away.

Forty-two

In Dean's pub it is always late afternoon, that's what he likes about the place. No point letting the sun shine through the window when all it's going to light up is a tired carpet, cigarette burns on the bar, the lines on the landlady's face. And his own. Dean runs a hand over his face, rough fingers catching on rougher stubble, he and the bar have seen better days, he has to admit. He certainly wouldn't normally come out without having shaved, he takes good care of his appearance, but things have been a bit rough for Dean the past few days, a couple of run-ins with Gina, a bit of bother between the two firms he works for, a low muttering that he might need to make a choice, Peckham or Brixton, not that it's come to anything yet, but Dean has always been a great one for no smoke without fire and there's been a few fairly clear signals recently. One or two more and he'll have to go and talk to someone, see what's really going on. Then last night, his boy, his younger lad, came home with a black eye and refused to tell him what it was about, no chance for Dean to go and sort it out. Everything feels a bit out of focus, a bit shit. It could just be that he's coming down with a cold, bones aching, chest heavy. Dean hates being sick, hates not feeling a hundred per cent at all times, which is why he's extra grumpy, sitting here, week before Christmas, rain pissing down outside, nursing a pint and whatever virus is working its way through his system, waiting for his mate Tim to get back from the flat he keeps quiet, so they can make a few deliveries, take care of business and get a bit of cash in for the shopping. As Gina's said half a dozen times already this morning, the kids' presents won't buy themselves.

It's all right in here though, in the pub. Dean knows everyone here, the blokes lining these bench seats have watched him grow up and he's seen them grow old. Seen more than his fair share of fights in here too, and those that carried on, out in the street, down the road even, once or twice, back in the day. Dean only has one scar that shows, but it's enough to look good, cuts across his left cheek, lifting it slightly higher than the right, always the beginning of a smile. Never mind that it's from when he came off his bike at thirteen, felt a right arse when he did too, it looks good, like he can handle himself, and anyone else who might need handling. But even Dean would admit he's getting tired, and it's not just whatever lurgy his body has got going on. He looks around the bar at the blokes he knows, always in here by mid-afternoon, the lags his dad would have been sitting with if the old man hadn't drunk himself to death years back, the old guys he'll turn into himself if he's not careful. He picks up his pint, takes another long sip, checks the clock on the wall, Tim's half an hour over time.

Dean's been thinking it might be time to move out, this coming year maybe. Not too far, not beyond a London post-code, but out. He knows he'd miss living round here, and of course it would make his work that much harder, he'd have to become something of a commuter, need to keep popping in here regularly as well, keep up the chat, the presence that means if there's a job needs doing, he'll be the one to get offered it first. This is where everyone is, especially now, coming up to Christmas, the kids playing on the pool table, the wives nattering, old blokes at the bar, in here most days from midday until teatime usually. Dean shivers, he really doesn't feel so good. Maybe it is time to knock it all on the head, his cousin has a business, house clearances mostly, legal and everything, has asked Dean to come in with him often enough. Steady job, regular income, regular hours. Dean thinks it almost sounds worth it, telling himself about the job, bit of driving, bit of delivering, a few pickups. Then he stops, shakes his head, holds up the pint glass to the smoke-stained window, bloody hell, what've they been putting in his beer? Christ, if Tim doesn't get a bloody move on, he'll be handing in his notice next, all too easy to sit in the half dark of the afternoon and imagine chucking it all in, very easy when he's indoors to think he can't be bothered going out and getting on with work. Except that even when he's feeling a bit sorry for himself, like he clearly is right now, stupid bastard, Dean likes his work and he loves the buzz and he doesn't mind the cut-price gear as well, every now and then, but what he really likes is the edginess. There's always the chance the two firms will give it over, this being-nice-to-each-other lark, or something will go wrong – like Tim taking so fucking long to get here – or just something, whatever, something new. Dean likes that he doesn't know what's coming next.

Then Tim walks through the door, big grin on his face, and Dean's up and ready, that ache in the back of his neck receding now, and he's punching Tim on the shoulder, once, twice, telling him he's a useless bastard, and they're out the door, Merry Christmas all round, he'll be back on the day itself, once the turkey's in the oven they'll all pop over for a few. Pushing through the door with Tim, Dean doesn't feel forty, he feels twenty-five or fifteen, and that's all to the good, because there's a fuck of a lot of gear to get rid of actually, Tim's really gone mad this time, and a few bills to pay and an enormous mother of a turkey Dean'll have to hand over a fistful of cash for, some bloke in the pub promising a job lot was coming at the weekend, your turkeys off the back of a Norfolk lorry, organic and all. Gina'll like that. And out here, in the cold and the drizzle, Dean doesn't feel so bad that he couldn't be bothered having a proper shave today, not now the wind's woken him up and he's looking forward to getting on with the job.

Then off on the rounds, first three fine, no problem, sweet as, and then it all goes arse over tit, arse over fucking tit, they're both at the door, just into the passage, Dean's handing over a bit of sulphur for the customer, and fucking Customs come crashing through the patio doors out the back, Tim gets grabbed, and he's kicking out at the bloke that's got him, he smashes a picture on the wall, sharp chunks of glass coming down on them and Tim gets cut which, even in the rush and the fighting and the shouting, Dean knows is shit. The fucking DNA crap these bastards have on Tim, he's been inside too fucking recently, and Dean doesn't trust they don't come and swab your fucking mouth in your sleep, that lot, these days. So now Tim's on the ground and this big Customs cunt has got him by the leg, Dean's halfway out the door, fuck knows where the customer whose house it is has gone, rushed off upstairs or out the back, wherever, and then somehow, God knows how, but Dean manages to pull away from the bloke who's lunged at him, and gets a free foot to the one who's still got Tim's leg, Tim pulling the bloke with him halfway out the door now. And Dean's left foot has always been good, always bloody has, smacks the bastard a good one in the face, boot-nose-hello.

Now Tim and Dean are off out that door, through the gate and fucking flying. All the way, no stopping, no looking back, Tim's gone one way, through the estate, Dean the other, straight down to Camberwell, further than he needed to go really, forcing himself to slow down by the Baptist church, put the brakes on, hands in his pockets, taking it easy, still half a dozen wraps in his pocket, he'd never carry more, not these days, but that might be enough if they thought they knew who they were looking for. Makes a decision, could go home right now, wonders if perhaps they do know who they're looking for, if this was the ache he'd been feeling all day, decides he's going to stay out and give himself something to do, something to say he was doing in case anyone asks questions later.

Dean takes himself straight into Woolies and buys the biggest fucking bag full of pick and mix he can find, not even bothering to nick one, just takes the lot to the till and hands over the cash. He's completely knackered now, heart still thumping in his chest, whacking against his ribs, and he's standing there at the front of the shop, where the heaters are blasting hot air on to the customers' backs as they come in, and he's handing out pick and fucking mix to every bloody kid that goes past, and half the mothers an' all, because actually this is why Dean doesn't want to stop. Yeah, it was just Customs and that means they're fucking lucky, whether Tim's cut bled enough for them to do anything or not, lucky it wasn't the Old Bill, just some fat arse who's going to spend the afternoon at A&E getting his nose seen to now. This is the good bit. How he feels now. Dean's forty, yes, he bloody is, Jesus, if he didn't know it before, his thumping bloody heart is telling him so for a fact, and he knows he can't keep on like this, he really can't, Gina's right, and now, after this, he'd better steer clear of the pub for a few months. Obviously someone's been talking, Customs didn't just happen to be passing that bastard's patio, so maybe a few months with his cousin might work out after all, keep the wife happy anyway.

Dean understands all this, and God knows he's not stupid,

so he'll lie low and watch his back and he won't go to the pub for a bit, not his pub anyway, keep his face out of it. But this is the part he likes, the thumping heart, the adrenalin rush, way more successful than half a gram up his nose, and better exercise too. Dean likes this feeling, and he knows he likes it too much, and so he'll be taking care and he'll stay indoors and be a good boy. He's lucky, it's not hard, he loves Gina and he loves his kids, he's a lucky man, he knows that, lucky to have it all nice. But bloody hell, handing over the last of the blackcurrant liquorices to an old Irish woman who looks at him like he's a fucking terrorist or something, but takes the sweet anyway, fuck me, Dean does like a bit of excitement every now and then, the heart beating, feet racing, rush. He likes it a lot.

His phone rings, it's a customer, his heart rate is almost back to normal, he walks through the door, stands in the street, takes the call. 'Hello, mate . . . Merry Christmas to you too. Lovely. What was it you were after? . . . Excellent. Excellent. I'll be on you in half an hour.'

Forty-three

There are many dead people in London, and they take up a lot of room. Graveyards splatter the city, have been turned into parks and recreation zones and motorways, the foundation stones of luxury conversions. Each cemetery has its own parking problems, borough councillor issues, local-paper human-interest stories, and every one of them has the same hierarchy of death – the dead may be all alike, but the grieving are very clear about their rank. In pole position are the newly bereft. These visitors are very aware that they have precedence, this is their time, bargained for, allotted, utilised to the full. Big city cemeteries run on a tight schedule and the newly bereft know their place – it is in the car park closest to the chapel, in a clump of black blocking the entrance, entitled to walk ahead of those who are here merely to visit, not to bury or to burn.

People dress simply when they are only attending the dead for a birthday or an anniversary, they wear everyday clothes, not funeral clothes. It is how they differentiate themselves from the buriers, the cremators, how the just-grieving pick out the ones they will become. The people who come to the cemetery accompanying a fresh coffin cannot imagine that grief could ever be anything but excessive. In many cases they are right.

Since Alice died, Robert has visited her grave every Christmas, but on few other occasions. Jean used to visit every now and then. She'd take Katie with her and the two of them would come, talk to Nana Alice, leave their white roses, then get the bus back down the hill, toast and tea in a café on the way home, side order of crispy bacon for Katie. Robert hated the cemetery, said he felt so out of place. Of course he had a right to be there, but not as important as the black-dressed, nowhere near as important as the earth-dressed, he always felt uncomfortable, the unwanted guest. It got into his bones, Robert said, even with the wide city view to the north and even on the brightest of days he still found the place so dark, as if the lights dimmed halfway up the Norwood hill, turned off altogether at the gates. For a while after his mother's death Robert made the effort, but he quickly found other places to talk to Alice, talk of Alice. Robert remembered his mother in the newly ordered store-room, or by the big press, dragging yet another twisted blasted duvet from the machine, watching a bridal car rolling off down Loughborough Road and knowing that Alice would have wished 'the poor bitch inside all the luck in the world – she'll need it'.

Jean tried to make it better for her husband, ease his guilt about not visiting, saying it wasn't Alice there anyway, not really. Jean had always tried to make it better, but she couldn't fix this, because no matter what she said, it really was Alice in her box and decaying. Alice dead in the ground. So Robert continued to feel guilty about not going to see his mother on her birthday, or her anniversary. Guilty, but not enough to put up with the creeping grief that settled on his skin the minute he walked through the big iron gates, grief sticking to him when he got home as well, lying around for a night or two, waiting to trip him up with a creak of the stair or a dress faintly scented with Paris Soir, a cup of tea left too long on the side, too cold to drink and Alice's voice chiding him, 'Come all the way from China just for you to throw it away?'

270

At Christmas, though, Robert always felt different about the cemetery. Alice had loved everything about the mid-winter festivities, the fuss and the lights, the drink and the food, every stretched excess suited her perfectly. Even when he was a little boy and there was nothing at all to spare, she would load down the top of the sideboard with mince pies, sausage rolls, a brandy-fed fruit cake and a crumbling chocolate log sprinkled with icing sugar for snow, the one-legged plastic robin redbreast pecking pointlessly at a dry holly sprig. Throughout the big build-up that everyone else moaned about, Alice would just turn up the volume on her portable record player, its red vinyl cover splitting and peeling more with every year, and sing even louder of calling birds and Rudolph and her favourite little drummer boy, handing out flaky-pastry mince pies to the ordinary customers, the same washed down with a whisky mac for her favourites. Come the end of January she'd be cursing the bills that rolled in, vowing to go easy this year. Until the first fat swallow bowing down the telegraph line reminded her it was time to think about making the pudding again and she would declare today was the day to shine up the pennies. She'd collect all the sixpences from the till, picking out the newest ones her customers had handed over, and get Robert to wash and polish them, rubbing them hard between his bitten thumb and his serge school shorts. A week or so later, long before they opened up, Robert was called out of bed and into the kitchen to stir the pudding mixture, a wishing stir, three times clockwise with the wooden spoon, through the lumpy paste of dried fruit and spices, eggs, flour and just a little more brandy and rum than the recipe called for, with a slosh of stout for good measure. Finally the mixture would be tipped out of the washing-up bowl, the only mixing bowl large enough for the job, packed into pudding basins, and Robert would have the job of pushing the polished sixpences deep into the centre. Then Alice would set the puddings to steam for the rest of the day; the scent of suet-warmed spices combined with cleaning fluid and drying clothes would forever be Robert's harbinger of colder weather. Four Christmas puddings made every year, one for the day, one for New Year's Eve, another to grow richer and darker until Easter Sunday, and a last one to give away. Alice maintained there was bound to be someone needing it at the last minute, and she was always right, inevitably some weeping new wife or grumpy old man in the shop on Christmas Eve, their smile in return for the gift of a pudding far outweighing the effort of making just one extra in the first place.

It was the year Alice died that Robert first went up to the cemetery on Christmas Eve. He didn't fancy it at all, not to mention the shop was getting busier every half hour as the day wore on. He went because it was the right thing to do, because Alice loved Christmas and, no matter how much he hated the thought, Katie had a right to a good Christmas too, so he should do as Jean said. Get up the hill and say your piece, then come back and be a proper dad, if you can't be a son any more, you can at least be a proper dad. Jean wasn't being nasty, not really, she just didn't know what else to suggest. Had tried kissing and holding, asking and listening, not mentioning and mentioning all the time. Every attempt was rejected, Robert didn't know how to move on from grief, but time was passing anyway. The chill and sadness up at the cemetery were as expected, how could they not be, but there was a surprising light too, and a bustle and warmth that Robert had never seen there before. So many had come with flowers and candles, bringing light to their dead ones for the shortest days of the year. It took him back to the Christmases when he was a boy, in that top-floor flat on Coldharbour Lane, people popping in for a quick drink and staying the evening, Alice's mates from the laundry arriving in a group and leaving two by two as the booze took its toll, Alice telling Robert to get off to bed one minute and then offering him sausage rolls and 'a drink to get him started' the next. The cemetery was busy, and bright. Alice would have liked it, the colours and the people and the crisp in the air. Throw in a few drinks and a gala pie, bright yellow yolk running through its mottled centre, and she would have loved it.

This Christmas Eve then, as ever, Robert will make the bus trip up the hill, dark red winter roses in one hand, three whisky miniatures in his pocket. One for Alice, poured on to the earth, the other two for himself for the trip home. There are families walking through together, leaving behind cards and mistletoe for kisses, long white candles in deep vases, high-sided to shield the flame from the wind. All of it left out for the absent ones to know they are still thought of, now as ever, now more than ever, all through tomorrow too, when the gates will be locked and the dead left in peace.

Robert is leaving Akeel in charge of the shop and the customers who come rushing in at midday wondering if there's any chance, any way at all that their favourite Christmas dress, or suit, or bloody hell, who cares, but yes, sometimes, their favourite tie – the one with last year's mince pie, or brandy butter, or office party detritus still down the front – can't be tidied up in time for another onslaught tomorrow. Robert has never understood how any favourite outfit can be so special as to be only worn once a year, but so be it. This year, it's not his problem. It's never going to be his problem again. He pulls on his jacket, wraps his scarf round his neck and pats Akeel on the shoulder as he goes.

'Won't be long, son. Hour and a half at the most. All right?'

Robert doesn't wait for an answer, doesn't care to. Leaves

the shop almost cheerily, happier than Akeel's seen him all this past week. Akeel nods, continues counting out one customer's change, while ordering new supplies for delivery in the first week of the new year and lifting a hand to acknowledge the three other people waiting. Akeel is only partly paying attention anyway, the other half of him is listening out for the dryer winding down from its latest cycle and the big washing machine spinning into action again and the answerphone clicking on after four rings. Akeel knows the sounds of his own business now, they are the background to every day. Right now they are the background to a different sound, that of the door closing on Robert's surprisingly tuneful whistle.

Forty-four

Marylin has been shopping in town. When Audrey was alive, the two of them always went up town on Christmas Eve. It was their ritual to buy last-minute little gifts for the tiny stockings Audrey left on each neighbour's door overnight. Now that she holds a Christmas Eve party for her neighbours, Marylin gives stockings to her clients instead. She'll drop one off with Mrs Erskinshaw on the Loughborough Estate, another for Patricia Ryan, and maybe one for Robert at the dry cleaner's — now he's announced his leaving date it feels like the last tie to Audrey and Aunty Irene is being cut. She barely exchanges more than a few words a year with Robert, but he's a link to her childhood, has always been there. His going feels like an old building coming down.

Marylin loves her Christmas party. The neighbours come over, several friends who prefer to leave the heat and family of their own homes, a couple of ex-boyfriends arrive with their wives and children. The flat is packed from the walkway across the front of the building to her balcony out the back, she wears one of Audrey's old dresses, with a full skirt and a low neck, and sashays around her little flat playing lady bountiful. Her neighbour's friend Dean usually turns up some time during the evening, stays for half a can of lager, leaving with his pockets empty and wallet full, an eighth here, a half wrap there. Marylin doesn't care who does what on Christmas Eve, just as long as no one ruins their appetite,

275

she'll be churning out little filo parcels of spinach with nutmeg, Stilton and pear tarts, chicken wings and sliced turkey, hot mince pies, gooey chocolate puddings, warm punch, mulled wine and cold champagne until at least two in the morning. And then, around midday tomorrow, when most adults across the city are coping with their fear of family and the impossible task of readying seven different foods for the same moment of presentation, Marylin will get up to a quiet flat, pour herself a large glass of champagne, cut a chunk of cheese and bread, and, wrapped in Audrey's old tartan rug, she will sit in front of the telly and watch three or four of the films she didn't get around to seeing in the year. She will pick at any leftovers, drink as much or as little as she likes, and go to bed when she wants. On Boxing Day she'll visit some of her old people, Mrs Erskinshaw again, Patricia Ryan, Jack Courtnidge, the ones who don't live too far and probably haven't seen anyone since she dropped off their stockings on Christmas Eve. It's not a work day, but Marylin knows not everyone is as happy with their own company as she is, too many of her clients see Christmas alone as a penance not a privilege.

The air is crisp, the early-afternoon sun half-set already, and, though her shopping bags are weighing her down, she makes a detour across Covent Garden, down to Waterloo Bridge, the stop for the 59 is a little out of her way, but she'd rather walk over the river whenever possible, and she has Audrey's Christmas present to leave. Since Audrey died eight years ago, Marylin has used the Thames for memorial. For the first year, she threw yellow roses into the river, anniversary Pooh sticks, twenty-five roses floating down to Tilbury, catching on the rubbish barges low in the water. Marylin does not believe her mother is in the water, any more than she thinks the real Audrey is in that rose garden up at Norwood, but if she's anywhere at all, she is more likely to be found in the middle of London, in the wide brown river that separates the centre from the south. To Marylin's right, Hungerford Bridge is a dream spider's web, sticky iron filaments holding up a toy train as it crosses south to north; she looks through the white threads of the bridge to the chocolate box Houses of Parliament and Big Ben. To her left, St Paul's is diminished by a Christmas-lit city crane, directly ahead, the National Theatre squats in great chunks of illuminated concrete. Walking further over the bridge, the angle of the wheel becomes so acute it is a single green cat's eye, turning slowly above the water, and every ripple below, every wave, is a Christmas sparkle in the slanting western light. Ten yards further on, and the sand on the southern shore becomes a humpbacked whale, waves idly sloping in to a mudflat beach. Behind the Festival Hall is a new building wrapped in scaffolding, like a Christmas gift or a sick patient hiding behind its screens, Marylin can't tell which. As with so much of her city's incessant reconstruction, it will take the removal of the building works to decide.

Standing in a scimitar wind off the bend of the river, she reaches into a Selfridges bag to offer the gift. The conversation in her head has Audrey horrified by the expense and Marylin giggling at the extravagance. She throws her gift, tossing love and gratitude to the water, and hurries off to catch the 59, there's a lot to get on with this afternoon, as well as a nice half bottle of non-vintage champagne to keep her company at the stove. A bus pulls up fifteen feet from the stop and Marylin runs to the door. Behind her, on the water, the seagull that alights on the soggy 'Authentic Individual Panettone' can't believe its luck, perching on its east-floating festive meal, nodding arrivederci to Gabriel's Wharf, hello to Baby Jesus.

Forty-five

Robert walks back into the shop and, before he even has a chance to take off his jacket, it's all rush. That Australian girl, giggling and silly, half-cut probably, on her way out with a couple of mates, the three of them standing outside and singing a loud 'Silent Night' to the passing cars, the girl herself rushing in to drop off a bag-load of clothes for her lawyer boss, none of it needed until New Year's Eve, which is why she forgot to bring it in two days earlier and then had a row with the woman about it this morning, the row hastening her opening of the beers in her little private fridge. Not that she cares, ticket finally booked back to Aussie she tells Robert and Akeel, and this her last cold bloody grey bloody London bloody Christmas. Robert wants to point out that the sky outside is clear and high, the air sharper than anything she'd get on some beach where every second family is burning burgers and filling the place with the stench of greasy sausages, but he doesn't. He wishes the girl well instead, reminding her to go easy on the booze, the tube won't be running late tonight. She's out the door and away with her mates before he can add Merry Christmas. Then there's Mrs Ryan on her way back from St Philip and St James, an afternoon novena under her belt and midnight mass to come, she says it smells like snow outside, and she could well be right, except that as Robert watches her go, she wanders off up the road towards Brixton, and he knows she lives Camberwell way, he's seen the view. Akeel serves the old father from the halal butcher's, the pair of them salaaming something to each other, a double-sided hug, and Robert feels a twinge of pride that Akeel has formed these local business bonds. Not the ones Robert's already made, those he'll pass over with the deeds, but these new ones Robert himself could never have forced deeper than a nod or a smile. Not Robert's fault, nor the butcher's either, one man's handshake quite clearly another man's hug and two-cheek kiss. That dancer funny fellow comes through too, some young man in tow, and Robert catches Akeel with a raised eyebrow to match his own, watching the two men walk away across the road, the younger landing a quick kiss on the other's shoulder.

'What?' Akeel asks.

'Nothing.'

'No, what?'

'Each to his own, lad.'

Akeel smiles. 'Didn't say anything, did I?'

'Me neither.'

'There you are then.' Akeel leans past Robert to drop another few used tickets into the bin. 'Tea? While we've got the chance?'

'Well noted. Hop to it.'

Robert's hands are warming up nicely when Akeel asks him how it was at the cemetery.

'Not bad.'

'Do you go every year?'

'Yes.'

'Is it traditional? Are you supposed to?'

Robert grins. 'That's likely, isn't it? Me going all the bloody way up there on one of my busiest days just because someone else thinks I ought to? No, I go because I want to.'

279

Robert goes because he needs to, but he doesn't know how to explain this to Akeel. 'Feels right. What she deserves.'

Akeel has no dead people, not really. One grandparent, one older cousin. He doesn't know how much he is allowed to ask, but he wants to ask more. He waits a moment, the moment that television and films have persuaded him is appropriate. 'Do you still miss her?'

The moment is not quite long enough, but Robert is ready to talk today, so he lets it slide. 'Course I bloody do, she was my mum. And I worked with her, twenty-odd years in the shop together. Course I bloody miss her, but you know, they're never really gone, can't go a day without hearing her voice, telling me off, having a go.'

Akeel takes the cups over to the sink to rinse. 'What did she have a go about?'

Alice over by the dryer telling Robert not to be such a bloody fool and get up there and tell Jean he's sorry about something he did or didn't do, doesn't bloody matter, boy, just say sorry. Alice taking one look at the shirt Robert has just folded and getting him to do it three more times until it's perfect. Alice glaring at the toast Robert has buttered for her and asking where's the ration book, did he think they were still at war and would he mind giving her some butter on the bread so she can actually taste the flamin' stuff. Alice unable to stomach more than a half sip of water and telling Robert if he doesn't damn well do it now she'll never forgive him. Alice holding her boy's hand alive. And dead.

Robert shakes his head. 'What didn't she have a go about? Thought I was a daft bugger half the time and no problem saying so.'

'But you were close?'

'Oh yeah, we were close.'

A car stops too suddenly outside, another screeches just

280

behind it, the thud and tinkle of glass shards on tarmac, Robert leans his head round the partition and looks out through the front window. 'Talking of daft buggers . . .' The drivers outside shout at each other, obscenities first, insurance details next, Robert and Akeel so used to the scene they carry on their conversation regardless, easier to look at the tumult than at each other.

'Not a bad view from up there though, the cemetery.'

Akeel winces as the first car driver squares up to the second. 'What of?'

'Down the hill to the river, right over the other side. Alice used to get the tram up with her dad to Hampstead, for the fair, and her old man always reckoned the view from the south was better than the one up on the heath.'

'You North and South Londoners are always comparing yourselves.'

'No, lad, not always. And I don't think her dad was right, as it happens. It is a lovely view from Norwood, from anywhere down that way, Crystal Palace, Gipsy Hill. Hilly Fields's got a good view too, but in a way, the North Londoners are right.'

Akeel is so surprised to hear this he turns back from the shouting men to look at Robert.

'Well, we've to look at that lot from over here, don't we? And they're no great shakes.' Robert is smiling. 'They, on the other hand, up there on their bloody heath, they get to look at us. And we're flippin' gorgeous.' He nods, point made, satisfied.

Six thirty comes and the shop is locked for the next week. Akeel pulls on his coat and scarf, still wondering if he should say what he's been thinking for the past couple of hours. In the end it comes out, just as he'd decided maybe it would be best to shut up after all. 'Robert, don't you get lonely?'

'You what?'

'Over the break? I mean . . . I know you miss Jean some-times, and your daughter of course, and Alice. So – don't you get lonely?' Robert doesn't answer at first and Akeel is flooded with a very British embarrassment. 'Sorry – I shouldn't have . . . I just . . .'

'No, you're right, son.' Robert nods. 'Course I do, but I am used to it, and it's not really lonely any more, not the same. If I've learnt one thing, it's that any feeling changes with time – loneliness, grief. Hurts, course it does, but you get used to it. Nothing's ever as bad as it is at first.'

'Or as good?'

'Oh, I don't know, some things get better with time.'

'Love?'

'I was thinking more of a good bottle of whisky. There's a joy you'll not be sharing.'

'No.'

'Still, nice of you to ask.'

Akeel is halfway out the door when Robert hands him the card. 'There, don't say I never give you anything.'

'But I don't . . .'

'And I do.'

Inside is a carefully selected non-Christian card, with its non-specific message of good wishes, and four fifty-pound notes. Akeel looks at Robert, uncertain.

'It's your bonus, isn't it? Don't need to celebrate Christmas to get a bonus, do you?'

'Yes. I mean, no. Thank you, Robert.'

'Thank you, son. Have a good one.'

At home that night Akeel offers gratitude for his good for-tune. He climbs into bed beside Rubeina, wrapping his cold body round her always warmer one, holding her waist, low-ering his hand to her belly, his touch intimating care and comfort, and father not fancy. And then, because of the way

Rubeina turns into him, turns him into herself, there is no more care and concern, it is all desire and hunger, and the touch is only lust.

The last of the Christmas Eve trains pass through Loughborough Junction as Robert closes his front-room curtains. He pours himself another two fingers of whisky, checks the *TV Times* once more, wishing futilely for a *Morecambe and Wise* repeat, and sits back on the settee, glass in one hand, shop-bought mince pie in the other. The pastry is too dry, the mincemeat too sweet. Years ago he'd have been eating it hot, straight out of the oven, overfull of brandied fruit, only ever made with Alice's own flaky pastry, whatever the recipe books say about shortcrust. She never said she was much of a cook the rest of the year, but Alice came into her own at Christmas. Since mid-afternoon he'd have had half a dozen mince pies, home-cooked sausage rolls as well, sent down every hour or so from the middle kitchen on a plate held in Katie's little hands, ready to sit on the counter tempting customers, and Robert, into 'just one more'. By eight in the evening they'd be on to their third or fourth bottle of whatever had been sent by the delivery company, bottle of whisky handed over, tenner in a Christmas card back to the driver, falling asleep, exhausted and happy in front of the tree and the electric firelight upstairs.

There is no tree in Robert's front room now, but he has put out a few decorations. He wanted to see them this year. There is the glass Father Christmas that Alice bought just after the war, only two years younger than Robert, so old he's lost most of his colour, is now just the translucent figure of a big-bellied man, waiting for light to shine through. There is one of a pair of dangly earrings he and Jean bought Katie one Christmas, when they'd been assured by the girl in the shop that long earrings were the in thing, only to see

283

their daughter's face fall when she opened the box. Naff apparently. Later that day, though, the pair of them looked lovely on the tree, hanging either side of the fairy's tiny feet. There's the glass bird, one of Mrs Swanson's decorations, the ones that came to Jean when her mother died, that she sobbed over as she decided which to hang on her own tree and which to throw out, many of them damaged beyond repair. That bird should have gone in the bin by rights, the little clip where it attached to the tree was broken, the end of its tail snapped off years back, but Jean couldn't bear to lose it. Now the one remaining earring and the Father Christmas and the bird sit on the mantelpiece, spaced around Alice's father's clock. When Jean and Katie left they took the Christmas boxes, Robert said he didn't mind, knew the girls would need some things to help them feel at home. He was staying in their real home after all, and Katie was just like Alice about Christmas, adored the lot of it, wouldn't be fair for her to have to do without the decorations she loved. That first Christmas, when Robert had been so damned sorry for himself he'd spent most of it over the road in the Green Man, Jean found him in a dark corner and made him come back to the flat and eat a proper meal. She'd left these bits and pieces with him, said she wanted him to have some Christmas, even if he didn't think he needed it. Made him promise to put them out. So he did, he does. Robert never breaks a promise, no matter how tempted he's been to take that bloody bird and crush it under his foot.

He pours another whisky. It's good this year, a gift from the plastic-bag people, very good. He's not lonely, he's not grieving, he is a little drunk. The lawyer's papers, words and deeds, are sitting on the sideboard, Robert will sign them soon. The shop is closed. He can begin clearing out some of his bits and pieces, make space for the larger boxes, get

284

himself organised. There are a few things he still needs to tell Akeel, to explain, make sure the lad has all the facts, and then it will be done. Robert didn't expect this time to come so soon, what's good is that he knows now, he's ready. It's taken him a long time to get here, but he's made the right choice. It's all going to be OK.

Forty-six

There is a single fall of snow between Christmas and New Year, and Robert takes himself off to the park before the fully risen sun melts it away. Patricia Ryan watches the white gusting outside her window and remembers that she used to know what this cold stuff was called. Remembers that she doesn't know now. Stefan and Mike call each other from their parents' houses, shy teenagers again from too much food and drink and not enough time naked together. Dan and Charlie spend some time at a shelter. Dan stays for one night, the walls are too tight for his body, Charlie sits, silent in a corner of a warm room, waiting for the holiday to end, and the street to welcome him home. Dean and Gina take the kids down to Karen's for the whole week, and actually, despite Dean moaning about not being able to work when they're out of town, it's brilliant. Games and food and drink and Karen and Dean taking the piss out of Nick as they did when they were kids themselves. At the bottom of Denmark Hill the 345 bus slides past Camberwell Green, no traffic to stall its route, an old man on the top deck proclaiming the words to 'Rudolph the Red-Nosed Reindeer' as if the lyrics have meaning and truth. 'Then how they loved him, he it was they loved oh yes, Jah how they loved him. As he shouted out, shout it to me, my man, my son of man, shout it out. I'm Rudolph. I am Rudolph. I am He . . . I and I, born today, my drummer boy, born today.' Helen takes the children up to the Horniman Museum for the morning. It is crisp and cold, London is stunning from high on the hill, the gardens are almost bare, their foreign fruits long gone. She stands beside a damp eucalyptus, stroking her hand along the rough, peeling bark, watches Freddie and Emily run rings around Simone. She is watching herself and her little brother in the Blue Mountains. They are eight and six, twelve and ten, sixteen and fourteen. They are all their ages and every holiday and Helen misses the smell of dry red earth more than she could have imagined. This is homesickness, stroking a eucalyptus trunk in London and watching someone else's children running off their energy in a snow-dotted winter garden planted with world flora, it is missing what she never much enjoyed in the first place. Homesick that feels like lovesick that feels like loss and all her own fault. She won't find a true love and nothing is going to change, unless she changes it, and that is why she has booked her ticket. It is nearly time for lunch and Helen pulls the children away from the gardens, a quick pop into the museum so Emily can see the butterflies, pinned out on the boards, their beautiful wings splayed and dry, and then home. Helen is going home.

Robert walks around Ruskin Park, like Helen he is looking down to town, from here he can see right across to the Wembley arch, grateful that the winter-bare trees allow him to see his city. He walks past that bloke who always sits at the Denmark Hill entrance to the park, the one with God knows how many cans on the bench beside him. Sometimes the old guy has mates with him, sometimes he's alone, but he always has his dog by his feet, in winter the animal is wrapped warm in a cape made of blanket and string. The two men nod to each other and Robert reminds himself to come up tomorrow, bring one of the coats he's going to give to the charity shop, he doesn't need them any more, and there's no point in packing them up. Up by the big old magnolia Robert sees a crow digging away at something in the ground, worms or soggy chestnuts. Closer to, he sees the crow is pecking at a squirrel, not yet dead. The squirrel keeps trying to lift its head, and every time the crow smashes down on its back with a stabbing beak. The squirrel is half dead and the bird remorseless. Robert hates bloody crows.

The New Year begins and the break is over. Robert has spent the time moving out his many boxes, filling black bags with all that past life he's held on to for so long, for just in case, now consigned to the bin and the recycling truck. He has made a good job of it, there's very little left to do. What there is, mostly involves talking. There's something he needs to explain to Akeel and, unlike the lists of important phone numbers and suppliers he must never offend and warnings about lean summers and busy periods, this bit is going to be hard to tell. But he needs to. And, in truth, waking up the morning after signing the papers, Robert finds he wants to. He wants to tell.

Akeel and Robert are standing in the back of the shop. Akeel stares at him, this man he has stood beside for almost a year. This man he has promised all his savings, all his hopes to. The kettle boils beside them. Tea bags sit in dry cups, tannin-stained, and Robert always refusing to allow Akeel to soak them in bleach, bleach is for toilets he says, bleach is for the loo, not for us, no harm in a bit of tannin and some London lime. Akeel has promised himself clean teacups when he finally takes over, when it is his name above the door, his certificate on the wall. There is an overflow pipe dripping somewhere out the back in the alley. Out there where it has rained all day and now cleared for a dry night with a high sky and plenty of stars, bright and very cold.

'I don't . . .' Akeel shakes his head at Robert. 'What?'

Robert nods. This reaction feels right. Not what he expected, nor what he didn't. He has no way to judge. The one other time he told this story he had no way to judge either. Misjudged. The kettle boils, its thick black switch clicks out and off, Robert reaches past the young man, this young man, his friend now he thinks, pours water into the cups, water that lifts and spins the circular teabags. Robert watches the water run clockwise and wonders if it goes the other way in Australia, as down the plughole, so in the cup. Probably not, unlikely. This thinking is a delay. He knows Akeel will not care about the clockwise motion, or otherwise, of water in the cup. He places the kettle back carefully, no more accidents.

'I said, I killed her.'

Robert nods as he speaks, confirming the truth with the simple physical action. Akeel opens his mouth. Doesn't speak, closes it again. He doesn't want to know this. And he does.

Robert continues. 'She couldn't stand it any more, the pain, the not being able to do anything. Not just for herself, for anyone. She was useless, and she hated it, it was unbearable. For her.'

Akeel finds his mouth. 'Right.'

Robert turns to the little fridge, the one he knows Akeel will want to replace soon. There is so much Akeel wants to replace soon. He takes out the semi-skimmed, twists off the lid, stops himself sniffing the plastic bottle because he knows the lad hates it, even though Akeel hasn't said, not once in the past year. 'I couldn't stand it for her, what she was. And what she wasn't.'

Robert pours in the milk and the tea bags bob under its heavier weight. He lifts them out with a teaspoon, wondering as he does so why people always say fishing when they talk about removing teabags. There is no fishing here, no patient waiting, nervous tension on the stretched line. He makes a judgement call, one sugar for Akeel, stirs it in, they listen to the grains grinding against the cup, against the spoon, dissolving into the heat. He pushes the cup across the bench top. Akeel does not look up, follows the swirl of brown liquid, Robert's aged hand leaving it there for him to reach when he will. When he can.

'How?'

'There were these painkillers she was taking. They've taken them off the market now, said they were too easy to overdose on, withdrew them. It was in all the papers for a day or two, not long. But you know, if it wasn't that it would've been something else. I helped her take them.'

Robert's speech is simple, there is no tremor in his voice, no sense of confession, he did not think it would sound like this. Thought perhaps there would be a feeling of something bigger when he told Akeel. It does not feel easy, but it does not feel hard either. Robert has felt this before.

Akeel is holding his cup now, one hand round the too-hot china, anchoring himself with the light burn. 'Helped her?'

'She'd been asking me for ages.'

'How long?'

Robert approves the specificity of the question, considers. 'Certainly months, maybe as long as a year . . . no, not quite. Just after Jean's birthday it got really bad. She did, Alice, got bad. So that's ten and a half, eleven months. Yes.' Robert nods, he is pleased to have worked this out, has never been asked before, never considered the length of her asking, the duration of her begging. 'She hated it, being looked after all the time. The final straw was when she needed Jean to take her to the loo. She was so humiliated, practically stopped eating, wasn't drinking much either, so she didn't have to go so often.'

'Didn't you get any help?'

290

Akeel knows the answer to this question. Has crossed London six days a week for the past year, was brought up in Stratford, now works a fifteen-minute walk from King's College Hospital and the Maudsley. He watched his own mother nurse her grandfather as the old man died in their back room, crying out every few hours to go home and knowing this was all the home he had time for. He walks past the corner drunks on their sofa every morning. Akeel knows there is so little help available, so much mess to be cleaned up.

'Some. Marylin used to come in once a week for a while, then when Alice was very bad we had a specialist nurse come in every few days, but she still wasn't sick enough to be hospitalised, or not what they called sick enough anyway, she just needed constant care. And Alice hated being cared for.'

The dripping continues outside. Cars pass. The shutter is fully down, though not yet locked in place. They are safe in the back of the shop, shutter and door and glass and counter protecting them from the rest of the world, warm air from the driers heats the room. Akeel shivers.

'And you . . .?'

'I ground up her pills. Fed them to her in warm milk with a bit of whisky.'

'Weren't you worried about being found out?'

'Not really. The new nurse was coming in regularly, the doctor once a week sometimes. So they wouldn't have needed an autopsy, even if there had been a chance they thought there was something wrong. But that was it, see, everything was wrong with her. She could hardly breathe, she had this bloody oxygen tank up there, her cough rattling round the flat and her lungs filled with fluid. Only they didn't know how long she'd go on. One doctor said a month or two at most – and she liked that, you know? She was pleased when he said it wouldn't go on too long. And then this other bloke, older doctor, more like her, closer to her generation, he told her it might be as much as a year. Thought he was doing her a favour, giving her more time. But she couldn't stand it. Really, she couldn't stand it.'

They pick up their tea, sip it. The cooling brown liquid tastes as familiar as dust. The room is small and feels smaller, darker. Robert looks up to check the lights, both bulbs are glowing down on them, the one he replaced last week slightly brighter than the other. It just feels dark.

'So she wasn't in physical pain?'

'Not much.'

'Then why . . .?'

Robert looks sharply at Akeel. 'You really think physical pain is as bad as it gets?'

Akeel doesn't answer. He doesn't want to have to think about it, doesn't want to think about this at all. Hates that Robert is telling him, must have been planning to tell him for ages, is waiting for another question, and another. Akeel hates this – and he is interested. As Robert had known he would be. As anyone would be. And so the question comes out, even when he doesn't want it to, even when his mouth is trying to close against it. 'Did she ask you . . .?'

'All the bloody time. Her dad, he'd had this long dying, stomach cancer, and she nursed him through most of it, her own mother was hopeless at looking after the poor bugger. He took so long to die. I remember, all that time, when he was sick, I was thirteen, fourteen then, Alice'd go round to theirs right after work, come back late on the bus, and before she went to bed, she'd come into my room and say promise me you'll put a bullet through my head before you let me get like that.'

'And did you promise?'

'No, I was a kid. And she was still gorgeous, figure like an actress – an actress from then, I mean, not like one of your

292

scrawny tarts nowadays – she had all this dark hair piled up on her head, stockings and lipstick every day, no matter what. I didn't believe she'd ever get like that, couldn't picture it.'

'But she did?'

'Just like. And worse, nasty. Alice always had it in her, a sharp tongue, a sly look. She was no bloody angel, but she got mean. Age and pain and then just how much she hated being sick, she turned into a right cow. Nothing we did was enough and nothing we did made her feel any better, and we bloody well did it all, the lot.'

'You and Jean?'

'Katie too, bless her, long as she could stand it. Even she gave up eventually, though. I told her she didn't have to keep going down to her nan, it was all just too much. She smelled, Alice did, in the end. The stink of dying, and worse. Made me spray perfume all round the room, every time I went in there, every bloody time. Didn't hide it, the perfume, made it worse in a way, more obvious. You know how it is when you're trying to hide something and everything you do just makes it stand out all the more. But she'd been such a lovely woman, not ladylike, I know that, but beautiful. Proud of her looks, proud of her body, and every right to be. Then there she was, laying in a bed she'd made filthy herself, couldn't help it, and she smelled bad. It shamed her. She would've died of the shame if she could. Only she couldn't die, poor bitch.'

Robert is crying now, and his hands are shaking. This seems odd to him. He remembers that when he did it, did as she asked of him, did as he was told, that his hands were shaking then too. But he was not crying. He didn't cry at the time or in the days to follow, not until the funeral. Then the tears came and he couldn't seem to stop them, every night without fail, he would shut up the shop and go upstairs to

Jean and Katie, and the tears would come. Jean said she thought he was having a nervous breakdown, and he knew that was probably what it looked like, maybe it was a breakdown for all he knew, but he didn't think so. Robert knew what the tears were for, that's what made them hurt so much. He knows he can stop these tears now, if he wants to, thinks he can. Has had years of practice in it, stopping himself crying, stopping himself speaking, not like Akeel who opens his mouth and out it comes, no matter what he's trying to hold in. But Robert finds he does not want to stop, not just yet, there is a relief here, washing his eyes, maybe he's learned something from the lad after all, a relief in speaking out. Akeel is leading him over to the old armchair in the arch, just half a dozen small steps, but he does need leading. And now he is sitting and his head is in his hands and he is rinsing his fists in wet salt. It was the right choice, Robert thinks, to share this story. These tears needed somewhere to go, they have been waiting a long time.

Forty-seven

Robert drains the tea Akeel has given him, milky with three sugars. He'd said not to, said he couldn't bloody well drink it like that, but it turned out he could. So now he has finished his tea and holds his cup out for another. 'Go easy on the sugar this time, lad. Those beet farmers won't know what's hit them.'

They sit in silence for ten minutes, each man drinking his tea, both of them ignoring the knocking on the door, someone who's seen the shutter not fully locked down, hoping to get attention from inside. Akeel has another question before he's ready to finish closing up.

'Did Jean know? What you were going to do? Did she know you'd done it?'

Then Robert's tears start again and Akeel doesn't know what to do. If this were Rubeina sobbing in front of him he'd go and hold her, she's only little, he'd put his arms right round her and hope that might make it better. But this is a grown man, taller and broader than he is, and Akeel knows this man now, but not well. Well enough for the man to confess to murder, not well enough to hold him as he cries. Akeel holds out his hand, aiming to touch, to stroke, to soothe, and Robert grabs it, squeezing Akeel's fingers, pushing the bones sharp together.

'I didn't tell her, Jean, not before. Didn't want her to get into trouble – you know, if anyone found out. But afterwards, after the funeral, once it was all done with, when I couldn't stop crying, well, she worked it out for herself. She asked me about it, and I had to say. Couldn't lie, could I? Even though telling her was putting her in an awful spot.' Robert clings to Akeel's hand, knuckles white from the tight grip. 'Told her about crushing up the pills, and putting them in her milk. I held Alice up so she could drink it, and she couldn't hardly talk then either, her throat was red raw, but she might have gone on for another month or more the doctor said, another month of it. When every bloody hour was hell for her. It wasn't fair. So I held her up and she drank the milk, like Katie when she was tiny, and they're so small and frail, and they have that baby smell, I mean I know they all have it, but you do think it's special to your baby, that your baby is extra precious, and you'd do anything in the bloody world to keep them safe, and warm milk – it's kind of sickly too, you know? It's sweet, but it's sour too. But then it's all right, because it makes them sleepy and it's so good when they fall asleep in your arms. Feels so bloody good, you'll see. And she did, Alice, fell asleep in my arms. I thought I'd buggered it up, that she was just going to fall asleep and it wouldn't work and then she'd be even worse when she woke up, so I tried to wake her. To see if she needed me to make more, do more – I mean, it was meant to be enough, but then she was sick, because I was shaking her, I think – not hard, I didn't shake her hard, just like you would to wake someone up – but her eyes were still closed, and it wasn't like we'd planned it to be, none of it. It wasn't easy and she didn't just slip away, it was supposed to be peaceful, calm after all the pain, only she was choking, on her own vomit, all this milky bloody vomit – and I do mean blood, there was blood in it – and I thought I had to leave her, in the bed, lying there. I couldn't sit her up now, fix it, help her get her breath. She was throwing up the milk with the pills in it, I'd have to do it all again. And I didn't think I could. So I got up and I walked over to the door, and I left her there, retching and choking. I didn't help her. I made her sick and I stood up and left her to choke to death. And it wasn't soft and it certainly wasn't bloody easy. Not for her. It wasn't any of what it was meant to be. It took so damn long. She was drowning in the sour milk I'd just fed her.'

Robert pauses, for a breath, to blow his nose. Akeel feels sick. A truck revs its engine at the junction, the lights change, the truck drums past, shaking the cups on the worktop. Robert sits back in his chair.

'Couple of months after, it was, when I told Jean. She thought that might help me, telling her what was wrong. Don't think it helped either of us. Then Katie started asking questions too, she was bright, knew something was going on, more than just me missing my mum. One night she asked me, outright. I'd never lied to her, neither of us had, it was one of the things we were proud of, me and Jean. I even thought it might be all right then, it was Easter and we were going away for a week, Katie had done her exams – the mock ones, done well too. I'd booked us a week in the Lakes, thought that'd be nice, we hardly ever had proper holidays, few days here or there, hard to take much time with the shop, but I thought we needed to get away, after everything that had gone on with Alice, only Katie said she didn't want to go. I thought she must've had a lad or something, didn't want to be away from him. There wasn't a row, she just said it. I don't want go on holiday with you, Dad, I don't want to be with you.' Robert shakes his head. 'I didn't think she was wrong. I knew exactly how she felt. I was her dad, and I'd killed a person, actually killed someone, her nan. And she could never make that be all right in her own head. She knew why I did it, and she said she thought it was the right thing to do, probably, as long as I was sure it was what Alice wanted, and I know my Katie believed me about that, only she couldn't forgive me either. Neither could Jean, they couldn't come to terms with it, so they left.'

'You saw them again?'

'A few times, we tried having a bite to eat, going to the pictures, it never worked. And then, you know, much later, Jean told me she got sick herself – Katie. And I think that made her even angrier with me. She used to send cards, Christmas, birthdays, but once she had her own kids she stopped.'

'But she was just a child, yes? When Alice died?'

'Sixteen, seventeen.'

'Why did you tell her?'

'Jean and I decided not to, but then she came to us and asked it right out. I said it's what your nan asked of me and I did it for her. And I did it for us too, by then Alice was pulling us apart with her nasty mouth, always having a go at me or Jean, even Katie too, in the last few months. See, that was the problem, I reckon.'

'What?'

'I think Katie might have gone along with it if she'd thought I only did it for Alice, because it was what Alice wanted – but she knew it wasn't just that. My Katie knew me very well.' Akeel waits for Robert to continue. The tears have stopped but Robert's hands are still shaking. 'Truth is, I did it for me too. She'd become this old bitch, never a good word for anyone, and that wasn't my mum, my Alice. Like all that pain had eaten out the good part and just left this nasty old woman. And I think that's what Katie could never forgive, that I did it for myself as well. I wanted her to die.'

'Oh.'

'And I think, actually, in the end, I wanted to be the one who did it.'

'Oh.'

'So then Katie said she wanted to move out. I suppose we always think about our marriages breaking up, you know, you have one of those weeks, or months, or years even, where it's all going wrong and you keep not getting what the other one's on about and you're just missing each other, not connecting, you and the wife, like spark plugs not quite firing, and you do, course you do, you think about how it would be if you weren't together. You with me, lad?'

Akeel wishes he wasn't, but he and Rubeina have had more than their fair share of these weeks, he knows what Robert means. 'Yes.'

'Right, but even when you're thinking like that, how it's all going wrong, you might think you'll lose your wife – break up or get divorced or she'll find someone else, and as you get older, you know one of you is going to go before the other, you do, it's inevitable – so I always knew there was a chance I'd lose my wife one day, but I never thought I'd lose my girl as well.'

'What happened?'

'Once she knew, she couldn't stop thinking about it, Katie. She started to hate me, I think. First she said she wouldn't come on holiday with us, so we just cancelled the week, lost the deposit. I thought when she went back to school it might be all right, got on with her year. We made it through summer, she was off with her mates a lot of the time, it wasn't too bad. Then, when school started again, Katie came home one day and just said she wanted to move out. And Jean went with her, she chose our daughter. Which is fair enough, she was only a girl, a kid really.'

'A girl with a lot of power?'

'Oh yeah, my Katie always had a lot of power. Even as a baby. I admired it, don't think I ever had the sway she did, Katie was so strong. And I reckon there's two types of women, there's the ones who stand by their man, whatever, they just need a partner for their life. Alice was like that – not that there weren't a string of partners, and not that she didn't love me, she was a bloody good mother – but she always needed a bloke. I don't mean she'd ever have traded a bloke for me, but her life didn't revolve around me, as her kid. Then there are women like Jean. She loved me, I know she did, but Katie always came first. I'm not saying one's better than the other, obviously you want to come first with your mum when you're a kid, and every bloke wants to come first with his wife, but the wife has to make her own choices. There are women who put the kids first, and women who put their bloke first. Can't do both.'

'Jean put Katie first?'

'They moved out.'

Akeel is washing the cups now, they have been closed for nearly three-quarters of an hour. 'So your daughter took your wife away from you?'

'She didn't mean to, she just couldn't stand it, what had happened. I understand that, I couldn't either. But I had to, I couldn't leave myself, could I? I wonder what kind of woman your wife is, eh?'

Akeel frowns, drags himself over Robert's leap from Alice to Jean to Rubeina, and answers more fully than he would have intended to had he had a chance to think. 'I suppose we'll find out. When the baby comes. I can't say this to Rubeina, but I'm not looking forward to it right now, it all seems like so much hassle, so much to get used to.'

Robert nods. 'Family, son, you wait. Two's good, really it is, or it can be, but three – that's when it starts to get fun.'

Akeel shakes his head. 'I don't know how you can say that, after what you've just told me, how can you say family is good?'

'Because it is, it's the best thing in the world, there's nothing like your own flesh and blood.'

300

'Even . . .?'

Robert smiles, it is a crumpled, tired smile, but it is there. 'Yeah. Even if you're the kind of bloke whose daughter hates him because he killed his own mother. Even me.'

'If they were so angry with you, why didn't they tell the police?'

'They weren't angry, they didn't think it was the wrong thing to do, neither of them, they just wished I hadn't done it. Or maybe they wished they hadn't known, I don't know. But once it was done, even though they both agreed it was the right thing, the only thing, they couldn't stand to be with me any more. Katie couldn't look at me. In a way, it was easier to have her gone, than turning away whenever I came into the room.'

'I'm so sorry, Robert.'

There is silence.

Robert gets up from his chair, his left leg has pins and needles, he stumbles a little, Akeel puts out a hand to steady the older man. 'The things people keep hidden, Robert, why are they always the hard things?'

Robert smiles, and it hurts his tear-dried face to do so. 'People don't make secrets of their triumphs, son.'

'Right, so why . . .'

'Tell you all this?'

'Yes.'

'Because I know you and I feel like I owe you. Because I never told anyone else before, aside from Jean and Katie. I needed to say it, for myself.'

'You need a witness?'

'Something like that. And because it explains things, explains me, some of me. And, well, because . . . you're my mate . . . I think?'

Akeel nods, sure. 'Yes. I am.'

Robert smiles properly now. 'There you are then.'

Forty-eight

Six twenty on Saturday morning and the 345 bus is heaving.
A few of the younger passengers are heading home after a
long night at the kind of club where there are still bouncers
outside at seven in the morning, but looking around her,
Helen thinks most of them appear to be on their way to
work. Work in town, work cleaning the bars that are just
closing, work while so many others are still sleeping. Work
for the heavily accented, work for the underclass, other
class, less-than-minimum-wage work. These are the workers this city, every city, thrives on, their willingness to get out
of warm beds at five in the morning, to travel long distances
on three buses because it is half the price of the tube fare,
their ability to turn need into willing. Helen is not going
to work. She is going home. Helen simply can't do it any
more, because as long as she is living the lie she's not
getting around to living her life, and she knows it won't
happen as long as she's sleeping with another woman's
husband and loving another woman's children. Not that she
has explained any of this to Andrew, or to Claire, or indulged
in long, snotty goodbyes with the children. She has left a
note on the kitchen table next to the kids' cereal bowls,
spoons, Simone's plastic cup. All of which she placed ready
before she left. Claire and Andrew are always rubbish on a
Saturday morning.

There is a man sitting behind Helen on the bus, a black

guy, long dreads, and he is whispering quietly to himself, singing too. When she got on, her pack smacking people behind her, her suitcase smashing against her shins, the man came forward from the back of the bus and helped her with her stuff. No one else offered. But then again, no one else looked anything other than exhausted, only the man with the dreadlocks and the quiet song seemed awake. Helen came into London on the Gatwick Express and she thinks it is fitting that she leave this way too – bus, tube to Victoria, then train, plane, home. She only called her mum last night to say she was coming. They're going to have a barbecue on the beach, an Aussie cliché to welcome her home. She can't wait. And she can't stop crying, and she loves Andrew, and she's missing the kids already, and she feels really bad, and so very relieved.

By mid-morning it's all done. Robert's flat is clear but for his last few bits and pieces, he's leaving on Monday. More impressively, the flat downstairs, that room full of other lives, is all cleared out. Akeel has spent the past couple of days watching Robert carry things down and cart them through the alleyway at the back. He has offered to help more than once, but Robert doesn't want help, he wants to do this by himself. Fair enough, maybe he doesn't want Akeel to see what he's keeping, what he's throwing out, maybe he wants it kept private. When Robert took the last of Alice's files to the dump, borrowing the van keys from Akeel so he could make the trip, he threw the final heavy box of 1976 files into the paper-waste skip and felt lighter than he had in years. All this time, all the hanging on, and storing, and saving. Everything kept, just in case, but the reason never came. Just after lunch he went for a walk, Katie's shoebox under his arm, and handful by handful he threw keys into the pond. Angry mallards and Canada geese hoping for winter bread, pecking instead at the glittering brass and sodden tags as other people's keys sank to the muddy bottom.

In the early afternoon, Charlie and Dan sit on the sofa together. It's only the second week of the new year, and is colder than usual, so they sit a little closer than Dan would necessarily like, than Charlie would admit to enjoying. Dan has found a globe, spun off its axis, nothing to keep it in place, and so he holds it as close to a 23.5-degree angle as he can manage and explains to Charlie why the sun is so cold today, so far away.

Just before teatime Patricia Ryan comes into the shop, she is looking for her Frank's overcoat. Akeel is polite, but when he tells her he doesn't know the coat she means, and asks for a ticket, her head begins to shake. For ten minutes she stands by the door, looking out, hoping to recognise something or someone. Robert comes back from dumping another pile of his old things, and asks Akeel what's going on. Akeel explains and Robert goes out back to the uncollected items. He takes an overcoat off the rack and is about to give it to Patricia Ryan, along with her own address, quickly scribbled on an old ticket and pinned to the coat, when he stops. 'Sorry, lad. Your shop.' He holds up the coat. 'What do you reckon? Mrs Ryan can take this home?'

Akeel nods. 'Of course. You right, love?' he asks Patricia Ryan, who takes the coat carefully, folds it over her arm so as not to crease it, and leaves the shop hanging on to the pin and the old ticket with her address for dear life. She needs to get home, Frank'll be wanting his tea, and he's a tartar if it's not on the table for six.

It is late afternoon. Stefan and Mike are in bed. Stefan has just called a friend to ask him to teach his class this evening.

304

Stefan is horrified at his own new attitude, and delighted, a bit giggly. He must remember to go in and say goodbye to Robert at the dry cleaner's, he's leaving next week, or this week. Damn, maybe he's missed him. Ah well, the old guy probably doesn't care, moving on, about bloody time, all those years in the same job, it would drive anyone mad.

At closing time Rubeina comes in. She wants to see Robert before he leaves, to thank him for everything he's done for Akeel, for both of them really. She's softer than she was the first time she came to the shop, seems less like she's sizing up the place to see what she can make of it, more like she'll give it time, let the building tell her. Of course she looks tired, getting to the end of her pregnancy, she's bound to have mellowed a bit, but a lovely girl, very nice. She asks him to show her upstairs, now it's all empty, and when Robert says it's Akeel's place now, the both of theirs, she doesn't need his permission to have a look around, she puts her arm in his and sets him straight.

'OK then, why don't you take me upstairs and show me round because I really just want a few minutes with you, by myself? I want to know what kind of a cleaner you think my husband's going to make.'

Later that night, at home in bed, after the handshakes and a quick, uncertain hug between the two men, Rubeina turns to Akeel, her hands spread wide over her warm belly. 'That poor man, I still can't really imagine being a mother, not yet, let alone losing the baby you've loved and brought up.'

Akeel is tired, the pressure of actually taking over after all this time, the solidity of his fears. 'Mmm?' he turns, holds Rubeina in one arm, the other joining her hands on the baby. 'Well, maybe he'll make the effort now, get in touch with her, see if he can't patch it up.'

305

'Akeel?'

Rubeina's voice is sharp enough for him to know he needs to wake properly.

'What?'

'Robert's daughter died, months ago. She's dead.'

Rubeina recounts the story Robert told her standing in his empty flat, looking out his front window and over to the railway bridge where the northbound train is speeding through, not stopping. He tells her about the trip up north and sitting at the back of the hall and talking to no one, and the colour of the fields as the train brought him home.

'How could he not tell me?'

'Men are rubbish at talking about themselves, you know that.'

Rubeina does not know about Alice, doesn't know why Robert and Jean broke up. Akeel has never told her, he's not telling her now. It's a secret, and Robert is his friend.

Forty-nine

Winter. Monday morning. Akeel stands on the platform at Loughborough Junction, walking away from the ticket office to the point where the bridge crosses back over Coldharbour Lane. He looks west to his empire, what is, from today, his own shop. He knows there will be problems to come, even the matter of crossing town to his lawyer later today is bound to be a hassle, there have been tube strikes threatened for the past week, the roundabout at the Elephant has building works, none of it will be easy, he knows this. He also knows this is a moment to savour, offers a prayer of gratitude to the cold morning, and then turns to walk back along the platform, down the stairs, into the new day. Just before he turns downstairs he looks across to the bright morning triangle of Canary Wharf, sharp January sunshine bouncing off the shard of glass, shining in praise. It all feels possible.

Out on the street, between the Celestial Church of Christ and God's Way Ministry, Akeel looks up the road towards Camberwell, he wonders if he should order lunch now, go across and pay for curry goat and vegetable patty, rice and peas, maybe some jerk chicken too, for a farewell meal with Robert. Pay for it now so that when Robert goes over to pick up their lunch, it is already there, waiting for them. Robert will be in today for the last time, to make sure everything is properly signed and sealed. Akeel is about to cross the road when he remembers Robert's disdain the last time he tried to pre-empt his mentor's desire. Ramadan and not eating himself, he'd come back from the shop with Robert's usual cheese and onion crisps, and instead of thank you, Robert had demanded to know why Akeel thought that was what he wanted.

'It's what you always have, every day since we've worked together.'

'But you didn't ask.'

'I didn't think I needed to.'

'Always nice to be asked, son.'

Akeel still isn't sure if Robert had meant it or was taking the piss, doesn't want to risk it though, today of all days. So he turns away and heads back towards the shop, noting as he does that the sofa the tramps are sitting on, under the bridge, looks just like Robert's old one, same heavy brocade around the cushions, same sagging middle. There must be thousands of these old sofas, littering railway arches and street corners, their mock-leather arms pockmarked with cigarette burns, plastic melted at the edges, the flammable stuffing protruding from their beige cushion covers. His parents had a similar one when he was a kid, but his mother had covered it with chintz furniture covers she made herself, more English she thought, more back home his friends mocked.

All morning Robert and Akeel pay attention to each other, closer attention than usual. Hand in the till, fingers on buttons, the rumble of the kettle, untangling plastic tags to load them in the gun, bright yellow litter of used tickets falling around the bin, this year yellow, last year pale green, next year for Akeel to choose a colour of his own. As well as the secrets, there has been so much that is mundane, so much that is ordinary, unpacking boxes, checking stock, keys to cut, the last shared duvet folding, 'You get that kid of yours to grow up quick, son – very handy for holding up corners, kids are.'

Then there is lunch. Everything Akeel would have ordered in the morning, but paid for by Robert. 'My treat, you're on your own after this.' And a post-lunch rush neither were expecting, school uniforms to be done by tomorrow afternoon please, three suits for a business trip, half a dozen shirts that should have been collected over six months ago and would, by rights, according to the sign Robert points out on the wall, have been given away by now.

Teatime. Akeel wants to say the last tea, so does Robert. Akeel makes the tea, neither makes a fuss. When Robert puts down his cup, he fiddles with the spoon, clinking it on the side, sounding the china and then he tells Akeel he is leaving.

'You're not going to wait and lock up? Last time?'

'Did that Saturday. After you and Rubeina left.'

'But you didn't say – I thought it should be special. I thought we'd – you know, mark it somehow.'

'What? Bottle of champagne? You'll break the rule of a lifetime?'

'No, just . . . locking up one last time, it's important.'

'It was. I did it. I don't want a fuss, lad, I'm not going far.' Robert looks at his watch. 'And I've a train to catch.'

Akeel's stomach flips. This is it, goodbye and welcome. What seemed exciting this morning is doubly so now, frightening too.

Robert grins. 'Come on, you've got a lovely wife, baby on the way, shop of your own. What more could you ask for, eh?'

'Someone to stand behind the counter with me?'

'You'll be glad of the peace and quiet soon enough.'

Robert is edging towards the door, he doesn't want this, would rather not say goodbye to his friend. He puts his hands in his pockets to stop them shaking, feels under his left hand a piece of paper. 'Oh yeah. I wanted to say . . .' Robert opens his mouth to speak again. But: 'I don't want to get it wrong, hold on.' He takes out the piece of paper, looks at it, puts it away. 'Go in the name of God.'

'Where did you get that from?'

Robert shakes his head. 'Spend nearly a year with me and you don't think I've taken in any of what you've been on about?'

'I mean, who taught you? I don't say it in English. I don't think I've ever said it in English.'

'No, but your mate from that mosque over the garage does. If you ask him nicely. Brought in one of his sharp suits Saturday, you were out back unloading the dryers. Bit put out he had to talk to me, I reckon, but I asked him anyway. He told me the English way, no point me trying to learn new words now.'

Robert's hand is on the door. He is leaving.

'Thank you, Robert.'

'You're right, lad.'

From the platform at Loughborough Junction train station, Robert looks down at the shop, he can see into the front window, not clearly, but it is darker now, the lights are on downstairs, and in the middle flat above, the rooms open and almost empty. Robert waves to Akeel who has come to the front window of the flat and is now staring up at him. Robert thinks he can see Akeel is holding a box in his hand, it may even be his own file, the one he left behind, the one with his own name and dates. Hoping to help, to explain, hoping that explanation will help. He can't really tell from this distance, though, can't even be certain it is Akeel standing there at the window, it could be anyone, might even be Alice. The light shifts, a cloud covers and uncovers the pared new moon, a late magpie laughs, a bus rumbles outside the shop, and then there is the reflected beam of a car's lights in the windows and Robert cannot see into the flat any more. Beneath his feet a 345 bus rumbles across the junction in the opposite direction, with a poet upstairs singing the praises of Zion from his seat on the left-hand side. Robert hears a shout from below and turns round to look back up Coldharbour Lane to where Dan is whooping and Charlie grinning from their perch on his old settee, the one he dragged out two nights ago. They lift their Special Brew cans like hand weights and belch belly laughs as one after the other, and slowly, half a dozen crates of carefully stacked tomatoes and red peppers and potatoes fall from their perfect positioning outside the halal shop and flow into the road, a guilty skateboarder racing off, the mix of brown and clashing reds running into the gutter. Robert draws his eyes up from the street, his street, to look further across the city, from the Salvation Army cross on Denmark Hill, to King's College Hospital, and past the church steeple at Camberwell, right out to Canary Wharf's isosceles angle.

There is a clicking on the line behind him, close now, he checks his watch and he turns back to be ready for the arriving train. He lifts his hand and waves to Akeel, to where he thinks Akeel might be standing, by the window, it could be Akeel. Then the clicking from the rail grows louder and the train arrives.

Above the junction and the street and the shops, the homes, the park, the people, a crow screams, flying north.

Much later a man walks to the centre of Southwark Bridge. Not Lambeth, but it'll do. It is a cold January night, there is a thin mist on the river. There is no one else on the bridge, Waterloo and Blackfriars claim the arterial routes, the Southwark crossing is always quieter. The view is not as pretty either, but beneath is the Thames, and that's all that matters. The man holds out his hand and lets a key drop from it, it has no tag and falls in a plumb line. Then he empties his pockets into the water below, letters and wasted lottery tickets float down alongside unread messages and a shopping list – milk, bananas, bacon, plums, dried fruit, toffees, wrapping paper. There is only one other thing to let go. The man is tired and ready. And he lays him down to sleep.

Or this. Robert gets the train to his new home. He is tired. He opens the door with a single key. He sits in his flat in Southwark, it is just a flat, one of so many adequate South London conversions. One house made into four homes, rooms carved out of rooms. But this flat is Robert's own. It does not belong to Alice or the shop or Jean or Katie or anyone but Robert. If he stands at his bathroom window, and leans right out, he can see the river. This is a man in his sixties. He does not like crows. He misses his wife, he mourns his daughter. There are sad things and they do happen. But they are not all, and this is not the end. And now he lays him down to sleep.

Acknowledgements

Thanks to Tamsyn Berryman, Stephanie Cabot, Donna Coonan, Sophia Dixon, Martyn Duffy, Courtney Hammer, Antonia Hodgson, Mobeena Khan, Rachael Ludbrook, Val McDermid, Faisal Naqvi, Lucinda Prain, Katie Purslow, Mari Roberts, Manda Scott, Shelley Silas, Lee Simpson, Kelly Smith, Mark Trezona, Harriet Wistrich, the friend in Kent, the Suttons of Waveney Valley, Ian Hodges and London Friend, the Buddhas of Brixton, everyone at Virago, and The Board who – as ever – make it all just about bearable.

STATE OF HAPPINESS

Stella Duffy

'Duffy is best known for her sharp insights and
sharper wit, and both are on display here . . . Brave,
understated and unforgettable' *Daily Mail*

When Jack and Cindy meet at a friend's party they are
immediately attracted to one another. Cindy, a celebrated
mapmaker, traces the contours of their relationship, from
New York to LA, from first passion to real love.

After five years together, Cindy and Jack think they have
tested their love to its limits. But then Cindy falls dangerously
ill, and the couple must face the hardest test of all.

Told with wit, tenderness and unflinching honesty, *State of
Happiness* is a captivating story of love and loss from a
writer at the height of her powers.

'*State of Happiness* is a sharp, sobering cocktail
spiked with metaphysic, immense good humour and
understanding. Stella Duffy gets better and better'
Ali Smith

ISBN 978-1-84408-023-6